Love, Judie Kate

A Novel

J.T. Allen

ISBN: 978-1-7357280-5-6

Allen. J.T.
Love, Judie Kate.

Edited by: Allie Coker and Melissa Long

Published by Warren Publishing
Charlotte, NC
www.warrenpublishing.net
Printed in the United States

This book is dedicated to all the Judie Kates who look in the mirror every day.

Acknowledgments

There are always many people to thank after finishing a book. I'll start with my publisher, Warren Publishing. I've worked with a lot of editors over the years, but Mindy Kuhn, Amy Ashby, my editor Allie Coker, and copy editor Melissa Long have been fun to work with. Positive yet professional, they took a chance on a man with a dream of writing a chick-lit book/beach read, and the finished product is now in your hands or on your tablet. Thanks!

Thanks to Bob Blackwell and Kathy Landis for their keen insights and critiques on an early draft. Thanks to Lynne Hinton, a friend from way back who has done well in her writing career, read the manuscript, and gave me encouragement during a rough patch. Make sure you read her books! Thanks to the ladies at Yesterday's Grill in beautiful downtown Snow Camp, especially Crystal and Britany, and my hairstylist Tina, who answered my questions about women's fashions and pop culture and movie hunks.

My wife Jackie deserves her special paragraph of thanks. She has tolerated my writer moods since 1984 and takes care of so much—both big and small—which allows me time to write. She also talked me through a time of writer's block with this story, and her wisdom made the plot better. Thanks, dear! I'll take you to Wendy's and get the Biggie Size!

My good friend Gerald Hampton, whose band Molasses Creek (Ditchville12 in the story) has been the driving force of the Ocracoke Festival for years, helped me with details of the island of Ocracoke and the festival. I modeled my character, George Wilson, after Gerald, and I trust we will still be friends as long as I continue buying lunch.

I began writing this story in the summer of 2018 and finished the manuscript just after Hurricane Dorian devastated the island in 2019. A seven-foot surge of ocean destroyed half the businesses, nearly all the cars, and most of the residences. Houses I stayed in while doing sound for the festival, restaurants I dined in, and friends on the island were all affected. The Ocracoke as depicted in this novel will never be the same. Islanders rushed to put their lives back together for the next season, but then the coronavirus hit in 2020, and the island was closed off as well. I hope my readers will book a ferry ride over to Ocracoke and vacation on the island. The resilient Ocracokers could use the tourist dollars, and the slow vibe, great local music, fantastic food, and pristine beach will replenish all who stay there.

Another form of thanks is necessary here. I have been friends with or professionally helped many women over the years who were abused—physically, sexually, psychologically—by spouses, friends, or clergy. I have also known many who were held back by issues of low self-esteem and poor body image. Thank you for sharing your pains with me. I combined many of your stories into the character of Judie Kate Wilson. I hope readers of this story will be empowered to recover their lives and claim their strengths.

Many years ago, my high school English teacher, Mr. Carlyle, handed back an assignment, told me I could not write, and said I would never be a writer. I have never forgotten those words, and the thought of one day relating this story has driven me through a long, exciting, and fun, if not necessarily lucrative, career of writing. This is my ninth published book. Thanks for the inspiration!

And lastly, thank you, dear reader, for turning these pages. If you come to the Ocrafolk Festival, held the first full weekend in June, come see me at the Workshop Stage area. I would love to meet you!

Yesterdays

Judie Kate Wilson took her diary out of the cedar box that had been handed down in her family for three generations. The box was well-worn and scratched from years of use, holding recipes, pictures, and receipts, but now it contained her diary, her good friend. She always brushed off the top of the cedar box for good measure, then looked at the abalone flowers inlaid in the fragrant wood. She took out her diary, which had a blossom of pink flowers and a purple ribbon for a bookmark. It was time to add a new character.

Sometimes, she envisioned being in a movie or a Broadway play, so she made a list of her cast of characters on the second page. There was her father, George Wilson. Famous mandolin player, Grammy award winner, traveled a lot with bluegrass bands, taught machining at the community college. Never at home. There was her mother, Ellie Wilson. Renowned educator, she also traveled the country promoting an alternative to the current troubled American educational system. Never at home. There was her dog, Duke, now gone. She had scratched out the name of the youth minister at church. Beside it she scribbled in "Jerk." Then, there were the names of friends from her high school, most of whom had been scratched out as well. It seemed like her diary was now her only true friend. At least it did not turn on you or call you names.

She wrote down "Joe" and then turned the page to a new entry.

September 16, 2007, Sunday

Yesterday, a young man came to visit Dad (shockingly, he wasn't on the road this weekend). He plays guitar (of course!) and they talked about music and things. His name is Joe, and he's so cute. Some guys are just cute, but Joe seems mysterious with his curly black hair and deep blue eyes. I think I heard him say he teaches at the community college—religion or maybe history? He's married, and Dad must really trust him because when he went out to run an errand, he left Joe behind with me. Dad's good at leaving me behind. We talked, and I got the feeling that Joe was really interested in what I had to say—total opposite of my parents!

He asked me what subject I like in school (math), if I have any boyfriends (seriously, how

can he look at me and say that with a straight
face?), what I like to do for fun (read), and what I
like to eat (ice cream). I had no idea what to do with
all that attention! Then, he asked what I dream
about. Weird question, but it got me thinking.
Boys, of course, but they only stare at me and not
in a flattering way. They only like skinny girls
like Britnee or Jalen or Pearson. Cheerleader types
or soccer girls. Boobs and short skirts. Lame. I
dream about Bon Jovi (who cares if he is a bit old)
and Justin Timberlake. I wish I looked like Jennifer
Lopez or Carrie Underwood. People really like Kelly
Clarkson. Why don't they like me?

Nobody has ever asked me about my dreams.
Mom and Dad always tell me about their dreams
for me. Educator. Period. Personally, I dream about
finding a boy who can really see me instead of just
my size. I secretly fantasize about going to the
prom. I'd be like Cinderella—and all the boys would
want to dance with me, and all the girls would
be envious! Cheesy, I know. I dream about being
pretty, not fat. Homecoming queen. I dream about
not being shy or ashamed anymore.

I can talk to Joe for some reason. I don't feel shy
around him. I wish he were my age. I bet he would be
my boyfriend! His wife is really lucky!

Love,
Judie Kate

November 8, 2007, Thursday

Tonight, I overheard Dad talking with Joe. He comes over nearly every week to talk guitars or music or other soundman things. Dad told him about the fight we had last weekend. About how I don't talk to him and Mom anymore. Great! Maybe this is why I don't talk to them—so they don't go blabbing all my business to everyone! Seriously, how can I talk when they keep telling me what they want me to say? It is SO FRUSTRATING! Dad never asks anybody for help, but he asked Joe.

"For some reason, that girl talks to you, Joe. Y'all seem to get each other. Maybe 'cause you're not a parent, she sees you as cooler. I don't know. Would you talk with her? Maybe you can get her to open up."

Joe must have said "yes" because he asked if he could take me out to get ice cream every now and then since that's my favorite food. Just a Sunday afternoon here and there, but still! He thinks it will get me to relax. Mom and Dad approved the plan, of course.

Joe makes me feel special. He listens, unlike that so-called youth minister who keeps telling me to honor my parents. How can I honor them if they are never at home? I get tired of staying with my friends on the weekends. One day, I will find somebody to make me feel special in the way that Joe does. That's my dream.

   Love,
   Judie Kate

December 16, 2007, Sunday

Joe took me out for ice cream this afternoon. He said it was a Christmas gift! He's so sweet. I got Rocky Road—two scoops, of course. He got plain chocolate, which I guess is an okay choice. We talked about school. He didn't know we're not allowed to have Christmas trees anymore. We talked about church some too. I told him the youth minister was a jerk—he stares at girls like Kaylee and Skylar because they wear push-up bras. It's disgusting and gives me the creeps. Joe warned me to keep my distance.

   "No problem," I told him. The popular girls always make fun of me and tell me guys don't pay attention or hit on fat girls anyway. So much for being Christian.

   We talked about Christmas gifts: he and his wife, Jay Jay, are giving to something called The Heifer Project. It's an organization that provides cows and water and chickens to poor people around the world. So cool! He asked what I wanted, and even though I felt a little bad about it, I told him

I want a new iPod. My old one is worn out, so I really miss my music! Maybe my own TV? Momma says "no" and Dad does what Momma says. Joe feels close like family to me. I wish he were part of my family in some way. All my aunts, uncles, and cousins live far away.

   Love,
   Judie Kate

January 6, 2008, Sunday

Got to have ice cream with Joe again this afternoon! Which is good because, so far, it doesn't feel much like a "Happy" New Year. It's back to school tomorrow, and I am dreading it. Joe could tell something was off with me, and he asked what was wrong. I told him about the bullies. I didn't mean to or want to, but it just kind of came out—the notes stuffed in my locker and in my book bag and how the bigger girls all sit together because nobody likes us. Christmas break was a relief from that. He told me I am pretty (!) and that sometimes it just takes a while longer to find someone who can see that. He reminded me there are other ways to be pretty too. I almost rolled my eyes when he said that part, but once he started talking, I could tell he really believed it.

   People who show kindness are pretty. People who love dogs like I do are pretty. His face lit up at just the thought of such "prettiness." I told him that sometimes, I don't think my parents consider me pretty or someone to be proud of, and that's why they are never home. Do they stay away because I am not pretty enough? Are they embarrassed about my weight? I'm not outgoing like them. I don't fit in with their crowd. Am I just one big problem to them? Joe says that Daddy worries about me all the time, but he doesn't know what to do with all his worry. He could stay home on the weekends! That might be a good start! Does his band need him more than me? Don't I count for something?

Maybe I'm an "oops" baby. That's what Kristal said one day. Since I was born when Momma and Daddy were older, maybe they don't like the mistake they made.

Joe said I could call him "uncle" if I wanted. Even if that's not exactly how I think of him, I like it as a nickname and think it will do for now.

I think Rocky Road ice cream is my favorite.

Love,
Judie Kate

February 14, 2008, Thursday

Valentine's Day is the worst. All the girls at school were dressed up and they got candy from secret admirers or their boyfriends. I just tried to ignore it all. I got a card from my parents, but that's about it. Momma's at a conference, and Dad's band had a job somewhere, so Uncle Joe took me for ice cream, and he brought Jay Jay! We had sundaes this time. I had strawberry, and he had caramel with nuts. Jay Jay had strawberry too! Too funny. She also said I have pretty eyes that are mysterious and deep. Honestly, I thought Jay Jay might be blonde and stuff, but she's normal. She's cool. I thought they might scoff at me crashing their date, but Jay Jay said she didn't mind sharing Joe.

She and Joe gave me a hug and told me, "Happy Valentine's Day, Judie Kate." I wish my parents were more like that. Maybe give me a hug once in a while? Take me for ice cream? Does a little token of love ever cross their minds?

Momma claims I have a crush on Joe. She says I am infatuated with him. I don't see how anybody wouldn't like him! I wish I were Jay Jay. She is so lucky!

Love,
Judie Kate

March 27, 2011, Sunday

Today was hard. Uncle Joe tried to cheer me up, but I wasn't having it. They announced the senior prom this week at school. I've been looking forward to

this since I was a freshman but also dreading it for
as long as I can remember. All the other girls were
excited. They talked about prom dresses, who they
hoped would take them, how they would do their
hair, blah, blah, blah. Hunter is bigger than me,
but she got a date because she promised to do it with
Blake. Blake tried that on me, but I told him to have
sex with himself. I guess that's not Christian of me,
but is that seriously all boys think about?

Anyway, Uncle Joe and I shared a banana split.
My side had Rocky Road of course. I jokingly
asked Uncle Joe if he would take me to the prom. I
told him about the dress I picked out when I went
to the mall yesterday. It's a simple, floor-length,
black chiffon dress with spaghetti straps that would
look good on just about anyone. Guess that won't
happen. But I am not going to have sex just to
preserve my dream. Joe was proud of my "scruples."

"Scruples won't get me to the prom," I told him.

I wonder what it's like to have a boyfriend. What
would it be like to hold hands and walk down the
hall or to kiss him? Would it be fun to sit together
at the game or share popcorn at the movies? I bet it
would, but I may never know.

No Love,
Judie Kate

April 17, 2011, Sunday

Joe secretly talked to Momma and Daddy, and they said we could go to the prom! They had to talk to the principal and sign some forms, but everyone said we could go, and Jay Jay said she would take me shopping for my dress! Dad said he would pay for it if it was under $200. Momma is flying in from a meeting that night and Dad is out of town that weekend (like we didn't see that coming!), so Jay Jay said she would help me with my makeup. I've never worn makeup, but this is major and so exciting! My dream is coming true!

Love,
Judie Kate

May 21, 2011, Saturday
(really Sunday morning)

I can't believe it happened! It was just as cool as I hoped it would be. Jay Jay did my makeup, and I wore heels, which I must admit, made me walk weird. She made me look in the mirror, and then she took some pictures. I started to cry, so we had to do my makeup all over again. Is this what beautiful means? I never knew I could look so good. Joe got me a corsage, and we even got to ride in a limo like the supercool kids!

We had dinner at a place called Sheffield's. I had never been to a fancy restaurant before, but Joe knew what to do. He made a big production of pulling out my chair for me and I ordered a steak with some shrimp. I ate every bite.

We got to the prom, and the driver opened the door for us, just like in Hollywood! We walked in, and everybody stared like we were on the red carpet. I guess they thought I wouldn't be there because I wouldn't be able to get a date. It felt good to prove them wrong. We got some punch and stood around. They had a DJ and there were strobe lights and fog machines. Joe said it was time to dance, but I suddenly felt scared. He said dancing isn't hard, it's just moving around to the beat. I watched and caught on—it was kind of funny, but Joe knew every song! Maybe he deserves more cool points—ha!

The DJ played a line dance, and Joe pulled me into it. Even though we messed up big time, I didn't worry about it or feel shy! The scariest (but most enjoyable part) was when the slow songs came on, and Joe took my hand to dance. He held me close just like they do in the movies, and over his shoulder, I stuck my tongue out at Blake when his poor, doomed date wasn't looking.

It's exhausting dancing in high heels, so after a little while, Joe asked if I wanted to leave and get some ice cream. We took the limo to the Ice Cream Churn and boy, the heads turned there!

We went back home around 11 p.m. Momma had returned from her trip, and she told me I looked pretty. Then she thanked Joe for doing this for me and gave him a hug. I took my shot at being brave and gave him a hug and a kiss on the cheek too.

I'll never forget this night! I was Cinderella for once in my life!

Love,
Judie Kate

June 9, 2011, Thursday

We had ice cream tonight, but things were solemn and off with Uncle Joe. I asked him what was wrong. Usually, he is so upbeat, and I am the one who feels down, but he pointed out I would be leaving for college soon, and with his schedule, he might not be able to see me again. He said he would miss our time together. It almost made me cry. He has been the father I never had, the friend I wished for. The only man who has ever believed in me or made me truly feel good about myself. He got me through so many hard times ...

He said something weird. He smiled, like he was telling a joke, and said if Jay Jay ever left him, I could be his wife. Well, that won't happen! Those two are so tight! Besides, he may be a cutie, but he is old enough to be my dad.

We hugged each other like we always do, but this time it seemed like our last time together.

Maybe one day, I will find me a Joe.

Love Forever Gone?
Judie Kate

* * *

September 2012
Revival Meeting, Lick Creek Baptist Church

The preacher railed from the dark oak pulpit as he slammed the worn, leather, King James Bible on it and walked back and forth. He was sweaty and gesticulated with his other hand while pointing his judgmental finger at unsuspecting people in the congregation. The plain white walls of the one-hundred-year-old church, accented by stained wainscoting, reverberated his voice, giving it a celestial force. The lights from the chandeliers did not illuminate the sanctuary well, thus making it seem as dark as the very souls he was preaching to. The ceiling fans whirred, but the air was still thick with sweat, sin, and the fear of Hell.

Pastor Amos Brown, all five foot eight and two hundred pounds of too many after-church dinners, wore out the carpet on the pulpit like a nervous father-to-be at the hospital maternity ward, as if he couldn't decide what to say next. He had removed his coat and then his tie, and his white shirt revealed pit stains from perspiration. Pastor Brown wiped off his brow and the bald crown of his head with a red handkerchief, picked up the Bible again, and continued, fire spewing from his green eyes.

"Men!" He pointed a shaking hand at several in the congregation. Some reared back as if lightning had touched them.

"You are to be the leaders of your family and then of the church and of this great nation. But we can't lead as men of God if we are distracted from the mission of God. The Apostle Paul commanded us to be the head over our wives and over our children, but we are allowing our wives and the women around us to enslave us to sin. King Solomon, led by God's Almighty Holy Spirit, was very wise when he warned us several times in the book of Proverbs, chapters one through nine, that there are two types of women to choose from: the beautiful Lady Wisdom, a true woman of God, and the temptress Woman Folly, who is the handmaiden of the devil himself. We see Folly all the time: She is before us, naked on TV and in the streets with short skirts and low-cut blouses and high heels and makeup. Her hair whirls around her head, seducing men and boys into temptation and to the very streets of Perdition itself. Her foul mouth is full of profanity and sex. The Apostle Paul warned us that women should keep their hair covered lest it be a temptation to men and pull them away from the paths of God, but they uncover their heads and everything else."

The guilty in the pews, male and female, did not have the chance to ask how the preacher knew of these things in such graphic detail, and none pondered the irony that it took King Solomon seven hundred wives and three hundred concubines to understand the difference between the two women.

The old, pine pew was stiff and uncomfortable, but that was not why one young man was squirming. He was feeling the heat of the Word of God. The description of the evil woman, rather than leading him down a path of virginal righteousness, brought about feelings in him. He had seen women in short skirts, tall boots, and skin-tight leggings that made them look naked. Women with cleavage, short shorts, and all sorts of undress flooded the stores, the movies, and the magazines. The girls at church wore some of those things when their parents weren't around, or they slipped out on dates and changed clothes at their friend's house.

They were of the devil, but he liked them, and now at this age, wanted them, desired them. Yet, the preacher was right about what God wanted, and America was riding in Satan's Black Train, anyone could see that, and God did not want women looking like that because it made men stray from the true path of God. Women should know better, and if they did, then men and thus the whole world would be servants of God and America would be great again. If women would just stop giving in to the devil and instead give themselves to Jesus Christ, who refrained from the evil wiles of women and remained a virgin savior his whole life, then America would be God's nation once more. The preacher railed and railed with biblical example after example of women leading men astray.

He slammed his Bible on the pulpit again and hollered out, "Can I get an Amen?" The people in the pews responded, more out of fear than faith.

As the young man sat restlessly in the pew, sweat beaded on his brow, and he repented for his lust as the preacher's fire and brimstone castigated and condemned women for leading men and the world away from God.

"That evil woman of Samaria, married five times and living with her sixth man, tried her best to seduce our Savior, Jesus Christ himself, but praise be to God, he did not give in to her deceptions and seductions, and he fought her with the true Word of God! But now, the Whore of Babylon herself is knocking at our American door and walking down our streets and is on our screens and in our computers and polluting our minds with filth, and America is going to burn forever because women today are giving in to sin!"

There were more "Amens" and some women started to weep, and men, feeling exonerated for their waywardness due to the seductions of the fairer sex, were calling for Christ to enter their souls.

"Men?" the preacher bellowed, pointing to each one in the congregation. "It is time you stand for God. When they want your attention, and that is what they want, you give your attention to God Himself! Turn the other way! Let them know right now whose side you are on! Take the lead in this war on decency! You tell them what God wants for them! Slay the evil spirit that is destroying our world! The Apostle Paul talked of the Sword of the Spirit. You take that Sword and slay that evil Woman Folly so that a true woman of God might bring us back to righteousness!"

Full of conviction, the young man made up his mind right there and then he would indeed pick up the Sword of the Spirit and slay the evil that was tearing America apart. During the invitation hymn, he walked down the aisle and gave his heart to Jesus Christ. He would fight the Whore of Babylon for the rest of his life.

* * *

FALL, 2014

Judie Kate sat in the tall chair at the small, round table and stared at the big screen on the wall above the bar. Another Friday evening at the Pizza Palace, alone. The décor consisted of dark wood walls, a squeaky pine floor worn from years of abuse, tables, short and tall, and creaking wood chairs with dark cushions. Three large windows faced the street, and one large window faced the side street. Booths lined the opposite wall, and tables in the front allowed a view of passersby. Outside, groups of students walked down the sidewalks of Wilmington, glad to be free for the weekend. No studying tonight. Beer, fun, and for a few, some all-night frolicking. Some students were on dates, some wished for dates, some were getting over dates. Regardless of their situations, everyone was hoping that the night's reverie, spent in a college town fit for living in the moment, would help them forget the past week.

Judie Kate took another bite of pepperoni pizza and wondered why so many restaurants had TVs. With no sound, the only thing making any real sense was the crawl that listed the same news bulletins over and over again. Another screen showed *Sports Center*. How many times can you watch the same play from a thousand different angles though? The waitress, Zoe, bobbed by with a tea pitcher.

"Need a refill?" She had short, dark red hair, and colorful tatts covered her white arms. Her Goth presence was completed by a tongue stud, nose ring, five piercings in each ear, and black fingernail polish. The required combat boots and black fishnet hose created an anti-establishment exclamation point.

"Sure," Judie Kate answered.

Zoe smiled, fully aware that Judie Kate was another part of the reason she hated society. Men don't date big women, and skinny women don't help the cause by remaining silent either. So many nights she had seen Judie Kate hang out at the Pizza Palace all by herself.

"Pizza good tonight?" She paused for a moment amid the mayhem of the Friday night crowd.

"Added some red peppers," Judie Kate answered with a grin. "Just right."

Zoe saw a hand waving at her that was connected to an angry face. She quickly moved along as Judie Kate slipped back into feeling isolated and melancholy. She looked at another screen and wondered what HGTV was trying to fix and flip when a stranger caught her off guard.

"Hi, uh, please pardon me if I am interrupting anything but—and I know this sounds awkward, and it's not a come-on or anything—but you sure do look sad for someone so pretty, all alone over here by yourself. Would you like some company for a while?"

She looked up and saw a broad-shouldered young man standing in front of her. He had a crew cut, and he was muscular but not overbearingly so. His mature face was weathered with freckles, and unlike Zoe, his thick forearms bore no tattoos like all the other soldiers who rushed to Wilmington on Friday nights looking for coeducational experiences. Her face must have looked offended, affronted, embarrassed, incredulous, or perhaps even stunned because upon seeing her reaction, his smile drooped a bit, and he backed up a step.

"I'm sorry, I probably shouldn't have ... I didn't mean ... you're probably waiting for someone."

Judie Kate stared at the handsome stranger for what seemed like a minute and then caught herself. She wanted to continue sulking in her self-pity, but suddenly, from out of nowhere, she answered in a forward way.

"Face it, the reason I am here alone is that most people don't think I am pretty, thus I don't get many pickup lines, but of the ones that have been thrown at me, that was either the most awful or genuinely very sweet." She grinned slightly, like a cat waiting for the kill, anticipating the punch line that would reveal the intent of the inquirer. In times past, they had all failed. She was ready to tell him to get lost.

He stepped forward again with a serious yet compassionate face. "I don't think that's necessarily true. I have been here for thirty minutes."

She glanced at the Miller Lite clock on the wall over the bar.

"In that time, you talked to the Goth waitress, who obviously has problems with anything that is status quo. I would think that means you are sympathetic to the marginal."

Judie Kate shot a glance at Zoe, who was also looking her way.

"I saw the way you looked at the three beauty queens when they pranced in, and that tells me you can see through their insecurities."

Judie Kate squirmed a little in her seat. *Hmm, didn't know I was that obvious ...*

"I saw your reaction when those supposed studs looked at you and then at each other and laughed. You hid your hurt, and that means you are aware of your own insecurities and yet are very strong."

Judie Kate's eyebrows raised. *Me, strong?*

"The fact that you put up with all this and still do your own thing tells me you are determined and yet also dream of acceptance by a world that has been taught, incorrectly, to look the other way when you come into the room." The stranger paused for a moment.

"And, FYI, some women tried to flirt with me earlier, but I was more interested in watching you."

Judie Kate suddenly felt warm. *Is my face flushing?* She was speechless.

He pulled out a chair, placed his tea glass down, and said, "I'm Don."

She motioned for him to sit.

"Judie Kate." And, for the first time in a long time, she felt like she was somebody.

Don was a Marine stationed at Camp Lejeune. When Judie Kate asked what he did, he would not answer directly but only said he could be called out anytime and could be gone for weeks at a time. He had a master's degree in psychology, spoke near-fluent Arabic, had been a Marine for years, and had been to Iraq, Afghanistan, and several undisclosed locations he could not mention. She knew all that was code for Special Ops, and when she said as much, Don changed the subject.

She shared her story—daughter of a musician who was always on the road and a respected educator who led workshops around the nation. Don intuited that her weight was the result of her insecurities and yet, at the same time, was a badge of her identity, and it did not bother him at all. He never tired of looking at her. Zoe had taken and returned their bills and filled their glasses five times before Don realized it was time for someone else to have the seat so Zoe could make more tips.

"Judie Kate, do you like ice cream?" He left a ten on the table for Zoe. "There's a little shop around the corner—"

"Cone Heads!" she answered with a bit too much enthusiasm.

Zoe walked by and mouthed "Nice!" at Judie Kate. She winked as Don got up and pulled the seat out for Judie Kate, who was taken aback by his gentlemanliness.

The evening was warm, and folks enjoyed dining and drinking outside the restaurants and cafes. There was nowhere to sit inside Cone Heads.

"Let's get a cone to go," Don suggested. "I'd like to buy, if that's okay?"

Judie Kate smiled and then said, "Rocky Road, two scoops, sugar cone, please."

When they arrived at the counter, Don called out, "Rocky Road, two scoops, sugar cone, and one scoop of vanilla, one scoop of chocolate, regular cone."

Just like Joe, Judie Kate thought and smiled. Cones in hand, they walked around the streets, sharing small talk and their Friday night together. Soon, they were back at the Pizza Palace.

"Judie Kate, I have to get back to the base. May I walk you to your car?"

She told him she lived in an apartment two streets back.

"May I walk you home then?"

Suddenly, her guard went up, and before she caught herself, she shot out, "Is that code for may I come inside?"

Don paused, realizing he had been misunderstood. "I'm sorry, Judie Kate, no intentions here. I just know it's safest for a woman not to walk alone at night, and I would feel more comfortable escorting you home."

She realized she had offended Don. "I'm sorry, Don, it's just that we're at that time of the evening when the boy reveals his true intentions. Once bitten, twice shy."

Both looked at each other and then smiled. To make amends, Judie Kate offered her arm to the soldier, and he took it like an usher at a wedding and led the way. The sidewalk turned into a dirty street with trash and large bins awaiting the garbage man. Old trees shaded the community with an ominous darkness. When they arrived at her apartment, really a room above the garage of a retired professor and his wife, Don paused.

"Judie Kate, I have had a wonderful night, and I hope you have too. Thank you for not turning me away. If you're up for it, I would like to do this again next Friday, same time, same place?"

"I would, Don. Very much. Thank you for a lovely evening."

They paused, feeling the awkwardness that every couple knows comes on the first date. Each stared at the other as ripples of love flowed from one to another. Kiss or no kiss?

Far away from her insecurities and skepticism came a sudden surge of joy and confidence. She leaned over, stood on her tiptoes, and kissed him on the cheek. "I'll see you next Friday night." Don gave her a polite yet hopeful embrace.

She walked up the steps and looked back at him again, as if he might have been a dream that suddenly ended. Reassured by his smile, she then went inside.

The calendar could not get to Friday fast enough for Judie Kate. Suddenly, her life was filled with joy, expectation, and renewal. After several dates, Don invited Judie Kate to his little vacation place in North Topsail Beach.

"It belonged to my grandparents," he explained as they cruised up the road in his old Ford truck. The interior was clean as a whistle, had vinyl seats, and there was no console between them. The radio had silver knobs instead of buttons and even a dial instead of numbers. The truck smelled of oil and dirt. For some reason, the old vehicle made her feel right at home.

He explained that his granddaddy bought the land way back when the island was undeveloped. He found out about it when he worked for the government in a program called Operation Bumblebee. It was a top-secret Navy project involving the new science of rockets and guidance systems. The Navy chose Topsail Island because it was basically deserted and because Camp Davis, a training site for antiaircraft training, was already there. The Women's Airforce Service Corp was stationed there as well. Tall, concrete bunkers were constructed along the beach to monitor the flights and speeds of the test rockets. The program only lasted three years, from 1946 to 1948, but during that time, his granddaddy got to know the area well, found a man who wanted to sell some land, and bought the little slice of heaven that became their beach home.

Soon Don and Judie Kate arrived at the beach house, which was really a short, 1950s trailer with a small deck and boardwalk over the dunes to the beach. The trailer was blue and white, with a rolled roof that looked somewhat streamlined. It seemed out of place parked between two modern, three-story beach mansions.

"Home sweet home!" Don called out as he shut off the engine and stepped out of the truck.

He unlocked the door and waited for her to go inside. She saw wood-paneled walls, linoleum floors, and faded, old curtains around the windows. There were two green, vinyl chairs and one brown, vinyl couch, obviously leftovers from years gone by. The small kitchen had a window facing the dunes and an aluminum table with red Formica and matching chairs. An old, green refrigerator whose edges were rounded as much as the trailer's balanced out the kitchen. Don went to the fridge and took out two bottles of water while Judie Kate inspected the rest of the trailer.

She saw more paneling down the hall and a small bathroom. There was a very small bedroom on one side of the hallway, and at the end of the short hall was a larger bedroom. She came back into the small living room and noticed a Bose Wave stereo CD player, a tall stack of CDs, and a bookshelf filled with paperback novels that would make any English Lit professor happy.

"I love it!" Judie Kate smiled as Don handed her the water. The vinyl chair cushion made a scrunching sound as she sat. She looked at the wall to the right of the window and saw a picture of an older couple. Don watched Judie Kate observing the photo.

"Grandparents?" she asked.

"Yes, Granddaddy Burton and Grandmother Patience. That was from the 1960s, I believe. Granddaddy was a B-17 pilot in World War II. He survived twenty-eight missions. Quite lucky since more than a third never made it back to the base. He met Grandmother at the hospital when he visited one of his crew members who had been hit by German flak. It was love at first sight, but she made him work for it!"

After they finished their water, Don reached over and grabbed Judie Kate's hand. "Let's go to the beach!" They smiled at each other, feeling giddy as teenagers.

He led her up the weathered and splintered boardwalk and over the dunes to the crashing waves. The sun was warm even though it was October, and it heated up the growing affections between them. Judie Kate pulled off her shoes and held Don's hand as they walked together, slowly, up the sandy beach. One wave nearly caught them, and they scrambled to avoid falling into the seafoam. In the mayhem, they crashed into each other and embraced, more to keep from falling than anything. Suddenly, though, it was more than that. Judie Kate kissed Don impulsively and then caught herself, as if she had been a bad girl. Don smiled, just happy to have Judie Kate with him, and seeing this, Judie Kate relaxed and held his hand. After a few more minutes, Don stopped and stared at the sand.

"Look at that, Judie Kate," he called out. He reached down and picked up a black, shiny shark's tooth.

"Wow, Don, how did you see it?"

He held it close for her to look at. "For you, my little mermaid." He made a grand gesture of presenting it to her.

"You keep it for me, Don," she answered. "I have no pockets." She saw it as a sign from Old Man Sea. This relationship was meant to be. Farther up the beach, Don paused a moment.

"Let's sit for a bit," he said.

They plopped far from the rolling and sometimes thunderous waves. Don started humming a tune. "Is that 'Toes' by Zack Brown Band?" Judie Kate asked. Don nodded and together they both hummed the song and then sang the final chorus. Life was indeed good today, Judie Kate mused. She snuggled up to her Marine and basked in the warm sun, the cool breeze, and an emerging dream of them together for the rest of her life.

For the next few weeks, there were Saturday picnics at the trailer. Bologna and cheese, peanut butter and jelly, and one futile attempt at burgers on the grill on a cold, blustery day. Don's schedule prevented them from having a lot of time together, but the few hours were like bits of heaven sewn together into a month of growing love. The sun of their relationship was rising.

Late in October, Judie Kate went for her monthly hair trim. Her stylist jokingly asked if she wanted to try a new style. It was a game she played. She asked this every time, and every time Judie Kate refused. But today, she felt different, flirty, whimsical.

"Why not?" Judie Kate answered.

"You're kidding!" was the shocked reply. But then she saw Judie Kate's eyes. "Wait a minute, girl. You got yourself a man?" Judie Kate nodded sheepishly and then smiled. "You go!" The stylist reached for a magazine and opened it up to a dog-eared page. "Look at this. It's a wedge bob cut. Been wanting to see that on you for months."

Judie Kate thought a moment. "Let's do it!"

Full of confidence with her new hairdo, she went to the mall to look for a new dress. She paused by a counter stocked with makeup.

A voice called out behind her. "Can I help you?"

Judie Kate turned to see a young woman walking her way. She almost scurried off, but suddenly a burst of curiosity swept over her.

"Well, I've never worn makeup before, well, besides for prom."

"Time for you to go to the prom again," the clerk answered.

The first week in November, the couple was walking on the beach. The new hair and the new face brought a new smile to Don's lips. He couldn't stop looking at her! As they strolled on the beach, he put his strong, protective arm around Judie Kate, but she sensed something different in his embrace. She wrapped her arms around his waist. The increasing passions she felt for Don were encouraged by his arm around her, as if to protect her from the waves, from the breeze, from anything that threatened her in any way. Like the sudden rush of warmth from drinking a glass of wine too fast, for the first time in her life, she felt appreciated, respected, and loved.

The sun was going down, and shadows from the dunes were catching up to the waves as they came inside the trailer. Judie Kate could feel the windburn on her face. Don reached into the fridge to get some drinks, and Judie Kate explored the trailer some more. She felt flirty, romantic, daring emotions that were entirely new for her. She wanted to twirl around on her toes. She fantasized about climbing into the small shower and playfully washing each other, exploring all the places that were, so far, left to their imaginations. Then they would dry each other off, taking time to tease each other in loving ways. She would grab Don's hand and lead him into the little bedroom where she would pull back the old sheets, rich with the smell of salt, and then they would enjoy the warmth of each other's body. They would snuggle together and make slow, beautiful, and everlasting love. They would peacefully slumber afterward, and in the morning, she would get up and make them breakfast as they watched the sun rise.

"There's a neat little restaurant on the way back home. Thought we could stop there and get a bite," he said. Her fantasy ended abruptly; her face filled with dismay although she tried to hide it.

"I'm sorry, I didn't mean to disappoint you," he said

She feigned ignorance but then confessed. "How did you know?"

"You went to the bathroom, moved the soap after smelling it. Then, you looked in the closet and found the fluffiest towels. Lastly, you looked into the bedroom and checked it out. Not too hard to figure that one out." Her face went red with embarrassment.

He walked over to her and pulled her up close. "I want that, too, but we can't tonight. I'm sorry."

He rubbed her back, ran his hand through her wind-tossed hair, and then looked her straight in the face. "I have to be back at the base tonight. The chatter begins around two in the morning, and I have to be there. It's something big, that's all I can say."

Judie Kate tried to smile, but it was like her parents all over again. Don saw her memories of past letdowns etch lines of pain and a slight frown all over her round face.

"Judie Kate, you are the most beautiful woman I have ever met. I knew that the first time I saw you." He paused to catch himself and then dove in. "I love you." He embraced her tightly and held her like there was no tomorrow.

Love. He said "love." The import of his words flooded her whole being with a rising tide of quiet sobs of joy. Even with the disappointment, could this be her dream come true?

Don, feeling her body shake, became worried, pushed her back a bit, looked at her, and said, "I'm sorry, I've done something to upset you."

She wiped her tears away with the back of her hand. Judie Kate was smiling, but Don was confused.

"You're gonna have to help me here," he said.

"Don, you said love. I never thought that anyone would love me. My Uncle Joe said that one day, somebody would tell me I was beautiful and I would be loved."

His worried brow turned back into a smiling face. "Your Uncle Joe sounds like a very wise man." Don pulled her close again, and they held each other for a long while. Then Judie Kate leaned back, wiped her eyes again, and smiled. It was time to live her dreams.

"Don, I love you too! Let's go get that dinner. I'll tell you all about Uncle Joe."

***

Two weeks later, Judie Kate walked around the mall looking at the Christmas displays, signs with "Happy Holidays" in the store windows, the shoppers with bags of gifts, and children racing to see Santa Claus. She was trying to find a gift for Don. A sweater seemed nice, maybe a flannel shirt, but it just seemed like he deserved more. Their relationship was going great, and their love grew like wildflowers with every moment together.

"What to get the man?" she whispered to herself. Her phone buzzed and she pulled it out. It was a text from Don.

Hey, bad news. I'm being deployed at this moment. This has been building for a while, and I hoped it would be after Christmas. I'll probably be gone for two weeks, maybe a month, tops. I can't call now, and I'm off the grid until I get back. We'll have Christmas when I return. I am so sorry. I love you.

Dejected, Judie Kate sat on the brick wall and stared at the reflecting pool as she reread the text through tear-filled eyes. On the overhead PA, she heard Don Henley singing "Please Come Home for Christmas." Her heart was broken.

After a moment, she composed herself and texted back.

I love you too. Please be safe. Merry Christmas!

* * *

On Thursday morning, January 8, there was a knock at Judie Kate's door. She opened it and saw two men dressed in Service Alpha uniforms and Dr. Hartshorne, her landlord, standing behind them with a distraught look on his face.

"Dr. Hartshorne, what is going on?" She started trembling as something arose deep within her, something she had feared all along but refused to acknowledge. The two soldiers introduced themselves to her. One stepped forward.

"Are you Judie Kate Wilson?" he asked.

She replied affirmatively.

"The commandant of the Marine Corps has entrusted me to express his deep regret that your friend, Master Sergeant Donald Brown, was killed in action in the Middle East on December 27. We are not allowed to explain the circumstances further, ma'am. The commandant extends his deepest sympathy for your loss. Per Master Sergeant Brown's instructions, there will be no funeral honors. He requested that these be given to you. More information will be sent to you in the weeks ahead."

Tremors rumbled deep within her. "No, *no*, this can't be true! Surely, this is a mistake." Judie Kate's body heaved, and she burst out in sobs. Never swaying from their protocol, the soldiers stuck to their script in the face of Judie Kate's grief.

"We are sorry for your loss, ma'am."

They handed her a large manila envelope, a decorative wooden box, and a triangular, wooden case with a United States flag inside. Shaking, she walked inside and placed the envelope and box on the table and hugged the flag close to her heart and cried.

"Ma'am, if you wish, we can stay with you for a while."

Judie Kate thought about their offer and then shook her head slowly.

"I just need to be alone, thank you."

After a moment, each man reached out and shook her trembling free hand, nodded sadly, and turned and walked back down the steps.

"What's the box for?" she called out.

They turned and one answered, "Cremains, ma'am. He had no kin and requested that he be cremated. With no family and no body, there was no need for a funeral service." Then they turned and perfunctorily walked away.

Dr. Hartshorne came up to her.

"What is this about, Judie Kate? They wouldn't tell me. They just wanted to know where you lived."

"My boyfriend, Dr. Hartshorne, my boyfriend. *He's dead!* He's dead." Grief overcame her, and she cried out loud as Dr. Hartshorne tried to give her a hug.

"I'm so sorry, Judie Kate. We didn't know you had a boyfriend."

How could he have not noticed? Don had come by every Friday or Saturday for weeks. Dr. Hartshorne gave new meaning to the term "absent-minded professor."

"What can we do for you?"

Judie Kate pulled herself together enough to pause for a moment.

"Thank you, Dr. Hartshorne. I just need some time alone."

He gave her another tentative hug, patted her on the back like she was a dog, and then quietly left. Judie Kate shut the door, sank onto her couch, held the flag close to her chest, and cried, quaking all over. "*Why? Why?*" she called to any deity who might be listening, pounding her feet on the floor in exclamation points. "Why?"

Hours later, Mrs. Hartshorne came by with fried chicken, potato salad, green beans, rolls, and cinnamon buns from the deli at Food Lion.

"We are so sorry, Judie Kate. He must have been very special." She held Judie Kate's hand, patiently waiting, sharing her presence and support. Judie Kate yanked out another tissue and blew her nose and tossed it onto the floor into a mound of wadded-up tissues and then told her all about their relationship and of the hope of a Christmas together. Mrs. Hartshorne saw a small Christmas tree on the table by the window with one present underneath it.

"He was the one, Mrs. Hartshorne. He was *the one*, you know?"

Mrs. Hartshorne waited a moment and then asked what she could do. Judie Kate's first instinct was to ask for her prayers, but why pray to a god who can't protect your boyfriend?

"Can I call your family?"

Judie Kate thought for a moment. *They didn't even know about Don. Would they care? Would they even be home?*

"I'll call them later, thank you." The silence became awkward, and Mrs. Hartshorne soon took that as her cue to leave.

"We're right next door, dear, if you need us." She got up and let herself out.

Judie Kate pulled the envelope over, stared at it, took a deep breath, and opened it. *You can do this, Judie Kate.* A set of keys fell out, along with a CD case, an envelope with a lawyer's address on it, and another envelope with "My Dearest Judie Kate" written on it. Her hands trembled as she held it, afraid to open it. Finally, she gathered up her courage and tore it open.

My dearest Judie Kate,

If you are reading this, then you know what has happened. I am so sorry I did not come back home. Every time I am deployed, I know I may not come back. I put my affairs in order and arrange things with my lawyer. This time, I arranged to have them sent to you. You would have been my new family.

First, please know that I have never met anyone as beautiful as you. I know that beauty has been a struggle for you, but you have never been a struggle for me. Every moment I was with you was a day in paradise, a walk in Heaven, a dance in the stars. Every time I held you close, life made sense and I felt complete, whole. Your lips touching mine was a new moment every time we kissed. I so looked forward to us being together, sharing our bodies and souls with each other. I will never be with you again, but I hope you will always leave room for me in your heart.

You have no doubt found the keys. I have no immediate family, so I have left you the trailer in Topsail. We had such a good time there, and we left some unfinished business there as well. I wish I had that moment back again. My lawyer will be in touch with you about the legal items. Do with the trailer what you please.

With that, when you go to Topsail, you will find some other things.

Lastly, on your way to the trailer, play the CD by the Platters and listen to the words of "Only You." Please

know that you were my dream
come true.

I will always love you.
Don

Judie Kate read the letter again and again, tears
staining the paper, trying to bring Don back to life,
only to find that he seemed farther and farther away.
She looked at the CD cover. She had heard the song
on the radio but could not quite recall the lyrics. She
was tempted to play it now but held off to stay true
to Don's wishes. She placed the CD on the table and
then picked up the wooden box. She had heard of
cremains but had never seen any. When she opened
the box, there was a small container inside. *Should I?*
She took a deep breath and opened the heart-shaped
urn, hesitantly peering at its contents.

"So, this is all that we amount to?" she said to
herself. "A handful of ashes." *This is Don. This is all
Don.* She put the top back on the urn and slowly, her
hands shaking now, placed it back into the box, which
she then set on the table. Then, she pulled the flag
close to her heart, laid back on the couch, and quietly
cried herself to sleep.

The next morning, she arose and looked around the
room, hoping that yesterday had never happened. The
flag lay beside her on the couch, the cremains box still
rested on the table, and the letter had fallen onto the
floor. She walked over to the small, used desk, turned
on her computer, and emailed Dr. Walters to notify

him that she had a death in the family and would not be in class that day. Then she took out her phone and thought about calling her father and mother but then wondered if they would really understand or even care, especially since she had never bothered to tell them about Don anyway. She would catch grief about not letting them know, and then they would interrogate her about the whole romance. Underneath the questions would be the insinuations: would he meet their expectations for their little girl?

Then, she scrolled down her contacts looking for one of the few friends she had. She stopped on a familiar name: Joe Clark. She had purposely broken off the relationship when she left for school. She knew she was getting too fond of him, but right now, she needed a friend who would understand her and not give her a lecture. She tapped the screen and waited anxiously while the phone rang.

"What's up, Judie Kate?" His warm voice and chipper tone brought back memories of long talks and ice cream, as if the years of separation were just a few days ago. She broke down immediately. "Judie Kate, what's wrong?"

"Uncle Joe, I, uh, I need someone," she sobbed. "I hate to ask this, but can you come see me? I could really use a friend, but I understand if you can't." She continued crying.

Joe became worried. "Judie Kate, are you in trouble? Are you safe?"

She sobbed and sniffed some more and then got herself together.

"My boyfriend, Joe, he was killed in action. I just ... Mom and Dad won't understand, probably couldn't care less. I could use a friend ... I just need someone ..."

"Text me your address, Judie Kate. I'll be there tonight. Are you sure you're safe?"

"I am now, Uncle Joe. Thanks." She ended the call and headed to the shower. She had a trip to make herself.

As Judie Kate drove up Highway 17, she held off playing the CD until she couldn't resist anymore. She came to an intersection and turned right on Road 210, headed into a somewhat deserted Surf City, and then turned left, staying on 210 headed toward North Topsail Beach. As she drove on, she decided to play the CD. She placed the disc into the player and The Platters sang away. As they crooned "Only You," she choked up until she had to pull over because her vision blurred with a flood of tears. It was as if the song were written for her and Don.

When she arrived at the old trailer, she picked up the cremains box and walked up to the trailer, but at first, she could not bring herself to go inside. What was waiting for her? The wind was cold, but the sun was warm, so she placed the box on the porch and took a walk on the beach, all wrapped up in her long coat. The waves pounded the beach and then ebbed back only to do it again. *The rhythm of life.* She remembered their first walk on the beach. She recalled when Don came over to her table that first night. She could taste their first ice cream together. She could feel his strong arms holding her. Now, she felt cold tears on her cheeks.

When she arrived back at the trailer, she hesitantly opened the lock, stepped inside, and placed the cremains box on the table. She looked around and found a note on the counter. *Ice cream's in the fridge.*

She pulled the chrome handle on the freezer door of the old refrigerator and saw a pint of Rocky Road. There was a frosted note attached with a pin: *Go to bedroom.*

She opened the ice cream, found a spoon, and then, dutifully following Don's directions, cautiously looked around the doorjamb of the back bedroom. She saw something on the bed.

She took a spoonful of ice cream and then cried a tear. There was a large, fluffy towel, and on top of that was a small mirror, a washcloth, and what looked to be a bar of soap. She also saw two jewelry boxes wrapped in Christmas paper. She unwrapped the soap and smelled the wonderful fragrance. On the wrapper, it said *Lavender*. She held it to her nose and inhaled once more. She looked at the boxes that were labeled 1 and 2. She opened the first box with shaking hands and took out a delicate gold chain with a shark's tooth dangling from it. There was a note: *We found this on our walk on the beach.*

She put it around her neck and connected the tiny clasp. It rested on her chest, a reminder of their time together on the beach.

The second box was wrapped in shiny gold foil with a bow on top. *Is it what I think it is?* She carefully unwrapped it, her nervously expectant hands hardly able to pull the wrapping, all the while savoring every moment. It was a ring box! She opened it and saw a gold, diamond engagement ring. The one-third carat solitaire diamond glistened in the light. She held it up, fascinated by the rainbows of fire emanating from it, and then she slipped it onto her finger. Perfect fit! How did he know her size? That she liked gold rather than silver? Simple rather than outlandish?

Tears ran down her cheeks as she thought of how Don could do all this on the spur of the moment. *He must have bought these for me for Christmas.* She thought of what might have been as she spooned out another bite of Rocky Road. *What is the mirror for?* When she picked up the towel, another letter fell out.

My most beautiful Judie Kate,

I see you found your presents. I was going to take you to the trailer on Christmas Eve, walk on the beach, come inside, and propose, and then we would take that shower together.

The shark's tooth necklace is made from the first shark's tooth we found on the beach. The soap is to remind you that you are beautiful. To celebrate your beauty, I want you to wash yourself with it right now and notice how wonderful you smell. The ring is to remind you of the fire that is within, beautiful and radiant but with a passion that is waiting to be released by the sun.

I know my passing will bring you much grief, but you are strong, you are beautiful, and you are Judie Kate! There is a dream inside you that will one day come true. Your fire and your brilliance will one day warm and brighten the lives of those who live in darkness. Live into that dream; become that dream.

For three months, I was the happiest man alive. I loved you so much. You were my dream come true.

After you shower, use the mirror to look at your beautiful face. Look deep into those mysterious eyes and know you are Judie Kate. When you fully know that, your dream will begin anew. I will always love you!

Don

Judie Kate put down the letter, looked at the ring on her finger, and stared at the mirror and then worked up the courage to see her face looking back at her. She saw the delicate necklace dangling on her chest. Then, she held up the mirror directly to her face and saw tears running down her red cheeks. She looked at her red and watery eyes and tried to see the mystery that Don saw. She remembered that Uncle Joe and Jay Jay saw that same secret.

As she sobbed, she tried to remind herself of who she was by saying, "I am Judie Kate." She repeated it, at first her voice quivering, then becoming increasingly stronger until it came out clear.

"I *am* Judie Kate!" She stood up, grabbed the towel and soap, and headed for the shower.

Refreshed yet still sad, she picked up the cremains box and took out the small urn. She carried it to the deserted beach where she sat down and took in the sounds, the smells, the very essence of the salty air and endless sands. She looked at her ring, fingered the necklace, and stared at the container. Sea birds began gathering around her, as if waiting for a bag of chips to be opened and shared. After looking out to the ocean for a long time, she slowly dug a hole in the sand and ceremoniously buried Don and her dream in the wet sand and cried. One by one, the birds flew away, and then she was left alone with just the agonizing refrain running through her heart of what could have been. The empty urn remained as a reminder of Don. *Story of my life.*

On the way home, she switched the radio to the mix station where she heard a song by the Moody Blues. "Your Wildest Dreams" seemed to be about her and Don. She suppressed her tears as she drove home and Tom Petty's "Running Down the Dream" played.

One dream was gone. There would never be another Don. Ever. What was the dream that Don was talking about in the letter? She remembered that Uncle Joe had said the same thing. What was her dream? She had always listened to others' dreams for her. Her parents wanted her to be a teacher like them. Her teachers wanted her to do science and math. That sorry youth minister said she should be a missionary, but he said it more because he thought with her weight she would never marry. Everybody wanted her to live their dream. *What is my dream for me?*

The miles went by as she headed back to Wilmington. When she came around a bend, she saw a sign for abused women, and suddenly, it hit her. *I want to help people like that, people who can't afford dreams, people who are shunned by society, people whose hope has been squashed. I want to help those who can't help themselves.*

She drove on, and reassuringly, from deep within, a surge of power and strength overwhelmed her and then she smiled.

I am Judie Kate!

Then it hit her. *Now what do I do?*

* * *

Joe arrived at eight that evening. It was dark, and he was not quite sure he was in the right place, but he saw a light over a porch above a garage and thought it might be Judie Kate's apartment. Before he could shoot off a text, he saw her come outside and wave. Joe smiled—it was good to connect with her again, but what were the circumstances this time?

Judie Kate ran down the steps and nearly leapt into Joe's arms, almost knocking him down.

"Uncle Joe!" she called out so loud people could have heard her down the block. He caught his balance as Judie Kate's emotions took over and tears soon drenched Joe's coat.

"Look at me," she sobbed, "that's no way to greet a friend." She backed off and pulled him to the apartment. "Let's get inside. It's chilly." Joe followed her up the stairs into the apartment.

"Home sweet home," she called out, turning to give him a hug after the door shut. She waved around the room in a circle. Inside, he saw a worn tan couch, some green and brown secondhand chairs, brown, green, and dark yellow drapes over the windows, and worn tables and lamps. Beach pictures, the obligatory decoy imitation, and other nautical adornments covered the walls and tables. The only thing modern was a modest-sized, big-screen TV and a stereo.

"It was a furnished apartment," Judie Kate explained. "I bought a bed and some other things for the bedroom. All I could afford at the time." She motioned for him to sit, and she sat on the couch under the dim light from a small lamp. Joe saw a lonely Christmas tree on a table with a present underneath.

"So, I wasn't sure about dinner. I have some leftovers the neighbors brought me," she said. Joe answered that he had stopped on the way down.

"Okay, then dessert?"

Judie Kate returned with two bowls of ice cream—Joe's with scoops of chocolate and vanilla and hers with Rocky Road. "Some things don't change, right?" she asked. They spooned several bites, both avoiding the inevitable.

"It's good to see you, Judie Kate," Joe said. "It's been a few years, hasn't it?" Judie Kate took a swallow. She wasn't sure if Joe meant that in a bad or good way.

"Yes, it has. I guess I should explain—"

"No explanation necessary, Judie Kate." He paused for another spoonful. "Tell me about this boyfriend. I get the impression he was very special." Joe noticed the folded flag on the coffee table.

She spooned more ice cream and then paused.

"He was my dream come true, Uncle Joe." Then she burst into tears again.

Joe moved over to the couch, patted the space beside him, and a shaking Judie Kate moved closer to him, like a teenage daughter to her dad. He put his arm around her shoulders.

"Talk," he said.

Judie Kate blubbered, sobbed, sniffled, reached for tissues on the table by the couch, and finally calmed down after ten minutes. She reached over for the flag, held it to her chest like it was her favorite stuffed animal, and then she told him the story. When she finished, there was silence that Joe honored for a while. She shifted on the couch and looked Joe directly in the eyes.

"Why, Uncle Joe, why? Why does our dream come true only to be taken away? Why is God so cruel?

What did I do to deserve this? It's not fair. Why did he have to die, Uncle Joe, *why*?"

She continued to cry, huge heaving sobs and loud wails erupting from deep within as the grief came back in swells larger than the waves of a tumultuous ocean. As the minutes went by, her body shook less, and the tears began to dry up. She muttered once more, "Why?" and then whimpered until she fell asleep, her head resting on Joe's shoulder. He looked at his watch. It was after eleven.

Soon, there were sounds, and Joe was in the middle of a dream where he was in a restaurant, waiting for his meal. He could smell the sausage and eggs and toast, but in the dream, he was asleep, head resting on the table next to a plain red bottle of ketchup. A flirty waitress from a bad movie was trying to wake him up. He opened his eyes and blinked several times until things became a bit clearer. Judie Kate was standing in front of him.

"One of us had to get up and make breakfast, sleepy head. Coffee, milk, tea?"

Joe was still in the restaurant.

"Uh, coffee."

Judie Kate, dressed in a long, gray, flannel nightshirt that reached to the floor, hair still wet from her morning shower, was already walking back to the kitchen.

"It's instant, make it yourself. Right cabinet over the sink. Sugar is in the bowl by the toaster."

This was a side of Judie Kate Joe never thought would emerge. Judie Kate the boss? He headed for what he thought was the bathroom.

"On the right," Judie Kate called out. She spooned out the scrambled eggs, placed a sausage patty on the plastic plate, and set it on the table. Joe ambled back into the small kitchen, looked around for a coffee cup, found one, filled it up, and placed it in the microwave.

He looked at Judie Kate and saw an older, more mature woman. College had been good for her in many ways, he could tell. She had short hair and was still overweight, but her carriage was stronger, despite her grief. There was something new about her he could not peg.

"What?" she said, looking at him looking at her.

"Sorry, I just have not seen you in three years. In some ways, you have changed, grown up. In other ways, you are still Judie Kate."

She set the plates on the table.

"Not sure if that is good or bad, Uncle Joe."

They ate their breakfast while talking in fits and starts. Then, Joe broached the subject that had him scratching his head.

"Why didn't you tell your parents about Don?" he asked, struggling with a mouth full of scrambled eggs.

Judie Kate responded, "You know how they are. I just didn't want to bother them with another letdown."

"You know, you three might connect better if you reach out to them more."

Suddenly, there was fire in Judie Kate's dark eyes.

"We've hoed that row before, right? If it fits into their grand plan for me, then we get to talk about it. If not, discussion over." She forked up some eggs. Talking with her mouth full, she continued.

"If I had told them Don was a soldier, Daddy would have said, 'Well, you know that's going to be a life of poverty, moving around, and constant worry about whether he will be deployed, and if he will come back. Not a good thing for my little girl,'" she said, mocking George's voice. "Momma would say, 'Well, you know that if you are moving around, you won't get tenure and your pension will probably be affected.'" She shook her head. "Besides, Momma would have asked me how I landed a soldier in the first place. That's insulting. Why couldn't I land a nice man, Uncle Joe?"

She got up from the table. "Strawberry preserves or grape jam?" she asked, going to the fridge.

"Both," Joe answered.

She brought out two jars of Smuckers jelly. "Only the best, right?" she asked. As they ate their jelly toast, Judie Kate's face turned serious and sad. "Thanks again for coming, Uncle Joe. It means a lot to me. You just don't know." She looked off in the distance out the window framed with yellow and black checkerboard curtains. The ocean waves were flowing in and out, the breeze was blowing from the south, and the sun was warm. She felt the spray cool their bodies. Don paused, pulled her close, held her tight, and kissed her slowly, passionately ...

Joe dropped a spoon on the table, making a loud clink. Coming out of her reverie, she looked at Joe.

"I didn't know love could hurt so much, Uncle Joe." She looked back out the window, but this time, nothing was there.

Joe walked over to the sink. "What are you doing? she said."

"Thought I would wash the dishes for you."

"Incorrect," Judie Kate responded. "Tell you what, you go get your shower while I finish up in here." Joe wandered off to get his bag and headed for the bathroom. In a few minutes, he came back out.

"Uh, Judie Kate, this is embarrassing, but I forgot my soap. Can I borrow yours?"

Judie Kate laughed out loud.

"Uncle Joe, seriously?" She laughed a bit more. "Sure."

Joe walked back to the bathroom and then paused.

"It's good to hear you laugh, Judie Kate," he called out.

He emerged from the bathroom a new man. Judie Kate motioned for him to sit on the couch with her. She told Joe about what Don said about a dream. Then, she told him about the sign she saw on her drive and how she wanted to help those who could not help themselves. She told him she was not sure teaching was for her, but she did not know what else to do.

"It's like I have a dream, but I can't get to it, Uncle Joe. You know, one of those dreams where you can see where you need to go, but the harder you try, the worse it gets? The obstacles keep getting thicker and the distance farther, and the dream ends with you being tired."

Joe thought for a moment, like he always did.

"Well, Judie Kate, who said it all has to come together at once? I know we teach people to pursue their dreams, make them come alive, but sometimes, dreams come to you, unfolding like a story, one chapter at a time. It's like a resume. You build it bit by bit until the dream finally comes true. Each experience is the foundation for what comes next. You know, teaching involves helping those who can't help themselves. Maybe that *is* the starting place. If that doesn't work out, then you scratch that one off the list and move to the next one. A process of elimination, if you will. Or, maybe teaching is what pays the bills while you work on Plan B."

Judie Kate thought it over while they sat silently on the couch.

Joe continued, "If nothing else, at your young age now, you know full well the pain and power of grief and loss. Very few women and men have experienced such a loss this early in life. Somewhere down the road, this will be valuable for you and others."

Judie Kate was slow to answer.

"I know that was supposed to make me feel better, Uncle Joe, but right now, it just hurts."

He squeezed her shoulders.

"And it will for quite a time to come. There is an old hymn that says, 'We'll understand it better by and by.' Many people say that this is simplistic, cheery, summery faith, but when you look at it from an

Eastern religious perspective, things will eventually come together. The brightness of Yang is tempered with the darkness of Yin to make life even overall."

After a moment, she said, "He was my dream come true, Uncle Joe."

Joe paused, picking his words carefully. Grief is not a good time to be logical, practical, or even truthful.

"Judie Kate?" He waited a bit. "Please take this the right way. I know this whole ordeal has brought you more pain than you have ever felt, but ..."

Now he had her attention. She pulled back a bit, worried that maybe a lecture was about to begin, and looked up at him.

"But what?"

"Maybe this was *a* dream come true but not *the* dream come true." Joe let the words sink in. Judie Kate relaxed and thought them over carefully.

"He was so much like you, Uncle Joe." She cried softly, and Joe put his arm around her shoulder. "I miss him so much. What am I going to do now?"

Joe looked around at the sparse room and its furnishings. He thought about the simplicity Judie Kate lived in. This was no doubt part of her insecurities, like the family whose yard is filled with junk, and the grass needs mowing, all symbols of low self-esteem. A mess for the neighbors to fuss about. She was old enough to deserve a neighborly intervention, but now was not the time.

"Right now, your past and present are so intertwined, the future is out of sight. Live this moment, the pain, the memories, the sadness. As the days go by, the pain will diminish, the memories will become more important, the future will be clearer. One day this will all make sense, but today is not going to be that day, and neither will tomorrow."

Joe squeezed her shoulder, and Judie Kate looked at him with a quivering smile. They sat in the quiet of the moment for a long time, then Joe broke the silence.

"Part of the grief cycle is dreams, Judie Kate. Sometime in the next year or so, Don will come back to you, and in that dream or vision, he will let you know that you will be fine and that the next chapter in your life is ready to begin."

* * *

A few days later, there was a knock at her door. Judie Kate opened it to see a handsome, chiseled soldier standing in front of her. *Oh no*, she thought to herself. *This can't be good.* The soldier spoke first.

"Are you Judie Kate Wilson?"

A bit suspicious, Judie Kate fired back, "Why do want to know? Who are you?"

"I'm sorry, ma'am. I'm Private Ronald Sanders. I roomed with Don. I have some packages for you."

Judie Kate softened up as she explained, "I'm sorry. I didn't mean to be rude. It's just, the last few days—"

Private Sanders interrupted her and said, "I understand, ma'am. We were close friends. I'm hurting too."

She motioned for him to come inside. He took off his hat and sat in the chair where she was pointing.

The two of them shared stories of Don. As the private spoke, Judie Kate began to understand Don even more than she had before.

"Ma'am?"

"Please, call me Judie Kate."

"Yes, ma'am, sorry," the private squirmed at the request to go against his military training. He tried again as an unseen drill sergeant screamed into his ear.

"Judie Kate, you need to know that Don was a private person, not one to share his feelings and emotions. What little he shared about his family was not good. In his line of duty, he saw things that no man or woman should ever see. He kept these things to himself. But after he met you, he became a new person. You were all he talked about. That man loved you, Judie Kate. I can't even say that in a way that gets across what I am trying to say."

Judie Kate began crying, and Private Sanders squirmed again, clearly uncomfortable with her emotions, and took out some tissues from his pocket.

"Figured you might need these." He handed them to her and sat back as the grief overcame her again. He let her cry for quite some time. After a few moments, she settled down.

"I'm sorry," she apologized.

"No apology necessary, ma'am, sorry, Judie Kate." He waited dutifully, proudly, like the guard at the Tomb of the Unknown Soldier, as she calmed down. Judie Kate sniffed, wiped her nose, blew her nose, then wiped it again, and sniffed one more time.

"Private Sanders?" she asked.

He corrected her, saying, "Ronald, ma'am, uh, Judie Kate."

She smiled, then asked, "Ronald, can you tell me what happened? Anything would help."

Private Sanders sat back, collected his thoughts, as if selecting what could be said professionally and what should not be shared for her sake, and then proceeded. He told her what he knew about Don's life, how he was engaged in top secret missions in the Middle East that often involved dangerous operations deep in enemy territory. Don worked with a small crew of soldiers who were specially trained in sophisticated, highly secret, tactics. Several times, Don had to fend for himself while trapped behind enemy lines, and once, he had to escape a situation solo through a thousand miles of Arab enemies to get back to a safe place. He had been wounded several times, survived IEDs, seen buddies blown into fragments, and even started one military coup.

Judie Kate shook her head and gasped. "I never knew."

She placed her face into her hands and tears came to her eyes. Private Sanders took out more tissues. She took them from him, wiped her eyes and face, and stared blankly beyond Private Sanders' head.

"Can you tell me anything else?"

Private Sanders shifted in the chair, folded his hands as if in prayer, looked down, and then looked at her.

"All I know is that he was behind enemy lines in Syria. It involved ISIS, and he was captured and then tortured until he died."

He didn't tell her that Don was dismembered and shipped in a box with an ISIS flag draped around his body to an American fort in Iraq. "I'm sorry, Judie Kate. I am so sorry." The bluntness of his response caught her off guard. The blow was intense, to the stomach of pain, the heart of grief, the mind of reality. She cried again, hurting over what Don had to go through—defending America, democracy, decency in a land that seemingly did not care, in a war that had never ended since the time of Abraham himself.

"*Oh my God*," she sobbed over and over again. "Oh my God."

After a while, Private Sanders got up.

"I've got two boxes for you, Judie Kate." He went out the door while Judie Kate got her act together. After a moment, she stood and waited at the door. He arrived back with one large box and then returned with another.

"What's inside?" Judie Kate wondered aloud after the boxes had been moved into the house.

Private Sanders took out a knife and cut the tape.

"CDs, ma'am, uh, I'm sorry, Judie Kate. A few thousand CDs. Don loved music. Figured you might want them. There's some knickknacks, some mementos, a napkin from an ice cream shop he said you guys liked, Cone Heads, I believe, and his Purple Heart. And, I found a pic of me and him when we were in Kandahar. As far as I know, it is the only pic I have of Don. Thought you might like it."

Judie Kate looked at the wrinkled picture of Don and Private Sanders smiling, a selfie from a strange land, mortar shells stacked behind them. Then she found the Purple Heart in a small case. She took it out and held it in her shaking hand, looking back and forth from the medal to her ring. She picked up the napkin and saw he had written *Rocky Road* on it. She smiled, remembering their many visits to the shop.

Then she ran her hand through the CDs. What would she do with all of them? She asked Private Sanders.

"Judie Kate, when I hear a song from his collection on the radio, I think of him. Maybe you can use the music to remember him too."

It was getting late, and emotionally, Judie Kate had worn out Private Sanders. He stood to go.

"I have to get back to the base."

She got up to let him out.

"Ma'am, sorry, Judie Kate, would it be out of line to give you a hug?"

Judie Kate was not sure, but there was something in his voice that reassured her the hug was truly from Don.

"I would appreciate that," she replied.

He walked over in strong military pose, as if the hug were from the Marine Corps itself, and wrapped his arms around her and patted her on the back. The embrace was full of grief, warmth, and genuine compassion. He pulled back and then looked her in the eyes.

"Judie Kate, just know that Don loved you more than life itself. Never forget that." He walked to the door, opened it, and then paused, assuming his former military air. "Ma'am, if I may say so, having met you, seen you, I understand what Don saw in you. You are one hell of a lady."

"Thank you, Private Sanders," she answered. "Thank you so much for taking the time to come here. You didn't have to do this, you know."

"You're right, Judie Kate. But I'm glad I did." He walked away, and the door shut behind him. She sat down on the couch and picked up the Purple Heart, clutching it in her hand.

That afternoon, she sifted through the CDs. Oldies from the fifties, big band music—Bennie Goodman, Glen Miller—New Orleans jazz, eighties rock and roll, seventies disco and southern rock, Motown, pop standards, even some old country.

She heard Private Sanders again: "Maybe you can use the music to remember him too."

"I will," she said to herself. And suddenly, her love for old music began. She pulled out the Doobie Brothers, put the CD into her stereo, and soon "Listen to the Music" was playing. The music got her through the grief and misery of the days ahead. It was like Don was with her all the time.

Every Sunday, she drove to Don's trailer and spent time walking on the beach and then time inside, reading, doing homework, making simple sandwiches for supper, listening to music, and grieving Don. As the weeks went by, the pain began wearing off, but the sadness remained. There was a hole to fill, and she was sure nobody could fit into that hole. Don was the perfect soul mate, and now he was gone.

One day, a man from the big house beside the trailer came knocking. She was lost in a treatise on educational theory, and the knock surprised her. She closed the book and set it down. "Come in," she said.

She stood up and welcomed the stranger, who then introduced himself. His stylish clothes, body language, and northern accent said a lot. The way he looked at her, the surprise on his face, said even more. She had seen it too many times. The judgment, the surprise, the inability of people to accept a person for who she was. Judie Kate tried to brush it off.

"Hi, uh, I am Billings Champlain. I own this house over here," he said, pointing to the one beside her driveway. "I saw your car outside. I had talked to Don about buying this place. Is he here?"

The question hit her hard. She guessed he did not know, would have no reason to know, about Don's death. She fought back a tear and related the sad story.

Billings was caught off guard. He saw the ring on Judie Kate's finger and quickly apologized. "I did not know. Please accept my condolences."

Judie Kate motioned for him to come inside and pointed to a seat. They both sat. He looked around the quaint, old trailer, at the cheap paneling, the vinyl chairs, the old fridge, and the metal windows. It was like the projects compared to his mansion with decks around all three floors, big screen TVs everywhere, and expensive cars parked in the sand and oyster-shell drive.

"We met in Wilmington, where I go to school," Judie Kate explained. "He was going to propose on Christmas Eve, but he was killed in action. He could never tell me what he did in the military, always top secret, but I think he was Special Ops or something like that." She looked at her ring, and Billings paused before asking her his question.

"Again, I am so sorry. We had some good conversations when he was here. Said this trailer belonged to his grandparents, I believe."

"Yes, as you can tell, it goes back a ways. He had no family, so he left it to me."

"Most certainly," Billings answered, not quite hiding his condescension. "I tried to get him to sell it to me, but he never would. It was all he had left of his family. So I feel bad asking you the same since this is all you have to remind you of him, but if you ever want to part with it, I am willing to offer a good sum." It was more an offer to get rid of the eyesore between his mansion and the one next door, and he wanted to beat his neighbor to the punch.

"Not to push you or anything, but you're in college, and the taxes here in North Topsail are quite high. Not to mention the insurance. Just something to keep in mind." He rose to leave, and Judie Kate stood as he headed to the door.

He handed her his card. "There's my number. If we are around and you need anything, come on by. And, again, I am very sorry to hear about Don. He was a good young man."

He shut the metal door behind him, and Judie Kate shook her head. She had not thought about taxes or even insurance. She liked the trailer; it was a second home to her now, and she often fantasized about living there when she graduated, but the reality was, where exactly would she work? Could she get a job in a school nearby? If not, what else would she do? Work at a restaurant? Or a beach shop? *Oh Lord, my parents would like that!*

She sat again and thought some more. *Dream, Judie Kate, dream. What is my dream? How would this fit into my dream?* She went to the shower, still thinking, as the scent from the lavender soap filled the air.

July 8, 2015, Wednesday

It actually happened! Uncle Joe said Don would come back to me in a dream and he did! I wish he could have materialized and stayed with me forever. Still, it was shocking and delightful to feel his presence again, even if it was only in a dream. He was at the beach, at his trailer. The sun was high, the day was warm, the ocean was glistening. He stood there on the beach and talked to me. He said he was fine, that life was good. He told me not to worry about him and to take care of myself. Then he said something I'm still pondering.

"When the old becomes new, your dream will come true. She will tell you when your new dream begins."

I wonder what this means?

Love,
Judie Kate

* * *

August 2015

He stepped onto the campus of Petros Christian College in the mountains near Asheville and felt the rush of the Spirit fill him. Maybe it was the mountain air in western North Carolina, maybe it was freedom of being away from home, maybe it was just the expectation of fulfilling God's will for his life, but he felt it. As he walked along the sidewalks lined with old oaks, his body tingled with the love and acceptance he had longed for all his life. He knew this was where God wanted him to be. As he walked toward what he thought was the administration building, he saw other students around him, smiling with joy and mission, empowered by the knowledge that they were doing the will of God.

He walked up to a table lined with boxes, folders, tote bags, and friendly faces.

"Hi," a chipper female voice called out.

He looked up and saw a smiling blonde with piercing blue eyes and a face full of excitement.

"I'm Kristi. Welcome to Petros! How can I help you?"

He looked around the room and then back at the table and met her gaze again. There was something about her. The way she stood, her confidence, her demeanor. It was as if energy exuded from her, radiating like an angel.

"I'm new. What do I do?"

"I'm here to help you. Step right over here."

Her movements were perky, quick, assured. She wore modest, blue jean shorts, black Converse shoes, and a maroon Petros Christian College pullover shirt. She awkwardly pulled out a box wrapped in shipping tape from underneath the table.

"Christian T-shirts," she explained. "All the newbies get one." She pulled at the tape several times but had no success.

"Here," he said, pulling out a knife. "Let me help." He made three swipes and then opened the box. "There," he said.

"That's some knife!" Kristi said.

He ordered it from Amazon after doing some Bible study from texts he found on the Christian survival weapons website. It was a basic survival knife, much like a Swiss Army knife. The verse "I can do all things through Christ" was etched by a laser into the wooden handle. Whenever he needed strength to resist temptations, he reached into his pocket and squeezed his knife.

"I keep it with me all the time. It's my Sword of the Spirit. When Satan comes and tempts me, I reach into my pocket and squeeze it. It reminds me I can fight off the devil with the Sword of the Spirit."

"What a cool idea!" Kristi said. "So, what size and color shirt?"

***

That night, there was a picnic and a bluegrass band. He listened as he ate his hot dog and potato chips and sipped his soda on the grassy lawn. The rhythms and sounds and harmonies of the voices, the banjo, the mandolin, the guitar, and the fiddle quieted the ever-stirring conflagration within his soul. He had never heard this kind of music before. His parents always listened to Christian music on the K-Love station. The mountain gospel music was filled with joy and a beat that made him nod his head, and suddenly, he knew that he had found something beautiful to give his heart to.

Kristi saw him and plopped down right next to him. She looked over at him as he gazed at the band. "They're good, huh? They go here. Good guys. All soldiers for Christ. They represent the college as ambassadors."

She took a bite out of her chili dog and listened. He looked at her face, the outline of it against the oaks and pines on the mountains far away. There was an attraction, unlike the feelings of old that he knew were evil. A softness, a peace, that overcame him. He had an urge to hold her and kiss her, yet within that desire was a new wisdom, a patience that felt comforting to him. He looked at her again and reached for his bag of chips.

"Want some?"

"Thanks!" she said as she smiled and took a small handful.

The band played a song they introduced as one of Alison Krauss's called "Shield of Faith." He didn't know who Alison Krauss was, but he nodded to the beat and understood the words. And for the first time in a long while, there was peace in his soul.

* * *

Wednesday, November 16, 2016

The hospice nurse sat quietly and patiently by the bed in a small chair, holding Jay Jay's wrist, taking her pulse. It had slowed dramatically in the last hour as her breathing became more labored. The room was dark except for a small lamp on the nightstand beside the bed. Jay Jay was comfortable, warm under the quilt, the morphine easing the pain. Joe had pulled up another chair beside her on the other side of the bed, holding her hand, savoring these last minutes together. He looked at her face, the lines that weren't there not long ago. The hair that had just started to gray. There was a peaceful smile that ignored the seriousness of the moment.

They had talked about this time for the last few weeks after she was diagnosed with stage four breast cancer. The cancer had developed fast, too fast for the doctors to catch in time. It was in the lymph nodes before they found out. The two had discussed it and agreed that no chemo or radiation would be used. Given the family history of breast cancer, even with treatment there was no guarantee it would not come back. Jay Jay worried she would lose her dignity through it all, so this was her choice. The reality tore them apart and then pulled them together into a spiritual embrace that was deeper than any love they had felt for each other.

Joe thought back over the years: how they met, how they courted, the early years when they could barely afford groceries. When they shared one lime freeze instead of having two because that was all they could afford. The attempts to have a baby, the decision to forgo adoption, finally landing good jobs, and beginning to settle down. Life was going well until a few weeks ago. Then, it crashed.

Jay Jay looked up at him through weary eyes and with all the strength she had left, pulled him close and hoarsely whispered to him. "I am going now. I have loved you all these years, but it is time for me to go. I know sometimes I have disappointed you, but I have always loved you and always will." She paused to catch her breath, her chest heaving deeply. "I will send someone to you, and you will know when she comes. She will be your new dream come true." She paused again. "I love you, Boo Bird. I have always loved you and always will."

She held his hand tight, and he leaned over once more to kiss her for the final time. She inhaled deeply, held it for a moment, and then exhaled her last breath, her hand cooling now, relaxing as her soul left for the next station in life. Joe cried, tears welling up, leaving it all behind. The nurse placed her stethoscope on Jay Jay's breast and held it there for quite some time. Joe looked over at her, hoping for one more breath, one more squeeze from her hand. The nurse looked back and shook her head, a tear emerging from her eye too. No matter how many times she did this, no matter how professional she tried to be, she still got attached to them. It was especially hard with Jay Jay and Joe. They were so close, so in love.

"I'm sorry, Joe."

She hung the stethoscope around her neck, packed up her things, and left the room to let Joe have his last moments with Jay Jay.

"I'll come back when you are ready." She looked at her chart and filled it in: TOD: 1:56 a.m.

Wednesday, November 16, 2016

It's 1:56 in the morning, and I feel like I'm losing my mind. I just had the strangest dream. I am literally shaking all over and have goose bumps. I can hardly write, I am shaking so bad. I don't know if it is scary or what, maybe a portent, a premonition. Joe's Jay Jay was dying, and she came to me.

She was wearing red overalls and she said, "I want you to take care of Joe now, but you must change. When the numbers add up, you will know. Tell Boo Bird I said so." Then, she disappeared, and that's when I was startled out of my sleep!

I have never had a dream like this. It was real, alive, spiritual, like I was connected to something deep in the universe. I don't know what to do. Did Jay Jay really die? That would be so terrible. I'll call Dad and Mom tomorrow just to make sure everything is okay. Do I tell Uncle Joe about the dream? What if he thinks this is crazy? Is this another "infatuation" that Momma worried about coming alive in my unconscious mind? Did I just make this up? I have seen Uncle Joe once since I left for Wilmington. I thought that was over. What did she mean that I would have to change? What numbers did she mean?

It's making me remember my dream about Don and what he said. When the old becomes new, your dream will come true; she will tell you when your new dream begins.

It can't possibly mean what it sounds like, right? Uncle Joe is twenty years older than me ... Am I supposed to marry him?

Now I am shaking again. It's like I am fourteen all over again and still have a crush on Joe.

Love?
Judie Kate

* * *

FRIDAY, MARCH 31, 2017

At three in the afternoon, Judie Kate sat dejectedly in the trailer and stared at the two slips of paper. The tax statement had arrived the same week as the insurance. Maybe she was just naïve, but she didn't know the taxes would be that high. And flood insurance? On her salary? She shook her head. Selling the trailer would be the last nail in the coffin. No more connection to Don except for her ring and necklace and CDs. She could ask her parents, but she knew that would go nowhere.

Tears came to her eyes as she reached for her pocketbook and searched for the card. Her hand shook as she touched the numbers. There was a voice, and after pleasantries, she explained her situation. She sighed.

"I'm ready to sell if you are still interested." She couldn't believe what she was hearing. "Three hundred thousand dollars?"

Billings said he would have his lawyers contact her the next week.

* * *

SATURDAY, SEPTEMBER 30, 2017
ASHEVILLE, NORTH CAROLINA,
BLUE RIDGE PRIDE FESTIVAL

The ministry team gathered in the lobby, held hands, and prayed openly as tourists stared in wide-eyed disbelief at the self-righteous display of faith. Then, empowered by the Holy Spirit, they left the hotel and took to the streets, which were filled with people of all descriptions. Gay and lesbian couples held each other's hands and kissed openly as they violated God's law and destroyed society and ruined the sanctity of marriage. The young man held up his placard: *Homosexuals destroy families!* One man stopped and looked him straight in the eye.

"Oh, honey, Jesus loves the little children. Red, yellow, black, white, queer." He stopped, and before he knew it, the gay man kissed him on the lips. "How's that for a holy kiss!"

Before he could restrain himself with Christian love, he hollered out, "Faggot! Burn in Hell!" Then he caught himself.

"I'm sorry," he called out, but the man was lost in the crowd. *Love the sinner, hate the sin,* he reminded himself.

He continued his lone ministry down the sidewalk, raising his placard in a pious display of conviction, living out his commitment to God, letting his works speak for his faith. Many ignored him, some ridiculed him, a few even confronted him, scolding his narrow-mindedness.

"It's the twenty-first century, Jesus," one called out.

"David loved Jonathan!" another announced to his face.

One more walked up to him. "Homosexuality is in the Bible! King David was gay!" he said.

"Tell me something, preacher boy. Why didn't Jesus ever marry? Ever wonder why he went about with all those male disciples?"

He continued handing out tracts that were tossed into trashcans or left to blow away in the breeze that wafted through the streets. As he walked by a club, he heard part of a song.

"It cuts like a knife ... "

It was a slow rock and roll song, so clearly of the devil, but the persistent rhythm, the strumming on the strings, even the raspy voice of the singer, caught him and ensnared him. He fought against it but recalled that God had used evil to promote the good of the Israelites, the salvation of the world through Jesus Christ. God used pagan kings from Assyria, Babylon, and Persia to promulgate His plan for Israel. God used the reprobate Samson to destroy the Philistines. God used the evil Judas to kill Jesus to bring salvation to the world.

He recalled Isaiah 45 and the prediction that the 45th President would make America great again. God was now using President Trump to make America great and get rid of abortion and sinful, murderous, rapist immigrants. With this justification, he looked around and saw no one from the ministry team on the streets, so he quickly dove into the club and listened to the song.

The bar smelled of beer, and he saw people he normally would never have associated with. Tattoos, beards, tongue studs and nose rings, blue hair, and skin peeking out through slashed-up jeans. He reached into his pocket and found his knife. The feelings that followed him everywhere were like a knife that cut deep into his very soul, slicing up his commitment to Christ. But like the Sword of the Spirit, he could use a knife with the shield of faith to fight for the Christian cause and defeat the devil within. This would be his secret mantra, his fight song, to conquer the Whore of Babylon.

The beat caught him, and he felt the pulse and power of the song. The rhythms filled him with, what? He could not explain it. It was as if there was a broader aspect of music that his narrow, theological ways had stymied, had blocked. It had guts, grit. Substance. That was it. Substance. Life. It was deeper than the Christian music he listened to. It had the same power as the spirituals he had discovered in the mountains. He asked someone who was singing the song.

"Bryan Adams, dude. Where ya been?" was the answer.

He stepped outside and googled the name on his phone.

* * *

REALGUYSLIKEME&U BLOG
JUNE 2, 2018 11:29 P.M.

So, I'm at the Ocrafolk Festival on Ocracoke Island in North Carolina. Hey, I play guitar and mandolin, so why not come here and check out the scene, right?

Dudes, you gotta check this out! Lots of hot chicks here. Man, bikinis, those real short shorts with the front pockets hanging out, skin-tight leggings, halter tops, even a tube top—remember those, guys? Whew, makes a man proud to be a man! I posted some pics on the blog here. They are dangling the lures, and I'm taking the bait.

So, I go to an auction tonight, thought I might pick up something nautical for the homeplace, ya know? I go in, and there's this hottie who gives me a real good smile, and I give her a wink back. So, like, I'm thinking we are making a connection, right? She was in a crowd, so I couldn't exactly get to her. Well, I go and sit and then as the auction begins, there's a sale, and here she comes up onstage to get her stuff.

Wow! She's got a figure, hips, and narrow waist, kinda like Beyoncé, you know, and brown hair like her too! What a tan! And it's all wrapped up in these white, tight skinny jeans, I mean *skinny*, and then a blue tank top that was tight and cut way down. So much cleavage, I mean, those puppies were barking loud, right? Man, match that with her long, brown hair, and like, I was beside myself.

I'm sitting next to an older couple, and she says to her man, "She just wants to be seen." And I'm like, hell yeah, she's getting her wish, right?

I mean, isn't that why girls wear these things? They want to be seen, and they want some too, right? Why else would they put that stuff on display? Check her out! I put her pic on the blog.

After the show, I find her and try to make some small talk, but she gives me the cold shoulder. So what's up with the smile, right? They flirt and dress up to get our attention, and they turn off the burner and then act as if we are the problem 'cause we want some home cooking, if you get my drift.

Okay, guys, sound off here. You can see her pic. Is she advertising or what?

As always, try to keep it clean so we can be respected! (Yeah right!)

* * *

REALGUYSLIKEME&U BLOG
JUNE 3, 2018 11:14 P.M.

To continue ... I find her again at the ticket booth this morning. She's got on this dress that is uneven, showing some side skin and then covering up the front and back. Teasing us, right? So I get my ticket and try to make small talk. She gets this attitude, like I am below her. Then, I see her at the storytelling that night. Man, she's got on this outfit, I don't know it's kinda like pajamas or something. Really short dress that flows all out, gives you the feeling you can look up her skirt, right?

Hey, dudes, I googled it. They're called rompers! And the top is loose. I'll swear she had on no bra! What did Eddie Money sing? Shakin'? Yeah, got me shakin', if you know what I mean. Check out this pic I snapped when she was turned around. I got one of her bending over too!

Hey, so I tried one more time, and she blew me off again! Said I wasn't her type. So I asked her what her type was, and she said she didn't like tattoos or beards or wallets on chains and stuff. What about the person inside, I ask? Maybe there is more to me than outward show, right? How do you know what's in the store if you don't go shopping? She walked off. Guess there is less to her than that outward show, right?

So guys, is this deceptive advertising? They're calling our name, but when we answer, then it's the wrong man. Sound off!

* * *

So, I'm leaving this place, man. Good music, but no scoring! I even shaved my beard off and put on my good pair of jeans and found her again. At first, she didn't recognize me. Good! But then she did, and she pissed me off with that attitude again. Makes you want to get even, ya know? Here are some more hottie pics on the ferry.

* * *

THURSDAY, SEPTEMBER 13, 2018

The young Christian man sat in Dr. Cranston's office, staring at the shelves on three walls filled with books and academic journals. Dr. Cranston was a short, balding man with stained teeth and splotchy hands who wore dark suits with starched, white shirts. On a lampstand in the corner was a pile of papers to grade. On the side of his desk was a stack of scholarly journals. There were artifacts and antiquities on his shelves from the Holy Land he brought back from archeological digs, and there were nine different Bibles on his desk.

"What's on your mind? You sounded pretty concerned this morning in class."

He talked about his calling, his desire for ministry. He talked about losing Kristi.

"Yes, son, she is a fine young lady, but she has had her heart set on missions in Africa for a while now. I know that one hurts, but who are we to argue with the plan of God? You'll find another Kristi. Just listen to God and He will lead you to the right one."

The young man asked, "Dr. Cranston, do you believe in dreams?"

The old professor replied that he did depending on the content.

"So, tell me, what was your dream, young man?"

He then related a dream he had the previous night. A dark-headed woman rose out of the blue ocean. On her head was a wreath of laurel, but there were blue and green flowers on it. She was beautiful, tempting, singing a song that dangerously, seductively, lured him like the Greek Sirens. He reached out to her, as if giving in to lust, but then the woman's siren songs abated, and she settled on the beach, dry, looking to him for acceptance, as if in need.

"Sing for me," she called out. "Sing for me."

Dr. Cranston nodded his head, thinking for a moment. He crossed his legs and looked to the right, as if an answer might be found on the shelves in one of his books.

The young man saw his professor looking around, so he explained his fight with his feelings, with the demons within. They centered around two things: women and music. He had read about the Ocrafolk Festival at the beach on Ocracoke Island and wanted to go. The problem was that he knew the beach meant bikinis and drinking and hedonism. He wanted to hear the music, but he wasn't sure of his ability to resist temptation. He asked about the Sword of the Spirit—could he use that to slay the demons within?

"First off, son, don't be afraid of the world. Jesus lived in the world. He ate and drank with the sinners of his day. They called him a drunkard and glutton, remember? And, he never shied away from women. Remember that Samaritan woman at the well? She tried to lure him in with her sexual wiles. He fought her off with wisdom from scripture. You can do the same.

"Now, to take that further, let's be honest here. If God leads you to a woman, you are supposed to have feelings for her, right? You can't 'be fruitful and multiply' without having feelings for her. Read the Song of Solomon again. That's an erotic love poem, son. It's a biblical way to have a relationship with the one God has led you to. Let's face it, if you are around women, you are going to have some feelings. That's only normal. If you didn't have feelings for a woman, then I would think you were gay, and that brings up another conversation. But it's what you do with those feelings, son. If you lust and dwell on them, then that is wrong. That's when the shield of faith and the Sword of the Spirit come into play."

He nodded his head. It was comforting to hear this wise reassurance from his professor. He saw a picture of Dr. Cranston and his wife on the shelves behind the desk.

"I think that is a good image to carry with you. The sword is Christ's word, the very words of God. Scripture, son, scripture is the Word of God, the sword you will use. Use that with the shield of faith

Paul talked about. Fight the good fight. I think the festival would be a good place to share the Word. Hand out tracts, preach on the streets like Peter and Paul. Hey, it's hot there. Hand out some water in Jesus' name. Be a witness, son. Sure, there will be temptations, but stand up to the devil. Slay the demons with the Sword of the Spirit."

He nodded his head, his mind and heart and body slowly filling with strength.

"So, let's get to the music. I know from your interest in the Psalms and from our other conversations that music is a passion for you. There's music all over the Bible, right? Why can't music be all over your soul? How can you grow this love of music if you stay away from it? And, I've heard you play on campus. Those Appalachian spirituals you keep digging up are good, and you've got a knack for singing them. And, I heard some other sounds in there as well. A little jazz, I think. You've got talent, son, talent. God has given you a gift, and sometimes, we don't know just what to do with those gifts. Now, what is this place?"

"The Ocrafolk Festival on Ocracoke Island, off the coast of North Carolina on the Outer Banks. Looks like mostly bluegrass."

"Think of the parallels, son. Jesus called the disciples to the Sea of Galilee. That's where the bulk of his ministry was. What better place to begin that ministry of yours? And, I bet the music will be good for your soul since you like bluegrass, right? Ministry does not have to be all serious. So, take some Bibles and tracts. You can witness on the streets, on the beach. And enjoy the music. You just might find a young Christian woman there too! Maybe that is why you feel this tug to go to Ocracoke."

He nodded at the professor's encouraging words.

"Yes, that will be the beginning of your mission. And like Jesus, you must go to the wilderness and be tempted by Satan. Maybe Ocracoke is your wilderness, son. Once you slay the demons, you can then begin your true mission for Christ."

That night, he looked up Ocracoke on the internet again. He saw the 2019 Ocrafolk Festival and thought once more that this would be a good time to go. He could listen to music and minister at the same time, and conquer the demons who plagued him, should they appear. He found the website of a hotel and made his reservation.

Thursday, May 30, 2019

Dad called me today and invited me down to the Ocrafolk Festival. He said he had something he wanted me to hear. I'm guessing it's probably some song he wrote. Who cares? I've never been to one Ocrafolk Festival, even though he and Momma go there every year. I think his band puts on the festival. Why do I want to go and be ignored by him and his music? Again.

BUT, he said Joe would be there doing sound, and maybe I would like to see Joe again. Is this part of JayJay's dream? Is this what Don meant? Is the

old turning into the new? I had always wondered
how we would meet up again. Is this the numbers
adding up? I never really understood that part. I've
lost a lot of weight, changed my hair, and wear
makeup now, so things have definitely changed.
Are these the numbers?

Time to take the plunge and see if this dream is
real. Hey, it's a free trip to the beach if nothing else!

Love Joe?

Tuesday, June 4, 2019

Uncle Joe arrives tomorrow evening. I am excited
and nervous. I have five days to convince him
about Jay Jay's dream. What if he doesn't believe
me? What if everything in the last three years has
been one big delusion? What numbers have to add
up? What if he has already found another woman?
What if he is not interested at all? Did he really
mean he would marry me way back when? What
if he doesn't remember saying that? What if all he
cares about now is the festival? Maybe I am going
crazy. What if this has been one crazy dream?

  Love (I hope!),
  Judie Kate

* * *

TUESDAY, JUNE 4, 2019

Joe lay in bed, thinking about the next five days. They would be frenetic, fast-paced, and furious to some extent. Deadlines, decisions to make on the spot, no time to stop running from here to there. Did he have all the things he needed? He worked through every scenario possible. Did he have enough connectors, splitters? Did he pack his small CD player? Cooler? Gatorade? Money for the trip? His gig bag was already in the truck. Ferry registrations? The orange power cord? He reminded himself that he had double-checked things twice over. *Chill, Joe, chill.* He always became anxious before a big gig—every time, like clockwork. He rolled over to sleep. *Five days to forget about the past, do man stuff, and just work sound.* It couldn't come soon enough!

* * *

REALGUYSLIKEME&U BLOG
JUNE 5, 2018 1:05 A.M.

Hey, dudes, I am heading off to the Ocracoke thing again. You guys remember last year, right? I was real into this chick who was making waves at me and then she blew me off because of all my tatts and stuff. Hey, she blew me off, so it was like she was blowing us all off, right? So, I'm back! I'm goin' to post some pics, and you can bet I'll find me some rompers again.

Those things turn me into a real man, get my drift? And you can bet I'm going to catch me a fish! Ain't no chick gonna blow me off this year, right? And if she tries, this real man is gonna show her a real man! Gonna get me some, or someone's gonna get it!

* * *

The young Christian man, full of faith and mission, packed up his Ford Escape with all the things he needed for his mission to Ocracoke: placards, boxes of tracts, King James Bibles, a large cooler, and several packs of water bottles.

"Give a cup of water in Jesus' name."

Tomorrow, he would pack his guitar and set out on his mission, ready to slay the devil within if Satan bothered him. He would sing, hand out tracts, witness, and if necessary, conquer the demons. He squeezed his knife.

Wednesday

Joe Clark reflected on the trip down from Snow Ridge as the diesel engines rumbled on the Swan Quarter ferry. He was on the outside deck, enjoying the sunshine and feeling the breeze as the wash from the ferry sloshed against the marshy banks.

While the ferry rumbled through the no-wake zone, Joe made his way to the observation deck and settled onto a very uncomfortable aluminum bench. The sun was hot, but the breeze was pleasant. He adjusted his hat and sunglasses and then watched a young couple who had to be on their honeymoon try to take a selfie. They couldn't take their eyes off each other, couldn't keep their hands off each other. She was beautiful in her loose, floral top that flapped invitingly in the wind, shorts revealing long, tanned legs; he was her hero, her knight, even if his armor was pastel and came from Belk.

"Can I take that picture for you?" Joe offered. She was quick to smile and say yes.

"You guys turn around, and we'll get one in front of the ferry."

They smiled, giggled, and held each other close. Joe handed the phone back to the young lady. She had long, dark hair; her partner's brown hair was long on top with a swoosh and short on the sides. His look was completed with a scruffy beard.

"Better make sure they are good," Joe noted.

They scrolled through, smiled, and then nodded.

"Thank you so much!" the young man said, a look of sheer joy and pride on his face as his dark brown eyes beamed his love for her.

"Honeymoon?" Joe asked.

"How did you know?" she said, taking her new husband's hand and sidling up close to him.

"Wasn't hard to figure out. You're smiling a lot."

They grinned at each other.

"That obvious, huh?" she answered.

"First time to Ocracoke?" Joe asked.

"Yes," the husband answered. "How about you?"

"Been there a few times before. I do sound for the Ocrafolk Festival. It's this weekend. You guys should plan to come. Lots of music, neat crafts, nighttime entertainment. Some of it local, some groups from far away. Neat show."

"Didn't know about that," she answered, looking at her husband as if gauging his interest. They sat back down again. "And," she said, "thanks again, sir, for taking our picture!"

Joe nodded and headed back to his seat. *Sir.* *Another sign that I'm getting old.*

As the ferry lumbered deeper into Pamlico Sound, Joe thought more about the drive that morning from Snow Ridge to Swan Quarter. Driving long distance was his time for music, relaxation, and escape. It was like when he was a kid, and he went to his room, put on a CD, cut off the lights, and laid down on the carpeted floor and closed his eyes while forgetting everything else. The beatings, the screaming, the threats, the chaos, the fear, all went away for a while as the music played. Sometimes, he played the old albums his dad had in a wish to be with him. Sometimes, he played his own CDs. He really liked the seventies and eighties rock and roll, R&B, and funk. Even disco was fine occasionally. His friends could not understand why he did not like nineties pop. It was like Joe was out of place, in the wrong decade. How could he tell them it was the only way he would ever be near his dad again?

He would look at the lights on the stereo and dream of being on stage, amps on, music loud, fans roaring. The music was the god who came to him and answered his prayers for peace and quiet. The angels were the bands, the musicians, the DJ on the radio. The scriptures were the lyrics, some as useless as the wars in the Old Testament or the begetting sagas, others as enlightening as Ecclesiastes, the Psalms, the sayings of Confucius, and the Beatitudes of Jesus. Worship was the venue with music and fans and stage lights and speakers.

The jams coming down from home were great. But it seemed like every fifth song was straight from

Jay Jay. The clincher was Chris Hillman's cover of Tom Petty's "Wildflowers," Jay Jay's favorite Tom Petty song. *It's like she is here! I just can't get away from her!*

* * *

While Joe reminisced about the old tunes he enjoyed so much, an anxious and impatient Judie Kate sat outside on the deck in a weathered Adirondack chair under the flapping canopy. The afternoon air was humid, more so than Tuesday. She finished filing her fingernails and then wiped them off with a damp cloth. After letting them dry, she opened the nail polish, Midnight Black with just a hint of glitter, and applied it to her thumb first, then the rest of her hand.

She wondered what Joe was doing on the ferry. Resting? Walking about? Looking at people, women? Reading? It had been three years. *What does he look like now?* Next door on the pier by the water, three young women types were sunbathing in their bikinis. *Tiny triangles on strings.* For a moment, she wished she could be like them. Dark tans, slim and exotic, cleavage and long hair tied up with cute clips. Wouldn't it be nice to have all the boys looking her way?

She thought about Joe's Jay Jay. *Wonder what she looked like when they got married?* She knew Jay Jay in her later years, and she hadn't been skinny or overweight. Did she have big legs or thin or regular ones? What color hair did she have? Chesty or flat? *I don't remember.* Did she dress fancy, simple, plain?

How tall was she? Funny how you look at people, but you never really see them.

She applied the polish to the other hand, slowly, carefully. *What if he doesn't like black nail polish?* The old insecurities began to rise from the dead. *Will he think I am going Goth?*

Her mother, Ellie, came out on the deck, her perpetual coffee cup in hand, and sat in the other chair. She stared at Judie Kate as she finished her right hand.

"When did you start using nail polish?" She set her mug on the table between them.

"About a year ago, Momma," Judie Kate answered, putting the pink divider between her toes, getting them ready for the polish.

"Just decided that I needed to look pretty for all the boys out there." She started with the left foot and looked at her silver toe ring. *Surprised she hasn't complained about that.*

"You get your presentation ready?" *She's always getting a presentation ready.* "I thought you retired last year, anyway."

"Still working on it and, yes, I did retire, but I still get offers for presentations. People read my book and want me to speak to them. It's in the third printing now. I don't want to disappoint them."

But you don't mind disappointing me, do you? Judie Kate hissed in her mind.

"Glad you're staying busy, Momma," Judie Kate lied. She pulled her right foot up and painted the big toe.

"When did you start wearing toe rings?" It was more a judgment than a question.

* * *

Back on the ferry, the sun was getting hot, so Joe went inside and found a seat as far away from kids as he could. *Does anybody have well-behaved kids anymore?* He leaned back and tried to nap. He thought about how many times he had come to Ocracoke for the festival. Joe had done sound a few times for the host band, Ditchville12, in the past, and Darren, the band leader who was ultra-picky about sound, liked what he heard. He knew Joe was doing sound solo, so he asked George, Judie Kate's father, if he could manage the Workshop Stage. George had helped Joe with two, big bluegrass festivals; George knew he could handle it and had recommended Joe to Darren.

Joe recalled how he met George all those years ago. The office next to him at the school where he taught had been open, so he had walked over and stuck his head inside. He saw an older man with a long, salt-and-pepper beard sitting behind a military surplus desk. ZZ Top was his office neighbor? On the wall were several photos of him standing by celebrity bluegrass pickers. He recognized J. D. Crowe, Tony Rice, Ricky Skaggs, Bobby Osborne, and Greg Luck. On the other wall was a scale drawing of a Martin D-28 Herringbone guitar.

"You into music?" Joe asked.

"A little," was the answer, which in music circles, meant, "Yeah, quite a bit."

"Joe Clark." He stuck out his hand.

"George Wilson." They shook hands and a long friendship began.

He wandered back to the soda machine, paused to stare at some young man reading a Bible, and reached into his pockets for some change. As he did, he overheard two women at a nearby table.

"So, it's your first time to Ocracoke?" the one dressed in a white, sleeveless blouse with blue shorts asked. Her light blonde hair contrasted starkly with her dark eyebrows.

"Yes," answered the other who was older and wore cutoffs and a tie-dye shirt that fit perfectly. She had short, black hair and a green, blue, and red tattoo of something unrecognizable on her left thigh. She looked out the salt-stained window at the endless sound and then back inside.

"We usually go to Nags Head or Atlantic Beach or even Myrtle, but that one is so crowded and commercial. We heard Ocracoke was quiet. So, here we are. We heard it was the best beach in North Carolina."

"Yes," the other nodded. "It is indeed quiet."

"Uh oh, you say that like a warning. I hope we didn't make a mistake."

The other leaned back, thought for a moment, and then answered.

"That depends." She explained that Ocracoke is a small village, not a sprawling beach city. There were about three blocks of shops and that was it. No malls, no movie theaters, no large-venue entertainment complexes, only a few places that could be called bars. No McDonald's or Pizza Hut or Walmart. No Wings Beachwear. No minor league baseball. No carpet golf, no go-carts. The beach, however, was long and pristine. Good shelling after a storm. No piers, no boardwalks, just sand, surf, and sun. A few ghosts, lots of lore, and three hundred years of taking care of themselves.

"Sounds like a good place to relax and just be," she answered.

"Exactly. There are a few boutiques for the ladies. The usual beach tourist traps with beach knickknacks from China, sunglass shops, the ever-present beach T-shirt shops, and good but somewhat expensive restaurants. Parasailing, fishing. If you like mosquitos," she said sarcastically, rolling her eyes, "take the trip over to Portsmouth and visit the old village there. Horseback riding. There is plenty of good music, and the Deepwater Theater features a few shows each week. Some restaurants have solo acts at night. There is no night life at two in the morning. Things start slowing down around ten at night. Overall, the groove here is quiet, slow. You must learn to relax and go with the flow of the island. Once you slip into that zone, you will have the vacation of a lifetime."

The tie-dye lady shifted her position and looked out the window at the sound again, trying to imagine a beach vacation without all the buzz, confusion, and mayhem of Myrtle Beach.

"Hmm," she replied. "Interesting."

Joe retrieved his Coke and settled down in a quiet spot for a rest. It was not to be.

A family of four came inside and sat in front of him, and immediately, the low roar of the ferry engines was overcome by the increasing din of family angst. *Great.* As they slammed down and then noisily unzipped backpacks and travel bags, the kids pulled out tablets, the wife some crocheting. Hubby was into history, and he had Alton Ballance's book on Ocracoke in front of him. He flipped through the pages. Just when it got quiet again, he became inspired.

"Ah, here is one. So, kids, did you know that the island of Ocracoke was formed about four thousand years ago?" The Historian had a deep, booming James Earl Jones voice that carried annoyingly far into the cabin of the ferry. "It is part of the barrier islands that block the ocean from the sound side. The barrier islands are part of the North Carolina Outer Banks."

The kids, a boy with long curly brown locks that covered his ears and his sister with braces and a whole face that said "attitude," remained glued to their devices. Momma crocheted and never looked up. Another man approached the family.

"Heard you talking about Ocracoke. Mind if I join?"

The Historian moved over.

"Maxwell Howard," the stranger announced.

"Oliver Newton," The Historian answered back.

Maxwell continued by saying, "I've lived on Ocracoke for a while. Want the inside scoop?"

Oh great, two Historians and one is connected to the Ocracoke Howards. This will go on forever, Joe thought.

* * *

While Joe fretted, Judie Kate worried. *Where are these insecurities coming from?* she wondered, looking at her toenails and fingernails, all black and deeply glittery. Was it being around her Momma and Daddy? Was she falling back into old patterns? Was it the anxiety of meeting Joe? Wanting his approval? His gaze? *His love?* Was she not sure about Jay Jay's dream? Maybe it was just an old crush coming back in anticipation of seeing Joe again? Was her mind playing tricks on her? What if all this was just one psychological screwup waiting to happen? Would she be embarrassed about getting ready for Joe only to find out this was all a fantasy? *How does one know for sure?*

She headed back into her room and closed the door. *What do I wear?* She pulled out light green capris and a yellow blouse. *I'll look like a cartoon bug.* Then, it was blue shorts and a cream peasant top. *Maybe it should be white shorts and a dark top?* A yellow dress seemed too much; jean shorts and a T-shirt was too little. *Why am I so nervous?* She plopped on the bed, stared at the mirror, and stuck her tongue out at herself.

* * *

Joe wound up near some young adults who were either older teens or in their early twenties. He overheard them talking music, a set list. His inner sound man woke up.

"You guys here for the festival?"

"Yes, sir," came the answer from the long-haired one. "*Sir*" again. "We're Cane Ridge Express."

He stuck out his hand. An older gentleman came over. *Gotta be the father. It's always the father.*

"I'm Joe Clark. I'm doing sound for the Workshop Stage. I've got you guys at eleven on Saturday. I looked up your website. Great credentials. Sponsors too! Looking forward to working with you!"

As he walked to the back of the ferry, the Historian had registered some new disciples. He was pointing out the window.

"Now, did you know that what you see out there is known as Pamlico Sound? It's about eighty miles long from northeast to southwest, and it varies from around fifteen to twenty miles wide. Some parts of it are about twenty-five feet deep, and most of it is around fifteen feet deep, but some of it is quite shallow. Did you know that it is the largest sound on the east coast of America? It's so big that one Spanish explorer thought he had found the Pacific Ocean when he sailed into it. In 2015, a great white shark was spotted in the sound."

Joe moved past the class as fast as he could. Soon, the nearly three-hour ferry ride was ending. The excited tourists gathered at the rails of the ferry as it approached Ocracoke Island. For quite some time, they had watched as the squat, white lighthouse grew larger and taller as the ferry chugged along.

"There it is!" cried out a middle-aged couple.

Squawking gulls sailed overhead. The tips of mainsail masts of boats in Silver Lake swayed in the breeze. The ferry engines slowed for the upcoming left turn into the harbor.

Suddenly, the Historian appeared out of nowhere and stood by a middle-aged couple. He pointed to the bay.

"That's Silver Lake, but the villagers call it The Creek." The couple seemed impressed, proud to know a tidbit that maybe others were not privy to, as if that made them true islanders. Their interest only encouraged him more. "Did you know the pirate Blackbeard came here?"

Locals were waking up in their vehicles while the tourists fled the upper deck and flocked to take pictures. Phones emerged everywhere, the rare camera aimed, autofocus on. Selfies were snapped and couples took pictures of each other with Ocracoke behind them. Children strained to see over the rails. A young girl in leggings and a GAP shirt tossed the rest of her breadcrumbs to the gulls.

Joe headed back to his truck. The trip had been uneventful. No harsh winds, no high waves. Once, a few years ago, a car had been parked with its sunroof open. The winds whipped up and the waves were intense. The ferry dipped to the side as a large wave suddenly crashed over the rails, filling the car with water from Pamlico Sound. Joe smiled with the memory. *Rookies.*

Joe settled into his truck, rolled the windows all the way down, felt the salty breeze flow around him, and thought about all the various people Ocracoke beckoned to its shores. There were the usual travelers in all kinds of vehicles with all kinds of license plates and a plethora of bumper stickers. North Face, Land's End, Old Navy, and other clothes, pressed, tattered and even torn, flapped in the breeze. Hats of every stripe covered balding heads. Enough fragrances wafted about to fill the perfume section of Macy's.

There were enough Simply Southern T-shirts to fill an entire boutique. Two older boys sported Confederate Flags. One professor type, nose up in the air like he was sniffing something, had a T-shirt that read "I took the road less traveled; now I don't know where I am." A mixed-race couple walked by and some people stared. Two kids ran between cars. Teenage girls touched up their makeup just in case. One skinny, tattooed guy, leaning against a rusty, blue Toyota truck, faded university hat on, wearing large gauges in his earlobes, stared at two young women in showy rompers who were leaning over the rails looking for dolphins. At the front of the line, a young stud, muscled arms straining his tight T-shirt, standing by his very conspicuous red convertible Corvette, sunglasses on a cord around his neck, glanced periodically to see if anyone was looking his way. Nobody was.

Joe watched as the tattooed man stared at the women and then took out a tablet and appeared to be taking pictures. Then, he held his phone up and apparently snapped even more. *Creepy.* For some unexplained reason, Joe pulled out his phone and snapped a pic of the tattooed man.

The ferry finished its slow turn into Silver Lake and positioned itself to dock at the loading ramp. There was an ever-imperceptible bump and the ferry engines eased off. Welcome to Ocracoke!

* * *

Judie Kate was standing by the deck rails, looking over the sound. She had seen the ferry come by and anticipated Joe's arrival.

"Sure you don't want any supper, Judie Kate?" Ellie asked.

"I'm fine, Momma, just not hungry."

"Are you nervous about Joe, Judie Kate?" Ellie put her book down on the table. *I'm scared to death!* Judie Kate thought to herself. "Funny, but I think I am, Momma. Don't know why."

"Well, it's been a long time, Judie Kate. Things change. He's probably much different than you remember him."

She turned around and looked at her Momma. *I just saw him three years ago.* She felt a strange shift in the breeze as she headed for the door.

"You're right, Momma, things do change. Probably anxious over nothing."

She went inside and headed for the shower. Everything had to be right. *First impressions are everything.* She paused in front of the mirror and pulled off her T-shirt and saw her hands shaking nervously. Then, chill bumps emerged on her arms.

"Okay, Judie Kate," she whispered to herself, "it's all or nothing." She looked back at herself in the mirror and remembered what Don had said.

I am Judie Kate.

* * *

Joe texted George: Here. The tourists—"foreigners," the locals called them—were tentative, not quite sure of the procedure of leaving the ferry, not sure of the route out, thus they slowly inched their vehicles forward, the staff impatient at their caution. Joe put the truck in gear and drove out. He pulled into a parking lot and waited for George's call.

"Change of plans. Meet me at the theater."

"See you there."

Joe pulled out of the parking lot and headed up historic Highway 12, known locally as Irvin Garrish Highway. He saw the old landmarks as he moved slowly along, dodging distracted tourists, long-haired skateboarders, errant bikes, and meandering golf carts. The Ice Cream Shack was still open in the newly redone community square. *Good to know!* He slammed on the brakes and heard something go thud in the trailer. Several women just decided to cross the road, oblivious to the traffic. *How do the locals stand this stuff for five months?*

At School Road, he turned left. To his right was the Live Oak Stage and the ticket and T-shirt booth. Beside them was Read a Bit More, where he found an interesting book last year. He drove a bit farther to the Methodist church and parked across from the Deepwater Theater on the right, where he saw George's truck in the sand lot. His good friend ambled up.

"Took you long enough!" he teased.

He looked like a character in the movie *Deliverance*. When he talked to you, he looked to the side, as if lost in thought. When he was finished talking, he just walked away. Nobody knew except those inside the bluegrass scene that he was an award-winning songwriter, blazing mandolin picker, and a former session player in Nashville. Teaching at the community college was something to do. Music was his life.

"You get in touch with the Methodist minister?"

"Yeah, said we could park the trailer on the lot. Thought we'd put it where it was last year."

Trailer parked, they walked over to the Workshop Stage area, checked it out, and sat down on the empty wooden stage that had been put together that morning. In two days, it would be covered in mic cables and stands, power cords, a bass amp, entertainers, and instruments, all facing four monitors, a hundred chairs, and five picnic tables.

Joe backed his truck right by the trailer. George nodded his approval while Joe took out his travel bag, groceries, and a cooler.

"Could use some help over here," he called as George lumbered back to his truck. After they loaded, George cranked up his truck.

"Let's get back to the house. You've got a surprise waiting on you."

"You made me dinner?"

"No."

"Where's the love? In that case, let's go by Salt and Sweet and get me a sandwich. I'm starved."

* * *

Not far down the road, the lonely young man picked up his travel bag and wandered into the lobby of the Crow's Nest Inn. The quaint establishment had a long list of admiring guests who returned year after year for its old-style rooms with rusty iron beds covered in faded, musty quilts, croaking floorboards worn from years of guests and sand, and knotted pine wood walls accented with lace-curtained windows that let in the ocean breezes. One guest never left: Mrs. Clampton's Ghost.

A beautiful, spectral face and shapely form visited rooms, moved items on dressers, closed open doors, turned on bathtub faucets, and occasionally hovered over unsuspecting guests in the night who either fled for their lives, endured the frights only to move to another room—or even another inn—the next day, or who just enjoyed the romantic and quaint presence of a wispy, old coot. The ghost especially loved to fiddle with women's cosmetics and would occasionally even find an item that was lost by a guest, and for reasons totally unknown, she preferred rooms 23 and 24 the most.

There were stained pine shelves close to the ceiling that displayed various duck decoys, some primitive and some carved and painted in such detail it seemed they could fly away at any moment. Old pictures of the inn and Ocracoke, sepia-toned and black and white, decorated the rustic, wooden walls. There was a large, nautical map on one wall. Two lamps, both with ship wheels, a barometer in one hub, and a thermometer in the other, stood on two end tables on opposite sides of the room. Magazines were arranged on the coffee table in front of a pillowed sofa: *Southern Living*, *Our State*, *National Geographic*.

They need a Bible, he noted to himself. He would get one and place it there later. A family walked into the room, a mother and father and two teenage girls trying their best to look like young adults.

"I'll be with you in a moment," the clerk called out. "You can tell the ferry just landed," he laughed. "Have a seat on the couch or go out and sit on the pizer." The family and the young man all looked back at him.

"What's a pizer?" the father asked.

"Oh, yeah," he answered, "that's what we call the porch."

The parents' clothes hinted of money and leisure. Their relaxed demeanor came from domestic and world travels and a reserved cosmopolitan lifestyle. The girls wore tight-fitting tops over camis with blue and red bras and frayed shorts that had more white pockets in the front than blue denim and showed more bottom than they covered. He wondered how any parent could let their children dress like that. The parents picked out several tourist brochures from a display by the map while the girls stared at their phones and giggled as they shared Instagram pics with friends far away.

One girl was curvy, tanned, her face dressed in flawless makeup, her adolescence accentuated with a plumpness that was sexy but in another twenty years would be a weight problem. The other was thin with braces and some freckles, a hint of blush that revealed less experience in the application of makeup, and dark red hair in a ponytail. They spotted him and immediately giggled to each other. The blonde, seeing his Christian shirt, decided to flirt. She looked down at her perky breasts and then back up quickly, as if asking him to check her out and let her know what he thought. He did and then caught himself.

Disappointed with his response, she gently dropped her phone, did an "oops" face, and then turned around, bent over, and let her two crescent moons do their job. He was sinfully smitten, and when she turned around, she cocked her head slightly to one side and raised an eyebrow in a "how's that?" grin and then looked at the other young girl and giggled again.

The freckled one whispered a bit too loud, "I so can't believe you just did that!"

Then they looked at his pants and giggled some more. It was then that he realized what was happening. He quickly reached into his pocket and grabbed his knife, repeated his mantra, *I can do all things through Christ who strengthens me*, and turned back around.

After the paperwork was finished, the clerk said, "Here is your key."

"Have a blessed day," the tall, clean-cut, young man responded to the clerk. He turned to go and then turned back. "Are there any churches here on the island? It's Wednesday, and I would like to worship somewhere."

The clerk thought for a moment and responded, "Up Irvin Garrish Highway, turn left on School Road and there's the Methodist church."

"The Methodists are sinners. God will punish them severely for thinking that gays and lesbians can be ministers. Are there any other churches?"

The clerk was caught off guard by his self-righteous judgment.

"Oh, wait a minute, I gave you the wrong key. I'm sorry." He reached down below the counter and pulled out another. "I'm sorry, again, sir, this is your room." Then he continued. "Well, there is the Assembly of God Church on Lighthouse Road. Good folks there, more conservative than the Methodists for sure. That might be more to your liking."

The young man looked at the clerk smugly. "We'll see."

Then, he turned and walked away, not paying attention to the teenage temptations, but as he climbed the stairs, he paused and feigned an interest in a picture on the staircase walls so he could look back at the plump one and stare at her bottom. When she caught him, she pooched her lips into a kiss, put her hand on her hip and thrust it at him, and then winked. He quickly carried his bag and his guitar up the creaking stairs, turned left, and entered his room.

The parents walked up and saw the clerk grinning.

"Interesting," the father said.

The mother chimed in, "I just don't see how people these days can be so misled by such primitive superstitions and antiquated sexual views."

The clerk answered back, "Yeah, well, you have to give him credit for speaking his faith. It must be tough knowing that all the world is laughing at you." The clerk took their credit card, still grinning.

"Anyway, the joke is on him. I put him in room twenty-four. That's the room with Mrs. Clampton's Ghost." The parents raised their eyebrows.

"Seriously?" they both said at the same time. He explained the story as they took their keys.

The mother replied, "Well, that should give preacher boy something to pray about, right? C'mon, girls, let's go."

* * *

At the Salt and Sweet Deli, Joe grinned as a cute and vibrant young lady handed him the sandwich in a bag.

"Thank you!" she beamed with a genuine air of appreciation.

Joe sat down by George at the table outside on the covered deck and opened the sandwich. An overhead fan took the sting out of the summer swelter. Taking a bite, he asked George about the changes for this year.

The plans changed every year. George and Ellie would rent a beach house for two weeks somewhere on the island during the festival. As part of his contract, Joe stayed for free with someone on the island, and it was usually with George and Ellie. Depending on the tourist market, the house George rented was different most years: three-bedroom, four-bedroom, two baths, one bath, on the sound, near a canal, tucked away in the woods, deck, handicapped ramp, pool table. Sometimes, George and Ellie shared a room with an entertainer, depending on how many rooms their rental had. Nearly every year, something unexpected took place regarding housing.

"We have an unexpected visitor whose car is taking up the place where your truck would normally be."

"That so?" Joe got up. "What kind of fudge do you like?"

George looked up at the ceiling and said, "Whatever you want."

Joe redirected, "What kind does *Ellie* like?"

George thought about that and guessed. "Peanut butter?"

Joe walked back inside to the counter, and the clerk rushed right over.

"A pound of peanut butter fudge, please."

"My favorite!" she beamed.

* * *

When they got to the beach house, George started heading inside.

"You gonna grab a bag or what?" Joe exclaimed while reaching in the truck to get his things. George was nearly at the back of the house. It was a three-story building on stilts with a truck, SUV, and a white

Mustang parked underneath. It was on the water, facing west, toward Pamlico Sound.

"Do I have to do everything?" George called back, turning around.

"You could start with *something*," Joe responded, handing George a bag with some groceries in it. George wandered off again.

"Yeah, no problem. I'll just get the other bags and cooler with my other four hands," Joe complained.

When Joe reached the top of the deck, he opened the glass door and stumbled inside, plopping his things on the table. He made another trip down and back with the rest of the bags while George recuperated from the single load. Ellie entered the room. She was a storied educator, well-respected in her field, the state, and even the nation. She received her doctorate from UNC-Greensboro where she challenged establishment educators across the nation with her contrarian views of the education system.

Her dissertation was published and her book, *Bring Back the Spartan Education*, made waves throughout the education scene. It was a call to arms that criticized the whole education establishment and suggested that America go back to the more disciplined ways of the Greek Spartans.

"George, you could have at least carried another bag," Ellie said. She gave Joe a hug and gushed, "Welcome, Joe. Glad to see you again."

"Hi, Ellie, good to be here as well." He looked around at the room and saw a shadow move in a dark corner. "Killer, is that you?" A canine blob of black and brown fur the size of a shoe made a beeline for him. "Hey, Killer!" Joe sat, and something that looked like a small, dirty mop landed on his lap.

"Why do you always call him Killer, Joe?" Ellie asked. "You know his name is Scruff."

"Scruff, what is your name?" Joe asked. Killer looked around the room as if Joe was talking to someone else. "Killer, what is your name?" The unkempt head looked right up at Joe, and the tail wagged so fast it made a hum. "See, Ellie, Killer knows his real name. You guys still feed him cat food?"

Ellie answered, "That's all the little booger will eat. We rue the day George accidently bought cat food and brought it home." She rolled her eyes in dismay. "He has refused dog food ever since."

Joe petted Killer a bit, roughed him up some more, and then stood up and looked around the room.

"So, this is home sweet home for a few days. Much bigger than last year. The view of the sound is wonderful."

George came back to life and noted, "Yup, three stories."

Joe looked at the tacky, multicolored fish lights hanging from the ceiling, all tied together with what seemed like the wiring used to connect Christmas tree lights. Tall windows on three sides of the room allowed for a good view of the neighbors on the right, the sound, and more neighbors on the left. Pine paneling covered the walls, and drab gray carpet completed the decor. Track lights illuminated it all.

"Yep, much bigger than what we had last year," Joe said, taking his groceries to the kitchen. He put the cooler on the counter. Beer, pimento cheese, and Ritz crackers emerged from the grocery bag. "Staples of life," Joe called out. He took out the fudge and waved it at Ellie, who had taken a seat on one of the cushiony chaise lounges. "George said you liked peanut butter."

Ellie looked over at George and frowned.

"George, how long have we been married?"

George looked up at the ceiling and mumbled, "I'm going to need a minute to do the math."

Ellie said, "How much peanut butter have you seen me eat in all those years?"

"Now I've got two things to figure out," George answered. "But I think the answer to one of them is none."

"Thanks for thinking about me anyway," Ellie said, wishing one more time that George had paid more attention to her in years past.

Joe finished putting out his goodies, then he walked back to the big table where he had placed his book bag, looked around, took out his computer, and positioned it on the table.

"Be all right if I do my work here?"

George was snooping around the goodies, helping himself to the fudge. Ellie was lost in thought, staring out the window as a small, fishing skiff zoomed through the sound, rushing home before dark. After Joe plugged in his computer, he looked around the room again and paused.

"So, does the Mustang belong to our guest musician?"

George responded, "Not exactly. That's the surprise."

Suddenly, as if on cue, the bedroom door on the right opened, and a young woman stepped out. As Joe stood up like a gentleman, every clock on the island stopped.

She was beautiful. Black hair cut in a bob circled her face, framing it in a halo, reaching down to just above her shoulders. There was a look of expectation on her face, with dark eyes that gleamed with excitement and just a hint of makeup to highlight her cheeks. A soft and simple lace-shoulder tank top snuggled across her body down to where black leggings took over. They hugged rounded hips and ample legs and then shimmered down to small ankles, the right one circled with a silver anklet, ending in cork wedge sandals with tan straps. Black toenails and one toe ring and black fingernails, along with a silver bracelet on her left wrist, accented the entire ensemble. She looked sheepish, tentative, hopeful, like a small puppy staring at potential new parents. *That is one cute musician!* Joe thought.

"Uncle Joe!"

"Judie Kate?" Joe stared in disbelief. "Is that you?"

"New and improved!" She did her best *Price Is Right* model pose, then ran over to Joe and squeezed him tight, nearly knocking him down. George and Ellie looked at each other, not knowing what had come over their little girl.

"Look at you!" she exclaimed.

When he came down after Don died, she didn't really have the wits about her to notice what time had done to him, and her apartment was so dark she could not see the details in his face and body anyway. Now, time paused for her. She looked at him closely. His black, wavy hair was accented with thin streaks of gray. His dark blue eyes, full of surprise, were highlighted with wrinkles around them, reminders of the years gone by. A faded Beaufort T-shirt could not hide a slightly bulging tummy, yet one more sign that time had crept up on him. Brown cargo shorts encased his thin legs, and he wore his ever-present, white New Balance shoes. Judie Kate beamed.

"You look great, Uncle Joe!"

They stood back from each other and stared, smiled, lost in years gone by, caught up in the joy and surprise of the moment.

Ellie, looking a bit worried, or perhaps perplexed, broke the reverie.

"Judie Kate, why don't you show Joe his room?"

She jumped into action and asked, "That your bag there, Uncle Joe?"

She did not wait for a response. She grabbed it and walked to the left bedroom door. "Welcome to the Hotel Wilson."

Joe watched her walk away, the way her hips wriggled, mesmerized as her hair bounced with each of her steps. Gone was the insecure, overweight girl with stringy black hair. This young woman was brand new. Before he caught himself, he felt tingles, urges, yearnings he had not experienced since before Jay Jay died.

"You coming or not, old man?" She paused at the door while he came back to earth and then obediently followed her into his room as she plopped his bag on the bed.

"You got the low-rent room, I got the luxury suite with the gorgeous view and deck," she said sarcastically as she lilted her way into the shared bath. "Here are your towels and washcloths—I took the purple ones; you get the slime green ones. If you leave the seat up, it is a ten-dollar fine per occurrence." She pointed to the toilet and then sashayed into the other room. "Here is my room with the view." She opened the blinds to the weathered deck that looked out over the driveway to the street and woods surrounding an abandoned and rundown A-frame house. "Romantic, huh?"

She turned and looked deeply at Joe, took his hands again, pulled them up, and then let them fall. She stared into his eyes, the eyes that saw her inner beauty years ago, and then again saw the wrinkles around them.

"It's been a long time, Uncle Joe."

He looked at her once more, not believing what he saw. It was the proverbial butterfly from the cocoon, but it was more. Those eyes full of mystery yet glossed over with shame and embarrassment years ago were now wide open with life.

"Judie Kate, I don't want to step out of bounds here, but gosh, you are beautiful. Look at you!" He gave her more than just another glance. She smiled and enjoyed his gaze, glad Joe approved of her metamorphosis, her emergence into a new life.

"Is this what you saw in me years ago, Uncle Joe?" She waited to hear what he said, desperately wanting his approval, hoping he might step into the new world of Jay Jay's dream.

Joe was caught in the moment, a moment in time years ago when he struggled to help a shy, young girl believe in herself, and the moment now as he realized this was more than what he saw then. It was like he was caught in a time warp, the warm uncle revered by his niece and the older man enthralled with a young woman standing before him. He still saw Judie Kate as the girl in high school, yet here she was, shapely, vivacious, and mysterious, slowly working a spell over him. It was like he knew her then and now, but the now was in a different way.

"Uncle Joe, remember we were having a conversation?" Judie Kate smiled as Joe came back around.

Now, he was infatuated with her; she could see it in his eyes. She hugged him again, but this time, it was not the innocent affection of a niece to an uncle. This time it was with the need of a young woman for a man's affection. Joe held her like she was still the shy girl, a little at bay, yet he felt a spark, something more in their embrace. It unsettled him, but he did not dwell on it, convincing himself it was just the rush and confusion of memories and emotions they had shared over the years, not to mention the touch of a woman on his body. She grabbed his hand and pulled him to the door.

"Come on! We got some catching up to do."

Joe dutifully walked behind her and was yet again caught up in her effervescence and the view he had. This Judie Kate was sassy, flirty, strong, confident, bold. *Oh my*, he thought to himself, *I never saw this coming.*

She could feel, sense his interest, his attraction. *Come on, Jay Jay, do your magic.*

George and Ellie were already into the pimento cheese.

"Caught cha' red-handed!" Judie Kate exclaimed as she aimed Joe onto one of the chaise chairs. She sat close beside him, patted him on the leg. Her parents came over to join in the conversation, each holding two crackers with pimento cheese on them.

"Got a little zip in it, Joe," Ellie noted, raising an eyebrow as the hot pepper kicked in.

"Thought I'd step out a bit from the mundane," he responded.

Killer jumped onto Joe's lap and settled in while Joe roughed him up some more, Killer's tail spinning like a whirlwind.

"So, Judie Kate, what brings you down here?" he asked.

Jay Jay, she almost slipped and said.

"I was talking with Daddy last week, and he told me about the show and that you were coming and that it would be neat for us to see each other again. So, I came on a lark."

"Surprised us," Ellie corrected like a schoolmarm. "She didn't say she was coming. Just showed up, called us when she rolled off the ferry, and thankfully, we had an extra room."

Judie Kate felt the motherly barb deep in her skin. "I've never been to the Ocrafolk Festival before, so I thought maybe it was time to come and see what Dad has been doing down here all these years."

Joe couldn't hide his surprise as he asked, "Seriously, Judie Kate, you've never been here before? How did that happen?"

She shrugged her shoulders and answered, "Wasn't interested, I guess." *Now I'm interested.* George walked back to the kitchen, grabbed another cracker, and spooned out more pimento cheese.

Ellie called out, "Yes, George, thank you for asking if we would all like some."

"I'll leave you all some right here on the counter." He smiled, stuffing the cracker into his mouth.

"Actually, I could use a beer," Joe said.

"Not so fast there, Uncle Joe. You don't want to get filled up on that. We have something important to do." Judie Kate patted him on the leg again. Ellie and George both looked unapprovingly at her gesture.

"That so? I don't recall getting an agenda in my email box."

"The Ice Cream Shack is calling our names. Remember how we would go get ice cream and talk about whatever?" she asked, pulling him up to his feet, Killer falling to the floor. "I figure we got four days to catch up on years of ice cream." She walked back to her bedroom, picked up her little pocketbook, pulled the thin strap over her head and shoulder, and came back into the room.

"Momma and Daddy, I promise to have him back before dawn," she said with a wink at both of them.

"Judie Kate, I don't have my truck. You driving?"

"No, silly, we're walking." She opened the glass door and stepped outside as Joe came along behind her. "I didn't get this figure by driving around!"

When the glass door shut, Ellie looked at George, who was after another cracker.

"George, I don't like this. Did you see the look in her eye? It's that infatuation all over again."

"What I saw," George answered, mouth full of the spicy treat, crumbs flying, "is the look in Joe's eye when he first looked at Judie Kate. I know Joe. He's never shown any serious interest in any woman after Jay Jay died. Oh, he has looked at some girls, like any man will do, but this look worries me. He's clearly interested in our little girl."

Ellie paused a moment, then got up and went to the kitchen, put a cup in the coffee maker, and punched the start button. While it gurgled, she looked around, worried, a scowl emerging on her already scowling face.

"Maybe they are just caught up in the old days. It has been a long time since she saw him. Seven years, she told me. She has certainly shown no interest in him until now."

"Well, maybe so," George responded, brushing the crumbs out of his beard with his hand, "but she has shown no interest in any boy at all, and now all she has talked about since she arrived is Joe this and Joe that. It is like she is obsessed with the man. There is something different about this. She does not seem to be that high school girl who was infatuated with an older man." George paused, as if gathering his breath, not being used to talking this much.

He walked over to the glass door and looked out at the sound for a moment.

"The clothes, Ellie, the clothes. She did not dress up at all on Tuesday, not today. Yet, she is dressed to the hilt tonight, makeup included. When did she start wearing makeup? It's like she is after him. Joe is still not over Jay Jay. I don't think he can handle this."

Ellie removed her cup from the coffee maker.

"You are right about that. I did not know she had such an outfit. It's too tight. She needs to wear something longer to cover herself properly. I don't know when she started using makeup. Did you see her toenails and fingernails?" Ellie put some milk and sugar in her brew and stirred it. "Still, maybe we should give them the benefit of the doubt." She took a sip and stared out the window as the day gave way to the night. "Maybe." The scowl turned to disapproval and then to deep thought.

* * *

Joe and Judie Kate slowly strolled down Pamlico Shores Lane as the evening turned into night. The road was narrow, with houses on the sound side and wooded areas with swamp water on the other. The wind blew strong enough to ward off the mosquitoes and occasionally ushered in a bit of a chill. As they reached British Cemetery Road, they took a right and headed to the happening part of Ocracoke Island.

After they passed the campground, Judie Kate surprised Joe when she hooked her arm around his as they walked along. Joe was increasingly confused. Was this the old friend showing affection and appreciation for years gone by? He was becoming more aware of his own awkward affection, however, and found himself pulling back, not comfortable with the sensations arising within him. It was as if every man's dream of having the hot, young thing pursue you with overt affection was coming true. *So, this is what it feels like.* Yet now that it was here, he felt oddly ashamed, embarrassed. Things were happening too fast for him to comprehend.

They dodged meandering tourists the whole way. Strollers, cyclists, skateboarders, large trucks. It was like wading through the stifling and indifferent crowds at a state fair.

Judie Kate and Joe engaged in chitchat as they headed to Irvin Garrish Highway. They talked about the past years, Judie Kate with her teaching, Joe with his tasks at the community college. Each wanted to delve into the deeper questions. Joe wanted to know what led to Judie Kate's transition. *Do I ask her about Don?* Judie Kate was curious as to how Joe was coping with Jay Jay's death. Both respected each other's privacy yet were desirous of the intimacy that would emerge if they were to ask.

Finally, Joe took the plunge and asked, "So, Judie Kate, George tells me that you got your degree in education but don't like it, that you are fed up with teaching. How come?"

Judie Kate answered that she had too much of her Momma in her. How she got tired very quickly with the whole thing. That there was no freedom for the teachers, and now, education was all about administration, rules, policies, procedures, lesson plans, twisted theory that had no common sense. Everything was scripted now, and originality was not allowed. They stopped for a log jam. There was a truck with wide mirrors coming at them with streams of walkers on both sides of the narrow road and an inattentive cyclist in everybody's way.

She explained that George suggested she get an MBA to help her prospects, maybe teach at the community college. She had just finished it but was frustrated with the whole business model. It reminded her too much of education, which took many of its theories from business. They turned left onto the busy street. Up ahead was the Community Square.

Now, it was time for serious reflection.

"Uncle Joe, how much ice cream do you think we ate in those years?"

"At least two quarts, Judie Kate, and you can just call me Joe now."

Judie Kate was caught off guard. *Hmm, Joe.* "Yeah, with all my weight issues, that probably was not smart, right?"

"In my desire to help, I was actually making the problem worse."

"Well, your intent was appreciated. I liked our times together. I miss them very much." She squeezed his arm into hers even more.

"Likewise, Judie Kate." Things were getting awkward again as they neared the Ice Cream Shack. Joe mentally veered around her tricky affections. "Still like Rocky Road?"

"Of course!" she exclaimed a bit too exuberantly, reminiscent of the youthful excitement of days long ago. "You still a boring chocolate and vanilla guy?" They maneuvered around a group of middle-aged tourists going the wrong way. Joe looked around and noticed that even with all the stores around the square, the area was quite dark at night. There was a line at the Ice Cream Shack, so they stood patiently, listening to the music in the background.

Judie Kate asked, "Isn't that Van Halen's cover of bluesman John Brim's 'Ice Cream Man'?"

"You know your music well, young lady," Joe answered. "When did you learn all these old songs? They are well before your time."

Judie Kate went silent for a moment as the memories brought back hurt.

"Don was really into the oldies. After he died, one of his friends brought me his CD collection. Said Don would have wanted me to have it and that if I wanted to keep his memory alive, then I should listen to his kind of music. So, that's when I developed a love for old music. They kept me going through some pretty rough times."

She turned back around and looked at Joe.

"Anyway, when I got my Mustang, my satellite radio had all kinds of channels, so I found the eighties station, then the seventies, then the sixties, big band, fifties, jazz, blues. There is something to that bygone era. The music feels honest, inspired, genuine, real. I just don't like today's stuff."

Joe looked away for a second, then asked, "When did you get your Mustang?"

She looked pensive for a moment, breathed in deeply, and then told the story while she looked out over the throng in the square. She told him about the trailer in Topsail Beach, how Don had given it to her. How she used to go there on weekends to relax and remember and dream of what might have been. She recalled the neighbor who wanted to buy the place and how he warned her that the taxes would be too much for a college girl. She began putting away money to cover them, but she could not believe it when she received the bill. She called the man, and he bought it for three hundred thousand dollars.

"How much?" Joe gasped.

"Three hundred grand, Joe. I had never seen that much money. So, I bought a small condo, got some decent furniture, bought my Mustang, and used the rest for my MBA. I still have a nest egg for just-in-case stuff." She turned around, and Joe saw the tear in her eye. She tried not to cry, but she was losing the battle. Joe, like old times, held her close to squeeze out the pain.

"It was like I finally said good-bye to Don, Joe," she said. It was the first time she had told the story to anybody, and it was cathartic. She sniffed and put herself back together and pulled away. "Sorry, Uncle Joe, uh, Joe. Didn't mean to ruin the moment."

Suddenly, Joe was lost in a song. He began humming a tune. Judie Kate, wiping her eyes, looked over at him and managed a smile.

"Is that 'Mustang Sally'?"

Soon, it was their turn.

"I'm buying," Judie Kate insisted, now recovered from her emotional moment. "Rocky Road, two scoops in a sugar cone and one scoop vanilla, one scoop chocolate in a regular cone for daddy here."

Joe looked at her and shook his head. "Seriously, 'daddy'?"

Judie Kate didn't miss a beat. "Better than 'grandpa,'" she answered with a wink.

While they waited, Joe noticed a few young men staring at Judie Kate.

"You have some admirers," he noted, nodding his head over to three guys.

"Watch this," Judie Kate answered. She put her arms around Joe and playfully snuggled into him. The young men's smiles frowned into disappointment, and they turned to find somebody else to stare at. "Another one bites the dust ..." Judie Kate sang, winking at Joe while turning him loose very slowly.

Soon their order was called, and they picked up their treats. As they came down the steps, to the right was a lone picnic table in the dark filled with vacationers, an old aluminum trashcan in the corner. They wandered around the dimly lit Community Square until Joe spied two empty rocking chairs on the porch of the Community Store. He pulled Judie Kate quickly to the chairs, and they sat.

"Better," he said as Judie Kate licked the side of her cone.

"What's in there?" she asked, nodding behind her.

"Little bit of everything," Joe responded. "Last time I was in there, they had fruit, potatoes, bread, antiques, art supplies, children's toys and crayons, old fishing reels, knives, wines, sodas, candy, and just stuff. Old country store feel. Quaint." He took a bite of his vanilla ice cream, saw Judie Kate lick her Rocky Road rather than bite it, and thought of how Jay Jay used to lick her ice cream as well.

As if on cue, the Historian appeared, staring at the Community Store, talking loudly to no one—save for the one bored-looking child he had in tow—in a strong, lecture-like voice. Joe looked at Judie Kate.

"He was on the ferry. Read a book about Ocracoke, met one of the Howards, and now he knows everything. Seems oblivious that nobody really listens to him. Guess he just enjoys being the center of attention." He rolled his eyes. "Now, how would you like to be married to him?"

I want to be married to you!

"Think I'll leave him for someone else!"

As they stared at the crowd, Judie Kate elbowed Joe.

"So, Uncle, uh, Joe, not rushing you or anything, but, you know, you're single. Who would be your dream girl?"

Joe took another bite off his ice cream cone and thought for a moment. "Just once in my life, I would like to be seen walking down the street with Kate Upton while Billy Joel's 'Uptown Girl' plays in the background. Just once."

"Joe, are you one of those twig lovers?"

"Not exactly. Some people say she is fat. But hey, she's cute! Girl next door, you know? What I wouldn't give to just experience that one time."

Judie Kate looked away for a moment, as if seeing a music video of Joe and Kate Upton. *My name is Kate.*

"Who else? TV gals? Movie babes?"

"Okay, A. J. Cook."

"The blonde on *Criminal Minds*?"

"Yes, that one. I like the way her blonde hair swirls around her face. And there's something about her lips." Joe looked far away again. "Okay, older than me, but I always liked Susan Sarandon."

"Sultry and sexy with that low voice. Interesting."

Joe paused for a moment. "You know, Meghan Trainor is kind of cute. So is Hillary Scott from Lady A."

"So," Judie Kate joked, "it *is* all about that bass, huh?"

Joe smiled at her quip. *Yes, it is!*

"Both are a far stretch from Kate Upton. You know, short and a bit pudgy compared to long and lean."

"And …?" Joe asked. Before he caught himself, he said, "You know, their bodies are quite like yours now."

Judie Kate was caught off guard. She had not made that connection. Now, Joe was saying he liked that kind of body.

"Are you calling me short and pudgy, Joe Clark?" she teased with fake indignation, licking her ice cream. "Are you saying I have curves?" She looked up at Joe like the Little Red-Haired Girl looks at Charlie Brown.

Joe decided to be honest. That is what he always taught Judie Kate.

"Okay, guilty. To be honest, Judie Kate, it is hard not to notice. Yes, you are quite shapely now. Very attractive. I think the word voluptuous would be correct here. And you should be proud. You've had a lot of young fellas looking your way tonight."

That was what she hoped he would say, but now that he said it, she was suddenly a bit shy, insecure, almost ashamed, not sure what to do with the attention, the affirmation, as if she was not meant to be pretty. *He really noticed! I have bass!*

Both focused on their melting ice cream. Then he turned the tables.

"Okay, now it's your turn. What celebrity do you dream about?"

Judie Kate paused, looked out over the crowd into the sky. "Well, I don't keep up with the celebs too much. But I hear from my colleagues that Jason Momoa, the guy who plays Aquaman, is hot. They like his long hair, I think. I'm not much into that. Actor Scott Eastwood is good looking. Nothing outlandish about him. Superman Henry Cavill has that British thing going on. Chris Evans in the Avengers. Those last three all look the same to me though. Oh yeah, there was that guy who played Thor a few years ago. I remember the trailer for that movie. Oh my God! Good muscles, but he had that long hair going on again. I had a crush on Bon Jovi. Oh yeah, who is that guy who played the new James Bond a few years back? What *is* his name? But if I had my way, Shemar Moore would be my dream guy. I never knew a SWAT team could be so sexy. And he doesn't have that scrubby beard thing going on. I can't stand that."

Joe thought a moment.

"Okay, so, we'll find reruns of *Criminal Minds*. You can stare at old Shemar, and I can dream of old A.J. Cook."

Judie Kate finished her ice cream and grabbed Joe's hand and hauled him out of his chair. As they walked down the steps and headed to the road, Joe recalled a conversation he had with Jay Jay years ago.

"Just an FYI: I always poked fun with Jay Jay that if she were to dump me, I would find me a young one," he joked to Judie Kate.

Like me? she hoped. The night was moving along too fast, even as they slowly returned home. As they headed back down British Cemetery Road, Judie Kate paused.

"Joe, if you don't mind me asking, what happened after Jay Jay died?"

Joe stopped, as if the past needed to catch up with him. Judie Kate noticed the decreasing pace.

"Joe, I'm sorry. I didn't mean to ..."

"It's okay, Judie Kate. Shrink says I need to talk about it more." He breathed in deeply but paused as the Niagara of grief roared in his psyche. Judie Kate held on to him when she felt his body stiffen up. Joe exhaled and relaxed. She waited patiently, anticipating what he would say. It was short and to the point.

"We had the funeral. Wish you had been there."

Judie Kate apologized and said, "Joe, nobody told me. I talked with Dad around that time, but he did not tell me."

"Yeah, that was my fault. I was trying to protect you. I was not sure you could handle it, what with Don's death fresh on your mind. I told George to keep it between us. Anyway, I hit a bad depression. I made it through the semester, barely, but then I hit bottom. With the holidays looming, I just broke down. Suicidal thoughts ran through my head. George and Ellie saw it coming. George called me every night and all through the weekends. Ellie invited me over for dinners. One day, when George called, I did not answer. He called all day. Finally, he came over to the house, saw my truck, knocked on the door. When I did not answer, he found my emergency key and came inside.

"I was on the floor, balled up, in a catatonic state. When I did not respond, he called 911. He went with me to the ER and stayed until they placed me in the psych ward. I stayed there a week, missed the first week of the new semester while they tried medications and therapy. When they released me, I stayed with your parents for another week, getting used to life without Jay Jay, life on medication, life with therapy. I went back to work, and that took my mind off her."

They turned the corner onto an even darker road, as dark as Joe's depression. Joe stopped, as if seeing a specter. Judie Kate became worried. "What is it Joe?"

There was a long period of silence.

"I would not be here if it weren't for George and Ellie, Judie Kate. I owe them my life."

Judie Kate sniffed, a slight sobbing taking over her body. She held Joe's arm closer, as if this time, trying to squeeze the pain out of him.

"I didn't know about the depression, the suicide attempt. Mom and Dad should have told me," she said.

"Don't blame them, Judie Kate. I asked them to keep it to themselves. Now, you three are the only ones who know."

On their left, they passed the marsh and its salty, rotten, stagnant smell. The pace decreased with the burden of sadness.

"What about your family, Joe?" It suddenly dawned on her that in all the years she had known and talked with him, he had never mentioned his family.

"That's something I don't talk about, Judie Kate. Only with the shrink."

"Wouldn't it be healthy to talk about that too?"

"Believe me, it is healthier for me not to talk about it."

The bluntness of his answer caught her off guard. But now she began to see a new image of Joe. In a way, he was the tall, dark stranger in her life. The weathered rider from the desert who was all about keeping the small-town folk safe from the thugs and villains while never revealing his past, including the days long forgotten and left behind that drove him to be the hero.

Who lives in that darkness of your yesteryears? she wondered. Suddenly, she was more in love with him than before. Now she was beginning to understand what Jay Jay had asked her to do and why. Joe was complicated, scarred, still limping along, in a sense alone, and he needed someone to care for him, to watch out for him, to stand guard over him. But the prize came with a disclaimer. Handle with care. Fragile. This end up. *Am I up for that?* she wondered.

They turned up Pamlico Shores Road, into even more darkness. A stray cat zoomed across the road, startling both of them. Judie Kate instinctively grabbed Joe around his waist.

"That was scary!" she called out, catching her breath. Joe protectively put his arm around her and then caught himself and brought his arm back. "Uncle Joe, uh, sorry, Joe, do you remember those times when you held me to let me know it was going to be okay?"

Joe took a moment to remember and said, "Sure."

Caught up in the moment, renewing her relationship with Joe, hearing his story, trying to fulfill Jay Jay's dream—suddenly she was overwhelmed by the task at hand. On top of that, being around her parents also led to a resurgence of old emotions and insecurities.

"I could use some reassurance right now." She pulled his arm back around her, and together they headed for the house. Her arms wrapped around him as naturally as a mother's around her newborn baby. As she settled comfortably next to him, he reminisced about the old times. She felt, she knew, it was more than that. Much more ...

* * *

After the Wednesday evening prayer service at the Assembly of God Church, the young Christian man chatted with the pastor for a few moments outside the sanctuary in the small, sandy parking lot. He shared his ministry plan to play guitar and sing on the corner and hand out cold water to all who were hot and thirsty. Reverend Todd Baylor agreed that it was a good plan, that the island needed more evangelism, especially with the tourist season beginning.

While they were talking, he noticed a small group of girls off to the side looking at him. When his eyes connected with theirs, they quickly looked away. The game of visual tag played out for the next few moments. All the girls were cute and modestly dressed, unlike other women he had already seen on the island. They smiled and giggled and nodded to themselves, stealing looks at him.

"I see you've got some admirers," the pastor noted, "and one is my own daughter."

He was embarrassed and looked away, as if caught in a sin trap. Their obvious attention produced the very feelings he constantly tried to escape. He was not sure what to do. These were good Christian girls, but now he had a sense of affection, an attraction for them. The one with dark hair really caught his eye, and she kept looking at him. It was different than his relationship with Kristi back at the college. He had always thought they would minister together in a small church. Now, he just wanted to be with the girls, hang out, be near them in a way he did not understand or even comprehend. *Desire. Flesh.* He felt his face redden, and suddenly, he was sweaty, nervous, and his heart pounded faster. *Run.* Was this of God? It couldn't be. Wasn't he on a mission? They could not interfere with the mission.

"I better go now," he hurriedly said, rushing down the narrow and ironically, very dark, Lighthouse Road, not looking back.

The girls raced over to the pastor.

"Where did he go?" his daughter asked in a disappointed tone.

Pastor Todd answered, "I don't know, dear. He looked like he had seen the devil himself."

A girl with brown French braids and a mouth full of braces exclaimed, "He is *so* cute! Who is he?"

Pastor Todd answered, "I don't know that either. He was a visitor tonight. He never told me his name."

Soon, he was out of sight, but for the preacher's daughter, he was not out of mind. Daddy Todd saw the look in her eyes, and it was the same as the ones he saw when couples sat in front of him for wedding counseling.

"Miller?" he said, putting his arm around her. "He'll be on the corner in the village, handing out bottled water and singing and playing his guitar tomorrow."

"Tyler!" she called out. A young girl with a head full of thick, curly blonde hair rushed over.

"What?" she answered, long used to the sudden, adolescent bursts of excitement from her otherwise reticent friend of seven years.

"What are you doing tomorrow?" Miller was about to explode, her eyes looking like sparklers on the Fourth of July.

"It's okay, Miller, remember to breathe," Tyler teased. "I have a guitar lesson at ten."

"He plays guitar too! He's playing in town. We've got to go hear him!"

Tyler saw the stars in Miller's dark eyes and instantly corrected her friend. "No, *you've* got to go see him."

***

He headed down the darkening road back to his hotel, a place of safety, but then realized he was not ready for bed yet. So he made a right off Lighthouse Drive onto Irvin Garrish Highway and narrowly missed three cyclists riding without lights.

The girls were cute. His emotions were confusing. He liked the tall one, the one with the long, black hair. Was she the one in the dream? He turned left on School Road. Annoyed by the crowds who impeded his progress, he felt his patience wearing thin. He held the knife in his hands and reminded himself of the love of Jesus. Slipping it back into his pocket, he saw the sign for Howard Street and thought he would explore the spooky, sandy road.

He initially worried about the darkness, thought about Satan, even ghosts, but then scriptures came to his mind and he relaxed. If Jesus could fight off the devil in the night, so could he. As he walked past one of the many cemeteries on the road, white picket fences and dark gray tombstones giving off a faint iridescence, he suddenly saw something. It was green, phantom-like, a woman. Just as suddenly, it was gone, back into the live oaks, back into the cemetery.

He nearly panicked at what he knew was a demon, but then a group of young women came by, giddy, looking for fun. They were holding onto each other playfully in a manner that unsettled him. Then, seeing him, they flirted, but being new at the game, he took it a different way. An eerie, increasingly foreboding, lusty desire overwhelmed his loins, swelling upward in his body, like a fever. It felt as if he was increasingly out of control of himself. *This is not right!* With ghosts and now the licentious flesh of the women, he knew the demons were obviously after him. He took his knife back out of his pocket and waved it, as if in a psychological fit, looking like he was swatting a swarm of pesky flies.

"He's got a knife!" one of the girls shrieked. They ran the other away as he wondered what they were afraid of.

"I'm not going to hurt you," he called out, confused and then frightened. He didn't understand why they fled. He was just trying to withstand the temptations. *Slay the demons with the Sword of the Spirit!*

The girls ran into the Craft Shack. "There's some creep out there with a knife!" they yelled at the clerk, who looked stunned. "He shook it at us!"

"What are you talking about?" the clerk asked. She worked part-time at the store just to supplement her social security. She had salt-and-pepper hair, a few wrinkles, and sharp, green eyes that hinted of a strong personality. Several curious and now-worried shoppers scooted over to provide support to the young ladies. She continued, "Nobody does that around here. We don't have any crime on the island. Not that kind anyway. Are you sure?"

"We were just flirting, that's all," one girl confessed. "Having fun, you know? He was cute in a goofy kind of way."

Another girl chimed in, "We saw that weird Christian shirt and, like, just wanted to make him sweat, you know?"

Another repented, "We didn't mean any harm."

"Did you get a good look at him?" a young man asked, walking over to them, suddenly shazzammed into a Marvel action hero.

"It was dark, you know, so, like, no, we didn't see him clearly."

The girls were visibly shaken. Goose bumps from their fear and the cool air of the store covered their arms and legs. The man rushed outside in a burst of chivalrous civic duty, stood in the small circle of light from the store, and looked both ways down the dark road, but there was no one there. He came back inside and walked up to the girls.

"Sure it wasn't a ghost? Lots of them here on the island, you know. Howard Street is full of them." A few of the shoppers smiled at his joke. The girls weren't smiling. Then, he saw an opportunity. "I could walk you to your hotel if you like."

Now they smiled, enjoying the attention again.

* * *

When Joe and Judie Kate arrived back at the house, they paused in the deep of the night before climbing the deck stairs.

"Look, Joe," Judie Kate called out, staring west into the sky across the sound, leaning on the wooden rail on the lower boardwalk. The weather was clear, with no clouds, and stars were all around. In front of them was the Milky Way, the night so dark you could make out two cottony strands. She reached out her hand, seemingly trying to touch the stars, and followed it all around the sky to the other side.

"Have you ever seen anything so beautiful, Joe?" The celestial light show was accompanied by the hypnotic lapping of the waves on the rocks. She hooked her arm in his again and held on, staring in awe. It was so romantic, just like in the movies. Oh, to just turn and kiss him slowly, softly, under the heavens as millions of tiny angels watched, a stray shooting star igniting the fireworks of a long, passionate, and intimate evening, the camera shot fading away.

"What we are seeing now happened millions of years ago, Judie Kate," Joe said, as if teaching a science class. "We are literally looking back in time."

"Maybe we could be looking forward in time as well, huh, Joe?" Judie Kate offered daringly, not quite sure of how to wrest him into Jay Jay's dream.

Joe stared, momentarily unaware of Judie Kate's clutch of his arm, missing her affectionate invitation. He was back in time, riding on a ferry.

"Joe, you there?" she asked, the magic moment suddenly stalled. The waves filled in the gap of silence as he came around. A whiff of fishy air wafted by.

Joe resumed as if he had never left the conversation.

"Three years back, we came to Ocracoke in late September or early October. I don't recall which. I think it was for an early fall break. Our one o'clock ferry from Swan Quarter was canceled because of a mechanical issue and the four thirty was already full, so they booked us on the six thirty ferry. We would arrive in Ocracoke at night. Not a cloud was in the sky when we departed. Jay Jay stood on the deck the whole evening, waiting like a child for anything new. We saw the lights of fishing boats far away reflecting on the water. She looked for the first evening star and found it, to the west oddly enough, as the sun was going below the waters.

"'Make a wish, Joe!' she said to me. She found another star, a planet actually. Then came more and more, as if the heavens were opening like curtains before a show. About eight thirty, we could see the wispy bands of the Milky Way from one horizon to the other, west to east. It was like a nighttime rainbow in black and white. It seemed like you could see deep into forever. The Milky Way bands formed a halo around the whole earth, like a fine lace all around the world. I had never seen the sky like that, and I have never seen it again until now."

Judie Kate thought it was an omen from the heavens orchestrated by Jay Jay herself, but she dared not say anything. Instead, she wrapped herself into Joe even more and looked up at him.

"Thanks for sharing that with me, Joe. That was beautiful." *And so romantic ...* She looked back into the sky and made a wish.

Joe brought her back to earth in a crash landing.

"Jay Jay died the next month," he sighed, his body going limp, the memory having sucked the air out of him. Judie Kate was stunned. *What should I do?* The moment of awkwardness seemed like an hour. But Joe never turned her arm loose and did not step away from her.

"Guess we better get inside before people begin to talk, huh, Judie Kate?"

She led him up the stairs and turned his hand loose just before reaching the landing. Joe went inside, but she paused for a moment, looking back out over the sound, letting the beauty of the night, the call of the constellations, the hope of forever, the sheer eternity of the universe, fill her soul. She breathed in the magic of the salty breeze and walked inside to reality.

"Well, you two must have had a lot to catch up on," Ellie exclaimed with a not-so-discreet look at the clock on the wall over the bar. It was past eleven. She was sipping some coffee while George scrolled through the Mandolin Café website, looking for an old instrument to bid on.

"It's been seven years, Momma, and you can't sum that up in a sentence." She sat down by Joe on the couch. "We didn't exactly run up there and back either. Those tourists just get in the way. I've never seen so many golf carts. Anyway, I was trying to find Joe a woman." She winked at Joe and gave her momma an indignant look. She crossed her legs and began wiggling one back and forth.

"Any success?"

"He's too picky. Wants a young woman he can raise up right."

"Teaching all those airheads at school hasn't taught you anything yet, Joe?" George called out, never looking up from the computer screen.

Joe was getting uncomfortable. He had been uncomfortable ever since he saw Judie Kate. He had been uncomfortable when she hooked her arm around him, sidled up to him, leaned into him. He was uncomfortable in the room with George and Ellie while Judie Kate patted his leg right under their noses. He was embarrassed and yet, deep inside, enthralled. *Impassioned.* Mostly, he was confused.

"Okay, too many Indians circling the wagon here. I'm gonna call it a night. So, folks, you know the drill. Remember that sometimes I have nightmares. If you hear me having one, just come in the room and shake me until I wake up."

Ellie laughed and answered, "Joe, you have said that every year you've stayed with us, and you have never had one. I think you just like to scare us."

"Just a legal disclaimer is all. See you all about six o'clock in the morning. George, I expect my grits to be thick and the sausage to be spicy."

George answered, "Hope you brought Pop Tarts."

Joe got up and headed to his room. Judie Kate noticed he did not tell her good night. *All this for nothing?* She stood up after Joe closed his bedroom door.

"Well, Judie Kate, how did it feel to see Joe after all these years?" Ellie asked.

Judie Kate sat back down near Ellie and recrossed her legs.

"I didn't realize how much I missed our talks. And our ice cream." She paused, looking away. "Different, Momma. He's older, but so am I. We've both changed. Jay Jay's death made him different, almost distant, cut off. Yet, he is still Joe, in a way. I don't know; it's hard to describe."

"You sound a bit disappointed, Judie Kate." Ellie faced her directly. "Grief does that to you, Judie Kate. It takes a part of you away and leaves an empty place. Joe is a lot different than he was when you left for college."

Grief did that to me too, Judie Kate thought to herself. Now, she was not real sure Joe wanted to fill that void. She *was* disappointed, even hurt.

"Well, I'm tired. Think I'll go to bed. Good night, Momma, Daddy."

When the door closed, Ellie got up and walked over to George.

"Well, maybe that will take care of that." She patted him on the head and walked over to the stairs. "You gonna be long?"

"Long for what?" George called out as Ellie headed up the stairs.

She shook her head and answered, "Never mind."

Judie Kate, sitting on the soft bed, heard Joe finish up in the bathroom and close the door behind him. She took off her shoes, her leggings, and her top and bra, found her baseball nightshirt and headed to the bathroom to wash off her makeup and brush her teeth.

Back in her room, she left the door barely cracked for some reason, reached for the flowered wooden case on the dresser, brushed it off, looked at her picture of Don, briefly held the shark's tooth necklace and the diamond ring, and then took out her diary.

June 5, 2019, Wednesday

I finally saw Uncle Joe again. (He says to call him "Joe" now). It's been seven years since we last shared ice cream and really talked, several years since Don died and Joe came to see me. He has changed so much since then. Older, a bit of gray in his hair, some lines on his face that weren't there before. There is something distant about him. I guess it has to do with Jay Jay's death.

Still, it was good to see him. I think (hope!!) he was glad to see me. When he saw me, I could tell he saw more than the old Judie Kate. He looked at me! He stared at me. I was a little embarrassed, shy maybe, but then I remembered Jay Jay's dream and I had to be strong for her and, hopefully, for him too. We went for ice cream (of course!) and I held his arm the whole way. I think he has a thing for young women and women who are my size!

I hope I did not come on too strong. He still has his heart on Jay Jay. I found out, too, that there is something in his past he will probably never share. It makes me hurt for him and want him even more so I can take care of him.

But tonight, after I dressed up for him and showed him some affection, he just went to bed like it was nothing. That hurts! Was this just a wasted dream of mine?

I realized tonight that I love him and that I have always loved him. I want him more than ever.

Does Joe want me more than anything?

Love,
Judie Kate

Tyler's phone vibrated. She looked at it. It read 12:53 a.m.

"What does she want?" she mumbled to herself.

Miller: **i can't stop thinking about him!**

Tyler: Who?

Miller: **the guy at church tonight**
Tyler: Why?
Miller: **IDK, there was something about him!**
Tyler: What does your dad think?
Miller: **he's not sure**
Tyler: Go to sleep!
Miller: **k**

Miller tried but to no avail. All she could see was his hair, his eyes. But, she saw more than that. She saw what she thought was an answer to a prayer. With her faith, her life as the preacher's kid, living in the fishbowl of ministry, boys stayed away from her like the plague. Life was lonely. While she had friends like Tyler, she longed for more. A hand to hold, a closer friend to confide in for life. Warmth that could not come from fellowship dinners or her teammates at school. A soul mate. *Bone of my bone and flesh of my flesh.*

Is he the one? she wondered, more a prayer than a thought. Could a prayer be a dream, a dream a prayer? *Why did he run? Why do boys run away from me?* She buried her head in the pillow and slowly sobbed herself to sleep.

* * *

Suddenly, there was a low moan, then an increasingly loud ethereal hollering that seemed of another language. Judie Kate woke up, confused, looking around the dark room, until her eyes could focus, and she listened. Then, she remembered the conversation that night. *Joe's having a nightmare!* She jumped out of bed and raced through the bathroom to the bedroom on the other side.

"Uncle Joe, Uncle Joe! Wake up!"

She stumbled into an unseen pair of shoes, then bumped into a wall before she could barely make out the bed in the dark room revealed by the red hue of the clock by the bed. It was 1:56. She plopped on the bed as Joe continued crying out.

"Wake up! Uncle Joe, wake up!" She gently shook him, and he shuddered until he stopped wriggling, breathing hard. "Uncle Joe, Uncle Joe, it's me, Judie Kate!"

Joe calmed down, still unaware of where he was, who he was. George cautiously opened the door and stuck his disheveled, sleepy-eyed head into the room, his hand flapping the wall for the light switch. He flipped it on, then saw Judie Kate on the bed with Joe, rubbing his forehead. Joe stared at the wall like he did not know where he was, like he was in another zone. He looked over at George and then to Judie Kate, who was at his side, but he could not comprehend who was there. He was still in another world, vague, fogged, shadowy, out of focus.

"Well," George said, "Now we know you actually have these things."

"Daddy! How insensitive!"

George noticed that she wore what seemed to be an oversized T-shirt. Killer slipped into the room, jumped on the bed, and stood guard next to a still-rattled Joe.

Joe stirred and worked up a faint smile, still shaking off the effects of the nightmare. He looked around the room again. The misty plane he was in began to merge into the room where he now lay in bed. While George remained at the door, Judie Kate continued rubbing Joe's head. The room still seemed dark, as if an ill presence was in the air.

The overhead fan thumped out of balance. Lights shining through dusty globes filled the room with a haze. Judie Kate wondered about the inviting picture of the mermaid on the wall by the window. *Are mermaids slimy like fish?* George stared at the painting of the scow in front of the lighthouse, black scribbles for gulls. *I bet every house on Ocracoke has one of these.*

"Told you," was all Joe could get out, still caught up in a place that was dark, shadowy, surreal, filled with specters, spooks, fear, and the past. George gazed around the room once more and noticed Judie Kate's legs, showing more than a lady should.

"Well, if you've got that out of your system, I'm going back to bed." George paused. "Text me if you feel another one coming on."

"Daddy!"

"It's okay, Judie Kate. Many years of this abuse. I can handle it," Joe said.

George paused again as he slowly pulled the door shut. This time his face looked serious. Joe had seen that face before when he was released from the psych ward and George picked him up. After Joe closed the door of George's truck, his friend had looked directly in his face and asked a blunt question, and Joe knew now that it was coming again.

"You okay, Joe?"

"I'm fine, thanks. Go back to bed. Won't have another for a few months."

George glared at Judie Kate. *Time for you to go.*

"I'm staying a few more minutes, Dad. Just in case."

"I'm fine, really. Been through this before." Joe breathed in slowly, exhaled, blinked his eyes a few more times. The fan thumped away the moments. "Tell Ellie I'm sorry for waking everybody up."

George closed the door but left the light on. Joe's eyes were still glazed with the frost of now-melting fear. This one had been intense, leading to an overwhelming sense of terror, stronger than in times past. He remembered to breathe, relaxed a little but still stared at something beyond the room, himself, something deep, dark, hiding in his soul.

"How long have you had these things?" Judie Kate asked in a worried tone. She scooted onto the bed some more to keep from falling off. Joe moved over to give her more room. He saw her legs and then tried not to see them. Killer repositioned himself.

"Since I was sixteen." Joe came back to earth, looked up at Judie Kate, and realized how pretty and caring her eyes were. He sat up in the bed, put the pillow behind him, and became aware of the closeness of Judie Kate.

She realized her shirt was creeping up her legs. She wondered if he noticed, *if he cared*. She pulled the hem back down. *If you're gonna get him, show some leg!*

Despite all the mental haze, Joe was disappointed that her legs went out of sight. He was so focused on psychological survival that he let down his guard for his feelings for Judie Kate. *I like those legs.*

Judie Kate took his still-shaking hand, laid it on her leg and rubbed it softly.

"But after Jay Jay died, they changed. I would see Jay Jay, then she would change into a young girl, lady maybe, and then a shadow would pull her away. I would call out, but the girl, Jay Jay, whoever, was gone." He looked at the wall, stared, looked back at Judie Kate, as if she were the lost girl, his lost wife, lines of confusion appearing on his face.

"I'm sorry, Joe," she replied, like she could fix it anyway. Her fingers soothed his soul as she rubbed his hand. She placed it back on his chest and got up, walked over to the light switch, and turned it off.

"I'm not going anywhere until you go back to sleep." She reached for the bed in the dark, found it, patted her hands on it, accidently patting his leg, until she found the edge next to him, pulled the sheet over, and sat down on it, leaving him underneath. "Don't give me any lip either."

Joe was still anxious, tense, worried that, should he fall asleep, the dreams would come back, and the nightmares would pick up where they left off. He fought the sleep that was now overwhelming him. As he settled down, he realized this was the first time a woman had been in a bed with him since Jay Jay died. Judie Kate rubbed his head slowly, and soon he was asleep with Killer stretched out on the other side of the bed, paws up in the air, snoring.

Soon, Joe was snoring too. Judie Kate reached for his hand and held it between hers while feeling the sheets rise and fall slower and slower as he ebbed into deep sleep. She thought she felt his hand tighten over hers, or was it just a natural reaction? Was he dreaming something? Then, his hand relaxed. A tingle raced up through her spine, her soul, the same tingle she felt when she knew Don, dreamed for Don. She felt Joe's warmth, wished for his love. *Please, Jay Jay, tell him it is okay. Give him your permission.* Then she leaned back on a pillow and wriggled close to Joe. Soon, all three were asleep.

Thursday

It was six o'clock in the morning, but the light through the blinds made it seem like it was noon. Judie Kate woke up, suddenly, realized she was still in bed with Joe, and swiftly but quietly left him.

She tiptoed through the bathroom, leaving both doors cracked in the secret hope that he might get daring, and crashed onto her bed. *What a night!*

Joe stirred from his deep slumber, having that sensation that someone was in the room near him. He reached around and, instead, found Killer in the bed, paws up in the air, sleeping on his back. The light in the room caught him off guard.

Did he dream Judie Kate was caressing him? He enjoyed it, wanted more, but then checked himself. Was this just Judie Kate's infatuation coming alive again? Was she flirting? What if it *was* flirting? What was she after? It was like she was fishing for something.

As he pondered this, he traveled back once more to when he first saw her standing there in her leggings and cute, little white top, taller with her wedge sandals. Her smile radiating like the sun at the sheer joy of seeing him, her dark hair surrounding her round face like warm hands holding a loved one, her eyes deep and mysterious like a cave. Even her earrings, dangling enticingly, pulling him closer like a shining lure for a starving fish. Along with the reverie came a deep stirring within his loins that moved slowly up to his heart, an electricity, no, a *burning* he had not felt in many years. He traced her outline repeatedly on a page that had been blank for some time. A spell had been cast upon him. *By whom?*

"Better hit the shower before she does."

Grabbing his kit, he went into the bathroom, but he noticed the door to Judie Kate's room was cracked open a bit. Suddenly, he was like the adolescent boy at camp seeing a crack in the girl's cabin window. *Should I, or shouldn't I?* He pondered the question while he took out his shampoo and looked for his soap. *Crap, no soap! I always forget the blooming soap.* He looked around the bathroom, but the only soap was Judie Kate's. He picked it up and smelled it. Chewing gum? Spearmint? There was another block beside it, so he picked it up and sniffed it, and he remembered a fragrance from years back. Lavender? *Jay Jay loved lavender soap.*

"I'll get her a new one," he mumbled to himself.

Back to the door. It was too tempting. What did she look like while sleeping? Curled up? Fetal position? All over the bed? On her back, on her side, on her tummy? Covers on or off or legs in the open and body covered? Hair wild? Did she snore? *Jay Jay did.*

He slowly pushed the door open and cautiously looked inside. She was sprawled out, no covers, just her night shirt on, bottom sticking out, hands under her face, pillow pulled up tight to her chest. *Pink panties.* Guilt overcame him. *Okay, too much here. I shouldn't have.* But, he felt a playful attraction, whimsical, naughty but in a fun way. He carefully closed the door.

With the subtle click of the latch, Judie Kate rolled over. *Took the bait, Jay Jay!*

* * *

Joe walked around in the kitchen, thinking, *Man, I smell like a woman!* He made his instant coffee and opened his strawberry Pop Tarts.

"Come on, Killer, let's go outside." He opened the sliding door and the furry mess raced to relieve himself. Joe placed his cup on the arm of the faded Adirondack chair, sat down, and stared north out over the sound. *Peaceful this morning.* A slight breeze carried the steam of coffee to the neighbor's house. His thoughts followed it along. Judie Kate and his conflicted emotions over her; George and Ellie and their possible reactions if this, whatever "this" was, played out; the nightmare. The show. Things were getting complicated, and it was only Thursday ... *I just wanted to get away from it all.*

Killer jumped back up the stairs and looked at Joe and then looked at the door.

"Okay, okay, I get it. Not an outdoor dog at all, are you?" Killer wagged his scraggly tail in affirmation.

Joe rose up from the chair and opened the door and Killer raced inside and parked by the food bowl. "Not too subtle either, huh?" He looked all around the kitchen and then found the cat food. "Here you go, Killer." The canine dust mop barked his approval.

Joe sat down at the table and fired up his computer to check his online classes. He clicked on the island station WOVV and live-streamed the morning jazz. Just five emails. *Slow day!*

He looked around the sun-lit room, stared at the windows, saw the rays from the sun to his left. There was a clicking sound, but he could not locate it. In fact, there were clicking *sounds*. He looked for a clock but could not find one. The faucet was not dripping. The breeze outside was not clanking anything against a window. The air conditioner inside was not blowing an errant blind cord against the sill. Killer was not scratching anything. *What on earth is it?* He clicked on another email.

After a while, Judie Kate came out wearing gray flannel shorts and a loose baseball shirt. She rubbed her eyes and looked over at Joe, who was staring at his computer. *Had I known he was in here I would have at least brushed my hair.* She saw the food on the table and shook her head.

"Seriously? Pop Tarts? You know how many grams of sugar are in a Pop Tart? She reached for a bowl and the container of homemade muesli, poured the cereal in, and added a bit of milk.

"And what's that? Tree bark?"

He took a swig of his lukewarm coffee. Judie Kate plopped beside him, suddenly filled with energy for the new day.

"I didn't get this body by eating Pop Tarts." She licked her spoon, maybe a bit too invitingly.

"I bring 'em cause they're easy to fix. Your dad's too lazy to fix anything. What I really want is a bacon, egg, and cheese biscuit."

"I didn't see a Hardee's or Bojangle's or McDonald's on the island. Where do you get those around here?" She ate another spoonful.

"Wild Herd Restaurant," George called out, wandering barefoot down the steps looking for reality, still asleep, pajamas wrinkled. "And you could fix breakfast yourself, you know." He wobbled through the kitchen as if unsure where the floor was, picked up a ripe banana, peeled it back, and then moved over to the bar to his computer.

"You over last night?" he asked, staring at Joe with a "why am I awake?" look. He powered up his computer and took a bite of the banana.

"Yup," Joe answered back, posting another discussion response in his online class. Judie Kate got up and walked over to the kitchen to get some water from the fridge. Joe glanced her way, paused, focused a moment, and then stared as her shirt pulled her shorts up just a bit too much. *Oh my!*

"Daddy, what are you up to today?"

George scrolled through the news posts, her question seemingly having to work through a maze of distractions until it hit a free synapse.

"Meet the band at ten to rehearse for tonight." He scrolled some more. "Work on a few things for the festival after that. Joe? Could use your help. I think we are fixing the speaker stands or something like that at the Live Oak Stage."

"That's why I am here."

Judie Kate frowned to herself, then pleaded, "Daddy, can I have him this morning?"

There was an awkward pause. Was George not comfortable with the question? Was he lost in the morning news?

"Daddy, you fall asleep over there?" Judie Kate went over and gave him an uncharacteristically warm hug. "Hmm?"

George looked up at his daughter, who never hugged him and answered, "We rent him out to people for ten dollars an hour, minimum of two hours, twenty-dollar deposit. Most people return him in thirty minutes and say, 'Keep the change.' Pay up!"

"Daddy!" Judie Kate responded, lightly smacking him on the head. She scooted over to Joe and rubbed him affectionately on the back, out of George's view. "Is he always this mean?"

"Actually, this is pretty mild." Her affectionate touch was reaching deep into Joe's latent yearnings and unleashing another quiet surge of interest in her.

"Not awake yet," George answered. "Promise to make it worse by noon!"

She sat and moved her chair closer to Joe. She so wanted to hold his face and kiss him good morning, sit with him on the chaise and roll onto his tummy and whisper little love things into his ear. To playfully rub his belly and remind him to watch his cholesterol.

"So, Mr. Heart Attack, work a deal with you. Go with me to keep me safe from the sea monsters in the ocean, and we'll get that biscuit for you on the way."

"Can we get me a Pepsi, too, Mommy?" Joe answered in a childlike whine, staring at her sparkling eyes full of adventure, her unruly hair bringing him back to reality, yet there was something innocent, cute, playful in the wayward locks. For some reason, Joe thought of a pillow fight.

"Do you know how much sugar a soda has?"

Joe ignored the interrogation and closed his computer. Judie Kate was up again, heading to her room. Joe watched her leave and felt her enthusiasm, her charisma emanating from her body. *Why are flannel shorts so sexy on women?*

"Suit up, Mr. Heart Attack!" She shut the door behind her, and Joe stood up to leave.

"Joe?" George asked. "I need a favor."

"You name it."

"Let's go out on the deck for a moment."

***

The young man woke to a room filled with the morning's light. After a prayer of thanks for the new day, he found his worn, leather-bound Bible and read a passage from Psalms, his favorite book in the Bible. He reflected over the day's passage and then headed for the shower. After he finished, he came back into the room and picked out his clothes for the day, dressed, and then reached for his things on the dresser. Wallet, keys, small wooden cross, change, guitar picks, and wait ... he couldn't find his knife. He looked on both sides of the dresser, thinking it might have fallen off or, maybe he knocked it off?

He pulled the antique dresser away from the wall and looked behind it. Nothing but some errant dust and spider webs. He looked into the trash basket and searched around the folds of the white plastic bag, but it was not there. He hunted around the room in a panic but still no knife. How could he fight off the demons and remain strong in his faith without his knife? *Maybe it's in the car.*

He ambled carefully and quietly down the creaking stairs and went to the front desk to ask the clerk where he could get some breakfast. Still moving slow from the early morning shift, she blinked her big, brown eyes several times and then offered some suggestions.

She carefully looked him over and noted how he didn't fit the usual type of tourist on the island. *Nobody wears long pants in the summer. And what's with that shirt?* She sipped her mocha as he considered the options.

"Thanks," he said in an uncharacteristically happy voice and then turned to go. Then he stopped. "You know, the funniest thing happened. I know I put my knife on the dresser last night, but I couldn't find it this morning. And now that I think of it, all my things were moved around as well. Maybe I'm sleepwalking, huh?" He laughed it off and walked out the door.

Looks like Mrs. Clampton's Ghost has found you, my friend.

* * *

While the young Christian searched for his knife and then headed to the Wild Herd, Judie Kate started to pull into the first beach parking lot on Highway 12, but Joe remembered there was another one up the road.

"Let's go up a bit farther." Soon they saw the entrance, right across from the wild ponies. "Better," he noted. "There are only a few cars here. More private."

Judie Kate got out and tossed Joe her keys.

"You're in charge now, mister."

Joe removed his shoes and socks as Judie Kate shimmied out of her long shirt.

"Let's see that bathing suit, Joe!" she commanded.

"Don't have one," he answered from the other side of the car while he stuffed his socks into his shoes.

"What?" she said incredulously. "You come to the beach, and you don't bring a bathing suit?" She walked around to Joe's side. "Who comes to the beach with no bathing suit?"

Joe, still absorbed in socks and shoes, answered her question as she rounded the door.

"I never have time to go to the beach so why bother?" As he finished his sentence, Judie Kate stood in front of him. He looked up and went back in time.

"You like?"

Joe gawked in a very ungentlemanly way.

"It's a retro suit." She modeled it for him. "Technically a Corinne, vintage, one-piece, halter sheath with a skirted bottom."

The black, one-piece suit emphasized her shapely body suggestively and looked like a skin-tight, very short, little black minidress. For some reason the word "pheromones" raced through Joe's electrified head. *Wow!*

Joe stood up, still overtaken with the young woman in front of him. He was indeed transported back in time, to the 1950s, bebop music coming from the jukebox, swing skirts and saddle oxfords, and the way women then seemed to have a Hollywood look about them that today's skimpy, barely-there clothes just could not replicate. *Boy, she looks good!*

Judie Kate grabbed his hand and pulled him out of his reverie. Joe quickly turned to go to the beach, as if to get away from lusty thoughts, but Judie Kate called him back.

"Whoa, mule! Sunscreen first! You need some suntan goop before we go out. I'll rub you down and then it's your turn for me." She pulled out a bottle of high sun protection, squirted out a glop onto her hands, and rubbed down Joe's white back and arms. "Here's some for your chest," she said, squeezing more onto his hand. "You get that done while I work on my legs."

Joe couldn't take his eyes off her legs. So full, so inviting, way too enticing for Thursday morning. After she finished, she asked him to do her back. Touching her so intimately raised a sudden chill all over him. He was tentative as he applied the lotion.

"Joe?" she asked. "I'm not a China doll. Rub it in."

When he finished, she tossed the bottle back in the car.

"C'mon, man-with-no-bathing-trunks. We got some beaching to do!"

The morning was still waking up. There was a blue sky accented by an occasional puff of white. The seagrass on the dunes leaned backward in the southerly winds. Sandpipers scurried to and fro, up to the water as it receded and away from it as a frothing wave came in, searching for morsels hidden in the sand. As the tide ebbed, a long *shhhh* sound followed as bubbles from unseen critters percolated up from the sand. Seagulls screeched and a line of seventeen pelicans floated with the breeze an inch above the ocean waters. Joe stopped to watch, ever infatuated with how large and ungainly pelicans could soar and never crash over the ever-undulating waves.

The winds were strong from the storm that was far off the coast, pushing swells that crashed and boomed on the long-beaten shore. There were three lines of breakers, one nearly a hundred yards away that rose, curled, and fell, then another line emerged just fifty feet from them, and the final movement of the ocean symphony crashed like a cymbal on the beach.

Ahead of them was a lone sunbather, stretched out on her beach chair, the back raised in a forty-five-degree angle. The young lady faced east, enjoying the warmth of the morning rays, and stared at her phone in her left hand while running her fingers through long, brown hair that wafted in the winds and fell just inches above the sand. Everything about her was serene, easy, a postcard for the "Life Is Good" line of shirts and placards.

Up ahead was a dark blue conch shell, bleached and worn from its ocean journey, accented with a stray barnacle, but still in good shape.

"Look, Joe!" Judie Kate ran up to grab it, held it up in awe, and then turned back to him. "I've never found a conch shell before!" She turned it over and over, like it was a lost treasure. "Isn't it pretty?" She held it up to her ear and heard the ocean inside, just like the legend said.

Joe had caught up to her by now.

"Beautiful. A gift from Old Man Sea to his lovely mermaid."

She handed it to him for his inspection and cheerfully cried, "C'mon, Joe, maybe there are more!"

She pulled him along, eyes wide open, looking like a child, dodging a pile of jagged oyster shells. All that was missing was a green plastic bucket and a red shovel. Joe stopped in his tracks.

"What?" Judie Kate called out, still tugging.

"Look down, Judie Kate." When she did, she saw a faint outline of a brown circle in the sand.

"Joe, is that …?"

He carefully picked it up, wiping the layer of sand off it as he responded, "Yes, it is, it's a sand dollar."

Judie Kate exclaimed, "Joe, we're rich!"

As they continued down the beach, Judie Kate suddenly realized that even though she had known Joe for years, she really knew nothing about him.

Like a boy and a girl on their first date, she started asking questions.

"What's your favorite color, Joe?" He answered blue.

"Dog or cat?" Joe had to think on this one. Jay Jay liked dogs, but he was really a cat person.

"Favorite food?"

Again, Joe thought hard about this one. He loved Mexican food; he and George had eaten enough over the years to feed all of Mexico. Then again, other favorites included real country ham and grits with red-eye gravy. Roast beef and ketchup. There was the dish Jay Jay made: turkey kielbasa, kale, sun-dried tomatoes, garlic and angel hair pasta. He could still taste it after all these years. Then there were the silly things. Marshmallow Peeps for Easter, chocolate-covered marshmallow Santas for Christmas. Some days, he could not get enough Pay Day bars. Then it hit him.

"Gingerbread. Three days old, a bit crusty and chewy."

"Seriously? Not hot out of the oven with some butter?"

"Nope. And I like the corner pieces. Two crunchy sides!"

She hooked a clammy arm around Joe's arm and led him along. The intimate gesture caught Joe off guard again. How should he respond? She playfully yanked him into her and then pushed him back again, like an infatuated teenager awkwardly trying to figure out what love is. She continued the Q&A.

"Okay, coolest song?"

Joe paused a moment and turned and faced her. *How does one go through sixty years of music and select just one cool song?*

"Songs," he responded.

"Okay, songs."

"'Car Wash,' by Rose Royce. B52s, 'Love Shack.'" He thought some more. "'Shut Up and Dance,' Walk the Moon. And Bruno Mars, 'Uptown Funk.'"

Judie Kate was caught off guard.

"Boy, I didn't think you liked modern music."

"It's not all bad. Just that disjointed crap."

"Okay, got it."

"And," Joe finished up, "'Cha-Cha Slide.'"

"Seriously?"

"Seriously."

"Favorite song. Ever."

Suddenly, she felt Joe's arm go limp, and he pulled it away. He kept walking but was silent. After a moment, it hit her: she realized she had gone too far.

"Joe, I'm sorry. I didn't mean ..."

But he walked slowly, quietly, too quiet, his mind far away from Judie Kate. *I miss you so much, Jay Jay.* He sang the lyrics to himself as the grief came back like a bad storm. Judie Kate gave him space but stayed beside him, hoping. Finally, he stopped and looked at her. His face was wracked with pain, and his eyes watered.

"Orleans. 'You're Still the One.'"

* * *

Back on the very opposite side of the island, Ellie came down the steps in a morning fog, eyes squinting at the light that rushed in through the three windows overwhelming the room.

"I need coffee, George."

She wandered over to the kitchen and fumbled around until she found the bag with the coffee pods. *Hazelnut, Breakfast Blend or Coffee Shop?* She selected hazelnut, placed it in the holder, closed the cover, and pushed the button. The coffee maker gurgled as the slow trickle of hot brew filled her coffee cup. Cream and sugar completed the task, and soon the aroma woke her up. She walked over to George and rubbed his back and then sat on one of the chaise lounges in the room.

"Where is everybody?" She sipped a bit and looked out over Pamlico Sound, the waves heading north. A kayaker was making his way around the shoreline. Killer came over and jumped up on the lounge with Ellie. "Have you had your cat food this morning, Scruff?" He looked up at her with a puzzled muzzle, as if he was confused. "Okay, *Killer*, have you had your cat food this morning?" He wagged his tail.

"You didn't answer my question, George." There was more silence as George scrolled through listings of old mandolins, looking for a steal.

"What?"

"Where are the children?"

"On the pier over there." George pointed northward as two children played on the boardwalk two houses up from them.

"Our daughter and our son."

"At the beach."

Ellie pondered that for a moment.

"George, was Joe okay this morning? He was hollering pretty loud last night. Does he ever talk about that with you?"

George could see that Ellie was not going to leave him alone. Agitated, he turned and answered.

"All I know is that he's had them all his life, and now they have something to do with Jay Jay." He walked to the back windows and stared at nothing, trying to make up his mind about whether to make a bid on a 1930s-era Gibson A-00 mandolin or not. Ellie continued.

"He has stayed with us five years out of six, and he has never had a nightmare." She took another sip and looked out at the sound again. "Do you think seeing Judie Kate had something to do with it? That's the only connection I can see here."

George turned back around.

"What I saw was Joe sitting up in bed looking like he had seen the devil himself. He was scared of something. What I saw was Judie Kate sitting on the bed with him last night, taking care of him like a mother takes care of a frightened child. She looked like she was not going to let anybody, or anything, hurt Joe."

"You don't think they …"

"We didn't raise Judie Kate that way, and Joe knows better."

"We didn't raise Judie Kate to be all sexified like she was last night either."

George returned to the internet while Ellie got up and stood at the sliding glass door, sipping her coffee, trying to make sense of the morning, Judie Kate, and Joe. George typed in a bid of fifteen hundred dollars and hit enter. Ellie went outside, Killer going with her.

She paused, looked back inside, and asked, "George? What time is practice today?"

"Ten."

* * *

Back on the beach, the temperature was rising, and a few more tourists were filling the sands. Judie Kate looked over at Joe and decided to take a dare. It was time to see if Jay Jay's dream was real or not. She took a deep breath. "Joe, do you believe in dreams?"

They walked along, the waves crashing to the right, sending salty spray at them.

After taking a moment to ponder the question, he finally asked, "What do you mean?"

"I mean, as in portents, to reveal the future. You know, maybe God or some spirit directing our lives, revealing the plan through dreams?" She could not quite put her finger on what she was asking. "Okay, let me change the question: do you think dreams come true?"

Joe became philosophical. "Should all dreams come true, Judie Kate?"

"You're analyzing this too much, Joe. Just make this simple. Do you think dreams come true?" She took his hand and pulled him back to the ocean, the beach, reality, from whatever mental time zone he was in. She stepped into the water.

"Ooh, it's kind of chilly!" Waves splashed around her ankles as she sloshed through the pools of ocean brine, and soon her feet acclimated to the temperature. She playfully yanked a reluctant Joe into the next wave.

"Woo, it *is* cold!" He pulled her back to the sand as the waters receded. "Yes, yes, I do."

They walked a ways, and Judie Kate asked, "You gonna tell me about it or just keep me in suspense?"

Joe kept walking but looked far away. "About the time your dad began making guitars, I began having dreams about a guitar. In the dream, it was black for some reason. I don't like black guitars—give me a nice wood any day—so I was perplexed by the dreams. And in the dream with the black guitar was the number three. I know, sounds weird."

Joe related the story as two women passed them, plastic bags in hand, picking up shells. An elderly couple approached, holding hands, lost in the years gone by and enjoying yet another moment that would be a pleasant memory in the few years yet to come. She was wrinkled and her one-piece suit held together years of wear and tear. His chest was filled with gray hairs, likewise his beard, and his belly bulged, but he looked at her with the excitement of a boy on his first date. Joe finished the story.

"So, when I played the guitar your dad made me, it sounded just like I wanted, and it also looked like I wanted. And—you ready—it was black, and it was the third one he had made. It was indeed a dream come true."

"You're kidding, Joe!" Judie Kate exclaimed, grabbing his hand and turning to face him. "Your dream came true!"

"So, I guess that means I believe in dreams."

But for Judie Kate, that was not enough. It was one thing to have a dream come true. It was something else altogether to believe in another person's dream.

"So, tell me, Joe," Judie Kate asked again, "do you *believe* in dreams?"

Again, Joe looked away, reflected a moment, became pensive briefly, and then looked Judie Kate in the eyes.

"Yes, I do. That dream surely came true."

A jogger rushed by, barefoot and shirtless, tanned torso taut, flimsy running shorts revealing long, muscular legs, phone attached to an armband, wires going to his ears, a faint *fush-fush* with each step of his feet. Judie Kate stared briefly at him and came back to earth. *Whew, what a stud!*

"Let's walk some more, Joe."

They listened to the rhythm of the waves, the pull of the water as it rolled into a wave, which then crashed onto the sands. The comforting, white noise released their tensions while the refreshing salt spray cooled them as the breeze took away their cares. The warmth of the sun caressed their skin and rejuvenated their souls, and the blue sky filled the day with hope and joy.

***

Unbeknownst to and not far behind them, the Christian man was on the beach handing out tracts when he saw her far ahead, walking with someone. He remembered his dream of the woman with dark hair rising out of the blue ocean. Was this what the dream meant? Something told him to reach out to her. He picked up his pace, paused to hand out a tract to a family with three rambunctious and squealing children, and then continued. A man on a mission, he caught up to them and snuck up behind them, his tender white feet quickly stepping over pointed shells. He stared at them with the look of an obsessed believer—or was it a crazy man?—then he became distracted by her bottom, the bend of her hips, the way the suit ended like a too-short miniskirt. He was too young to know that the Corinne bathing suit had a panty to it. To his burning mind, she was wearing nothing underneath and was nearly revealing her womanhood.

Fueled by the sun, a surge of burning lust overcame him like a wildfire, arousal consumed him, desire turned dangerously, devouringly, deeper into a lascivious yearning to grab her, but he caught himself and stifled his consuming passion. *Was this what Dr. Cranston was talking about?* He said a silent prayer for strength and walked faster. When he passed them, he quickly and awkwardly turned about and faced them directly, blocking their way in an eerily intimidating fashion. Joe and Judie Kate nearly collided into him. This had to be the dark-haired woman coming up out of the blue ocean. She was so pretty. Was God leading him to her? *Why* was God leading him to her? He was conflicted, confused, and the message, the images, were contradictory.

Joe and Judie Kate saw the wide-eyed bewilderment in his face and were caught off guard. The stranger was staring at Judie Kate in a way that seemed creepy, manic. Joe, aware of the awkwardness, stepped forward to speak, but he was interrupted.

"Hi, sir, have you and your daughter thought about your salvation?"

He didn't wait for an answer, a bit out of breath, distracted by Judie Kate, rushing through his nervous spiel as if it would temper and then subdue his overwhelming interest in the young woman standing in front of him.

"If the world were to end today, where would you spend eternity? These are important questions that nobody in our secular, hedonistic world is asking today, but as a Christian, I am asking them because your spiritual lives matter to me, and I want you both to be saved."

He took a deep breath, trying his best not to look too much more at Judie Kate. Her black hair, black bathing suit, dark eyes, coupled with her fair, angelic skin, all pulled him into a new yet frighteningly confusing world. He wanted to ask her out but was intimidated by her, by her soft skin, by her smile. He wanted to put his hands all over her. Despite her puzzled look, there was a radiance in her, about her, that was captivating. She was an angel in white skin, but she was also a demon in a black suit, beautiful yet seductive. Bathsheba and King David. The Samaritan woman whom Jesus faced. King David gave into lust, but if Jesus could overcome temptation, so could he!

"So, here is a spiritual tract that I hope you will read today," he blurted out. His sweaty hand was shaking as he handed it to her. "Please read it because I do not want you both to burn in Hell for the rest of your lives." He handed Joe a tract as well. "And have a blessed day."

He then turned and walked briskly away, as if fleeing temptation or maybe fear, but like Lot's wife, he couldn't resist the impulse to look back. He turned and ogled her one more time. Sensing something troubling, Judie Kate spun around and looked back at him and saw him lecherously looking her over. He was embarrassed and hurriedly bolted away. Not sure of what he was feeling, he instinctively reached for the knife in his pants pocket. But then he remembered it was missing from his room. Now what would he do?

Still, as he walked back down the beach, he recalled the discussion with Dr. Cranston. Maybe she was the reason he felt led to the beach. Maybe God was sending him to her. Maybe she needed salvation. *She needed to stop wearing such revealing clothes!* Then, it hit him out of nowhere: maybe God was leading him to change her so she could be his wife. Could it be?

"Whew, that was weird," Judie Kate said, her eyes getting big and then relaxing as they watched the young man race back down the beach.

"Well," Joe responded, "either that was the best pickup line ever, or he's yet another example of why people don't go to church anymore." The Christian stranger stopped to talk with another family, and he handed them some tracts. His long pants were clearly out of place on the beach, and Judie Kate commented on his T-shirt.

"Did you see his shirt?"

"How could you miss it? 'The Lord's Gym' is clearly a takeoff from a fitness center. That man bearing a huge cross while doing a push up. I don't know how they get by with that."

"Kind of obnoxious, huh?"

"Well, anyway, where exactly is someone in a swimsuit going to put these?" She handed hers to Joe, and he stuffed them in a side pocket.

"Maybe he wanted to see you try to put them somewhere," Joe answered, smiling devilishly.

She popped him on the arm. *Maybe you would like to see me put them somewhere?*

Having survived beach evangelism, they walked farther, listening to the waves crash onto the sand and tinkle like a hundred bracelets on its return to the sea. But Judie Kate's radar was up. There was something dangerous, threatening about that stranger.

They continued down the beach, the sun warming them, and the breeze cooling them off. A sand crab scurried away from them, and a seagull squawked out a warning.

"Let's sit for a while, Joe."

She motioned to a place back from the waves and they rested on the beach, the wet sand soaking their bottoms, and they placed their sea treasures behind them. Judie Kate breathed in and out, working up her courage, and then spoke.

"I need to share a dream with you." She pulled her legs up to her chest and placed her arms around them and then looked out over the ocean. Joe leaned back on his hands and extended his white, hairy legs out. Several waves came and went, and two gulls parked nearby, hoping for some treats as Judie Kate wrestled her nerves to bare her soul, her dream, to Joe. *Here it goes!*

"A few years ago, I woke up shaking in the night. I saw Jay Jay in a dream. She said, 'I want you to take care of Joe now. But you must change. When the numbers add up, you will know.'"

While the ocean came and went with thunderous booms of varying degree, the silence between Joe and Judie Kate was deafening. She stared at the sparkling waters as if Joe's response might come from that direction, afraid to look directly at him lest he question the truth of her dream. As his reticence continued, she began to have doubts. What if this was purely her imagination? What if it was her infatuation? But, she knew the dream had come around the time Jay Jay had died. In the greater realm of energy, spirit, it had to be real!

Joe surveyed the ocean as well, but what he saw was Jay Jay. Jay Jay drying off after her shower, washing dishes at the sink, screaming as she stepped off the platform on her first zip line. He remembered peculiar things: the way she held the spoon when stirring ingredients in a bowl, always putting her left shoe on first, using the blinker even when nobody was behind her.

Then, he saw her dying, whispering to him words he had forgotten but now were as clear as the sky above: "I will send someone to you, and you will know when she comes. She will be your new dream come true."

He had put her words away into a trunk that would never be opened again, stored in an attic of No More, perhaps in loyalty to her, in vain hopes that by remaining true, she would never go away, maybe return one day. But now, Judie Kate had opened that trunk like Pandora had her box. Is this what Judie Kate's dream meant? Was Judie Kate the reincarnation of Jay Jay? What did "take care of Joe" mean? And what did "your new dream come true" mean?

Judie Kate thought the numbers had added up. She thought this serendipitous weekend was the right time. She remembered seeing Joe's eyes light up when she walked into the room. She sensed his excitement, off and on, still a bit reserved, as they walked around, as she held his arm. When the nightmare occurred last night at 1:56, the same time Jay Jay had appeared to her, she knew the numbers were in place. But, she worried now that Joe's silence meant she had opened an old wound that was best left untouched.

"I'm sorry, Joe. Maybe I shouldn't have brought this up."

Her apology brought him back to her side. He turned and looked at her.

"When did you have this dream?" If it was recently, then he would dismiss it as yet another bout of infatuation for him, something that needed to be nipped in the bud right now. He didn't have time for this, not during the festival.

Judie Kate turned his way and calmly answered, "November sixteenth, twenty sixteen, at one fifty-six in the morning. I remember it like it was yesterday. I wrote it down in my diary that morning, and I have never forgotten it." She paused and then stepped into the abyss. "Wasn't that right around the time Jay Jay died?"

Joe squirmed uncomfortably, crossing his legs under him, placing his hands in his lap. Lines appeared across his brow; a seriousness rose like a stormy morning all over his face. His eyes teared and he rubbed them with his salty hands.

"Joe, maybe we should not talk about this anymore. I'm sorry ..."

"She died at one fifty-six in the morning on November sixteenth."

He looked down at his feet, embarrassed to let Judie Kate see him so saddened. But there was more to it. He couldn't face her because he was still putting it all together, and the emerging picture from the puzzle pieces from the present and past was a picture he was not sure he wanted to look at.

"When Jay Jay died, she said something to me. I did not believe it, did not want to believe it. I thought it was just one of those things people say to each other when they die. But now, with your dream, I have to rethink this."

Judie Kate, filled with a sliver of hope, instinctively reached for Joe's hand and held it tightly, anticipating, anxious.

"What did she say, Joe?" She looked at him with a warm yearning, a wish that this was the moment when the numbers added up.

He took a deep breath, the kind you take when you are about to admit the truth, to let out the hurts of the past, to say something you hoped you would not regret.

"She said, 'I will send someone to you, and you will know when she comes. She will be your new dream come true.'"

Judie Kate smiled cautiously, her face slightly beaming with a deep wish that this meant her dream was real, she had not made it up, and her desire for Joe was not just an infatuation from days gone by. She knew what she wanted to ask but hesitated, waiting for what seemed like the right moment. Finally, she took the leap of faith.

"Joe, this brings me back to my original question. Do you believe in dreams? This is not just my dream, this is not a coincidence, it is Jay Jay's dream. She told me the numbers would add up. Remember when she died, when I had my dream? Do you know what time your nightmare was last night? It was one fifty-six, Joe. I looked at the clock when I came to your room. She told me the numbers would add up. Joe, we were meant to be together. Jay Jay set us up, Joe!"

It was more than he could handle. He wanted to believe, and he certainly had the feelings to carry the dream to fruition, but something still fought it deep inside.

"How do we know for sure, Judie Kate? How do we know? Maybe she just meant for you to take care of me while I am in transition, while I look for somebody else. Maybe it is your turn to talk me through my grief, my pain, my issues, like I helped you through yours."

Judie Kate was not giving up, and a fire ignited inside her. She stared Joe in the face and hit him hard with one simple fact.

"Joe, how exactly am I supposed to take care of you when we live half a day apart?" She waited for his response, which was not coming soon enough, her consternation rising like an out-of-nowhere wave. She leaned closer toward him.

"Hmm?" She waited. "Joe, let it make sense, okay? Jay Jay wants this, remember?" She shook his hand for emphasis.

The breakers came and went, as did several beach walkers. Joe wrestled with the past, the present, and the future. It was certainly time to let the past go. By still holding on to yesterday, he was keeping Jay Jay alive but to what good? He had only felt heartache and loneliness that kept him in a perpetual state of despair and sadness. When he saw Judie Kate, when she took his arm, when she walked close to him, it all went away.

But then, the fear of losing Jay Jay forever would creep back into his mind. To keep her with him, he thought of excuses based on the future: What would George and Ellie say? What would his colleagues say? How would people react when they saw the old man and the young girl at the mall? *Hi, sir, have you and your daughter thought about your salvation?* Could Judie Kate, would Judie Kate, take care of him when he was old while she was still in her prime?

The ingredients of conflicting thoughts boiled up into a stew of doubt and reluctance that still steamed with passion for this woman beside him. How could he want something so desperately and yet run away from it so hard at the same time?

Judie Kate stood up, wiped the sand off her bottom, and motioned for him to get up.

"Turn around," she commanded. She playfully wiped off his bottom as well. After they picked up their shells, she took his hand. To her, it was like they were in middle school, and she had answered Joe's letter: *Will you go out with me? Check yes or no.* After a while, she stopped, turned toward Joe, and took a chance. She placed her hands on his hips and pulled closer to him. She looked up to him and smiled.

Joe looked over at the dunes, most standing fifteen feet high, covered in sea grass. He could see the different colored layers in the sections carved out by the storms of the past few years. *Each layer had a history*, he thought to himself as Judie Kate held on tightly. Life has its own layers, each laid down by the years gone by, like silt in a riverbed, each layer a tale, and as the years go by, the story emerges. But sometimes, life interrupts with storms and takes out a chunk of the story, like Jay Jay's death. Would Judie Kate fill it or build a boardwalk over it?

"Joe?" Judie Kate asked. "Let's please give this a try. For Jay Jay's sake, okay?"

Joe breathed in and held his breath for a long time. He was hesitant, not sure, fearful of what might be, yet, deep within, he felt the pangs of love. He was nervous, like a boy asking the beauty queen out to the prom.

"Okay," he reluctantly exhaled. "For Jay Jay's sake," he said while still not quite convinced.

Then, he tentatively reached for her hand, like it was a burner on a stove, and he was checking to see if it was still hot, and she squeezed it tightly, like two teenagers in love at the Friday night ball game. A stray wave crashed into them, as if baptizing their new relationship, knocking them down on each other, both now sopping wet. Her face hovered over his, and she impulsively kissed him. For a brief moment, all sense of worry and the unknown fell aside, and they both laughed together.

She got up, and Joe followed her, both wiping sand off themselves and then off each other, accidently touching places that were off limits just moments ago. The wave had loosened propriety, and smiles covered their faces. There was a playful glint in their eyes, and youthful devilment filled their souls. Relief relaxed their inhibitions, and they kissed each other again. For Joe, finally, the spell of the past had been broken. All that mattered was the present. The worries of the future would take care of themselves.

When they turned to head back down the beach, holding hands and soaking in the rays of the sun and joys of love, Joe reached into his pocket and realized that the sand dollar was broken.

Ready to head home, as they left the parking lot, Joe saw the ponies across Highway 12.

"Have you seen the wild ponies?" he asked.

"Nope," Judie Kate answered, pulling on her seat belt as they inched toward the intersection.

"Okay, then let's cross the road. Looks like a crowd. Might be something to see!" There was an excitement in Joe's voice Judie Kate had never heard before.

She parked the Mustang in the last space, and they walked over to the railing. She put her arm around him, and they enjoyed the pastoral peace while standing at the fence, the breeze rustling the limbs of the trees, a song from nature gracing the moment. The ponies grazed serenely in one place for a moment and then slowly walked about to new patches of grass as the breeze from the east blew their tails and manes.

"So many colors, Joe," Judie Kate said in muted amazement. There were several painted horses with large swaths of contrasting colors of fur. A lone sorrel horse stood to the left, and two white horses grazed together. Joe pointed to the barn in the background.

"Look, Judie Kate!"

There was a gray foal wobbling on weak legs next to the bay mare who stood guard.

"Joe!" Judie Kate exclaimed like a child.

"That foal is not too old, Judie Kate. See how unsteady he is on his legs." They both stared in quiet wonder as other horses wandered off to farther parts of the pasture. Caught up in the moment, just the two of them and the tranquility of the ponies, Joe wrapped his arm around Judie Kate's waist and pulled her closer. Even in the heat of the June summer, he felt her warmth radiating into him, and for the first time in years, his soul smiled.

* * *

After the ride back down Highway 12, Judie Kate dropped Joe off at the Workshop Stage area and drove off. He walked over to the theater where Ditchville12 was practicing, waved to the band, and went to the back room and stole a Coke from the fridge. Refreshed by the fizz, he came back into the room and plopped on a chair. George noticed that Joe's face was radiant, an aura he had not seen in years. It was not so much the skin overall—or the slight radiance from a morning in the sun on the beach—as it was the aura his face revealed, like that unseen glow a pregnant woman has. It worried George quite a bit, so much so that he missed his break.

"George, still hung over from Wednesday night?" Kimber Lee, the bass player, teased with squinting eyes as the band paused for the mistake. Darren, on guitar, scowled.

"Let's try that again." Bow String Bill tapped off the beat with his fiddle, and the band jumped back into "Waterbound."

Joe left the theater and trudged back over the sandy path to the Workshop Stage. The event crew was busy setting up the tents for the entire festival and mesh screens to cordon off the concert areas from the rest of the grounds. Tomorrow, the place would be alive, electric.

He walked up the weathered steps onto the porch of Read a Bit More and paused for a moment. Turning a tarnished doorknob, he stepped inside and instantly enjoyed the cool air and the peculiarly musty smell of books. He walked around the tightly packed shelves of novels, self-help tomes, and children's books and found the local history section, and picked up a new book by journalist Andrew Lawler about the search for the Lost Colony of Roanoke and read the inside jacket cover. *Hmm.*

"Another chapter in the long history of that tragic settlement," he mumbled to himself.

"Excuse me?" a woman said, standing behind Joe.

He looked around and saw an attractive forty-something with sparkling green eyes and a few lines on her somewhat rounded face that was accented by thick sandy hair brushing down behind her shoulders. Her body language was that of lingering shame of a marriage gone bad mixed with the resolve to do better this time and find someone who would treat her with respect and love.

"I'm sorry," Joe apologized. "I was just muttering to myself."

She wore a soft perfume that wafted about like a fresh breeze, and her cream tank top revealed enough cleavage to spark more interest. Joe tried not to look, but he noticed brown legs and cheap flip-flops below a short, jean skirt. She noticed that he noticed.

Once she moved beyond Joe's blue eyes and wavy black hair, she wondered why his shorts seemed a bit damp and had sand on them. Then, she saw his shirt was wrinkled also, but his shoes were perfectly white. The man standing in front of her was something of an anomaly, handsome and striking yet perfectly unkempt in a boyishly innocent way. *He's cute.*

"I sometimes mutter to myself," Joe explained, face reddening by the second.

"Oh, okay. I thought you were talking to me." The moment was now awkward. She looked down and then back up and met his eyes. "So, what brings you to Ocracoke?" she asked, somewhat casually but with a hope of something more.

"Festival," Joe answered, a bit uncomfortably. He never could speak to pretty women. He always got flustered and tongue-tied. "The Ocrafolk Festival. I do the sound at the Workshop Stage." The tight space between the shelves made their encounter a close one. Joe backed up but hit a bookshelf.

"Me too!" she answered back with a bit too much enthusiasm. "I mean, not to do sound, but for the music." Now it was her turn to be awkward. She smiled in a hesitant way that begged for more conversation. "Think it will be a good show this year?" She relaxed a bit and shifted her legs, crossing one foot daintily over the other. "I enjoyed the folk music last year. I'm not a child of the sixties, but that was some good music back then."

"Should be a good show this weekend," Joe answered, recovering his confidence. "I've seen the program already. There is a nice mix of genres and special events. We are having the folk song sing-along at the Workshop Stage at nine on Saturday."

"Sounds like a plan," she answered with a bit of anticipation in her voice, suddenly looking very young. Was he inviting her there for a reason or just being polite? "See you there?" she asked before she realized that, of course, he would be there. He was the sound man. "I mean, see you there."

"It'll be fun," Joe answered. "See you then." He turned and walked into another shelf, and she smiled, watched him gather his wits and direction and then walk to the checkout.

"Hmm," she mumbled to herself. "Nice. No ring either. Folk music it is!"

Joe paid for his book and went back outside into the humidity. He returned to his truck where he deposited his purchase and then headed for the theater. The band would be finishing up soon and then he and George would head for lunch.

* * *

While the boys did their music thing, mother and daughter wandered about the village, each trying to think of a way to repair years of distance without seeming obvious or touching a nerve in public. Leaving one store, the Slushy Mushy caught Judie Kate's attention.

"Want a slushy?" she asked happily. She was in such a good mood she didn't mind splurging on the calories.

"Not in my diet," Ellie answered, looking back in the store as if she had missed something.

"Well, I'm getting a slushy."

They paused for the slow-moving traffic and then dashed across the road and walked over to the stand, climbed the ramp and steps, dodged three indifferent tourists, and went inside and stood in line.

"Look, Momma, they have smoothies. You know, yogurt, healthy."

Judie Kate ordered two that were strawberry-peach flavored. Judie Kate paid the bill and mother and daughter sat down on a bench on the side porch of the Slushy Mushy.

"All right, Momma, talk. You've been quiet all morning long. What's bothering you?" She strained to slurp some smoothie through a straw that was really too small for the thick refreshment.

"My hip is hurting, that's all."

"Incorrect. Try again. Something's on your mind. Out with it."

Ellie looked worried, awkward, hesitant, and then wondered when her daughter became so brash. She glanced out at the tourists, then back at her smoothie, took a sip, and stared far way one more time.

"Okay, since you asked … why are you so taken with Joe? Why can't you look for men your age?"

Thought so, Judie Kate thought as she responded, "Momma, you don't get it. I just—"

Ellie interrupted by saying, "What I get is that you have been infatuated with this man since you were fourteen. George and I saw it; Joe knew it too. We thought you had gotten over it when you left for college and got out on your own. Why this renewed interest in Joe?"

This again. Judie Kate mentally rolled her eyes.

"First off, Momma, I am well aware of my infatuation with Joe when I was young. He filled a void that, frankly, you and Daddy were too busy to fill. Yes, I had a crush on him. All teenage girls have a crush on an older man. All teenage girls have a crush on a man who pays attention to them."

"Well, I'm sorry you feel that way. We had jobs to do so that we could take care of you, provide for you. That's what paid for your college, your car, the rent on your apartment. We just wanted to be good parents." Ellie looked disappointed at her daughter's unappreciation for their sacrifices.

"And for that, I am very thankful, Momma. I really am. But all I wanted was a Momma and Daddy, not money. What I got was a Mother and Father and no bills. Your generosity is lovingly and graciously appreciated, Momma. But this is water under the bridge. I'm moving on now. I want to live my life my way, and that, hopefully, includes Joe."

Ellie, caught off guard that her daughter finally admitted she wanted to live with Joe, was not giving up. She explained her side the best she could. She and George just didn't understand why she could not find someone her own age. Ellie worried that people would talk; they would say things about Joe, about Judie Kate, and about them. She shifted around on the weathered wooden bench, clearly uncomfortable with the direction of the conversation.

"Judie Kate," Ellie said, "He's old enough to be your father for Christ's sake. That doesn't bother you? Have you thought about what happens when he gets old? You'll be stuck taking care of him when you could be enjoying the prime years of your life."

Some sunburned customers in bathing suit cover-ups sitting at the table next to them realized that the conversation was becoming heated and awkward. They picked up their slushies and hurriedly scampered down the steps. Three teenage girls with espressos over ice rushed to their seats.

Judie Kate turned directly to Ellie and became very intense. "Okay, here is the thing. I just don't fit in with this current generation. It's like I was supposed to live twenty years ago, not today. I don't like this culture."

It took ten minutes to explain why. Ellie was caught off guard, not quite sure of the flow or the logic of Judie Kate's vitriol. She was also aware that Judie Kate was tapping into the very culture she had derided in her work. *In some ways Judie Kate is so like me!* She was also aware, however, that she had tapped a nerve, a very big nerve, in her daughter.

"Looks like you have thought this over quite carefully," she responded, somewhat shocked that her little girl was this astute. She took a sip from her now-melted smoothie.

Judie Kate stared as several young men strutted by, flipping a football between them, hoping to turn a few female heads. "And don't get me started on the narcissistic men," she said.

After a brief explanation, Judie Kate stared directly at Ellie with a stern face. "Why would I want to marry a man who looks better than me? Who smells better than me? Is that the kind of man you want me to marry?" She glared at a twenty-something in plaid shorts and a polo pullover who paused to look at her. He quickly walked away.

"See what I mean?" she asked Ellie, pointing as the man passed by. "Seriously, plaid shorts in pink and baby blue, yellow pullover? Is that supposed to turn me on? Do you want that for a son-in-law? Shallow, smooth-skinned, and self-absorbed?"

Ellie shook her head again, and Judie Kate was not clear if she was shaking her head about the men she just described or her daughter's rant. A shiny Land Rover slowly drove by, hip-hop loud, college kid with greasy, dark hair, shades on a rope around his neck, staring at the ladies, letting his money and smile do the talking. Two lithe, attractive, young women in skimpy bikinis and sarongs highlighted with dark tans paused, caught up in the attention he was giving them, letting him dream of things that might be. Did they like the car or the guy? Judie Kate pointed to herself.

"Look at me. I have big bones. I lost weight, but I am still big. Men don't want this. Men don't want me." She sat down with frustrating sadness all over her face. But then she collected herself.

"But," she said, slowing down, taking a breath and suddenly feeling appreciated by a man. "Joe does." Judie Kate smiled slightly, and Ellie looked away in a sense of out of sight, out of mind.

"Momma, you see what I am talking about? Joe is not like that. That is why I am 'infatuated' with him," she said while making air quotes. "He has depth unlike so many people I've run into who are my age."

Ellie nodded her head, not entirely convinced, more to say that she was ready for the conversation to be over. She swirled the few drops of her smoothie with her straw and then drank the rest.

"Just wish he were younger, that's all."

Just wish he were mine, Judie Kate answered to herself. She stood up, grabbed her Momma's empty cup and threw both cups in the trash.

The two women excitedly jumped into the Land Rover, clearly loving the attention of being seen in the expensive vehicle, in the company of apparent money.

"Come on, we gotta find me some earrings," Judie Kate said.

As they got up, they saw a young man park his car in the sandy parking lot. He was tall, somewhat big, with wavy brown hair. He was boyish in a way. He unloaded a cooler, then filled it with water bottles and covered those with ice. Then, he took out a package and placed it beside the cooler. He pulled out his guitar and began playing. Curiosity got the best of Ellie and Judie Kate, so they walked over. A small crowd gathered as he began to busk, playing bluegrass gospel music, Appalachian music, and African American spirituals. When he finished a song, he paused and asked if anyone wanted some cool water. As a few tourists walked up and took the water bottles, he handed them a tract. Suddenly, Judie Kate realized who he was.

"Let's go, Momma." She pulled her away in a huff.

"Where are we going? He was playing gospel music. You know I like that kind of music. I bet he is down here witnessing. It takes a lot of guts to witness in this world, you know? He must be a very strong young man."

"He's a very weird young man, Momma."

"Now, you don't know that, Judie Kate. You haven't even met him yet."

"Oh yes, I have. He stopped us on the beach this morning. He stared at me a little too much for my comfort. Then he handed me and Joe a tract and walked off. He's creepy, if you ask me. He can keep his self-righteous Christianity to himself!"

Ellie was caught off guard and irritated by Judie Kate's blasphemous tone. She had raised her daughter in the Church, but now it seemed she was against it.

"When did you get so angry about the Church? Did that happen in Wilmington?"

Judie Kate, now full of indignation, turned and stared at her mother straight in the face.

"It happened when I was thirteen, Momma. That youth minister everyone loved so much, the one you and Daddy loved so much. He put his hands all over me when I was thirteen, Momma."

Ellie's jaw dropped in disbelief.

"Judie Kate, surely he did not mean anything. He was a fine person. Maybe you misunderstood. You were so pretty at that age ... "

Now, Judie Kate was hot. *Are you saying I'm not pretty now? Are you saying that gives him the right?*

"What I understood, Momma, is that his hands had no reason to be all over my breasts or on my butt when we passed the peace or had a prayer circle. You didn't see him staring at the other girls my age either." Then, she looked angrily at her mother.

"And, by the way, thanks for taking his side rather than your daughter's side. You'd be a good priest in the Catholic Church."

The words stung, and Ellie was about to fire back in defense, but then she realized something else: Judie Kate's problems began when she was thirteen.

***

He saw her in the crowd, realized it was the same woman from the beach, and felt that God had brought him to her, her to him, again. But then she walked off. He didn't understand. He picked up his guitar, checked the tuning, and began playing "Poor Wayfaring Stranger" in a minor key. Several folks walked up and dropped money into his guitar case. He nodded in thanks and kept playing, watching the dark-haired woman from the ocean and his dream walk away.

***

As the Christian busker continued singing, mother and daughter went next door to Rags 2 Riches and looked around. Trinkets abounded. Wooden pelicans, nautical gifts with different sea birds, boat miniatures, puzzles, cards, framed sayings, racks of shirts, and other clothes. Judie Kate found a dark blue bracelet and matching anklet that matched her dark blue romper with floral accents.

"I'll take both. Plastic, okay?"

The transaction complete, Judie Kate told her mom, "Now, we have one more thing to buy." When they went outside, they saw the busker again, this time with a trio of young girls around him. They were singing Christian pop tunes. The girls were clearly mesmerized by the singer, but when he saw Judie Kate, his attention went straight to her.

"C'mon, Momma," she commanded, grabbing her hand and pulling her to the right. *Why is he staring at me like that?*

***

It was lunch time, and George and Joe drove over to Amigos Taco Stand. The short trip over was tense, with both men needing to say something to the other but neither wanting to test their relationship. Amigos was a food trailer in the same parking lot as the grocery store, the hardware store, and the ABC building, and it featured authentic, made-from-scratch Mexican food.

"Pork burrito and a drink," George said.

George paid his bill and took his number and stepped to the side. Joe ordered a chicken burrito and a drink.

About five minutes later, they took their food and headed for a picnic table behind the trailer. Large umbrellas provided a break from the hot, June sun. George sat down on one side, and Joe took the other.

As George opened the wrapper of his burrito, Joe spoke up.

"I had forgotten how big these things are. Definitely takes two hands."

George took another bite and kept going.

"George? I'm in a bit of a pickle here."

George was lost in thought, running through a riff in his head for a song in the set list for the show that night.

"I don't think Amigos has pickles," he joked. "Hmm. Pickle tacos."

"Not that kind of pickle, George." Joe munched some and swallowed. "Boy, these things are hot today. Anyway, your daughter, Judie Kate—I think she has a thing for me."

"*Think?*" George responded. He looked over his reading glasses at Joe. "She's had a thing for you since she was fourteen. Thought she got over that when she went to college, but now, after last night, I don't think so." He took another bite, wiped the sweat off his brow from the hot sauce, and continued. "You're all she's talked about since she got here Tuesday. She's been on you like a tick since then."

Joe knew that look and the tone of voice. He had observed both when George was fussing at students. *Here we go.*

"Well, it got more interesting this morning." Joe put his burrito down and looked directly at George. "George, do you believe in dreams?"

George looked up from his burrito, a drip of sauce caught in his beard, incredulity oozing all over his face.

"Ah jeez. Is this some of that new age stuff you teach in those religion classes? What's Judie Kate gotten herself into? Did she channel some spirit from fifteen thousand years ago like that video you show your classes?"

Joe looked at George, enduring another jab at his topics in his religion classes.

"You have a glob of sauce in your beard, Grandpa."

George wiped it off with a napkin. Joe paused for a moment to collect his thoughts. He had to say this just right, but then again, no matter how he put it to George, it was not going to go well. Best to just spit it out.

"Judie Kate told me about a dream she had. She said it was on November 16, 2016. It occurred at 1:56 a.m. She said Jay Jay appeared to her in the dream and that Jay Jay had on red overalls—"

"Oh, this is going to be good," George said.

He took a bite from his burrito, shaking his head all the while. Bikes and golf carts careened into and out of the parking lot.

"George, I'm trying to be serious. Judie Kate said Jay Jay appeared to her and said she was to take care of me now. That she would have to change, and when the numbers added up, Judie Kate would know what to do."

George stopped chewing and looked over his glasses at Joe. "I'm no psychologist, and I barely made a C in that class in college, but that dream came a few years after she left for college. Maybe it was just her infatuation coming back. She never really dated anyone in college, so maybe she was lonely, inventing something to get back with you. Women are strange, you know?"

Joe knew this was going to be awkward. "George, do you remember when Jay Jay died?"

George shook his head. He knew it was a few years ago.

"November sixteenth, twenty sixteen, one fifty-six in the morning. When she died, she told me she would send someone to take care of me."

George looked straight at Joe. "How do I know that you aren't making that up to jibe with Judie Kate's dream? I always thought that you, in some odd way, had a thing for our daughter too. To me, this sounds like you two connived together this morning and made up a good story to convince us that you two were meant to be together. That seems mighty convenient, you know?"

Joe was stunned and hurt by the accusation from someone who could be called his only friend. He looked away to calm down for a moment. Two young couples sat beside them at the next table. They giggled as they unwrapped their food and then smiled as they took their first bites.

"George, you know me better than that. I have never taken advantage of Judie Kate even though I have had many opportunities to do so. The last person I would ever take advantage of is Judie Kate, if for no other reason than she is the daughter of my best friend." Joe looked down at his half-eaten burrito as if searching for inspiration.

"George, man to man here. You know me better than anyone. I have never recovered from her death. You saw me through the suicide thing, the recovery, the medicines, the therapy. You and Ellie are the very reason I am alive now." He paused, feeling a tear come to his eye as the leftover emotions from those years came back.

George looked away. He never could handle tears.

Joe continued, "George, when I saw Judie Kate last night, for the first time in over three years, I felt something. A spark, a light, shock, fire. I don't know what to call it. I could use all the love metaphors, but you would just laugh."

George looked at Joe. "Lust? She dressed mighty spiffy for you last night. You haven't been with a woman for a long time. Just saying."

Joe glared back at George at the insinuation.

"Interest, George, *interest*. I have not been interested in any woman since Jay Jay died. *Not one*. And you know that. The pain was just too hard to overcome, my loyalty to her too strong to even consider that. I can't explain what I felt last night in terms that you would understand. Hell, George, I don't even understand this at all. But when Judie Kate told me about the dream this morning, it made sense. It makes sense, George, *if you believe in dreams*."

George, impatient, refusing to accept it and now just annoyed, balled up his wrapper loudly and angrily and took a last swig from his drink. He was feeling things deep inside and emotions were not on his list of things to do today.

"What I believe, Joe, is, you're right. You *are* in a pickle." He got up and tossed his wrapper in the trash can and placed his bottle in the recycle bin. "And you know how I don't like pickles."

* * *

Unaware of the argument between her father and Joe, Judie Kate led her flagging mother to yet another store.

"Down here, Momma," Judie Kate said, pointing to Island Artworks. "This looks good!" They went inside to a dim room with wooden and glass showcases filled with handmade jewelry.

"Hi," a quiet voice called out. "Make yourself at home."

The clerk looked back down and picked up a bead. Judie Kate stood over one case and eyed the copper earrings and necklaces, then she turned and saw the display stands and cases of other jewelry behind her. She stared at the sea glass pieces until one grabbed her eye. It was dark blue glass with silver wires and copper backing. She asked to see it up close. There was a mystery deep inside the blue orb, as if a light, a spark, was hidden there. A secret to discover, a riddle to be explained. *Joe's blue eyes!* The clerk rose up and opened the case, picked out the earrings, and Judie Kate held it up to her ears.

"Perfect!" she said.

"They go well with this necklace." She pulled out a necklace from another case, and the disparate pieces of jewelry matched as if they were siblings. Judie Kate took the other jewelry from her bag and laid them out on the counter. "You have good taste," the clerk noted. "They all match, like pieces in a puzzle, each with its own character but all coming together with the same theme." She paused for a moment then continued the metaphor. "There is a story in these pieces of jewelry, isn't there?"

"What do you mean?" Judie Kate asked.

"I mean, who's the lucky man? All jewelry tells a story." Suddenly, Judie Kate saw it all in her selections: from head to toe, her jewelry told the story that she was smitten with a dream slowly coming true …

"Will that be all?"

She woke up from her reverie.

"I hope it will be just the beginning," she whispered to the clerk, who smiled and nodded her approval. She handed the bag to Judie Kate.

"Me too."

* * *

The heat was becoming oppressive as Darren Edwards walked up on the deck of the theater, only ten minutes late. He was tall, bearded, wiry, tanned, and walked like a dynamo. His eyes were sharp, and they peered with a poet's depth behind wire-rimmed glasses. Sandals over his dirty feet complimented his shorts and faded shirt. He stepped inside and sat in one of the green chairs, looking around as if assessing a situation.

"Feels good in here. You guys do lunch?"

"Amigos," George answered.

Darren was already off to the next topic.

"So," he started off hesitantly, as if gathering his thoughts or possibly recovering from the stupor of an all-night drunk. Joe and George waited for the next phrase. "Uh, we need to mount some speakers on the ceiling. Any ideas?" All three walked around the stage area, sized up the speakers, walked around some more, and then sat.

"The problem is the slant of the ceiling," George offered. Joe looked around some more. Then it hit him.

"Instead of hanging them straight up and down like normal," he suggested, "why not hang them sideways, parallel to the ceiling."

Darren looked at George, who looked at Joe and then back at Darren.

"Unconventional, but it solves the problem."

Darren nodded his approval. "Okay, then you guys go to the store and get the hardware—some eye screws and steel cable with clamps should do the trick. I'll find a ladder, and we'll get this done."

* * *

It was midafternoon, and Judie Kate drove around the island, totally lost. Even with a map, she could not find her way. All the roads seemed to have a "B" in them. Back Road, Old Beach Road, British Cemetery Road. And everything seemed to be in circles. Just when she thought she was near her destination, she was lost again. She was trying to do it on her own, but she finally gave up and initiated the GPS device in her car.

"Ocean Lights, Ocracoke Island, North Carolina."

Out front of a weathered house stood a bottle tree. Beside it was a small zen sand garden with a rake leaning against the wall of the house. A dream catcher hung beside the front door, and Tibetan prayer flags flapped in the sea breeze.

"Hmm," Judie Kate mumbled to herself. "What am I getting myself into?"

Inside, a waft of incense overwhelmed her as flute music floated throughout the rooms. In one room hung numerous placards with motivational sayings and proverbs. In another room were soaps, bath oils, lotions, herbs, and fragrances. On one closed door hung a sign: *In Session Do Not Enter*. In a back room was a small stage area and a few chairs. To her right was a shelf of New Age and Eastern religion books. Buddha and Ganesh statues, cairns, small shrines, stones, and other spiritual implements rounded out the selection.

A voice called out, "Be there in a minute."

Soon, a young woman in a flowy, long dress seemed to float out of nowhere. "I'm Angel. Welcome to Ocean Lights."

Judy Kate was taken aback. She expected a thin, vegan with starry eyes and an ethereal aura. Instead, she was being hugged by a stout and energetic yet oddly calm, grounded female.

"What brings you to Ocean Lights?" There was an almost devilish grin on her rounded face. But her eyes looked like they could dig up mysteries from the past.

"I was looking for handmade soaps, and I found your shop online."

"Right over here," she pointed.

"Are these handmade with real ingredients?" Judie Kate had purchased some "handmade" soaps before, only to be disappointed.

"Yes. Any particular kind you're looking for?"

There was a pause, and Judie Kate called out, "Found it. I love lavender. But these other ones are nice too. Smells like spearmint, like chewing gum." She picked up several bars and smelled the oatmeal in one. "Is the oatmeal soap good?"

"Yes," Angel called out. "I like it a lot. Makes the skin smooth."

Angel then cut to the chase. "Okay, what really brings you here. Lots of folks sell soaps on the island."

Judie Kate, initially shocked at the blunt question, still felt welcomed by Angel. She introduced herself and then slowly opened up about her dreams, her love for Joe, her parent's disapproval, and her latent fears of the whole thing being a bad case of misplaced infatuation. "Thought I might find some energy here to help out."

"Where is your negative energy coming from?" Angel was suddenly serious.

Judie Kate was caught off guard. She listed potential problems as Angel listened. After a moment, Angel went into a room, took down a placard, and then handed it to Judie Kate. *The only thing standing between you and true love is your self.*

"Hmm. Never thought of it like that."

"Judie Kate, if you've got an hour, I can help with the energy. Ever heard of Healing Touch?"

An hour later, a refreshed and renewed Judie Kate paid for her items and therapy.

"One question, Angel. Where can I buy some gingerbread mix?"

* * *

George and Ellie got in the car to go to the restaurant. Ellie resumed their conversation.

"So, Joe told you that Judie Kate had these dreams about Jay Jay coming to her and saying that she needed to take care of Joe?"

George turned right onto British Cemetery Road. "Uh huh," he muttered.

"I don't buy it, George. I'm all aware of the theories of Freud about dreams and the unconscious and how his protégé Carl Jung worked on dream theory even more and discovered mythical images in them. That gave them a religious or spiritual meaning. Some New Age religions are into that now. Therapists put a lot of stock into dreams. But dream theory says you are everything in the dream. How do we know that Judie Kate's unconscious was not just a new manifestation of her infatuation with Joe?"

George said, "Hmm. Mentioned that to Joe."

"Well, aren't you the budding psychologist?" Ellie teased back.

George paused for a few tourists who were watching a stray cat cross the road.

"He said it was at the time of Jay Jay's death. Judie Kate and woman's intuition?"

"Okay, I'll grant that given the mystical folks on your side of the family. But we know that children who are interviewed by therapists often make up answers to fit the therapist's questions. Their imaginations control their answers, not rational facts. Some people have been wrongly convicted because of so-called evidence by these children. We know that deranged people often recall dreams that led them to their destruction."

"You saying that Judie Kate is deranged?" George asked sardonically. He turned left on Back Road.

"I'm saying something drastic made her lose all that weight. She's never told us what that spark was. What if it was something psychological, some trigger tripped in her, some influence that was not healthy? Her infatuation with Joe may be manifesting in imaginative dreams in order to justify a misguided desire to be with him. Or, maybe in seeing him yesterday, she made up the whole dream story and told him about it this morning to hoodwink Joe into a relationship with her. He has clearly taken the bait."

"Sounds like you don't trust our little girl."

"I'm saying that we don't ever get to see her, and the Judie Kate we have seen since Tuesday is not the Judie Kate we've known in the past. I mean, look at the car she bought not too long ago. A sports car? We thought the Camry we gave her was too much for her. Now this?" Ellie shook her head. "Did you ever tell her about your conversation with Lane the other day?"

"Nope. He wanted to keep that between him and her."

"Well, if it works out, what if Joe gets in the way of that? I'm just worried she is making a big mistake based on her past relationship with Joe. And, admit it, Joe has sexual needs as well. Her dressing up like that, sitting close to him, patting his legs. No wonder he's smitten!"

George turned into the Fishnets' parking lot.

"Big crowd tonight," he observed, putting the car into park.

"Did you hear anything I said, George?"

"There's Darren on the porch. He brought Betty with him."

***

It was nearly time for dinner if Joe and Judie Kate were to make the theater on time for the Ditchville12 show. She nervously wrestled with the clasp on her romper and finally got it hooked. She stood and looked in the mirror.

"Is this okay on me?" she wondered out loud, full of doubts and insecurities. She turned her hips one way and then the other.

Now, in the quiet and privacy of the beach house bedroom, Judie Kate stared at herself in the mirror once more, getting ready to meet Joe. The romper was dark blue with gray and white florals, half-sleeved, the V neckline nearly uncomfortably low, not that she had anything to show anyway. The legs came to well above midthigh—maybe a bit too high? The polyester fabric was flowy, suggestive, ephemeral, so that with a good breeze, something might show. She was still not sure, having never worn anything this daring before. But this was Joe, and Jay Jay's dream had to come true.

She took her new jewelry out of the bags and looked at the earrings, bracelet, necklace, and anklet. She carefully put each one on, and they all added to the mystery of the dark romper, bringing sparkle to the sexiness she embodied. Suddenly, she felt exotic, sultry, feelings she had never experienced before. They brought back her insecurities.

"I'm not meant to look like this," she said in despair, turning away from the mirror and flopping on the bed. She sat for moment and then looked back up into the mirror. Her black hair circled her face, and the copper earrings dangled about as she nodded her head, playing hide and seek like a child looking for attention, hoping to be found. She thought about that for a moment.

"That's it," she said to herself. "I am like a child, hiding but looking to be found. No more Judie Kate the shy teenager. No more hiding from my fears and insecurities. No more getting in the way of finding my true love! I want Joe to find me!" She reached down, pulled her wedge sandals on, and stood up, three inches taller. "I am Judie Kate!"

* * *

Joe waited on the balcony, humming Brad Paisley's "Waiting on a Woman" while Judie Kate finished dressing. He was nervous about their date. Today had moved too quickly for him. In fact, the last twenty-four hours had moved too quickly. It was like a fast-developing storm had hit him, leaving a path of emotions, feelings, and confusion for miles. The talk with George sobered him up, but it did not quell the feelings that were once dormant but now full of life. It only made him want her more. Now, they had a date.

He looked down at his brown shorts, wrinkled from being tossed into the travel bag. Was that a stain that did not come out after the last wash? He licked his finger and then rubbed it. *Not coming out now!* It never occurred to him after Jay Jay died that he might meet someone on the island. There was that flirty fifty-something last year at the party. She was slim and chesty with vixen-like, long, dark hair. She had a money style to her and was eager to meet someone new since her husband had left her for his secretary and flew off to South America where he had that big construction deal. Okay, on second thought, there was the island lady who always treated him nicely whenever he was there for the festival.

"Leslie," he mumbled to himself.

She always remembered his name and made a beeline for him when she saw him. Was she just nice, or did she really have a thing for him? Now that he thought about it, for two years in a row, there was the woman who hung around the sound table. She was blonde, wore a jean miniskirt, and when she sat down beside him, she showed a lot of leg. She asked a lot of questions about sound and music and things in general. Was he that blind? Was he rude? Why didn't he see what he was looking at? *What am I looking for?*

He heard the sliding glass door open and turned around. Judie Kate stood before him, looking sheepish, shy, hesitant, and with the eyes of a daughter looking for daddy's affirmation. The wind caught her hair and tossed it aside, revealing the dark earrings dangling beside her neck. He followed her rounded shoulders draped in dark fabric that flowed down her arms and waved in the breeze. The romper loosely embraced her waist and then shimmied around her hips, pausing tantalizingly above midthigh. The anklet accentuated her daintiness. *I'm a lucky man.*

"Does it look okay, Joe?" a very unsure Judie Kate asked, almost stepping back into the room in case he disapproved.

"Judie Kate, okay doesn't even begin to describe it."

He took her hand and pulled her out the door. But he felt desire deep inside, and suddenly, he wanted to touch, hold, embrace her. Was it the outfit, the beach sun and breeze, the joy he felt inside, the rush of freedom from the past? Restraint was an emotion Joe had not felt in a long time. He put his arm around her waist, playfully squeezed her with his hand, and felt her hip rise and fall as they walked to her car. Stopping behind the trunk of the car, she gave in to a rising surge of love, whirled around, and hugged him tight and kissed him softly. As they held their embrace, the attractions, urges and desires they had worked to restrain now surged into each other. Joe started humming a tune.

"Joe? Are you singing 'Uptown Girl'?"

* * *

After dinner at Aleta's Pub, they came back to the theater.

"You can park down by the school in the roundabout," Joe instructed Judie Kate as she turned the Mustang down School Road.

She found a spot and pulled in. Joe got out of the car and watched as Judie Kate got out as well. He was absolutely taken with her. He stared as she came around the car, as first her head and shoulders and then her waist and finally her legs appeared, all highlighted by her outfit that danced enticingly and playfully around her body, drawing his eye to every inch of her. He was proud to be her man tonight!

Judie Kate saw his appreciation in the aura around his face and the way he now walked with a lilt in his step, and she basked in the attention like a star on the red carpet at the awards shows. Her smile said it all, and her eyes dazzled with love as she hooked her arm around Joe's arm. As they walked up the road, she heard him humming a tune but could not make out the song.

"Joe, what are you singing?" Joe looked at her and took it all in one more time. Could this be real? Was what he was feeling right now a fantasy? A dream? Was it a dream come true?

"Clapton's 'Wonderful Tonight.'"

"Aw, Joe," Judie Kate answered in her sweetest voice. "You're gonna make me cry." He pulled her left, down the small dirt path to the theater, where a line was gathered at the door.

There were all sorts of vacationers and locals anticipating the doors opening. Some were dressed in relaxed attire, others looked like they had just come in from the beach, although they smelled better than sweat and suntan lotion. They were mostly middle age, but there were some teens, forced to come with their parents, who stared boringly at their phones, and a few young adults as well who mostly were there because there was not much else to do on Thursdays on the island. Some were locals, but most were first-timers who either had read about Ditchville12 on their website or who had seen advertisements on the various island websites.

Joe spotted the creepy tattoo man from the ferry who was taking photos with his phone. He instinctively steered Judie Kate away from him back into the crowd. The tattoo man tried to strike up a conversation with a young woman. Soon, he walked away, obviously disappointed and very visibly miffed.

Joe noticed that some people were looking in their direction. A few women stared at Judie Kate, and Joe could not tell if they approved of what she wore or did not. The few teenage girls at the show saw her, and they smiled their approval. He also noticed several men looking in their direction as well. The attention was unsettling.

Ellie and George stepped outside the theater to get a breath of fresh air. A moment later, Darren appeared on the deck, and he and George walked off to the side for a moment. Joe and Judie Kate both saw Ellie glare at them. When they turned around to avoid the stare, they saw George looking at them with muted disapproval as well. Darren spotted Joe and headed toward him.

"Hi, Joe. Thanks for coming to the show." He looked at Judie Kate. "Are you George's daughter?"

Joe handled the introductions.

"Seriously, Joe, is this young lady George and Ellie's daughter?" Joe had forgotten that Darren had never met Judie Kate.

"Oh, you don't know her, do you? Yes, this is her, the real Judie Kate Wilson." She grabbed the sides of her romper, gave a slight medieval curtsy, and smiled.

"I heard about you before, but George had not told me how beautiful you are."

They talked briefly, and then Darren asked if he could talk with Joe about something at the Workshop Stage.

"If you boys are going to talk sound, I'm going to stay here. Is that okay, Joe?"

She watched as they walked away. She wondered if Joe was like her father, putting the show before everything else. Suddenly, she went into panic mode. Was she making the right choice? What if Jay Jay's dream was just all wrong? Maybe this was a big mistake. When she turned around, the Preacher Boy was standing in front of her, staring. *Not him again!*

There was much too long of a silence that made her feel a bit wary, even afraid. He seemed to practice mouthing words, as if looking for the right thing to say. Or was he praying? For a moment, Judie Kate felt sorry for him. It was like she had put a spell on him. But then, she saw his eyes, and what they revealed was more than even he understood. He was infatuated with her in too many conflicting ways. She looked at his shirt, which featured "Enjoy Jesus Christ" styled like a logo on a soda can.

"Hi, uh, I saw you on the beach this morning with your dad."

Judie Kate almost corrected him but thought better of it. Maybe thinking Joe was her father would spook him off. She tried to be nice.

"Yes, I remember. You gave us some tracts to read." She paused. "By the way, FYI, you need to know that women wearing bathing suits have no place to put those."

He seemed caught off guard, as if God had not thought about that. Why would God tell him to hand out tracts to women who had no pockets? Suddenly, he felt more awkward than normal. The sheer presence of Judie Kate standing in front of him was one thing. Having doubts about God was not helping. Maybe he was wrong about this whole thing. He thought about running away, but he wanted to see the show. He wished he had his knife to give him strength.

He looked at her again and remembered St. Peter's admonition that women should be modest in appearance and adornments. The Apostle Paul said the same thing. Would God lead him to a woman who clearly did not live by the rules of the Bible? But he was mesmerized by her soft and round face, the way her hair formed what seemed to be a halo around it.

Her lips were so inviting, and even though she was not smiling, he could tell that her smile would be warm and loving. Suddenly, he wanted desperately to kiss her. He looked at her body, trying not to lust but at the same time recalling his professor's advice about love and feelings. Solomon wrote about his feelings for his lover. He could have feelings too. The breeze caught the folds in her outfit, and it wafted like a flag, saluting her body. There was something about her fingers, gentle, yet long and thick. He wanted to hold them, her. He was convinced God had led him to her. Now, he needed the courage to make the next step. *Help me, Lord!*

"I saw you again today while I was playing too. I think coincidences are God's way of showing us His will. It was like God was leading me to you. I'm not really good at this, but I was wondering if maybe I could sit with you tonight during the show? Maybe we could get some ice cream afterward?"

The tone of his voice was one of pleading, almost desperation, as if he needed her to accept his offer to affirm God's calling. Judie Kate was flattered by his attention and his proposal, but then something funny hit her. Did Jay Jay's dream trump God's plan? What does one say to a person who is convinced that they are part of a divine will? It was time to nip this thing in the bud.

"I'm flattered by your interest in me, but I don't think I'm the one God is sending you to. I know you feel led this way, but I am not feeling this divine calling."

The curtness of her retort caught him off guard. He stepped back, as if the earth would open up or a plague would hit.

"But, maybe God has not spoken to you yet. Maybe God wants me to lead you to the right path. Why else would He lead me to you three times in one day?"

Judie Kate was getting worried. Maybe this guy was just a religious loon. Maybe he was dangerous. Was this like an episode of *Criminal Minds*? Was he using God to attack and rape and then do who knows what? Her radar beeped danger. Then, she thought of something.

"I saw three pretty young ladies standing with you today while you played. Maybe God was leading you to them? Maybe God was leading one of them *to you*? Might that be part of God's plan? Maybe coming to me was just a mistake, you know, a wrong decision made with good intent. Sometimes, coincidence is just that, a coincidence, nothing more. Maybe something else led you to me."

She meant maybe his feelings, maybe a twinge of lust, some psychological thing where he was projecting his mother onto her. Whatever. What he heard, however, was, "something else." If God had not led him to her, then Satan had misled him. This could only mean she was of the devil. *She was dangerous.*

Confused, he abruptly turned and walked away, leaving Judie Kate both relieved and worried. Just in time, Joe walked back up.

"Preacher Boy after you again tonight?" he joked.

"Thinks God led him to me to ask me out or save my soul since he saw me three times today. Maybe the two are intertwined in his mind? Says coincidences are God's way of talking to us." She shook her head and her earrings bobbled enticingly for Joe. "I didn't get that email." She grabbed Joe's hand and held it tight. "Then, he bolted like he had seen the devil himself."

"Maybe he did," Joe teased, squeezing her hand.

The young Christian man stood off to the side, wondering if he was wrong or if she was wrong. Why would God send him to someone who refused to follow God's plan? *Why was she holding her father's hand?* He was sure it was God and not Satan. But what if she was right? Then, it hit him. The demons had spoken the truth in the gospels. Maybe she was a demon sent to tell the truth to him. If she was a demon, then she had to go.

Doors now open, Joe and Judie Kate took their place on the lone pew in the back of the Deepwater Theater, hiding from the crowd and leaving others to sit in the green plastic chairs. Ellie found a seat up close to the stage beside some Ocracoke friends. On the walls were pictures from the old days of Ocracoke. In the back corner, displays of mugs, crafts, T-shirts, and previous years' programs lined the wall and countertop. An old Carvin soundboard rested on a dusty tabletop behind Joe and Judie Kate, meters illuminated and ready for work.

Individual voices combined into an electric buzz as the gathering crowd settled down for the first Ditchville12 show of the summer season. The band members were scattered about, talking with the crowd, some of whom were old friends and others who were new to Ocracoke and the theater itself. At eight o'clock, the house lights went down, and Darren walked toward the stage and picked up his guitar, followed by George on mandolin, Bow String Bill on the fiddle, and Kimber Lee heaving her big, upright bass into position. Darren fiddled with the mic stand, adjusting the microphone height to his liking.

"Well, welcome everybody to the Deepwater Theater tonight. We are Ditchville12," he said. There was applause as Bow String Bill came over to the microphone and took over, giving the count for the first song. The band led off with an instrumental, "Blackberry Blossom," that featured the hot licks of Bow String Bill and George on the mandolin, and it brought a loud round of applause as the crowd showed its pleasure in the number. They moved right into their next song, "Waterbound." After the song, Bow String Bill took over. He was big and tall, with gleaming eyes and short, fuzzy hair.

"So, how many of you have heard us play before?" About half the audience raised their hands. "Ah, so, you all remember how we got our name, right?" They applauded. "For the newbies, we are called Ditchville12 for two reasons. When you come into Ocracoke on the Cedar Island or the Swan Quarter ferries, you enter the body of water we call Silver Lake. But before that area was cleared out during the war era, it was called The Ditch. And the main road out there is called Irvin Garrish Highway, after one of our prominent and revered locals. But it is also the beginning of the historic Highway 12 that goes from

Ocracoke nearly up to Virginia on the Outer Banks. Thus, Ditchville12."

The crowd applauded their understanding of the band's name. Then, Darren introduced the next number. Ditchville12 settled down into its set list. As the show progressed, Judie Kate took Joe's hand and placed it in her lap, patting it in excitement with her other hand. Joe listened, seemingly ignoring her while she was trying her best to keep his attention. She shook her leg some, squeezed his hand tighter, pressed it down onto her leg more, and then sidled up close to him. Joe stared at the band, oblivious to the young lady trying her best to seduce him from the music.

Then, it dawned on her. Joe *saw* and *heard* what other people missed. He had always seen beauty in her when all anyone else saw was obesity and shyness. He heard what she was trying to say when her parents, friends, and church leaders missed it completely. It was like he *knew* things and *understood* things others were not aware of. She looked at him as he stared intently at the band, listening to every nuance that emerged from the stage, from the speakers, seeing every glance and nod that came from the singers.

That was the mystery in Joe that attracted her to him. She could see it in his eyes, in his face, in his posture. Now, she could feel it in his hand, his arm. She leaned into him more and rested her head on his shoulder. It was like her body fit exactly into his, like a piece of a puzzle being set into the empty space in the corner. *Is he listening to me now?* She felt his warmth, but there was something missing that she literally could not put her hands on. Soon, another question loomed in her mind.

After their discussions last night and then on the beach today, she realized there was another element in the equation. *Feelings.* Could Joe feel anything for her? Was he so caught up in grief over Jay Jay that he had blocked off all his feelings for anyone? What if he was not able to feel anything anymore? What if the music kept him from experiencing feelings? It sure kept her dad from feeling anything.

Now, Joe became much more intriguing. Now, he was a cause. Judie Kate had to save him from himself. She grabbed his hand with both of her hands and pulled it close to her belly, squeezing it all the time. A moment passed and then another. Then, he squeezed her hand ever so lightly. Judie Kate played with her bracelet as the music continued, fingering it along like a rosary. *It might take more than a dream to get Joe.*

When the first set ended, the crowd stood up, stretched their arms, and mingled about. Several people rushed to the musicians, and some went to the back of the theater to purchase CDs and shirts. Bow String Bill handled the sales and talked music. Joe pulled Judie Kate up to Darren and described the sound of the first set.

"Good to know," he responded. Then, a fan stepped up and butted in with a question for Darren.

"We'll see you at the house tonight," Joe said as he stepped away, taking Judie Kate with him.

"Tonight? At the house?" Judie Kate asked in a sour tone.

"The band always gathers at someone's house, either George's or Darren's, after the gig. They have a beer, eat a few snacks, wind down, and talk about how the show went." Joe led Judie Kate outside to the deck for some fresh air. Oddly enough, Joe did not like to be in crowds.

"Oh," she answered in a disappointed voice. She was now bored and wanted to have an evening with Joe, not the band, not music.

"Joe, can we skip the second part and get some ice cream?" she asked. Joe wanted to hear the second set, but he was suddenly caught in the spell of Judie Kate, who was squeezing his arm and looking up at him coyly. She did not wait for an answer, pulling him down the steps. They followed the sandy path faintly lit by clear Christmas tree lights out to School Road, where she paused.

"Is that your stage area?" she asked, looking at the tent across the road and to the right. The darkness and emptiness brought up a whiff of devilment, an embrace of a dalliance, and Judie Kate saw her chance to get Joe's mind off the music and into her heart. He answered affirmatively, and she pulled him in that direction. "I wanna see it."

The light over the front door of the Methodist Church did not penetrate the canopy of the tent, and the live oaks lent a spookiness to the side yard. It was dark under the tent as they stopped for a moment. Joe's heart beat a bit faster, and a warm tension coursed through his veins. Judie Kate felt it too. Joe suddenly wanted to kiss her but was afraid of being too forward. Judie Kate felt his apprehension and pulled him close, sending him an invitation to open up. She looked at him and cautiously pressed her lips to his. His body still felt tense, but slowly, ever so slowly, she felt him relax and give in. *Feelings!*

Joe held her tightly now, and Judie Kate laid her head on his shoulder, like they were dancing at the prom, and she enjoyed the warmth of his body next to hers. The thin fabric of her outfit allowed his very soul to flow into her flesh. He felt her breathe, and with each breath, her soft skin melted deeply into his. Suddenly, Judie Kate felt desire. It was overwhelming, rising too fast like a flood after a downpour, and she was nearly out of control, hydroplaning on primal urges she had never felt before.

"Joe?" she asked, looking up at him, reluctantly, slowly, pulling back from his embrace.

"Yes?" He felt the flood, too, and was near a line of inhibitions, moving toward a place of no return. His hands ached for intimacy, exploration, pleasure.

"I think I need that ice cream now." She took his hands and led him out of the fantasy back into Ocracoke. Joe was disappointed, or was it confused? She backed away from him and led him back into the light. As they walked up School Road, she looked right down a dark path.

"Where does that go?" she asked.

"That's Howard Street. It goes by houses, the Craft Shack, and several cemeteries."

As they strolled down the dark lane in a narrowing funnel of live oaks and cedars, the haunting mood of the night took over. There was a back-porch light that was blocked by low-hanging limbs. But after that, the road was barely visible, lined with dim white picket fences haunted by barely visible tombstones and grave markers. She thought about the cemeteries.

"Ooh," Judie Kate responded, tapping into the mystique of old graves that somehow led couples to them. "Cemeteries are kind of scary, Joe. Let's head that way."

Joe felt it, too, and said, "You know, Judie Kate. In medieval times in Europe, lovers would date in cemeteries."

Hardly any light filtered into Howard Street because of the old live oaks that covered it, turning the street into a black tunnel. Judie Kate held on to Joe, wrapping her arms around his waist, using the dark as an excuse for more connection. They walked slowly on the one-way dirt road that was barely wide enough for one car. They could just make out some of the cemeteries as they strolled past the Craft Shack. Outside the store, a small crowd had gathered. Joe paused.

"That's Mary," he said, pointing to the slim young lady with dark hair. "She's probably getting ready for the ghost walk tour." Then, Joe spotted the skinny, tattooed man in the crowd. He held back as the crowd walked away. When the coast was clear, he resumed their walk.

"Is this another stage?" Judie Kate asked. Joe explained about the Howard Street Stage, how it was separate from the Live Oak Stage on School Road, and how entertainers who did not sing at the Live Oak Stage during the festival often thought they were lesser than other talents at the show because they sang at the Howard Street Stage.

Suddenly, Judie Kate froze.

"What is it?" Joe asked. She felt a cold chill run down her spine as she faced the darkening road ahead. "Afraid of ghosts?" Joe asked jokingly. Judie Kate resembled a dog sniffing the wind, looking about cautiously. "I didn't see any ghost," he continued.

"Let's turn around, Joe, and go up that lighted path." Her tone was serious. Joe headed onto Lawton Lane, not quite sure what got into her so fast.

"You okay?"

"Something's wrong, Joe. We need to head to the main road." When they arrived at Irvin Garrish Highway, they turned right onto the main drag. The main road was not much brighter than Howard Street, and they were nearly hit by four cyclists with no lights on their bikes.

"Feeling okay now, Judie Kate?" Joe asked. She turned around, saw nothing, and turned back again.

"That was weird, Joe."

"What was?"

"It was like something was following us."

"Cemeteries got you spooked?"

"Let's get that ice cream, Joe," she said, looking around one more time. They headed to the Ice Cream Shack.

* * *

As they waited in line to order their treat, the Christian man wandered around the Community Store, looking at all the oddities on the old, dusty shelves, from vegetables to antiques, trying to make the connections between all the disparate merchandise. He continued his aimless wandering until he found a lit showcase with knives where he paused to look at the collection. *I need to replace my missing knife.* There were pocketknives and short and long single blade knives with leather sheaths. He remembered the advice from the Christian fighters' website about the appropriate knife to own. The clerk with a German accent walked over to him, noticing his interest in the knives.

"May I help you?"

"Yes, I'd like to see that one, to the left. Yes that one." She retrieved the shiny knife for him to inspect. "That's a popular one," she noted.

She looked him over carefully. He was tall, imposing, broad-shouldered, with big hands. There was an odd combination of grace and intensity in his dark brown eyes. As if there was a subtle motive beneath a compassionate demeanor. His Christian shirt was curious, and she could not figure out why a Christian was so taken with a knife that was so potentially dangerous. *Maybe he likes fishing and needs a good knife.* Still, there was something about him, almost sinister, that did not add up.

Just then, a skinny, tattooed man came up and stood by him.

"Great knife there, dude!" He watched him look it over. "Can I hold it for a moment?"

He quickly pulled it back and loudly said, "No! It's mine!"

"Whoa, dude, plenty more in that case. Wow, didn't know a knife was such an emotional thing."

He glared at the skinny man, who walked away and looked at other items.

"I'll take it," he told the clerk, who was now looking at him with a big question mark on her face. He paid her cash and left, brushing brusquely in a self-righteous mission past ambling tourists who turned and stared at his rudeness.

The skinny, tattooed man walked back up.

"Wow, that was one keyed up dude!" he called out to the clerk, who was still looking spooked.

"Creepy, if you ask me," she responded.

"Anyways, can I see that same model? Got something to take care of tonight."

"Night fishing?" she asked, hoping to ring up the sale.

"You could say that."

* * *

While he purchased his knife, Judie Kate and Joe stared at the menu on the wall at the Ice Cream Shack.

"Joe, time for a change. A new us, so a new tradition. Want to share a strawberry parfait? Maybe they could add some hot fudge to it, hmm?"

The crowd was slim in the Community Square, so they found an empty picnic table. Judie Kate sat beside Joe as close as she could get, nearly knocking him off the bench.

"Oops," she grinned with a devilish smile, patting the empty place beside her. "Get back over here where you belong, mister." Each took a spoonful and watched the crowd walk by, caught up in the moment, enjoying each other.

"Tell you something, Judie Kate," Joe said with a mouthful of ice cream and fudge. "When Jay Jay and I were first married, we were a bit poor. We would go to a small soda shop and get a single lime freeze and two straws and share it. Many folks would come over and comment that we looked so romantic, sharing our freeze together. We didn't dare tell them it wasn't romance. We were just too poor to afford two lime freezes."

"Joe" Judie Kate said with a sad face, "that is *so* romantic!" She took her spoonful and placed it at Joe's mouth. "Eat, my love!" she commanded, and Joe did as he was told. Together they shared the parfait, each other's attention, and the warmth of the salty, ocean air.

Suddenly, Joe noticed the skinny, tattooed man staring at them. He caught Joe's look and quickly glanced over in another direction. Joe became worried. He had seen this man one too many times, and it bothered him.

"C'mon, Judie Kate," he commanded, standing up and grabbing her by the arm. She was confused. What happened to the romance? Did she do something wrong? Joe glared at the creepy man and began walking in his direction.

"Where are we going, Joe?"

Suddenly, a small group of teenagers barged right in front of them, cutting them off from the man. When Joe and Judie Kate finally got around them, he was gone. "Joe, what's going on?" Judie Kate asked, now worried. Joe stopped in the middle of the parking lot, looked around several times, appeared puzzled, and then looked at Judie Kate.

Not wanting to alarm her, Joe lied, "Thought I saw an old sound friend." He scanned the parking lot and stores again and then protectively put his arm around Judie Kate and slowly walked toward the road. "Sorry, didn't mean to scare you."

Now at the road, Joe waited until a group of people wandered by, and then he pulled Judie Kate along behind them, holding her close just in case. Judie Kate, unaware of the possible danger, reveled in the renewed attention of her man. They walked farther up the dark road, terrorized by bicycles with no lights, tourists with no manners, and golf carts that seemed to have minds of their own. Going around the curve and dodging several roots in the sidewalk, they soon turned left onto School Road and found her car and headed back to the house. The young Christian man, standing in the shadows, watched as they headed down the road, tightly clutching his new knife.

* * *

After the show, back at the house, Ellie was clearly upset.

"Did you see what she had on tonight, George?" She tossed her pocketbook on the couch in a huff. "It was next to nothing. Could you see through it? I think I could."

"Now, Ellie," George answered, coming down from the show, trying to dodge the emotional confrontation, "it was more than several other women had on. At least hers had sleeves." He placed his mandolin case on the floor next to his guitar case and then headed over to the computer to check on his bids. "She shows more legs in a bathing suit than she showed tonight." He grabbed the mouse, clicked on eBay, and then scrolled through several pages looking for the mandolins.

"She was showing too much cleavage, George!" Ellie snorted back.

"Ellie, Judie Kate has never had any cleavage."

"George, you saw her back. I bet she had no bra on either. What do you think?"

George, annoyed, paused from looking up eBay items, and looked at Ellie with an irritated expression. "Ellie, I try not to look that closely at our little girl."

"Maybe if you did, you would know her better. I don't like what Joe has done to her. That was not our Judie Kate tonight."

George turned around and looked at Ellie. "Maybe Judie Kate did that to get Joe. Maybe it is not Joe's fault at all."

"You're just saying that because Joe is your friend!" Ellie retorted, heading to the kitchen to make some coffee.

George was becoming heated, something he was not known to do. "Ellie, Joe is my friend, and I know him pretty well. We talk a lot when we eat out, when he goes with me on the road." George could not get to what he wanted to say, the curse of being a musician. If he had his mandolin out, he could say exactly what he was thinking. "What I am trying to say is that while Joe may be intrigued by what Judie Kate wears or what any woman wears, he is smart enough to know there is more to a woman than that."

Ellie put a cup in the coffee maker and pressed the button.

"It's not his IQ that worries me, George."

* * *

Joe and Judie Kate paused under the house, the darkness suddenly opening new doors for intimacy and romance. She pulled him up tight once more and held him there in the privacy of the quiet evening. The silence was passionate, and waves lapped against the rocks on the sound. Joe, still a bit cautious and tentative, placed his hands on her waist, squeezed softly, as if a signal for permission to hold her, and then shifted to the small of her back. Given what took place and what nearly took place at the Workshop Stage, he was now hesitant, as if needing some assurance that all would be well if he pursued the relationship further. Yet, Joe felt the warmth of pure, innocent, and trusting love reaching into his body as Judie Kate pressed into him. As each enjoyed the embrace of the peaceful and warm salty breeze, she wrapped her arms around his neck and kissed him slowly.

"Joe?" Judie Kate asked. "Can we do this forever? Can we hold each other like this and sway to old songs and new love?" She looked at him and then kissed him softly on his neck. "This day has been so beautiful, Joe. We walked on the beach and found shells. We talked about us, about our future. We spent time apart, only to come back together like real couples do. I enjoyed dressing up for you and making you proud to be seen with me. Sharing our ice cream like young lovers. Having you around me, near me, holding me, it is so …"

The words fell away as she shook slightly. Joe asked if she was cold.

"No, Joe, I am shaking because I feel joy. And I am scared something will take it away from me, from us."

The lapping waves and the breeze took over the conversation as they held each other silently, closely.

"Are you talking about your parents, Judie Kate?"

She was hesitant with her answer because Joe was asking about the wrong person.

"Joe? I am talking about you. We can do this, Joe. We did this, Joe. Today. All day long, it was us, Joe. And when you relaxed and just let it be, it was so wonderful. But, I can still feel you pulling back occasionally. When we get near my parents, you pull back. Tonight, we have to go inside where my parents are, and you are already pulling back," she said.

Knowing she was right, he remained quiet, but he brought her up close, desperately holding her, nearly squeezing the breath out of her. She almost said something but realized he was holding on for dear life. Joe felt the foundation of grief, sadness, depression, and disconnection he had constructed after Jay Jay died was cracking and crumbling. The demolition had been all day long. Brick by brick, with every touch and word from Judie Kate, like a soft hammer, gently tearing down the past.

He remembered his first fight with Jay Jay. It was while they were dating, and she was trying to win his heart, but he kept pulling away as if he was scared she would hurt him in some way. All he would say was that he had been hurt and betrayed before and that he was scared to trust someone again. Jay Jay pried and pried, but Joe would not crack, would not share what was keeping him from her love. Finally, she threw the gauntlet down.

"You talk to me now, Joe Clark, or I'm gone. I don't know what's in your past that you keep holding on to, but you can live there forever, or you can live with me. What's it gonna be?"

Joe eased up on his embrace.

"Judie Kate?" He paused as if he was about to dive off the thirty-meter platform. "I'll talk with George tomorrow. We'll talk about this man to man."

"Are you saying what I think you are saying, Joe?"

He wasn't sure if he was thinking what she thought he was thinking. His head was spinning, seemingly out of control, but at the same time, feeling like a merry-go-round, with lights flashing and reflections off the mirrors and horses and a young girl giggling, reaching out to her boyfriend on the horse beside her. Suddenly, he was like a kid again, a kid he wished he could have been many years ago, finally living a life he had hoped for all his young years. It happened with Jay Jay, and it was happening now with Judie Kate.

They held each other again, but this time, it was different, deeper, passionate, as if gates had been opened and pent up waters were flooding downstream. They grabbed each other and kissed, rubbed their hands on each other, looking for that one place that revealed their truest affection for each other. Joe held her waist and moved his hands up slowly, feelings intensifying. Now, Joe wanted her, had to touch her, not like a bumbling adolescent boy looking for his first score, but in a way that would tell her she was special. Intimacy seemed the next step. As he reached for her breasts, she pulled back gently, took his hands, and placed them back around her.

"Not yet, Joe, please?" She led his hands back to her hips. "I want that, too, Joe, to share myself with you, but not just yet." Still, the desire was becoming intense, and like a southern California wildfire, once it started, she knew it could not be doused. Judie Kate wisely, disappointingly, brought them down to earth yet again. It was a hard landing for Joe.

"We should probably go inside." She paused, as if thinking to herself. He could see a faint, but devilish grin emerge on her face. "Me first."

"Why you first?" Joe asked. The desire was slowly abating, but a sudden playfulness took its place.

"Joe Clark, to be so smart you can be dense. What is that beach song, 'Backfield in Motion'?" She headed toward the steps that led up to the deck. The spotlights along the staircase shone into the sound.

"You wait right here and enjoy the view."

She stepped lightly up the stairs while he stared until she reached the top of the deck, the romper flitting playfully, enticingly, as if it had fingers calling him to come closer, look deeper. *Jay Jay did the same thing when she went up the stairs to the attic.* He watched, ogled, and then realized what it was about rompers that was so enticing. The way the fabric jiggled around her bottom that was jiggling as well. It was like it was all winking at him, flirting with him, a hand balled up with one finger pulling him to her hips. Judie Kate opened the glass door and went inside.

"It's about time!" Ellie said with a little too much consternation in her voice, giving Judie Kate a motherly look. "Ice cream again, I suppose?"

"Yes." Judie Kate answered, plopping down on the couch. She looked around the room. Darren and another man were there, drinking a beer with her dad. "Strawberry parfait this time."

"Where's Joe?" Darren asked. George glared. Ellie stewed. The stranger was not sure what was going on.

"He's outside." She paused a moment. Then she lied. "He saw someone at the ice cream stand who reminded him of his wife. I think that brought back some memories. He just needed to be alone some." *He just needs to cool off!*

There was an awkward silence. How to answer that one? George and Ellie had been joined by Darren and a new man Judie Kate did not know. He was shorter than Darren, and his face radiated devilment. The site of a pretty woman brought even more excitement to his face.

"I'm Mike Scott," he announced, nodding at Judie Kate. Ever the life of the party, he picked things back up. "I've known your dad since he got off the ark, and I wish I didn't know Darren, but sometimes, God just needs to punish people. I'm gonna guess that you are Judie Kate." He grinned at George and Ellie, then looked back at Judie Kate with a different kind of smile. "I saw some heads turning at the theater tonight, mostly in your direction, young lady. Or maybe they were staring at that ugly, old escort of yours?" Darren laughed out loud. George rolled his eyes, and Ellie harrumphed with a scowl.

Judie Kate blushed, tugged at her outfit as if to cover up, and forced a smile. She did not know quite how to respond but felt positive rather than hesitant.

"Thanks, Mike! This was a new departure for me tonight. Sometimes, you just gotta make the boys look." George rolled his eyes again, and Ellie perked up.

"Maybe not make them look so much next time," Ellie said.

"Loosen up, Ellie." Mike smiled. "She can't get a man if she wears a sack. Make 'em look, Judie Kate!" She blushed even redder. "Look, now she has red cheeks like Santa Claus!" he cried out.

Darren changed the subject. "Got any food around here?"

"Sausage balls in the fridge," George muttered.

"Wait a minute. You guys didn't tell me about the sausage balls. When did you make those?" Darren called out. George answered that Ellie hurriedly made them that afternoon. Darren searched around in the fridge and took them out, placed some on a paper towel, and put them in the microwave and punched the one-minute button. "There's nothing else here? What are you guys eating during the day?" The microwave dinged. Mike went to the fridge and took out another beer.

Joe finally came in. He ignored Judie Kate and took a seat at the bar, looked over it, and grabbed a box of Cheez-Its crackers and reached in. Killer, sensing Joe was in the room, came crashing in and stood at attention at Joe's feet.

"What did you think of the show tonight?" Darren asked Joe. "I noticed that you left during the intermission. Were we that bad?" About that time, Kimber Lee came in and went straight to the fridge.

"Free food and beer tonight?" Picking up on Darren's comment, she asked, "Yeah, how many of my mistakes did you catch?" She smiled and opened her beer and took a seat at the bar while Ellie continued thumbing through posts on Facebook. "First show of the season and not my best night," she continued.

Joe answered, "Well, the band as a whole seemed tentative. I think Bow String Bill came in with the wrong break on one song ... Darren, did you flub some words on the third tune? George, you looked a mile away tonight."

Mike agreed, "Yes, tentative is a good way to put it. Where are those nuts?" He reached for the can and took out a handful.

"Well, you all are talking shop, so I'm heading for bed." Judie Kate yawned, getting up, making sure her romper fell properly into place. "Good night." She walked past the bar and subtly poked Joe in the ribs. The room was silent as she shut the door to her room.

"George, Ellie, Judie Kate is a really beautiful young lady. You two did good on that one!" Mike nodded at both parents.

"We're just glad she trimmed up. She was so overweight. We were worried about her health," George answered.

Mike came back. "You're kidding? You wouldn't know that by looking at her now," he said.

"We're glad she has lost the weight, too, but we don't like all the skin showing," Ellie responded. "That isn't our little girl."

Mike shook his head. He had known George and Ellie for years and couldn't believe they were still treating their daughter like a child.

"I didn't see a little girl sitting over there. I saw an attractive young woman. Ellie, she's not a teen anymore." He paused to sip his beer and then continued. "She keeps looking like that, she's gonna take a young man home with her after this weekend." He grinned at George and winked at Darren.

"You're not helping," George replied with an open-eyed glare.

"I thought she was cute," Kimber Lee answered, taking Mike's side. "It was a very feminine outfit. Rompers are in this summer. Several at the show tonight. I saw the heads turning too. Not all of them were young."

Joe's phone beeped.

"Text," he said as all looked at him. "Probably a student with another dumb question. One has pestered me all day." He swiped the screen and saw the name. Judie Kate. He touched the screen and saw her text.

I can hear everything you guys are saying about me.

Joe typed while everybody stared. He put the phone on the bar and grabbed a handful of nuts.

"This student has annoyed me ever since we started the summer semester." He paused. "You know, gang, I bet Judie Kate is enjoying hearing us talk about her." He nodded to the bedroom door. Silence was their answer. One of the fish lights blinked.

"Back to the show," Darren said. "Mike, have you looked over the lineup for the Howard Street Stage?" While he answered, Joe's phone beeped again. He looked at the screen. Judie Kate.

"Jeez, again?" Joe called out. "They just won't leave you alone sometimes."

He read the text: THNX.

After an hour, Mike, Darren, and Kimber Lee left, and George and Ellie headed upstairs. Joe checked his emails one last time, let Killer out and then let him back in, and then headed for his room. He cleaned up and then lay in bed, thinking of the day. He was just about asleep when his phone beeped. A text from Judie Kate.

You awake?

Yes.

Need to talk.

Meet on the deck.

Joe climbed out of bed, put on a shirt and shorts, and headed outside the glass door with Killer right behind. He sat on the picnic table bench and stared at the dark sound, listening to the waves lapping in a quiet rhythm. The door rumbled, and Judie Kate appeared, wearing an oversized night shirt, the long sleeves covering her hands. She sat down on the other side of the picnic table, looked down at her fingers, and fidgeted a bit. She wrinkled her lips and looked far to the side of Joe, as if she were embarrassed.

"Were they right, Joe?" She looked to the other side; her dark brown eyes almost afraid to meet his eyes. "Were Momma and Daddy right?"

"About what?" Joe wanted to take her hands but thought better of it.

"My clothes tonight. Was it too much? Please be honest."

Joe looked at her face, her watery eyes, felt her insecurities returning. It was like she was back in high school again.

"How did you feel tonight?"

It took a moment, but soon a small smile came to her face. She looked up at the sky, the stars, the few clouds that wafted by. It was as if she were in a dream, caught up in reverie, living a fairy tale. She remembered the kisses, Joe's hands, his desire pressing deep into her soul, the point of no return having been reached.

"Pretty, Joe. Pretty." She paused. "Special. Sexy? I'm not used to that." *Yours?* "Like I was somebody. Like I dreamed I could be when I was fat and ugly. Like when I saw the other girls who got the dates, who turned the heads of the boys in the hallway." She paused. "Like Cinderella, Joe." Judie Kate stared back in time.

He watched her face, her eyes again, her eyebrows. One of them rose up slightly.

"But ...?" Joe started.

"How did you know there was a but?" She thought some more, started to answer, paused, looked down at her hands, up at the night sky, and then back at Joe. "Joe? Tonight, people looked at me. Men stared at me, up and down, and they smiled. One even winked. It was like they were feeling me with their eyes, their minds. The creepy Christian guy, that tattoo man? The women, most of them, glared at me like I was going to take their man or like I had crossed some sort of line. Some approved; I could tell by their faces. The young girls looked at me like they wanted to be me. The boys couldn't stop looking. Joe, you couldn't stop looking! It's what I wanted, but I don't know how to handle the attention, good and bad. What does it mean when people stare at me?"

She began to shake.

"I just wanted to be pretty, Joe." She sobbed quietly, fidgeted with her sleeves, pulled them down over her wrists, as if to hide her skin, then rubbed her eyes and nose. "I just wanted to be beautiful for you, Joe." The breeze blew her hair around her face. She pulled it back and looked at a very fuzzy Joe through tear-filled eyes for an answer. "Maybe being beautiful is a little more complicated than the pretty girls admit."

The lights from the house next door went off. The deck was now dark but for the dim glow the fish night-light gave off in the kitchen.

"Joe?" Judie Kate asked in a quietly desperate tone. "Tell me what you thought."

"Did you get the reaction you wanted tonight?" Joe asked, afraid to admit what he really thought deep down inside.

She remembered his look when she came out of her room. How Joe's eyes lit up, how they looked her up and down and then all over again. How he beamed like the prince at his wedding with the bride of his dreams. She thought about their moment under the Workshop Stage tent when things almost got out of hand and their heated time under the house. Their embrace, his touch, his hands on her body, how the fabric seemed ephemeral, dreamlike, when he touched her. She so wanted him close to her, around her, in her.

"I don't know, Joe, did I?"

They heard bumps, and then Judie Kate saw her father coming to the door. George looked perplexed, or was it worried, when he saw the couple outside. He opened the glass door. Killer scooted back in.

"Hi, Dad, come sit beside me!" She patted the picnic table bench with fake enthusiasm and George sat. Then, she rolled her eyes at Joe.

"High-level meeting here?" George asked.

"Well," Joe answered, "we were on the verge of figuring out who was in Grant's Tomb when you came out."

"The world will have to wait then, huh?"

The three of them chatted about the weather.

"What are they saying about the storm off the coast, Dad?"

"All depends on whether the high moves south or north. Nobody seems to know."

"Sometimes, my head can feel the pressure changing. Like a nail through my eyeball," Joe commented.

"What do we do it if rains, Daddy?"

"We panic, that's what."

The small talk withered as sleep finally hit all three.

"I'm going to call it a night, folks," Joe said, getting up. "You two can do that father/daughter thing."

Joe went to his room, closed the door, and sat on the bed for a moment, reflecting on the day. He wanted to run, to stay, and hide all at the same time. Was it time to say good-bye to Jay Jay? *How do I do that? Am I being disloyal to her?* How long should one grieve? Does grief last differently for different people? When does "till death do us part" end?

On the other hand, he couldn't deny what he was feeling. Seeing an adult Judie Kate Wednesday night lit a spark he never thought would light again. But what did it mean to have feelings for *Judie Kate*? Then there was Judie Kate's story of Jay Jay's dream. How could he know if Jay Jay's dream was true? And sitting over all of this was George and Ellie. If he pursued Judie Kate, then that would jeopardize their relationship. It would destroy everything. *Yet if I don't, I might lose the whole world.*

He reached for his phone, and with a shaking finger, texted Judie Kate and answered her last question.

Yes, and it scares me. BTW: you were beautiful tonight!

Thursday, June 6, 2018

Today was interesting. Okay, thrilling. Or maybe just scary. I don't know which. Joe and I walked on the beach. We talked about Jay Jay. He still misses her a lot. More than I thought. That is something I don't understand. After three years, shouldn't you be ready for the next chapter in life? I'm over Don now. Why can't Joe be over Jay Jay? I asked if he believed in dreams, and he told me about one he had that came true. So, I finally told him about Jay Jay's dream.

I am not sure if he really believes it. Maybe I did make it up. But what if it is real? I truly believe it is! What if we don't follow Jay Jay's dream for us? I told Joe I was going to try to make it come true and asked if he would just give it a chance. I held his hand on the beach as we walked. It is like I am holding on to everything I have ever wanted in my life. I hope Joe feels the same way.

Tonight, I took a dare and wore my romper. That was tough. It is so flimsy, so revealing. I don't see how other girls do it. I thought it would bring the dream to life, but I think it just complicated it more. Joe was caught off guard. I will never forget how he looked at me! That is what I wanted! But other people looked at me too. I am not used to that, and it scares me.

What do they think of me? Of Joe, who walked beside me and sat beside me? Did they think I was a gold digger? He walked a little prouder tonight though. I kissed him tonight! It was so romantic. I felt beautiful, loved. We felt an attraction and had to stop before it went too far. Momma and Daddy disapprove of this whole thing. They don't understand at all. I am not sure if even Joe understands. But I do know that he wanted me tonight. And I wanted him! And that is what Jay Jay wants as well.

Love,
Judie Kate

* * *

She closed her diary, locked it, and placed it in the special flowery box on the dresser. She looked around the room, as if trying to find something, flipped the light off, and sat on the bed. She was restless. *I'm scared, too, Joe!* She held herself tightly and thought for a moment. Was she scared of what might happen or of what had already happened? She remembered the placard from the store. The only thing standing between her and true love was her self. But, there was something else she could not place her finger on. Something deeper looming ahead, she could feel it, like the storm off the coast. *What is it, and why am I afraid?*

She got up, tiptoed to the bathroom door, opened it slowly, then went to the other door and opened it carefully. The room was dark, but she could make out the bed, Joe curled up in it. She wondered, *Which side?* She pulled the sheet up and sat on the bed.

Joe stirred, then realized what was taking place and whispered, "Judie Kate?"

She put her finger to his lips, crawled into the bed, and pushed her back up to Joe.

"Joe? I'm scared. Please hold me," she whispered. His face felt her hair, and he slowly, reluctantly—or was it carefully and longingly?—put his arm around her. He felt the soft fabric of her nightshirt and bunched it up in his hand. Judie Kate was shaking. She pulled his arm across her breasts and held it there. *Exactly like Jay Jay,* Joe thought.

* * *

REALGUYSLIKEME&U BLOG
1:23 A.M.

So, dudes, like, I am walking around today at the festival and spot some cuties at the theater with those romper things on. You guys know what I think about those outfits, right? Damn! So, there were a couple of girls that looked too old for their own good. How do we tell the difference, right, guys? I mean, makeup and hair and titties and you trying to put the whammy on them, and then daddy comes up looking all mean. I mean, come on, man, you let 'em dress like that and then get all mad cause we looking?

So, I check out one of the romper chicks. Seriously, that off the shoulder stuff just kills me and then, no bra, no way I'm looking the other way, man, right? So, I go up to her, and she blows me off! She's a goody-two-shoes girl! Dressed like that? So, I'm getting tired of this BS. I chased her down tonight and gave her a big what for, right? I showed her what a real man has to offer! That'll fix her! She won't blow me off again, that's for sure!

Anyway, I spotted another cutie! Look at her pic. Whoa! I mean, like she's got a curve or two, right, guys? So, I snap a few pics and follow her around, but her daddy, or is he a dirty old man, caught me staring! Run for it! Better leave her alone, huh? No way! I'll get to her soon!

Oh yeah, the music was real good tonight! Check out that Ditchville12 bunch!

***

REALGUYSLIKEME&U BLOG
1:31 A.M.

You know what? I'm going after her tomorrow! One down, more to go!

Friday

There was light in the room at 5:00 a.m. Joe slowly woke up, wondered what, then who, was beside him in the bed. It was nice to have a warm body to sleep with, to hold. But then, the guilt hit. *What was she thinking? What if George or Ellie had become suspicious?* He looked at her lovingly as she lay in the bed, pillow pulled tight against her tummy. *When did Killer get into bed with us?* He grabbed his clothes, went to the bathroom, and prepared to take his shower. There, on his washcloth, Judie Kate had placed one of her soaps. *When did she do this?*

Fresh from the shower, Judie Kate still unresponsive in his bed, Joe wandered into the great room. The strange clicking sound was in the sunlit room again. He looked around but could not find anything shaking or rattling or moving. Then, he noticed several bobbleheads in the window. The heads were shaking, but he had not touched them that morning. Maybe a breeze from the air conditioner? A draft through the window? He went over to investigate but felt no air moving. Sitting back down, he listened to the clicks and then realized that the bobbleheads were in sync with the clicks. *Hmm. Solar-powered bobbleheads?* He googled the phrase, and sure enough, there was such a thing as solar-powered bobbleheads. *Mystery solved!*

Emails done, Joe fixed his instant coffee and heated up his Pop Tarts. Remembering the sausage balls, he turned around, grabbed a handful from the fridge, nuked them, and then found his seat on the deck. *This is the life!*

Outside, it was already warm. The breeze was out of the west, boats were racing to the best fishing holes, and despite the storm off the coast, there was blue sky above. Killer scratched the door, and Joe let him out. He headed down the steps to take care of the morning business. Joe popped a sausage ball, nibbled on his Pop Tart, sipped his brew, and breathed in the salty air. *What a day!* Killer came back up, sat down in front of Joe, and stared.

"Hungry?" Joe took a bit of crust and laid it at Killer's paw as he just stared back in a "you're kidding" way and Joe grinned. "Okay, try this." He tossed a crumb of sausage ball. Killer looked the other way. "Only cat food, right?" He got up and retrieved a can of food, plopped it in Killer's bowl, and returned to his morning thoughts outside.

He couldn't get Thursday off his mind. Judie Kate kept coming back to him again and again. He shook his head and remembered the kiss on the Workshop

Stage, their walk to the Ice Cream Shack, the kiss under the house, his sudden desire for her, things nearly getting out of hand, Judie Kate telling him not yet, waking up with her in his bed. *When does "yet" come?*

He heard George fumbling around inside the beach house. *Oh yeah, George and Ellie.* Suddenly, his five days of getting away from everything had turned into getting into everything. *Not what I had planned ...*

George fiddled with the glass door as if he had never opened one and then came outside, peeling a banana in a morning stupor and finally finding a seat, as if the latter was a taxing task. Killer took his place at the edge of the deck, the canine lookout in the crow's nest of an island rental. After a few moments of silence and slowly waking up, George spoke.

"No dreams last night, huh?"

"Thought I'd give you guys a rest."

George chewed more banana.

"So, what's the agenda today?" Joe asked.

George placed the empty peel on the arm of the Adirondack chair. He paused for a moment, as if he were trying to pull up the day's agenda from an old file.

"Well, Darren and Bow String Bill are on the radio this morning for an interview."

Joe waited for more details, but George seemed to have stalled somewhat. "Interview about what?" Joe asked. Sometimes, a conversation with George was like pulling teeth.

"Talking about the show, you know the twentieth anniversary and all." Joe waited for more details, but none were forthcoming. He continued his part of the conversation.

"So, what time is the interview?" George looked out over the sound, waiting for the answer to arrive on a slow-moving wave.

"About eleven thirty, I think."

He wondered how George could remember the exact month when Gibson guitars began using screws to hold bridges in place and when they ended that practice; when Martin Guitars shifted from one style of bracing to another; engine sizes, horsepower, and torque ratios for muscle cars in the 1970s; sparkplug gaps for the chainsaw; but could not remember exactly the time for an interview today.

The glass door rumbled and out stepped Judie Kate, hair in place, smile beaming brighter than the sun, dressed for the beach in her long cover-up.

"You boys talking man stuff?" She plopped on the bench of the picnic table across from Joe and popped open the top of her yogurt. Joe was mesmerized by her eyes, her face, her joy.

"Just planning out the day is all," Joe answered back, trying hard not to stare too much at her while George was around. It wasn't working.

"Pencil in a beach date with Judie Kate, Joe," she responded. Then she caught herself. "If that's all right with Daddy."

George woke up with the word date. "Joe's day begins this afternoon," he noted. "We don't need him until then. If you can keep the sharks away from him, that would be nice."

Joe finished his Pop Tarts, tossed in the last sausage ball, and emptied his coffee mug while Judie Kate spooned around in the yogurt cup, and George ate the last bite of banana. All enjoyed the quiet of the new day, slowing down in the casual vibe of Ocracoke Island. Judie Kate turned her spoon upside down and slowly licked it clean with a tongue that was a bit too enticing for Joe and remembered her father's request.

"I'll see what I can do." She got up and looked at Joe. "You coming?"

For a moment, Joe was reluctant, caught between what he perceived was George's disapproval and Judie Kate's effervescence. He looked over at George, who was staring at the sound as if in a sense of "if you can't see it, then it ain't happening."

"I've got my phone, George, if you need me."

Killer barked as a line of pelicans whooshed by.

***

The young Christian man walked down the highway, quietly praising the Lord for another day. The sun was just rising over the live oaks and cedars, and the morning air was thick with salty humidity and the mixed fragrances of coastal flowers. When he arrived at School Road, he saw the clamor of excitement as the event staff feverishly prepared for the festival beginning that afternoon. He walked over to the big Allen & Heath soundboard under the awning at the back of the seating area and introduced himself to Rex. Two handfuls of Chihuahua stood on the chair with front paws on the soundboard.

"That your dog?" he asked.

Rex crushed out his cigarette. He was the stereotypical sound man. Wallet on a chain, ponytail, T-shirt hanging out, black Converse shoes. A slightly off-in-space look and an air of intensity mixed with a slow pace of indifference.

"Nah, man, that's Abner the Sound Dog. Lives on the island. Just walked up here like he owns the place. Did that last year too."

He wandered farther down the road and turned left onto Howard Street. *Why did the girls run from me the other night?* He walked past the Craft Shack up to the Howard Street Stage and paused to look at the stage. There were mic stands, cables, amp cases, power cords, monitors, and main speakers, but there was nobody around. *Did they just put things there and leave them? Don't they worry about somebody stealing them?*

He looked up and saw yellow crime scene tape across the road just beyond Lawton Lane, the road he strolled late last night. He walked up to the tape, and then a sheriff came out of nowhere and asked him to go back.

"What happened, sheriff?" he asked.

"Mister, I just need you to move on."

"I'm sorry, sheriff." He turned and walked back down Howard Street.

Another sheriff came over.

"Did you get a good look at him?"

"Yup. They say they always come back to the scene of the crime."

"I got a pic of him just in case."

"That shirt sure was interesting, wasn't it?"

"'Jesus Delivers' and the pizza place logo. Cute."

***

Walking down the beach, Judie Kate held Joe's hand as they strolled along together. The waves were quiet, and the water was nearly smooth, accented by diminutive, rhythmic waves. The sun sparkled off millions of briny sequins stitched by Mother Nature onto the pale greenish-gray fabric of the ocean. The young woman from yesterday was in the same spot, her hair pulled back over the top of her chair, dangling down in a soft dance just over the sand that would lure any young man. She was fast asleep, enriching her tan, basking in the warmth of the sun, and losing herself in a dream far away. Judie Kate felt something missing in Joe's hand. He seemed distant, preoccupied.

"You okay, Joe?"

"Just thinking about the show, that's all."

She felt there was more to it than that. After a few more minutes, she stopped. An older man walked by wearing a shirt that said "Fishing Buddy" with a cat on the front. Joe sat, and Judie Kate made a place beside him.

"Jay Jay loved the beach. Said the ocean talked to her. The louder the better. She loved crashing waves. Our favorite place was Beaufort. We went there several times a year when we could afford to. Stayed at a bed and breakfast. We would go over to Fort Macon State Park and walk the beach there. It must be a mile and a half one way. I bet we walked a thousand miles on that beach. No houses, no piers, no bait shops. Just beach. Sometimes fishermen, sometimes people flying kites. In the fall, winter, and early spring, there would sometimes be nobody on the beach but us. We have a box full of sand dollars that we found there."

Joe paused, and Judie Kate noticed that he said "we" like Jay Jay was still alive. She almost said something but thought better of it. Pelicans skimmed the glistening waters, and Joe momentarily forgot his memory, distracted by the grace of the ungainly birds.

The tide was coming in, and the waves were catching up to them, so they scooted back. An older woman looking for shells walked in front of them and gave them a look over her shoulder. Two teen girls giggled as they walked by, staring at their phones, oblivious to the beautiful day. A young man jogged by in a tight shirt and short running shorts, looking like he was heading for the finish line. Joe looked at Judie Kate for a long time. Finally, she could not take it any longer.

"What?" She turned to face him directly.

The sun was behind him and shining on her face, giving her a radiance that was like life itself. Her large dark-framed sunglasses lent even more mystery to a latent sexiness. The slight breeze blew little strands of her hair around her face. There was something about her shoulders that he couldn't resist. He just wanted to run his hands softly over them and then come back up and do it all over again. Then he realized he wanted more than that, her hands on his waist, pulling him closer, tighter, his arms around her shoulders ...

"Joe? You're worrying me."

He was worrying himself.

"Talk," she said.

Joe looked at her again, but, this time, his face was different. "Emotions, Judie Kate, emotions. My emotions are all over the place. When I'm alone with you, I want you so bad, to feel you, hold you, do other things with you, to you. But then, I get around George and Ellie and things shut down. Last night, we nearly lost control, and then we cooled off. I want to be with you, but I have a show to do. Men look at you, and I get jealous and then I feel proud. Women look at you, and I wonder if they approve or not. People look at us, and I feel like a man on the moon, and then I worry that they think you're a gold digger, and I'm a sugar daddy." He held his head low and then looked back up. "And then Jay Jay comes to mind, and it just starts all over again."

She was not sure where he was going with this admission, confession, or whatever it was, but she was sure where he was not going with it. Filled with determination, she scooted over and sat on his lap and wrapped her legs around him like she was never letting him go. Ignoring whoever walked by and whatever they thought, she slowly rested her arms around his neck and kissed him softly and then with a rising passion that even surprised her. Every inch of Joe responded back, and she felt his passion in her embrace, in the kiss. She leaned back and looked him in the eyes.

"What are your emotions right now, Joe Clark?"

"I am feeling a lot of things, Judie Kate, wonderful things, but most importantly, right now I can't feel my legs."

"Huh?"

"Legs, Judie Kate, my legs are numb. You're squashing my legs."

"I'm sorry, Joe!" She jumped up and tried to pull him up, but he reminded her that he could not feel anything, and so he could not stand. She plopped back down on the sand beside him. He reached over to her and pulled her close.

"I think I need some more practice feeling things again." He rubbed her legs and her body, and Judie Kate repositioned herself in front of him, now looking out at the sea. She pulled his hands around her waist and held them there, and together they stared at the ocean blue and sailed away into each other's dreams.

After a long time on the beach, they realized that both needed to return to the house. On the way back, Joe asked Judie Kate if she had seen the lighthouse yet.

"You're kidding. You have not been there yet? Everybody goes to see the lighthouse." They were driving down the highway. "There," Joe pointed to the left. "Turn left there."

She slowed and waited for some bikes to clear the intersection. She carefully drove down the narrow Lighthouse Road until they came to the historic white sentinel. There was one parking space left in a tiny parking lot.

Those staring at the lighthouse were silent, as if in a house of worship, in awe of something that had withstood the storms of life for ages. In the brief silence, they leaned into each other. They wondered at the romance, the stateliness, the stability of the stubby, white lighthouse. It stood like an old grandpa, weathered but still wise, resisting the push of the present as it held onto the stories of the past. There was a feeling of comfort, safety, security in its powerful yet understated presence. They could see the lighthouse straining against the hurricanes of past years, sending its light out to worried, storm-tossed sailors, saying good-bye to one keeper and his family after years of dedication, and then welcoming the next keeper and wondering if he would be as loyal as the last.

"Reminds you of that song by ... what was the group? Nickle Creek?" she whispered in his ear. He looked off to the side, looked back at the lighthouse, and then it came to him.

"'The Lighthouse's Tale,'" he whispered back to her. They cuddled closer, floating slowly back into the mysteries of the lighthouse.

"Wonder what tales this one would tell?" she asked.

"Want to see it up close, Judie Kate?"

"Actually, I need to go to a store to see about something."

* * *

Miller felt her phone vibrate in her back pocket. She pulled it out and swiped the screen to read a text from Drew.

Drew: If ur interested, that guy is playing near Cat's Meow

Miller: thnx

Then Miller texted Tyler.

Miller: he's at cat's meow playing

Tyler: you going?

Miller: duh! where r u?

Tyler: school road hanging out

Miller: come on!

* * *

Judie Kate parked her car in a sand lot just off the highway.

"Where are we headed?" Joe said.

She pulled him along to the shops in the village. "I need something for tonight. We're going to the restaurant, right? You're doing that thing for the jazz people. So, I wanted to look good for you." She pulled him inside Cat's Meow. "Saw this place yesterday and wanted to go in, but Momma was getting tired. Bet they have something pretty."

Joe dutifully stood by as she looked at the fashions, rack after rack, flipping one garment after another on each rack. She saw a long, black maxi dress and pulled it out, held it up to herself, and looked at Joe. It was sleeveless, with little spaghetti straps and an elastic band that would fit snugly on her chest.

"What do you think? Good enough for tonight?" Joe's face lit up. "I'll take that as a yes. I'll try it on."

The black maxi dress was simple, casual, yet in some way, also elegant. It flowed enticingly down to her feet. The tiny straps tied neatly into pretty bows gave her shoulders a new meaning, a new lure. The dress was a bit loose but clung to Judie Kate's curves just enough.

"Like?" she asked, but she did not need an answer judging by Joe's face.

After she paid for the dress, they walked back outside and found an empty bench. They watched the tourists amble by, lost in thought, in memories, in dreams, or just plain lost. One group of women, who could have been the characters in a summer beach read, paused a moment, trying to decide which way to go, one looking at a map. Joe was staring off in their direction, but it was not them he was seeing.

He was too caught up in a fantasy to see the tourist drama. He was holding Judie Kate close, feeling her body conform to his, running his hands over her black dress, its soft fabric directing his hands to explore what lay underneath. As he ran his hands up and down her back, the dress pulled up. He let it fall, ever the gentleman, but the passion that was building moved his hands to her hips, and they flowed over the curves to her small waist, where they lingered, tempted to move higher up the mountain. She leaned into him, as if urging him on, and he hesitantly slid his hands over the soft fabric to her breasts, teased them for a moment as if asking permission to explore even more.

She pulled back, giving them room. After a moment, she leaned back into him, trapping his hands, and kissed him, her full, moist lips meeting his, first slowly and then passionately. Then, she took his hands, placed them on the small of her back, and pulled her dress up slightly, giving him permission once more to delve deeper into the mystery of Judie Kate. He slowly pulled her dress up ...

"Uh, Joe, you with me here?" Judie Kate was watching Joe look at the women, her jealous bone taking over, making her hand reach for his, as if she needed to put a leash on him. She saw a faint smile on his face. "Hello? Staring at the ladies?"

Joe came back to earth. "Thinking about something."

"That something sure is making you smile, Joe." She stood up, pulled him up close, and kissed him like there was no tomorrow in plain sight of everybody. "There. That'll give you something to smile about."

They started walking, but Joe suddenly stopped. He spotted the Christian man on the corner.

"Hmm," he said to himself. "That guy is busking. I have never seen that so in the open down here, usually it is done a bit out of sight. Sometimes, there is a busker across from the Community Square."

"Joe?" Judie Kate asked. "What's a busker?"

"A guy who plays in public. A musical beggar, if you will."

"Joe, that guy gives me the creeps. Remember how he stared at me on the beach yesterday? Momma and I saw him yesterday afternoon. That annoying Christian T-shirt thing. He stared at me the whole time then. Remember, he was at the show last night. He stared at me then too. It's like he is infatuated with me, obsessed with me. And if he wasn't staring at me, he was looking at other women. It's like he's from the hills and has never seen a woman before."

Joe was torn. He was not a fan of the Church—the hypocrisy of his devout deacon father beating his son for religious infractions was too much for him—but he loved music, any kind of music, and he was always interested in any kind of live music. He was not sure about Judie Kate's worries either, but he did not want to make her uncomfortable.

"Just for a bit? I just want to hear what he is playing. Must be pretty good. He's got a crowd around him."

He pulled a reluctant Judie Kate across the road and paused to listen. He heard the busker finish up a soulful rendition of the African American spiritual "Deep River." The small crowd, mostly of young girls who seemed to be taken with him, clapped their appreciation. Two folks dropped dollar bills into his guitar case. He thanked them and then made a small spiel about Jesus, offered a bottle of cold water to anyone who was thirsty, and then resumed with a finger pick version of "There is a Balm in Gilead." The crowd was mesmerized, caught up in his deep voice, feeling the passion and conviction of his music.

"He's good, Judie Kate. Look at the crowd. Look at how they are staring at him." More people had paused, caught up in his music, his brash yet innocently daring display of his faith. "He's got a good command of the song; look at his chords. Many are quite complex, like jazz chords. But there is a bit of blues in there too. He's done his homework."

The busker sang away, looking up to the sky, then back down to the ground, immersed in the moment. But then, something obviously caught his eye. Now, he was staring directly at Judie Kate. His face changed, indeed his very demeanor. He flubbed a chord. To Judie Kate, it was like he was demonic. It was as if he were being directed to reach out to her. Then, she spotted the big knife resting on top of the tracts. The hair on the back of her neck rose and chills covered her body.

"See what I mean, Joe? He's looking directly at *me* now, nobody else. That creeps me out. He had that same face on last night at the theater. What does he want from me? I want to go now, Joe."

He turned around and led Judie Kate the other way.

"Sorry, just wanted to hear him play." They walked a while, Judie Kate holding Joe's hand limply, clearly spooked by the singer, the knife, the whole scene.

"Ice cream?"

* * *

While Joe and Judie Kate enjoyed their treat, George and Ellie gathered around the computer just before eleven thirty in the morning. Ellie sipped her coffee, still waking up. George, as always, fidgeted, this time hooking up the computer to some speakers after checking out Yahoo News. He plugged them in, and soon, radio station WOVV was playing.

"When do you meet Darren?" Ellie continued.

"After the broadcast. We might have some lunch. Want to come along?" George ambled over to the counter and grabbed a handful of nuts and crunched away.

The announcer came on air, interrupting the music. "This is an emergency bulletin. Early this morning, a young woman was assaulted, raped, and then beaten and cut by an attacker. We have no description of the attacker at this time. The sheriff's department warns the public to always be aware of their surroundings, gather in lighted areas after dark, walk in groups, and stay off the streets late at night into the morning. We are placing this announcement on Facebook, Twitter, and Instagram, so please share with your friends."

Ellie got a worried look on her face and then began rattling away.

"Joe and Judie Kate were out last night. What if that was them? I don't like this whole situation. What was she thinking wearing that outfit last night? Now there's a stalker out there … what if she dresses like that again, and the stalker gets to her? Is Joe making her do that? This didn't start until Joe came in. That's just inviting an attack." She paused. "Are you listening to me?"

"What?"

"Where did they go this morning?"

"Judie Kate made him go to the beach with her."

"I don't like this one bit."

"What exactly are you going to do about it, Ellie?" George turned around and stared at her over his reading glasses.

"I was hoping you would say something to Joe. He gets you. He respects you. Say something!" Ellie was now visibly upset, shaking her head, walking heavily around the room. She grabbed her phone, sat in a chair, and scrolled through Facebook. "I don't like this one bit!"

A few moments later, Peter Vankevich came on air with "What's Happening on Ocracoke." It was time for the interview. George turned up the volume.

"We are celebrating the twentieth anniversary of the Ocrafolk Festival this year. With me, I have Darren Edwards, leader of the local band Ditchville12, and Bow String Bill, also known as Big Bill Dawson, fiddle player with Ditchville12 and President of Ocracoke Alive, who is presenting the festival this weekend. My guests will be talking about how the festival began and what is involved in the production of such a big undertaking as this festival. Welcome, gentlemen."

Darren and Bow String Bill thanked the host for the opportunity to talk about the festival.

George turned up the volume a bit more. "Be interesting to hear what stories they share this morning."

Ellie did not respond.

"So, Darren, I understand you were the brains behind how this festival started. Can you take us back to those early days?" Peter Vankevitch said.

Darren cleared his throat. "Well," he started off with a pause.

"George! Come over here!" Ellie shouted, interrupting the interview. She was holding her phone, her hand shaking.

George ambled over, obviously annoyed, not in any rush. "What?"

Ellie put the phone in front of his face. "It's Judie Kate. Her picture is right here on this man's website. He's got pictures of other women as well."

George looked at them as Ellie scrolled down with her twitching finger. "These are all from the show last night at the theater." George pointed at the screen. "How did you find this?"

Ellie was having a difficult time holding her phone still. "I googled the theater and the date and got a few hits on Facebook, Twitter, Instagram."

George looked over the site. "What does that say there?" He reached for his reading classes.

Ellie gasped. "'Got me one last night. Plenty more to go!'"

"Does he have a name? Was he stupid enough to put his picture on there?" George asked.

"No picture of himself, but he has a graphic of a knife cutting a blue apple shaped like a heart." Ellie paused. "That's weird. His name is iheartbryanadams. Who is Bryan Adams?"

George thought for a moment, went back in time. "Rock and roll." He walked around the room and recalled the hits of the past. "I can't remember." On a hunch, he went over to his computer and typed in Bryan Adams. The website popped up, and George saw the graphic of the knife slicing the apple and a list of hits from the singer. "Damn!"

"What is it George?" Ellie exclaimed.

"Bryan Adams had a hit song called 'Cuts Like a Knife.' I think you just found the page of the rapist. I'm calling the sheriff." He dialed 911, gave them the information, and was informed a sheriff would be dispatched soon. Then he called Joe.

"Where are you?" he asked in a demanding tone.

"Ice Cream Shack. What's wrong?"

"Judie Kate with you?"

"Sure."

"Get her home now, and don't let her out of your sight!"

"George, what's wrong?

"Get her home *now*!"

* * *

Joe put the phone back in his pocket.

"That was your father. Said to get you home and not to let you out of my sight."

"Did he say what was going on?"

"Nope. But I know that tone of voice. Something's not right."

They left the Community Square and hurriedly walked back up the highway and passed the entrance to Howard Street.

"Hmm, that's strange," Joe called out, stopping in his tracks. He saw the yellow crime scene tape across the road. "Didn't see that on the way down. Wonder what's up?"

A sheriff walked up, looking very serious, and waved him onward.

"It's closed, sir, please move along."

Judie Kate pulled him forward, but Joe looked back again.

"Very strange," Joe said, more to himself than Judie Kate.

"What's strange, Joe?"

"There is never any crime here. Wonder what all that crime tape is about?"

Suddenly, Judie Kate felt a cold shiver run up her spine.

"Do you remember last night, Joe? We were walking up that road, and when we got to that intersection, you wanted to walk farther, but I stopped?" Joe nodded. "I didn't want to say anything, but I had a strange feeling, something evil-like, when we stood there. It ran all over my body." She began shaking, and despite the hot and humid air, goose bumps rose on her arms. Joe looked at her closely.

"Judie Kate, are you alright?"

"Evil, Joe. Something evil happened down there last night. I can feel it."

* * *

Interview over, Darren rode his bike from the radio station to the Live Oak Stage. On the way, he thought about the rapist and what it might do to the show, the 20th anniversary. He could get fliers made and distribute them around the crowd, but that might spook the tourists. Or he could have the stage hosts make announcements to the crowds, but that would ruin the moment, take away the excitement.

Or they could do nothing at all. The show must go on. But that seemed irresponsible. They could bring in more sheriffs to patrol the area. That would lend a sense of security. He thought it out some more and decided that was what he would do.

When he turned the corner, he saw the Christian busker. He hit the brakes and paused, staring at the small crowd. If there was one thing Darren didn't want, it was a busker drawing people away from the show. He had no power over a lone busker, what he might do, what he might say, how he might act, and he didn't want anybody associating the busker with the show. If the busker was bad, what would people say? They would think the promoters had brought in sorry talent. What if the busker said things the show did not approve of? There was no control over a busker, and this one had to go. Time to nip this in the bud.

He walked up to the crowd and noticed the Christian T-shirt with its restaurant logo take off.

"Can't they be more creative than that?" he muttered to himself. He was about to say something when he heard the singer. Darren paused, for once pulling back from his need for control.

The busker was singing Ralph Stanley's "O Death" acapella. When he finished, the crowd applauded enthusiastically. Darren stayed for a bit, intrigued, listening to the boy's brief message. Several folks thanked him for the water and tossed some coins, some dollar bills, into his guitar case. Two people asked for one of the tracts he had available. He took his knife off the stack—the knife kept them from blowing away in the breeze—and handed them out.

"Sure is a big knife," Darren mumbled to himself.

He picked up his guitar and tuned it up, getting ready for the next song. Darren noticed it was an old Gibson sunburst. Soon, a heartfelt version of "Working on a Building" was flowing in the breeze. One bystander, caught up in the moment, started clapping her hands. Another started clogging.

After the song, most of the crowd dispersed, except for the three girls. Darren knew them well. Miller Baylor was the preacher's daughter. She was on summer break from Mount Olive University, where she was on the women's volleyball team. She was tall and her long, dark hair matched the darkness of her green eyes. Like her father, she was unassuming as well, ordinary by many standards, but there was something about her—her smile, her exuberance—that made her stand out in a crowd. She was athletic with girl-next-door looks.

Tyler Samuels was the daughter of the Samuels who ran a local restaurant. She, too, was athletic in shape but shorter than Miller. Her long, blonde hair was a favorite for the boys, and the double French braids she often sported didn't hurt either, but she had other things on her mind, mostly music. She played keyboards and the guitar and was teaching herself drums, and she was beginning to get a few local gigs. Her family had moved to Ocracoke some years ago from Ohio.

Drew Layton was in Ocracoke on a summer mission project for the second year in a row. She did youth work at the Assembly of God church, where all three sang in the youth choir, put together a Vacation Bible School, and led other volunteer activities for the tourists. She had beautiful, thick brunette hair, the kind that stayed in place no matter what the humidity was like. She was big-boned and had large, dark eyes and facial features that were large as well: thick eyebrows and full lips with a wide smile. She was stout in stature, but her face was that of a Greek goddess.

All three had on tank tops, Tyler's glued to her lean body, and modest jean shorts, Tyler's being the tightest, with phones sticking out of their back pockets.

"Ladies, how are you all today?" Darren asked.

"Doing great! Isn't he good? Can he sing for the festival?" Miller asked, nearly begging for a yes.

Darren explained to her that the performers and the schedule had already been arranged.

"He could sing with us on Sunday morning," Miller offered, not giving up. "Please!"

Darren paused. "Well, now, that's a good idea. He could certainly join your choir." He saw a bit more in her face than just wanting him to sing. Her eyes had an excitement in them. He had seen that before with his own daughters. He leaned over to her. "Got a little thing for him, huh, Miller?"

She blushed and looked down but then looked back up with a sheepish grin. "He *is* cute."

The busker started up another song, "Just a Closer Walk with Thee" and, like magic, another small crowd formed around him. Darren was intrigued by his musicianship. There was a lilt to his voice that gave the song a lift out of the ordinary, making it more than just another gospel song. When he changed keys and did an extended instrumental solo, Darren knew what he had to do.

The crowd applauded, and he thanked them for their appreciation. Then he tuned his guitar way down and began a mournful intro, leading into a haunting version of "Two Coats." Darren was majorly impressed. The singer finished up and looked around as people clapped their approval.

"So, folks, I'm going to take a break. Please feel free to have some water." More people talked with him briefly and tossed money into the case. Soon, all had left except for the trio of female fans.

Darren stepped forward. "Ladies, could I have a private moment with this young gentleman?"

They reluctantly walked away, wondering if Darren was going to shoo the singer away. Miller crossed her fingers and sent out a quiet prayer.

"Hi, I'm Darren Edwards. I'm the promoter for the Ocrafolk Festival. You're quite a picker there. What's your name?"

"Zach, Zachary Daniels." He was a bit shy, and a bit skeptical of others until he knew them. "Good to meet you, sir."

Darren pointed at his guitar, and they traded tales of past guitar experiences. Finally, he got to his point.

"Zach, I've been in the music business for nearly forty years. Many of the groups that have come here for the festival have gone on to the next level.

I've got a good sense of the industry. You're good, very good. You have a gift that needs to be given to more people."

Zach was almost embarrassed, but he knew deep inside that he had talent. Still, his Christian humility would not allow that feeling to surface. It was pride, and that would not work in the Kingdom.

"Thank you, sir."

"You can call me Darren. Anyway, I have some advice and then a proposal. First, the advice. I appreciate your Christian witness, but the whole idea of witnessing is to bring people in, right? Your shirt will drive away more people than it will pull in." Darren was quite blunt, short, curt, not known for keeping people's feelings above all else. Everybody on the island and all the entertainers invited to the festival knew that. He had ticked off quite a few people in order to keep the integrity of the show intact. Zach was clearly offended in a self-righteous manner.

"So, I'll work you a deal. I'll get you three festival shirts and put you onstage Sunday morning for the Gospel show if you'll quit wearing those church shirts. Miller can get you in with the church choir and then you sing one yourself. In one sitting, you'll reach three hundred people. That's a lot of exposure. And if that goes well, and I think it will, I'll bring you back next year to do a full set on Appalachian and African American spirituals. What do you say?"

Zach thought about it carefully. Was he selling his soul out? Was he giving in to mammon? Or was this Christ reaching out to him to reach out to others? Was it the door Jesus talked about? *Behold, I stand at the door and knock* ... He was torn, confused. Giving up his Christian shirts was a major step. How would people know of his faith?

Miller overheard the invitation and walked back up, sensing Zach's hesitation. She knew the reputation of the festival, how it had helped several groups take the next step in their careers.

"Zach, I heard what Mr. Darren said. You don't know how big this is. You need to do this."

He was not used to a woman telling him what to do. Was God speaking through Miller? She did have black hair, and she lived at the ocean. Was she the one in his dreams? It was a step of faith, more like a leap across a canyon of doubt and fear. Zach looked around as if there were some writing on a wall somewhere. The wheels of Ezekiel's chariot were turning in his head, and he was going back and forth between what he had originally felt was his mission on Ocracoke and the new opportunity now in front of him. Something had to give.

Miller moved her red lips enticingly: *do it.* There was something angelic about her face, the way her mouth moved, her lips forming the word *do*, the way her dark green eyes radiated depth and wisdom, the way her body exuded joy and strength, that moved Zach to try the unthinkable.

"Okay, uh, I'll do it, uh, Darren," he answered, still unsure of himself and the decision. Miller grinned, and Drew and Tyler came running up. She told them of the news, and they shrieked for joy. Their hero was going to be on stage, and the message of Christ would be shared with more people.

"You're gonna be *so* great!" Tyler called out. Darren patted him on the back.

"Good choice, smart choice. So, I'll get those shirts and be back in a jiff. Come to the show Saturday and walk around some and get to know us better. I'll be at the Howard Street Stage, so come by and we can talk. Be at the Live Oak Stage Sunday morning around eight thirty." Suddenly, Zach realized the import of his decision. He would be singing in front of a large crowd, witnessing.

Darren brought him back to earth. "By the way, you're at the beach. Put some shorts on." Darren got back on his bike.

"Uh, thanks, Darren!" Zach called out, a bit excited yet still not quite sure what had happened and whether it was good or bad.

Miller beamed. "Thanks, Mr. Darren!" she said. As Darren rode away, Miller looked up at Zach, throwing up her hands in excitement. "Do you know what this means?"

Zach picked up his guitar, hooked up the strap, and strummed a chord to see if he was still in tune. He looked at Miller, then Drew and Tyler. "Yeah. Where do I buy some shorts around here?" he said.

Miller jumped at the chance to have more time with him. "We can take you. Finish up here, and we'll go this afternoon."

* * *

As Zach finished his set, George, bad knees and all, was nervously pacing back and forth in the hot sun in the driveway. The sheriff pulled up at the house, and George met him as he got out of the cruiser.

"Are you George Wilson?" the sheriff asked.

"Yes," George replied in an uncharacteristically quivering voice. "Please come inside."

Ellie was a quaking mess and so shaken she forgot the formalities and blurted out, "Can I get you something to drink, sheriff?"

"I'm fine, ma'am, thank you."

George motioned for the sheriff to sit down.

"Sheriff, we think we have found the web page of the rapist. It has a picture of our daughter and other young women on it." He got his computer and brought it over, and Ellie grabbed her phone, typed in iheartbryanadams, and the page came up.

"Here it is, sheriff." She scrolled down and showed him the pictures of Judie Kate, then she scrolled through the others. "All of these were taken at the theater last night. We know because we were there—"

George interrupted. "I'm in the Ditchville12 band."

Ellie continued, "And these pictures are all from that area." Ellie handed him her phone.

The sheriff looked at the pics, scrolled up and down, then back through them again. "Well, these women all seem to have nothing in common—they have different hair, different heights, faces—except for one thing: the same style of outfit. What do you call these things?"

"Rompers," Ellie said with a voice of disgust. "Rompers. Apparently, all the women are wearing them. They are too showy if you ask me. Might as well walk around naked."

"Yes, ma'am," the sheriff answered. He scrolled through the page again. "And, this bothers me." He pointed to the stalker's statement: *Got me one last night. Plenty more to go.* "Look at the time of that post," the sheriff said as he pointed to the computer screen. "One twenty-three. The attack occurred last night after eleven."

"What on earth was that young woman doing out by herself at that time last night?" Ellie asked.

"I don't know, ma'am. Tourists do strange things. We don't have much crime here. Maybe she was out for a walk? I guess she felt safe, even on the dark road. Maybe the attacker forced her down the road?" The sheriff reached for his phone. "Let me make a call." He scrolled through the numbers and touched one on the screen. George and Ellie could hear the phone ringing.

A groggy voice answered.

"Hello?"

"Sammy, Bill here. Hate to bother you, but I think we have a lead in that attack last night. Can you get on the computer?" There was a long pause. The sheriff looked over at George and Ellie. "Sammy worked the incident last night. He saw the victim. It was bad."

A groggy voice answered, "Uh, yeah, okay, I've got it up."

"Good, so look up 'iheartbryanadams.'"

"What? I who?"

"Spell it out Sammy—'iheartbryanadams.' Like the singer, Bryan Adams, just all small letters."

There was a pause as Sammy typed it in.

"You got it, Sammy?" Another pause.

"Yeah, so what am I looking for? Just a bunch of cute women on here. Not much to go off of," Sammy said.

"Look over the women carefully. Recognize any faces or even clothes from last night?"

Another pause as Sammy looked over the page again.

"Damn. Oh my God. That's her. The third woman on the page. I recognize the polka dot outfit and her face. It took a minute. There was so much blood from that cross cut on her chest ... the bruises on her chest and face ... she was scarred up some. Yes, that is her."

"Sammy, this does not look good. Serial rapist, you think? Look at what he says on the page: 'Got me one last night. Plenty more to go.'"

"Yeah, Bill. This is serious."

"On it, Sammy." Bill closed the call. He looked up at George and Ellie. "So, folks, I don't mean to frighten you, but this is very serious, very dangerous. Your young lady needs someone around her all the time. She does not go anywhere without someone with her, preferably a male as a show of strength to this pervert. Everywhere you go, keep an eye out. My guess is that he will only attack at night, but like these pics show, he is stalking her during the day. He may try to abduct her. Sounds like that's what he did last night after the show."

"Sheriff?" George asked. "Did he say a cross cut on her chest?"

"Yes, he cut a cross on her chest, the long piece between her breasts and the cross piece above them. There was bruising on her face, probably from a struggle. Maybe a cult thing?"

At that moment, Judie Kate and Joe rushed in. She tossed her package on the futon. They looked at the sheriff and then at George and Ellie.

"Dad, what is going on? Why is the sheriff here?" she called out in a panicked voice. "Are you two okay?"

"You haven't heard?" Ellie asked, rushing over to her daughter.

"Heard what, Momma?" she answered, not quite sure what the sudden surge of affection from her mother meant.

The sheriff interrupted. "Ma'am, there was a sexual assault last night on Howard Street, around midnight. An assailant attacked, beat up, raped, and then cut a young lady." The sheriff continued. "Anyway, the victim is still alive. We don't have a description of the man; the victim has blanked out all memories of the attack." The sheriff looked directly at Judie Kate. "But your parents happened on a website that probably belongs to the assailant. Your picture is on it, and we think you are in very grave danger. He knows your face and is probably stalking you and others during the day and most likely at night."

Ellie showed Judie Kate the pics on her phone while George pulled Joe over and showed him the website as well. The sheriff continued.

"A picture of the victim is on the webpage along with yours and several other women. There is one common factor: all of you are wearing the same outfit. He seems to claim to have attacked one woman and that another one is next. I think we have a very sick man who is a serial rapist."

Judie Kate sat down on the chaise. "Oh my God, Momma!"

Joe sat down beside her and put his arm around her. The room was eerily quiet as the emotions took over, no one knowing exactly what to say and do, George and Ellie caught up in the tension of wanting to help a daughter they had never really been able to get close to.

Then, Joe looked up, as if he had seen a vision on the ceiling.

"Sheriff, I think I might know who the man is." He pulled out his phone and scrolled through the pics. "Here." He showed the sheriff the pic of the man on the ferry. "I saw him on the ferry taking pictures of women, some wearing rompers. I saw him last night at the theater taking pictures and then saw him staring at us while we were at the Ice Cream Shack last night."

The sheriff handed his card to George, another one to Ellie, and one to Joe and Judie Kate, and then stood up to go. "Joe, you have my number. Would you send me that pic, please? Thank you all for this information."

Joe nodded, and then he got up to go outside for a moment. Judie Kate followed him out on the deck and closed the door behind her.

"Ma'am, sir?" the sheriff said as he left, looking back at Ellie and George. "Someone needs to be around her at all times. This is very serious."

"Thank you, sheriff," Ellie said as he walked out the door. Then she turned to George. "What are we going to do? This is our daughter, George. She's in danger." Ellie teared up.

"Ellie, I know we don't like what is going on between Joe and Judie Kate, but this might be a godsend. I'm going to ask him to watch over her as much as he can from now on."

Ellie looked back at George with a worried face. "How is he going to do that when he is doing sound, George? Doesn't he start up tonight? And you know that this will only encourage them more."

"Yeah, I had not put that together yet. I'll think on that some more. In the meantime, I'll make sure they don't feel too encouraged," George said.

There was a heavy, haunting, and seemingly helpless quiet in the room as both thought through various scenarios. Then Ellie raised her eyes.

"We find her someone else to be with. Aren't we having dinner tonight with Lane and his wife, Brooklyn? You know, the doctor? Don't they have a son, pre-med fellow? We met them last week at Aleta's Pub. He seemed nice. Maybe they could bring him along to meet Judie Kate?"

"I'll call and see," George answered, reaching for his phone.

After the sheriff left, Joe and Judie Kate remained on the deck. She was crying softly, and Joe was rubbing her back, trying to calm her down.

"Nothing is going to happen to you, Judie Kate. I promise." He rubbed her back even harder and then her shoulders and then held her close.

"Why is this happening to me, Joe?" she sobbed. "That poor girl, Joe. Why?"

Joe had no answers other than a protective hug. "You got your car keys?"

"Where are we going, Joe?"

"I'm going to the Variety Store."

"You want to go shopping now, Joe?"

"You go inside and rest and get cleaned up for this evening. Lock your deck door. I'll be back in a bit," Joe said.

"Joe? Please be careful. He knows who you are too!"

Joe was already heading to her car. She remained on the deck, looking out over the sound, crying quietly, trying to make sense of it all. *If I hadn't worn that outfit, none of this would be happening!* She chided herself for being so showy, so out of character from who she was. *What was I thinking?* Well, at least Joe will have to be with me more! She smiled to herself, wiped the tears from her eyes, and then worried again. *What if he kills Joe?* The breeze, now from the west, tried to take her worries away, but the load was quite heavy. Suddenly, she noticed dark storm clouds far away over the sound. She turned and walked back inside. George was just getting off the phone.

"Judie Kate," he said, coming over to her, "This is serious. You know that. The sheriff wants someone to be around you at all times. Ellie and I don't approve of you and Joe together—"

"This would not have happened if Joe had not been around!" Ellie shouted out in exasperation. "It's his fault, Judie Kate. You getting all dressed for him. What is this fantasy all about anyway?" Her stoicism finally cracked, and she started crying and stood up to walk around.

"This is Joe's fault?" Judie Kate shot back. "It's that creep's fault. How dare you blame Joe for some pervert's crimes!" Judie Kate walked back around and faced her mother. "This is not about Joe, Momma!" she stomped back to the window and looked out over the sound. It was now a standoff at the Ocracoke Corral.

Ellie, having calmed down, became more logical and continued. "Judie Kate, you need somebody around you at all times. Joe is doing sound, so he will be preoccupied. Tonight, you can be with us. Some friends of ours wanted to meet you, so we are having dinner with them tonight. They have a son, pre-med, so there will be someone you can talk with as well." She paused for a moment. "Maybe it's time for you to move on from Joe, Judie Kate."

Judie Kate turned around. "I guess I don't have any say in this, right? Somebody must be around me all the time, and Joe can't, but you guys can? And I guess it is out of the question that I can just stay here?"

George answered. "Judie Kate, you can't stay here by yourself, so this is the best we can do. And tomorrow, you can sit with me at the Howard Street Stage. Between me and Darren, we can keep watch over you."

"I want to stay with Joe tomorrow!" Judie Kate demanded.

"Joe is what got you into this mess, Judie Kate!" Ellie shot back indignantly.

Judie Kate looked back out over the sound again. She thought through the whole evening. "Isn't Joe doing sound for A Tempo?" she asked.

George answered, "Yes, he is, but he won't have any time for you."

"Fine. I'll go to the restaurant. Time for me to take a shower!" She grabbed her package and headed back to her room, a tempest waiting to explode in thunder and lightning.

"George, why didn't you tell her about what Lane wanted to talk about?"

George was ready to move on from the tensions in the room.

"My job was to get her here and to the dinner. It's his job to talk with her."

* * *

A half an hour later, Joe arrived back at the house, carrying a small bag. He was running out of time. He needed to get to the restaurant to set up, but he had to stop and get his equipment before that. George would have to get him to his trailer. That was going to be an interesting ride. *Guess there will be no lunch today!*

George walked up to him, blocking his way to his bedroom. "Joe, we need to talk."

Joe raced around him. "We'll talk on the way to my trailer. I'm running behind, and I need to change shirts before I go."

He closed the door behind him and walked softly to the bathroom door. It was cracked open a bit, so he carefully walked in. Seeing nobody there, he stepped over to the other door, which was slightly open as well.

"Judie Kate?" Joe whispered.

"It's okay, Joe," Judie Kate whispered back.

He hesitantly walked into the room, as if George and Ellie might come in and catch them together. She was lying on the bed, resting. Her eyes were red, and her face was covered with worry and fear.

"I got you something." He laid the bag on the bed along with her keys. He walked over to the sliding glass door and made sure it was locked. "Make sure this stays locked from now on! I've got to go. I'm running behind."

"Joe?" Judie Kate rolled over and got up from the bed and stepped over to him. She noticed his worried face. "Please be careful!" She held him close and kissed him softly, but all he felt was her shaking. Fear, not love, was in her embrace.

He pulled away and pointed to the bag. "Take those with you everywhere you go from now on. They'll fit in your purse."

He hurriedly left the room, grabbed a fresh shirt, changed quickly, and raced out the door. She picked up the bag, hands shaking, and looked inside and took out two items: a small container of Mace and a compact emergency air horn that boaters often kept on hand. *Joe, you think of everything.*

"Let's go, George," Joe called out, racing out of his room.

George ambled out the door behind Joe, carefully negotiating the steps to take care of his knees.

Get ready for the riot act, Joe thought to himself as he climbed into George's truck. As they headed toward British Cemetery Road, Joe broke the silence. "All right, what's on your mind?"

George negotiated a clump of errant tourists and stopped for a stray cat. "Geez, let's see. A creep who attacks women is after my daughter. A man twice my daughter's age is after my daughter. My daughter seems hell-bent on pursuing a man who is twice her age. My daughter does not like her father or her mother right now. Somebody needs to be around my daughter at all times, and oh, I've got a show to do. I would normally ask you for help, but let's see, I don't really like what is going on between you and my daughter." Now that the cat was way out of the way and out of the bag, George moved on.

Joe was cringing in the discomfort of the rant. *Five more minutes to go.*

"So," George continued, "we're having dinner tonight at the Sea Dogs with some friends who just happen to have a son. We want Judie Kate to meet him." George turned onto Back Road and then looked directly at Joe. "Stay out of the way."

When they arrived at Joe's truck and trailer, Joe got out and then looked back around at George. "You guys ever gonna let Judie Kate live her own life?" He slammed the door and walked off.

George drove around the roundabout in front of the school and sped away.

* * *

Joe arrived at the restaurant at four. He opened the screen door and was met by a tall, dark-haired waitress with black-rimmed glasses and an island tan.

"Can I help you?" she asked with a huge and welcoming smile. She was Joe's age, and it was not clear if she was just a professional host or a woman looking for love, possibly even both.

"Yes, I'm Joe Clark. I'm doing the sound for the band this evening."

She answered back, "I'm Beth. I'll show you the stage area." She led him off the porch into the restaurant with a swing in her hips.

Inside, there were funny signs on the painted wooden walls. The stage was small, maybe ten by five, with a railing around it. It would be tight to get four musicians on there plus equipment.

"Not much room here," Joe remarked.

Beth agreed. "Usually, it is small groups, duo, trio, or DJ. You got a big group?"

"Four-piece tonight. Keyboards, upright bass, singer with harmonica, and percussionist," Joe said.

"Yeah, that's gonna be tight. Can I get you something to drink while you bring your stuff in?"

"Thank you. Yes. Sweet tea."

"Coming right up. Make yourself at home." She smiled one more time and then turned and walked away, a little more swing in her step as Joe headed toward the door.

After five trips to the truck, he was sweating, and the cool air inside the restaurant felt good. He downed the tea and looked for Beth for a refill. He remembered he had not brought in the power cables. When he came back, there was more tea in his glass.

Beth came back up, gleaming. "Want anything to eat?"

"Maybe some fries to nibble on?"

"How about some bacon cheese fries?" Beth said.

Joe nodded his head.

"Coming right out!"

***

Early birds were arriving and taking their places, most far away from the stage. As Joe fretted and fumed and frantically put the stage together, Judie Kate retied the thin straps over her shoulders. The black maxi-dress flowed over her body, covering up everything but her feet, arms, and shoulders. She purchased the dress for Joe, hoping it would be elegant, inviting, sexy in a subtle, mysterious way. Now, it served another purpose. Whoever this new guy was, she was not going to give him the benefit of seeing her in full view. She put on her earrings and necklace and readied herself for what she knew would be a long night.

On the way over with her parents, Judie Kate learned all about Dr. Lane Winston and his family. He was a successful and recognized gynecologist from Winston-Salem. He and his wife were pillars in the Presbyterian Church. Their son had just graduated from UNC-Chapel Hill and was headed to Duke University to become a doctor.

"These are good folks, Judie Kate," Ellie pointedly informed her. "She does a lot of volunteer work. They would be good people to know in the future."

Know for what? Judie Kate wondered.

George took the bend in the road, then swung left and continued the sales pitch.

"I've known Lane since college. We played some music together. Then after we graduated, he went into med school, and I went on the road. But we stayed in touch through the years. He bought one of my guitars last year. He fronted us the money for our first Ditchville12 CD years ago."

Judie Kate remained silent, a prisoner to a stalker, a man she had never met, and now her parents. Was Lane the next warden?

They arrived at the restaurant, and just before they went inside, Judie Kate saw the Christian man again, across the road, staring at her.

As they entered, Ellie called out, "There they are."

She waved to a family, and Judie Kate instantly noticed the young man. He was dressed in plaid pastel shorts with a pink dress shirt on, sleeves rolled up midway on his strong forearms. He wore loafers with no socks. His dark brown hair was full of gel, short on the sides and poofed up in a slight curl or wave on top, and he wore his sunglasses on a rope around his neck. Something about him seemed familiar, but he had that money-jock-frat boy look, and she thought maybe he just looked like a million other materialistic men whose sole purpose in life was wanting people to see what they saw of themselves in their mirror every morning. *Great.*

George introduced his daughter to the couple. "This is Doctor Lane Winston and his wife Brooklyn."

Lane reached out to shake Judie Kate's hand, holding it in both of his hands like a preacher greeting a parishioner, and Brooklyn offered a pleasant and welcoming social embrace to Judie Kate. He was handsome and distinguished, and she exuded elegance with her flowery yet simple halter dress. Both were tanned, in shape, and had that style, confidence, and grace only found in the upper crust of society. Their smiles were genuine and filled with interest in Judie Kate, yet there seemed to be a purpose behind them as well.

George continued. "Judie Kate, this is their son Drake."

Drake nodded in her direction, tapped his phone off, and then offered her a handshake. He looked her over quickly. *Not really my type. A bit chubby, dress is too long. Show me some leg, for Christ's sake! Good for a weekend fling.* He politely if indifferently motioned to a chair beside his. Judie Kate took his instead because she could look at Joe from that angle. He tapped his phone back on and, bored already, scrolled through Facebook.

The band was already into the set with a version of "Ain't Misbehavin," and the crowd noise was annoying, so when Lane looked over to Judie Kate and asked a question, she could not hear very well. Brooklyn got up and offered her seat to her.

Lane leaned over to talk. "So, Judie Kate, George tells me that you are not very satisfied with your current job situation."

Okay, here we go again. Meddling in my life. She looked at her father and forced a smile and turned and answered Lane politely. "Yes, education was not as fulfilling as I was led to believe. Dad suggested an MBA to give me some more options, but the business world does not excite me either. Too cutthroat, too numbers-oriented. So, I'm kind of looking for something, but I don't know what that is yet."

"Well, something will turn up soon," Lane said. "You just have not found it yet. After dinner, come join us at the house. Brooklyn and I know some folks. Maybe we can get you connected with someone." Lane winked at George, but Judie Kate did not see the wink.

She was looking woefully at Joe. "Yes, thank you, Doctor Winston, I'll do that."

"Please, call me Lane. Drake can drive you over. Give you two a chance to get to know each other a bit."

Yay me. "That will be fine," Judie Kate lied. She gave up her seat and sat down beside Drake again. He glanced up from his phone briefly, looked annoyed, and then continued typing. She turned her attention to Joe and saw his phone on the power head, so she took out her phone and texted him *I'm sorry*. In the background, the band was into a soulful rendition of "Summertime."

Joe's phone vibrated. He swiped the screen and saw it was Judie Kate. *Wonderful. I can't get the band dialed in and now this*. He read the text, looked over at Judie Kate who mouthed the words "I'm sorry" real slow, and then typed an answer.

Me too.

She typed back. *Momma and Daddy set this up*.

Joe was not in the mood for text chitchat. *Time to stop being a daughter and be Judie Kate?*

In a huff, she put her phone back in her purse, crossed her arms over her chest, and stared away at the wall. So, it stung. Maybe it was time to draw a line. Joe could not intervene in the matter. It was up to Judie Kate to decide who to please. She was incensed, but she did not know who to be mad at, Joe or herself or her parents. Drake was no distraction, still scrolling through his friends' posts.

Brooklyn started up a conversation with Judie Kate and commented on her dress, earrings, and necklace. She loved her sandals and said the whole ensemble brought out the beauty of Judie Kate. The affirmation caught her off guard. Brooklyn was so refined, so petite, so beautiful. Her long and thick black hair was perfect, her makeup was like a Cover Girl ad. Her nails were painted in a deep red that matched the flowers of her dark yellow dress. Yet, here she was complimenting her. It was girl talk, and it was nice to have a break from all the tensions of the day. Finally, someone other than Joe appreciated her for being her. For a while, Judie Kate forgot she was the target of a stalker or the date for a preppy boy who could care less.

The band played on. They changed genres and Amos, their lead singer, belted out a version of "Bourbon Street Parade" and then played his harmonica on another number. Judie Kate decided to try and make the best of the situation. She asked Drake about school.

He had just graduated from UNC-Chapel Hill, studying biology and preparing for a career in medicine like his dad. He had been in three consecutive summer internships at leading hospitals. He was on the school lacrosse team, which won the Atlantic Coast Conference championship, but they lost the national championship by one goal. He was a member of a fraternity, and he would be traveling to their annual meeting later in June before he began his medical studies at Duke University in July. He had just arrived back from Cancun for his graduation trip where he and his buddies, in his words, "stayed drunk most of the time and met a lot of women."

Drake did not inquire about Judie Kate at all, but he did stare at three teenage girls in very short skirts sitting with their parents across the room. George and Ellie kept up a long conversation with Lane and Brooklyn while eating their dinner. Judie Kate was miserable, and she poked around her salad. She looked up at Joe, who was staring at the band, obviously hearing something, focused entirely on the gig.

"I've lost him," she sighed to herself.

***

Joe saw Darren come in the restaurant and head for George and Ellie's table. He knew why he was here. Darren ran the festival like a well-oiled machine and constantly checked the stages and other venues for quality and to see how things were going overall. Some might say it was over-the-shoulder micro-management, but there was another side of him that many did not see, a side that truly cared about the craft of music, the traditions, the quality, the very soul of the music, along with the joys and appreciation of the crowds, not to mention the tourist dollars that came with the festival. There was a year's worth of work that boiled down to three days of nonstop entertainment. Everything had to be right. If it wasn't, then you didn't come back next year. Neither did the tourists. The Ocracoke economy was at stake.

Darren made the rounds, talking with George and Ellie, then Lane and Brooklyn. Lastly, he briefly conversed with Drake and Judie Kate. The band finished the final song in the first set and then took their break. He walked up to the sound table as Joe was talking to Amos about a squeal at the beginning of the set that maybe came from the harmonica mic, and then he talked with Reynold about the upright bass. The band was satisfied, so he walked back to the sound table.

"Good sound out here, Joe," Darren exclaimed. He looked back at the crowd. "Wish they would talk less and enjoy the music more. Thought folks might hear the band and be polite. What was I thinking? Things going well?"

Joe nodded yes and then gave him a breakdown of the first set. He told him about the squeal. "Yeah, I didn't have room for the big set up, so I just have my power head, and it has minimal EQ. If I had the big stuff, I could EQ it out."

Darren nodded his approval. "Yeah, no room up here for sure. Smart move, but it does limit the control over the sound."

Joe was not sure if that was an observation or a critique.

Darren turned to walk away and noticed Drake and Judie Kate. He turned back to Joe.

"Things not going well?" He nodded to the couple.

"George and Ellie don't approve of us, but with the rapist, sheriff said somebody has to be with her all the time. I'm busy, so they set her up with him," Joe said.

Darren paused and thought a moment. He was about to become Father Darren. "Well, Joe, to be honest, if she were my daughter, I would feel the same way. There is a big age difference between you two." Darren paused again and then a smirk came across his face. "Plus, you're a sound man. Who wants their daughter to marry a sound man?"

Joe smiled, but deep inside, it hurt. He watched Judie Kate feign interest in Drake while sneaking peeks at him.

Darren continued. "I hear Drake's a good kid, although I don't know him personally. Pre-med if I understand correctly. His family is a major donor to the festival. They sponsored two bands this year and put up performers in their house as well. Lane is a doctor, and when he is down here, he volunteers his time so the nurse practitioner at the clinic can have some time off. Good folks."

Joe disagreed. "I guess that's good for Judie Kate, but there is something about that kid that I don't like."

"Hmm, a little jealous, perhaps?"

"No," Joe shot back, "if she wants him, then fine. But I get a bad vibe just from looking at him. There's more to him than what we are seeing."

Darren had other things to do, and arguing the fine points of a kid he really didn't know and did not care about was not one of them.

"Gotta go."

Joe turned around and took a sip of his tea and sat down.

"Hi there," came a vaguely familiar voice. Joe looked up with a slightly puzzled face.

"Remember me? Yesterday, the bookstore?" She was more attractive than yesterday, wearing frayed tight jeans that were maybe a bit much for someone her age, as if she were trying to be twenty again. But they did the trick. They got his attention with tanned legs peeking through the holes. Her yellow blouse was unbuttoned enough to deserve a second and even third look, which he did not disguise very well. She had on more makeup than yesterday, but her perfume was the same. Her eyes were filled with a gleam of hope, and her smile was filled with genuine warmth. Given the dynamics of the evening, she was suddenly very attractive. And she was his age for goodness sake.

"I'm with my girlfriends tonight." She pointed to the side of the restaurant where three other women, drinks in hand, were now laughing out loud. They paused as she waved to them and all smiled their approval and raised a silent toast as she continued her conversation.

"So, I'm Pamela." She gave Joe the once-over one more time. *Is he always this disheveled?* He seemed like a kid in adult's clothes. His hair was a mess, his green Ocrafolk shirt wrinkled from the back and forth of moving equipment, sweat, and then air conditioning. *Surely, those aren't the same shorts he wore yesterday?* But, there was something oddly endearing about him nonetheless, kind of like Pig Pen in a Charlie Brown TV show.

Joe was caught off guard but politely responded. "Joe," he said, sticking out his hand. At the same time, he noticed Judie Kate staring at him with an alarmed face. Her eyes flared as she watched them talk. His heart sank and he felt disloyal to her, but what could he do? George and Ellie had made it plain that Judie Kate was off limits. They set up the date. It also seemed that she was reluctantly resolved to the situation. He looked at her again. Or was she? Now, there was flame in her eyes, and it was setting Pamela on fire.

"Come over and join us," Pamela said with a nod toward the group.

Joe paused, thought about it for a moment, and then decided what the heck. "Sure. I've got a few minutes before the second set." He walked behind Pamela to the table where the ladies were giggling away. Her middle-age body filled out her jeans very well. Too well.

When they saw Pamela with Joe, they gave her a sly smile and nodded very slightly in a "good catch" kind of way.

Pamela introduced him to her friends. "Joe, this is Carmen," she said, pointing to a woman with thick, brown hair and large, dark eyes and a somewhat rounded face.

"Hi, Joe," she nodded.

Joe smiled back, not quite getting a "hi" out of his very dry mouth. "This is Mysty, Joe," Pamela said.

Mysty was a thin, petite blonde with big coils of hair that flowed down her body and a dark tan complimented by long fingernails. "Hi," she said coyly.

Joe nodded, rendered speechless by her sexy hair and tropical tan. *Wow!*

"And, last because she is indeed least—" Pamela said.

"Really, you set me up like that?" the woman answered, shaking her head to move her curly raven hair out of her piercing blue eyes. "Ignore her. I'm Lynda." She stood up, intentionally revealing a tall and lithe body seductively wrapped in skinny jeans and a clingy, white cami. Joe immediately thought of the word "vamp." Something about her reminded him of Cher.

Pamela laughed and pulled a seat over for Joe to sit in. "So, Joe, having fun tonight?"

Joe was very clearly uncomfortable, but he was trying to overcome his shyness and general fear of small groups, not to mention very attractive women.

"Always fun when doing sound," he answered awkwardly. "When it is going well, you just sit back and listen to good music. Does it sound okay over here?"

The four women nodded. They all wanted to know about Joe, where he was from, how he got into sound, where he was staying. Joe was not used to such attention. Band members got the attention; sound men were ignored. Now, it was like he was a celebrity. Eventually, they got to the real question.

"Are you single?" Carmen pointedly asked, leaning forward, elbows on the table, pushing her breasts up even more dangerously into view.

It caught him off guard, and he immediately retreated to his safe zone. He noticed that the band was back, and he pointed to them.

"Well, uh, duty calls. Nice to meet all of you." He nodded and walked back to the stage and talked briefly with the band before sitting back down. He looked out in the crowd, but Judie Kate and Drake were gone. George, Ellie, Lane, and Brooklyn were heading out the door.

* * *

Judie Kate climbed into Drake's Land Rover. She had never seen such a finely appointed vehicle. Drake bragged about it as they headed to the house.

"Graduation gift. Cum laude," he said.

His demeanor changed inside the vehicle. He reached over and more aggressively than invitingly rubbed her leg as they turned off Irvin Garrish Road.

She placed his hand back on his side of the vehicle. "Not on first dates," she advised.

Then it hit her. She had seen this vehicle before. Yesterday, while shopping with her mother. That greasy-haired guy cruising by who picked up the two women in bikinis. She knew there was something she didn't like about him. *What does he see in me? I'm clearly not his type.* Now she was worried about the apparent incongruity. *I don't like this.* She moved over to the right as far as she could.

"Let's drive around a bit," Drake suggested, turning left down Irvin Garrish Road. "I'm still getting used to this beauty," he bragged, patting the dashboard.

Lots of tourists were clogging the road and quite a few caught Drake's attention. He smiled and pointed at the pretty ladies and dared the men to try to cross in front of him. It was as if Judie Kate was not even in the vehicle with him. He turned right on British Cemetery Road and then right again on Back Road, once more dodging the walkers, cyclists, and golf carts, staring at the girls and nearly running over anyone else in his way.

Judie Kate was disgusted. "Drake, can we just go to your parent's house?"

They arrived at a large house on the backside of the island. It was a three-story structure on stilts right by a canal with expensive boats lined up in it. Decks circled the whole building, and steps zigzagged up the sides. Drake pulled up, got out, and walked up the driveway, leaving Judie Kate behind. She dutifully followed him, shaking her head, climbing the stairs to the third-story deck where their parents and two other people were already standing around inside, drinks in hand. Judie Kate was not comfortable. In her mind, she knew she was there for only one reason: to keep her from Joe.

Brooklyn and Lane met her at the door with welcoming smiles.

"Come in, Judie Kate. We're glad you decided to come by," Brooklyn said cordially, ushering her into the large kitchen. *Like I had any other choice?* "Can we get you anything to drink? Beer? Wine? Mixed drink?" Brooklyn led her to the bar, where a variety of bottles and mixers were ready for a crowd.

"I'm not really a drink kind of gal," Judie Kate responded. "Do you have some water?"

Lane retrieved a bottle from the fridge and brought it to her. "So, Judie Kate, let me introduce you to these two folks."

They walked over and stood before a middle-aged woman, plain yet strong in stature, depth to her green eyes, wisdom and experience emanating from her, who reached out her hand.

"Hi, I'm Susan Avery, the woman said. "This is my husband Carl." He was strong in build, skin weathered.

Lane continued the conversation. "Susan is our nurse practitioner on the island. I give her a break when I'm down here. Bill is sort of a jack-of-all-trades. Carpenter, electrician, web builder."

Gonna be a long night. She reached out her hand. "Hi, I'm Judie Kate."

* * *

Drew, Tyler, and Miller walked around with a very awkward Zach in tow. That afternoon, after he had finished his ministry of busking, they took him to several stores to find him some shorts. He was clearly uncomfortable with the three ladies helping him find and try on various shorts. He wanted something plain, but they insisted on more fashionable attire.

"You need to make a statement for Christ, not for boring," Drew advised. Tyler had a better fashion sense than the others, so she picked out several pairs and held them up to his body, making him very nervous with a woman's hands on him. Miller gave her opinion after Tyler found some that Zach liked, hoping all along he would wear them for her. After three stops, he had found two pairs he could afford. Then, they rushed back to his hotel, where they insisted Zach put on one new pair before they went out again. Zach thought they meant they were coming up to his room, but they knew better, so they stayed in the lobby while he changed.

While he was away, Drew gave Miller a hard time.

"Well, you keep opening the door, but I think you're gonna have to push him through," Drew said.

"I know, right?" Miller answered, looking away from her phone for a moment. "I don't get it. Maybe he's just not interested in girls."

Drew leaned back a bit on the couch. "Oh, he's interested. He looks around quite a bit. I don't think he has been around this many ladies in his life. He seems to be overwhelmed. Too many temptations for him to choose from."

"I think temptations is a good word," Tyler answered. "It's like he's scared of us."

"Scared of God," Drew corrected.

"What do you mean?" Miller asked, suddenly worried and curious at the same time.

Drew leaned forward to give her ministerial opinion as Tyler faced her more and Miller crossed her long legs.

"He's a fundamentalist, a very strict form of Christian. He takes the Bible very literally, more so than we do. He has some very narrow understandings of what the Bible says. Just from what I've picked up on, he thinks that women lead men astray, that they are to be feared and, therefore, dominated by men. You saw how he reacted when we began giving him some advice about what to wear. Then, when Tyler held those shorts up to him, it was like he was naked and ashamed. But at the same time, he looks at women with interest, maybe too much interest. It's like he does not know what to do with us. And put all that together, here we are with our hands all over him and telling him what to do ... he's getting the very attention he wants deep inside, but he's convinced it will send him to Hell. So, he's afraid of punishment, and that means he is afraid of God."

Miller and Tyler nodded. Miller looked at her phone again and hurriedly typed a response to a text. Tyler looked around the lobby as the clerk came back to the desk.

"Can I help you all?" the clerk said.

Tyler answered that they were waiting on a friend. She looked around some more. "Never been in here, but heard a lot of stories about this place. Is it true that a ghost lives here?"

The clerk straightened up some items on the desk. "Yes, rooms 23 or 24, depending on what mood she's in." He laughed, but Tyler was a bit spooked.

"Seriously, for real?" Tyler asked.

"So, like, she is an old woman, you know, Mrs. Clampton, and she, like, visits here, right?" He talked with his hands, like he was doing sign language, and his inflection was always up. "She likes to move things around on the dressers and stuff. Sometimes, she hides them, sometimes, she, like, takes them away. Had an instance Wednesday night. The guy in 24 lost his knife."

Zach came back down the steps, and the clerk nodded toward him.

"Dude, you ever find that knife?" the clerk said.

Zach shook his head no. "Bought a new one."

Miller shot up off the couch.

"Zach, look at you. Nice shorts. Where'd you get those?" she teased. Zach was perplexed, not understanding the humor.

Tyler caught on. "Zach, that was a joke. Loosen up."

Drew shot a look over to Tyler as if to say "Careful, you'll spook him," but Miller was back in action again, standing beside him, pulling her phone out for a selfie, more to keep than to send. Tyler showed her approval, Drew nodded her head, and Miller selfie snapped and tried not to swoon too much.

Other than his white legs, he now looked like a real tourist at the beach. Miller had lived on the island for ten years and had seen all kinds of tanned legs: muscular, skinny, long, short, hairy, and smooth. But Zach's legs made her go "oooh" deep inside. And the way the new shorts hugged his bottom sealed the deal. Darren was right. She definitely had a thing for Zach.

The group left the hotel and walked around. They stopped at all the tourist souvenir shops and acted like they had never seen the trinkets before as Zach saw them for the first time. Blackbeard mugs and shot glasses, pirate flags, seashell crafts, post cards with beach scenes and bikini-clad women, beach towels with all kinds of prints, sunglasses, beach games, Confederate flags, and the ubiquitous saltwater taffy. Then they went to the Ice Cream Shack and waited in line, watching tourists walk by.

Zach was amazed and mesmerized by the pretty women, the different kinds of men, the smorgasbord of kids, the constant noise, the crowds in general, like a child's first time at the circus. He was intimidated by it all. He was shy by nature, hesitant except when around close friends, and so he kept to himself while the girls tried their best to get him to come out of his shell. He could handle playing music in front of small crowds, but being *in* a crowd was another thing altogether. Socially awkward was something quite fine with him. And it kept him away from temptations, one of which was becoming more and more apparent.

Tyler was curious. "Zach, do you like contemporary Christian music?"

Zach took a respite from staring at the women going by. "I play it, but not really," he answered, as if the conversation was done.

"Why not?" Miller asked, anything to get him to look her way.

Suddenly, Zach perked up. Nobody was pointing fingers at him, no one was making fun of him. No one was trying to make him feel guilty. Instead, someone wanted his opinion on something. *Somebody cares.*

"My parents listened to that stuff all the time. It was either gospel or K Love on the radio. It seemed okay at the time, but when I got into mountain music, when I found the spirituals, I suddenly realized there was no depth to it at all." He paused to eat some more ice cream, licking up the drips on the side of the cone.

Miller, fixated on his licking the ice cream, was filled with infatuation, Tyler was quite interested in where this was going, and Drew was just enjoying watching the whole show.

Zach continued. "Then, I stumbled into rock and roll and even old country. I know, it's the Devil's music and all, but at least it has some guts to it. When Christians try to do their music, it just comes out soft. I know, I know, rock and roll talks about life, most of it about sex and parties, but it drives, it has a beat, the licks are strong and creative, *it's alive*. But all Christian music does is sing about Jesus, praising Jesus, singing 'Alleluia' a hundred times, or inserting 'Amazing Grace' into every third lyric. It's like they all sit round heaven and just stare at Jesus and sing. There's no originality in it, no creativity, *no life*. Can't we do better for God?" He licked his cone again and stared as two temptations with dufus boyfriends walked by.

Miller was frustrated because he would look at them but not at her. *Maybe I need some frayed short shorts and a tan.*

"Boy," Tyler shot back. "Heaven's gonna be a bit disappointing for you, huh?"

Zach came back to the conversation and suddenly became very direct. "But, Tyler, we live here on earth. Why can't Christian music sing about earth? Why doesn't somebody write a song about Joshua and Jericho, like the spiritual? Drums and cymbals and a heavy bass beat to make the walls come down? What about Elijah, fighting the prophets of Baal on Mount Carmel? Guitar licks and pedal effects for the lightning bolts consuming the sacrifices! What about Isaiah's vision? Dreamy special effects, flutes, background voices? What about Sarah laughing about being pregnant at an old age? Taylor Swift could write that one! Find me a Christian song about a boyfriend and

\$1000 Walmart gift cards or 1 of 750 \$100 Walmart gift cards.

Díganos acerca de su visita a Walmart hoy y usted podría ganar una de las 5 tarjetas de regalo de Walmart de \$1000 o una de las 750 tarjetas de regalo de Walmart de \$100.

http://www.survey.walmart.com

No purchase necessary. Must be 18 or older and a legal resident of the 50 US, DC, or PR to enter. To enter without purchase and for official rules, visit www.entry.survey.walmart.com.

Sweepstakes period ends on the date outlined in the official rules. Survey must be taken within ONE week of today. Void where prohibited.

THANK YOU

How was your experience?

Tell us about your visit today and you could win 1 of 5 \$1000 Walmart gift cards or 1 of 750 \$100 Walmart gift cards.

Díganos acerca de su visita a Walmart hoy y usted podría ganar una de las 5 tarjetas de regalo de Walmart de \$1000 o una de las 750 tarjetas de regalo de Walmart de \$100.

http://www.survey.walmart.com

No purchase necessary. Must be 18 or older and a

Walmart ⚡

Save money. Live better.

336-226-1819 Mgr:TBD
530 S GRAHAM HOPEDALE RD
BURLINGTON NC 27217
ST# 03612 OP# 001572 TE# 54 TR# 02402
RX# XXX2787   D38 QTY 1H   59.10 0
                    PAI
                SUBTOTAL   59.10
                   TOTAL   59.10
      FSA/HRA MCARD TEND   59.10
ACCOUNT #   **** **** **** 8467 S
APPROVAL # 054051
REF # 1042000314
          11/25/20   16:40:48
              CHANGE DUE   0.00
          # ITEMS SOLD 1
FSA/HRA items are indicated with a
"H" to the right of the UPC.
FSA/HRA DETAILS:
TOTAL RX   59.10
TOTAL NON-RX FSA/HRA   0.00
TOTAL QUALIFIED FSA/HRA   59.10
     TC# 1293 1235 3191 2200 5347

|| || ||| | ||| || | ||| ||| | || |||| |

Save time with Express lanes
When you use the Walmart app!
      11/25/20   16:40:49
       CUSTOMER COPY

moved beyond the loss of life and into the gain of life again. He had found the key that unlocked the door of darkness, letting in light that illuminated his dark life again. Judie Kate made him feel alive, walking off the ground, playing with the stars. It was like the energy at the beginning of a show, when the once-empty stage was now filled with musicians, and the air was vibrating with sounds, and the crowd was singing and swaying to the beat. Smiles were everywhere and applause reverberated while all was forgotten as a new memory was being created.

Joe threw the drink can hard to the back of the tent. Then he heard the applause of the crowd up the road at the Live Oak Stage. It was like salt being rubbed into a fresh wound. *Life is cruel.* He wondered what Pamela and her friends were up to.

*   *   *

As Joe sulked in self-pity, Judie Kate was still not quite sure what all the fuss was about. It was like something was going on that all were privy to except her. Brooklyn and Lane, George and Ellie, and Susan and Bill had retreated to the living room and were engrossed in stories of Ocracoke, past festivals, and their professions. Tired of water, she picked up a soda and walked around the kitchen, trying to stay away from everybody, especially Drake, who was an octopus, two arms like eight tentacles, pulling on her from every direction.

She saw the address of the house on a plastic-sheathed realtor paper stuck on the refrigerator and something hit her, an intuition. She pulled out her phone and began a text to Joe, including the address. Two hands grabbed her waist from behind.

"You've got some very nice curves there, Judie Kate. Very nice."

She turned around and found Drake's face coming toward hers, smelling the beer on his breath.

"Not on first dates, I said," she warned again, this time firmly taking his hands away from her body.

"Okay, I get it." He paused, a slight hint of contrition on his face. *They always say they don't want it.* "Anyway, it's too noisy in here. Want to go to the back of the house or out on the deck where it is quieter?"

It felt more like a command than a suggestion. Judie Kate weighed her options as Drake's arm pulled her against her will. Her radar went off as she looked down the hall. It was too dark, too narrow, too far away from everybody. The deck was a better option, but there was no one else out there. Something did not feel right.

"Actually, Drake, I need to go freshen up a bit. Where is the ladies' room?" she asked, putting on her best coy face.

Drake took the bait. "Right here on the left," he answered, taking her arm in a misleading act of chivalry and leading her to the door.

"I'll just be a minute," she noted, shutting and then locking the door.

She sat on the edge of the bath, took out her phone, and finished her text to Joe.

Where are you? She waited for a moment. *Come on, Joe, don't let me down. You have every right to be mad. Please answer!*

Joe's phone vibrated, and Joe took it out and stared at the screen. Judie Kate. *Great.* He was not sure he even cared now.

He placed the phone on the stage and muttered, "I need a beer." He sighed heavily while staring at the ground. The screen had gone blank, but the green light still flashed, as if pleading for his attention. He picked up the phone, swiped the face, clicked on the text button, and there was her message with an address. *This is odd,* he thought. He texted back.

You ok?

Can you come get me?

R U Safe?

Not sure. Hurry!

She flushed the toilet and hoped the hallway would be clear as she opened the door. Drake was standing there in her way. He would not let her pass.

"Come on, me and you, just a little summer fun." He grabbed her dress and lifted it up.

"Drake, for the last time, please. I said no." Judie Kate took his hands away from her body, but he shook them free and then grabbed her arms tightly, his hands strong from years of lacrosse, squeezing hard, pushing her against the wall, against the corner, himself into her. Her arm slammed into the doorframe.

"Come on, you know you want some of this." He yanked up her dress again and groped under it, his large Rolex watch scratching her thigh. His other arm pushed against her throat. Judie Kate was pinned.

"*Drake, I said no!*" Judie Kate screamed.

The guests stood motionless, stunned by what they heard.

"Aagghh!" a voice called out.

There was a pause, the loud and disturbing retort of flesh slapping flesh, then another blood curdling scream. Drake came running into the kitchen, doubled over, raced to the sink, grabbed the dish sprayer, and shot water into his face.

Drake's father ran over to him. "Son, are you all right?"

"That fat bitch kicked me in the nuts and shot me full of *Mace*!" Drake said. His father took over the sprayer as his mother came to his rescue with a dish towel.

"Honey, are you okay?" Ellie stood motionless, not knowing how to react. Susan and Bill, confused, walked over to the mayhem. Then Susan became worried. This sounded too familiar.

George trudged over to Drake. "What did you just call my daughter?" Lane stepped forward as Ellie scooted over to refrain her very agitated husband.

"George, let's see what is going on before tempers flare, okay?" Ellie said. George paused as his daughter came steaming down the hallway.

"You two need to teach your cum laude son that when a woman says no, she means no!" She headed to the door that opened to the deck.

"Judie Kate," Ellie called out, "where are you going?"

"Back to the house. Joe is waiting for me outside." She stepped out on the deck.

Ellie answered, "Judie Kate, it's not safe out there."

Judie Kate wheeled about in total fury. "*Safe?*" She paused to catch her breath, heaving in and out as the full import of what had occurred now began to hit her. Then she pointed around the room. "Like *this* was safe?"

It was then that Susan saw the red handprint on her face.

"Judie Kate, what did you do?" George asked.

"What did I do? What did *I* do?" she answered, now crying and shaking all over.

Susan ran over to Judie Kate and looked back at George.

"Look at her face!" Then she stared at Drake. "Did you hit her, Drake?"

Drake, regaining his composure, defended himself. "She fell in the bathroom. I was trying to be a gentleman."

Susan shot right back. "Did you think smacking her in the face was going to help her get up any faster?"

By this time, Judie Kate was storming down the steps.

George glared at Drake, grabbed his shirt collar, and got right in his face. "What did you do to my daughter?" he demanded. Lane intervened.

"Now, George, let's be calm about this until we get all the facts," he said, slowly realizing all the while what the facts were.

George clenched Drake's collar tighter and looked at his friend of many years. "Lane, I'm not feeling very calm right now."

* * *

Like an angry mom after the umpire at her son's ball game, Judie Kate approached Joe. He jumped out of his truck to see about her. She was crying, but her face was angry, and he could feel the earth shake with every footstep.

"Get back in there!" She climbed into the truck and slammed the door. "Take me to the house, *now!*" She was still shaking, trying to breathe, sobbing.

He backed out and headed for Back Road. The short ride home took forever. Finally, they arrived. Joe saw a driveway just up from theirs in front of a vacant house, so he parked the truck there. Judie Kate didn't wait for him. She got out, slammed the door, and plowed forward, hurrying to get away from everybody's stares and questions. Joe diligently followed behind her, trying to catch up.

When they got inside, Judie Kate pushed Killer out of the way with her foot, turned around and stared at Joe, and pointed to his bedroom. She was shaking so hard that her words warbled as they came out.

"You go in there and you ... take a long ... shower. When my parents get here ... " she said. She took a long breath, then began again. "Armageddon begins. I d-don't care what you hear. Don't come in here ... to save me, protect me ... defend me, nothing. I've had enough! Go!" She stared at Joe with a what-are-you-waiting-for face. "I ... don't ... mean tomorrow. N-n-now!"

Joe, confused, followed orders, still not clear about what had happened. He closed the door, grabbed his night clothes, went into the bathroom, and found Judie Kate's soap placed on his bath cloth. Turning on the shower, he jumped in when the water got hot, wondering if Judie Kate's Armageddon would bring an end to the world, his world, any world.

Still full of adrenaline yet shaking in shock, she pounded the floor back and forth, waiting for George and Ellie to get home. Her face was hurting now, and the marks on her arms were becoming more obvious. Shame and fear, violation and rage consumed her. She was crying and could not catch her breath. Killer sat to the side, just in case, still not sure what he had done or what he was supposed to do. Soon, she heard footsteps on the stairs, and then she saw her parents at the door. When the door opened, the Gates of Hell unleashed their fury.

"What were you thinking?" she screamed, tears streaming down her cheeks. "What in God's name were you two thinking?"

Ellie was caught off guard by her daughter's tirade; George, still seething at Drake, yet ever one to defuse a situation, looked puzzled and hurt. They had never experienced a hurricane, but the increasing gusts of their daughter were beginning to take their toll. Judie Kate beat a path around the room, circling the furniture. Finally, she collapsed on the couch and heaved in heavy sobs, holding herself in shame to keep anyone from seeing her. Ellie sat beside her and tried to hold her.

"Don't touch me!" Judie Kate screamed.

Ellie jumped back in shock, for once wanting to physically console her daughter but now feeling the sting of rejection. George stood in confusion, wanting to reach out to her, scared of her reaction, his feet locked in place.

After a few minutes, Judie Kate began to calm down. She rested her arms on her legs and saw the welts. George, standing back, saw her face and the marks on her neck and arms. He wished he had punched Drake in the face. Ellie, wanting to hold her hurting daughter, could only stare at the imprint on her cheek. She got up and found some tissues and handed a wad to Judie Kate.

"I don't know where to start," Judie Kate began quietly. She blew her nose and then wiped her face. "Was Drake supposed to be your answer to Joe? Was I supposed to be safe tonight, maybe in your sight all the time?" She paused to wipe her nose again. "Are we still on the clothes thing?" She threw her hands up in the air in disgust.

"Judie Kate?" Ellie asked, clearly upset about the attack and the questions. "We don't understand you anymore. This is not our little girl. This is not what we raised you to be—"

Judie Kate lifted her hand to stop her Momma's words. "All my life, I have tried to be what you two wanted me to be, tried to live up to your expectations. It made me fat and lonely. It led me to a job I hate.

It brought on debilitating insecurities. I have parents who don't have a clue, who have *never* had a clue, who I am. The only person who has ever understood me—and you two know this!—is right behind that door. For once in my life, I have an interest in a man who fills me with happiness and cares about me, and my parents don't want him in my life." She paused, teared up, and exclaimed, "*Why? Why?*" She rubbed her hands together as if trying to wash the whole night away and cried.

"It's hard to explain, Judie Kate," Ellie said, cautiously rubbing her back.

"Why must it be explained? Why can't you two just let it be? Maybe for once, trust me. Or do you still think this is just childhood infatuation? Or are you blaming Joe for leading your poor little girl astray? Thinking maybe he is just a horny old man looking for a hot young woman, no, excuse me, a defenseless little girl. Why do you think this is his fault? Why do you blame him? Maybe there is something greater working here. Maybe this is fate." Judie Kate looked up at Ellie. "Maybe I want to be a hot young woman! Did you ever think about it that way?"

She wiped the tears off her face. "I can't win! When I was fat and ugly, I was not approved; now that I am more secure with myself, I still don't get your approval. What does it take?" Again, she threw her hands up in the air in total confusion. Silence filled the room, and all they could hear was Joe's shower running.

George walked around, fidgeting, uncomfortable with the whole confrontation. It was worse than a band fight over a song.

"Daddy, I have a question for you. Why did you call me last week and tell me that Joe would be here and maybe I should come down to the festival? Why? If you don't want me to be with Joe, why did you tell me he was here?"

George was quiet, as usual.

"Exactly!" Judie Kate fumed. "Twenty-five years of not saying what's on your mind! It's never gonna change, is it?"

George, filled with emotions he could not express, felt like the Hoover Dam about to burst.

"Judie Kate," Ellie responded. "We just don't want you to make a decision that will be bad for you. We want what is best for you, that is all. We were just trying to help." Now Ellie teared up, torn between caring for her daughter, realizing that her plans had not worked, had even jeopardized her daughter's life, and trying to understand that it was time to let Judie Kate make her own way in life, no matter where it took her.

"We're just tired of seeing our little girl hurt, sad, and living a life that is going nowhere. And I'm sorry, Judie Kate, but we just don't feel Joe is going to help this situation. He's older than you, much older. He needs to move on with his life, find someone his age who knows about his needs at this point in his life. That is just how we feel. We really care, Judie Kate. We really do."

Judie Kate paused for a moment before speaking. "Momma, do you care enough to turn me loose and let me fly on my own?" She let the question sink in. "Let me change that. Do you *trust* me enough to turn me loose and let me fly on my own? With Joe?"

The silence was the answer.

"Just as I thought," she muttered, standing up, straightening her dress. "So, it's either Joe or your blessing. I get it now. Guess I have a decision to make." She went to her room and quietly shut the door. Killer scratched at the closed door; it opened enough for him to come in, and it closed again.

Ellie rose up and turned on George.

"Why didn't you say anything?" she hissed angrily. "Why didn't you tell her about the job? Are you ever going to learn and try to talk to her?"

George stood up and whispered back. "Because she just told us she is tired of us meddling in her life. If I had told her about the job, then she would have had more reasons to think we were meddling in her life. And, frankly, we are. Let's just let this ride a day and then see what happens. After tonight, that job is probably history anyway."

"But," Ellie retorted, "what do we do about Joe?"

George walked over to the sink and got a cup of water. "We let them be together tomorrow to keep Judie Kate safe. The show is over for Joe tomorrow night. I'll tell him he must be on the first ferry Sunday morning. End of story." George drank his water and set the cup down. "Now, I've got a long day tomorrow, so I'm going to bed."

* * *

Judie Kate sat on the edge of the bed, stared at herself in the mirror over the dresser, and sobbed away. Killer, strangely, stood stock still in front of the sliding glass door, growling in a low tone. She reached down and ruffled his fur and then ran her fingers through it again and again.

"I'm sorry, Killer, for pushing you out of the way. Right now, you are the only thing in my life that makes any sense." Killer wagged his tail and licked her fingers, then turned right back to the door and began growling again. She was too tired to wonder why.

After a while, she heard a tap on the bathroom door. The door slowly cracked open, and Joe's head cautiously appeared.

"Judie Kate, are you okay? Want to talk about this, whatever this is?"

Judie Kate shook her head no and began to cry again. "Joe, please understand, I just want to be alone. Nothing makes sense right now, nothing. I don't want to talk to you or anybody else. I just need to be alone. Please understand, Joe. Please, just leave me alone."

Rejected, hurt, and still confused, he quietly shut the door as she cried even more, knowing she had just pushed away the only person who ever seemed to really care for her. She cried, knowing Jay Jay's dream might be coming to an end. She cried because it seemed that it was the only thing she could do right without being the object of somebody's mistaken opinion, well-intended care, or dysfunctional, debased sexual pursuits.

After a while, she ran out of tears. She stood up and looked at herself again. Emotions crashed about in her mind. She looked at her black dress, recalled why she bought it, seeing Joe's smile when she modeled it for him. Then, she felt Drake's hands pushing into her, and she looked away from the mirror.

She so wanted to hold Joe again tonight, to feel his body next to her, to feel his hands caressing her, gently exploring her, the soft fabric slowly riding up and down her body. She wanted him to reach for mystery, to let their romance move a little deeper into the dark cave of love. But Drake's hands made her feel dirty, and then she felt shame and despised herself. She would never let any man touch her again!

She noticed the bruises, the abrasions. She took off her dress and saw the scratch on her thigh that had dried up, the tear in her panties. Again she felt dirty, as if Drake had covered her in shame. She wanted to wash it all off, remove the whole episode from her life, her memory. She took her bra off and went to the shower, turned the water on, and climbed inside. As the warm water cleansed her body, the tears came back.

Joe lay in bed and listened to Judie Kate wail in the shower. The crying tore into his soul. He wondered if, indeed, he was the problem here. Maybe George and Ellie were right. This was a bad idea. Judie Kate was doing fine with her life before this week. Seeing him just renewed old feelings that were misplaced then and were still misplaced now. Maybe it was time to end this and move on. That's what he would do. After the show, he would have a long talk with Judie Kate, try to help her see things differently.

The conclusion suddenly hit Joe hard as well, and tears came to his eyes. If this was Jay Jay's dream and he ended it, he also ended his life with Jay Jay. Good-bye to Jay Jay, good-bye to Judie Kate, *good-bye to hope*. All he could see ahead was a life of loneliness and despair. For two days, he felt renewed, alive, joyful, *in love again*. He sat up and looked at the mirror, at his reflection, but all he saw was a body of emptiness, and he sank back onto the bed.

He pulled back the covers and turned off the light and lay down. The light from the bathroom peeked out under the door. There was no more crying, just the shuffle of feet, the clink of a toothbrush, and then the light off. Everything was quiet now, just as from here on, everything in his life would be quiet too. Judie Kate brought him the singing of birds, spring breezes through green leaves, the soothing roar from a mountain waterfall, the warm crash of waves on a summer beach. Simon and Garfunkel's "The Sounds of Silence" came to mind. Silence is deafening when life is filled with nothing.

Having calmed down and begun to adjust to the new reality, Judie Kate opened the box, took out her diary, and plopped on the bed. Killer was still a canine sentinel at the door.

Friday, June 7, 2018

Today began with wonder and beauty and ended with pain and heartache. Joe and I walked on the beach, and we talked about us. We agreed to talk with Mom and Dad about our relationship. It was so nice to hold his hand, to feel his body next to mine, to kiss him on the beach!

But there is a rapist on the island, and he has posted a picture of me on his website along with other women. Momma found the site by accident. Now I am a target. I must have someone around me all the time. Trapped! Joe would be that someone, but Momma and Daddy disapprove of us, so they set me up with the son of some rich friends of theirs. He tried to rape me, but I fought him off. Glad I took that self-defense course. Glad Joe bought me that mace. Still, I'll carry that shame with me for the rest of my life.

When I got home, I let my parents have it! I've had enough of their manipulations and dreams for me. All to no avail. They want me to leave Joe. Now, I must decide.

Jay Jay, do dreams have to hurt to come true? Does everything have to fall apart before a dream can come true? When people say they always dreamed of being president, a star athlete, a great humanitarian, a beauty queen, did they have to go through this? Am I supposed to make my dream, your dream, come true?

Tonight, I hurt Joe's feelings. I told him to go away and leave me alone. Just when he wanted to take care of me, just when I needed him most, I turned him away. I would give up everything I have to take that back, to make him feel better. Is that what love is?

I just don't have any more fight in me.

Judie Kate

She put the diary down for a moment, looked away, looked down, and then back into the mirror. She saw something, a man's face. At first, she cringed. Was the stalker in her room? She fearfully looked around her. But the face became clearer. It was Don. He was talking to her. What was he saying? Then, his words became audible.

You are Judie Kate. You are Judie Kate. You are Judie Kate.

At first, it was a whisper, like Don was far away in the universe. But each time the words came, they were louder, clearer. Her spine tingled, goose bumps instantly arose on her arms, and she trembled all over. A strong burst of wind shook the trees outside.

She began to whisper, "I am Judie Kate." Again and again she said it, getting stronger, more confident, each time. Finally, she cried out, "I am Judie Kate, and I love Judie Kate! I will not get in my way of true love!"

Don's face disappeared. There was a period of silence. But again, her spine tingled, goose bumps rose on her hurting arms, and the wind rustled the leaves on the trees.

Take care of Boo Bird.

She grabbed her diary. She had forgotten about that part of the dream! She started writing again.

> I have a mission. In times past, I would just give up, give in, and only hurt myself more. Now, I realize that when I give up, it hurts others as well. No more! I will fight to the end to take care of Boo Bird because I am Judie Kate!
>
>   BTW: I Love Judie Kate!

She placed her diary on the dresser and curled up in the bed. Killer jumped up and briefly snuggled beside her. She ruffled his head and closed her eyes. *I just want this day to end. Tomorrow will be a new day!* Then, Killer jumped off the bed and stood by the door and growled again.

Joe woke up with a start. *What did I hear? Why is Killer barking?* He looked at the window, through the cracks in the blinds, and thought he saw a movement, a shadow on the deck outside of Judie Kate's room. *Are those footsteps?* He rushed through the bathroom doors and stood at the sliding glass door, pulling the drapes back. Nothing. But Killer was standing at the door, now growling quietly. Something was not right. Joe could feel it. Killer knew it too.

Judie Kate rolled over, a sleepy stupor clouding her senses, her vision.

"Joe? Is that you? Why are you standing there?" She instinctively pulled the covers up to her neck. "Was that Killer barking, or was I dreaming?"

"I thought I saw something on the deck." He pulled the drapes back a bit more and looked out over the deck and the driveway. Killer growled louder.

"Silly, it's the American flag. The wind blows it around. I was tricked by that, too, several times, but now I ignore it," she said.

Joe checked the lock on the door. It was unlocked. "Judie Kate, you need to keep this door locked, especially given what is going on now."

She was confused. "Joe, I checked it before we left for dinner and went out the other door. I don't know how it could have become unlocked." She sat up in the bed, covers falling back down into her lap, and rubbed her eyes.

"Did you see your Dad or Mom lock that back door?" Joe asked. "You know how people are on Ocracoke. Nobody locks their doors."

"No, and I didn't know that." She pulled the covers back up and held them against her body. "Oh my God, Joe, you don't think … "

"I don't think, I know. That creep was in here while you were away. He intentionally unlocked the door, hoping to get to you tonight. He was just outside. I bet Killer spooked him." He opened the door and stood on the deck, looking all around. Nothing. Killer ran out and raced down the steps, growling the whole time. He ran down the driveway and stopped at the road, barking. Joe saw nothing.

After a few minutes, Killer came back up the steps, went inside, and turned and stood at the door, facing out. Joe shut the door, double-checked the lock, and then sat on the bed.

Judie Kate grabbed him and held him close and started shaking. "Joe, Joe? What are we going to do? What *can* we do, Joe?" She shook even harder, scared, terrorized.

He went back into the kitchen area and locked the sliding door, returned to the bedroom, sat on the bed, and held her tight, squeezing away her fears.

"I know you said you didn't want me to bother you tonight, but, right now, I am not going anywhere. I'll sleep by the door."

Judie Kate was hurt by his gentlemanly virtue but recalled what she had said and then was oddly proud that Joe still honored her request even in this dangerous time. His willingness to sleep uncomfortably on the floor made him even more appealing to her, her knight in shining shorts and a T-shirt.

"Joe, I appreciate your honesty and integrity but please forgive me. Right now, I need you beside me more than ever. Please?" She made room for him in the bed, lifted the sheet to cover him. Joe sat on the bed but remembered his decision earlier. It was time to cut things off. Still, he knew Judie Kate was frightened. He pulled the sheet down and lay on top of it, facing the door instead of her.

"Judie Kate, I have a long day today. I need to get some rest."

His coldness stabbed her heart. "I understand," she whispered, feeling the tears coming again, knowing she caused this. She rolled over the other way, trying not to cry, but the pain of reality set in, and soon her body quivered. She pulled the sheet over her face as if it would hide her crying from Joe.

"Joe?" she asked, rolling over again. "I know you don't want to hold me right now and that I hurt you tonight, and I don't blame you, but please don't push me away. You're the only thing I have left. Tonight scared me, Joe, and then I had the fight with Momma and Daddy, and now the rapist was standing at my door. I can't take any more Joe; I just can't take any more." She cried while respecting the distance between her and Joe.

Joe turned over. "What exactly happened at the house tonight, Judie Kate?"

His question opened the lock on her emotional gate. Floods of anger, fear, shame, guilt, and insecurities that she had bottled up while dealing with Drake, his parents, and her parents poured out as she shook and cried, heaving with sobs and moans. With Joe, she could finally feel vulnerable and safe.

"He tried to rape me, Joe!" she whispered frantically. "He tried to rape me!"

Joe, now filled with manly rage, pulled the damsel close, and her tears soon drenched his shirt. He held her tightly until the quakes subsided into tremors and then into a calm that ended in sleep. He held her head in his hands, ran his fingers through her hair, and listened as she began to quietly snore. The sheet was still between them, and now Joe wished it weren't. Now that Judie Kate was asleep, he turned over to keep watch.

Killer stayed right by the door.

Saturday

*J*oe woke up, looked around, and lay in bed for a moment. Judie Kate's arm was around him, holding him tightly. Killer was curled up by the sliding glass door, facing out. The morning sun was just coming up, illuminating the island with a brand-new day. *Maybe I got three hours of sleep*. He walked to the bathroom and closed the door and took his shower.

Joe wanted to get out of the house before George woke up. The last thing he wanted was a confrontation today. He needed to be clear-headed and focused for the show. He would deal with George and Ellie tonight. Leaving early would put him at the stage an hour before he really needed to be there. Now what?

He fixed some coffee and munched on a Pop Tart and a few heated sausage balls while he prepared his cooler. *Sure would like a biscuit, but nothing is open this early.* As he quickly checked his student emails, Killer strolled into the kitchen. He opened the sliding door to the deck so Killer could take care of his morning business. While Killer was out, Joe found a can of cat food, opened it, and forked it into Killer's bowl. He heard Killer scratching on the door and let him in, and the scruffy blob of fur raced to his food bowl.

"Long night, huh, Killer?" He growled in agreement.

Joe brushed his teeth and grabbed his wallet. He stopped for a moment and then looked into Judie Kate's room. She was still asleep, holding a pillow like it was a baby. He quietly closed the door and then headed out to his truck.

* * *

Around the Workshop Stage, even at that early hour, all was a bustle with the excitement of the day. Joe finished setting up the stage and then took a breath. *Well, let's see if it all works.* He connected the CD player, inserted Steve Martin's *The Crow*, eased up the volume fader on channel sixteen. *Yes!* The hard part was done, and it was only quarter to seven.

Joe turned everything off, left the stage, and wandered up School Road, looking all around, killing time. Up at the Live Oak Stage, volunteers were wiping the dust, leaves, and dew out of the folding chairs, all three hundred of them. Bow String Bill directed two young boys to put a cooler full of bottles of complimentary water by the stage.

"The other two coolers go by the Howard Street Stage and the Workshop Stage at the Methodist Church. When you get done, I've got another job for you." They bobbled off together, each holding the handle of a huge and very heavy cooler.

The sound crew was waking up after getting in late that morning.

"Let's uncover the amps, turn them on, check for overall sound, then work on the stage area for an initial sound check," Rex told Bill. "Hopefully, putting that fan on them all night kept the condensation out."

Abner the Sound Dog dutifully followed the crew around. Bill headed up front while Rex inserted a CD into the player, punched channel twenty-four on, and then waited for the amps to kick in. Soon, there was bluegrass background music. Each main speaker was checked, then the two subwoofers, and then each monitor as well. Bill gave the thumbs up to Rex, who crushed out his cigarette and walked up to the stage.

Joe wandered over to Rex, and the two sound men talked shop for a while as early birds, looking for that just-right seat, milled around. Rex shook his head, then looked at Bill.

"Bill, I think we got some percussion today. Let's get an overhead condenser ready just in case."

Joe walked away, wandering about, dodging chairs, people, cables, golf carts, cars, and errant, sleepy-eyed children trying to follow in-shape parents. Abner followed him and then turned left to check on the Howard Street Stage.

At the Information Tent, volunteers prepared for the onslaught of visitors with questions, smart and not-so-smart. Along School Road and Howard Street, vendors set up canopies, putting shelves together, unloading their wares, checking their pay apps on their phones, and arranging everything in preparation for the crowds.

As the minutes ticked away, the electricity in the air rose like the humidity. The usual walkers, strollers, and lost people milled about, causing more congestion and confusion in the narrow road as the vendors emptied cars, trailers, and SUVs. The two volunteer boys came back from placing the coolers at the stages.

"Now what?" they asked Bow String Bill.

"We need to get the schedule for the musicians who need help getting to the stages. You guys can drive a Gator, right?"

Joe arrived back at the Workshop Stage and looked at the time on his phone: 7:45. At this point in the setup, George came in helpful. Joe needed to do a sound check for the mics. It was hard to do alone, but it could be done. He sat down on the stage and wiped the sweat off his forehead. *It's too early to be this hot.*

A familiar voice shouted out over the din of the morning.

Inspired by Don, rejuvenated by Jay Jay, trying her best to love herself, Judie Kate called out, "Hey, you ready for some breakfast?"

Joe looked up and saw a bright red body with legs carrying a white bag. Judie Kate moved toward him full of energy and with a big smile. He caught himself staring. Again. Then he saw the bruises. Her neck, her arms, her legs. He tried to hide his anger. It must have worked.

"You drooling over the food or over the woman bringing it to you?" Judie Kate beamed, hoping with all her might that today would be better than yesterday. *I am Judie Kate. I am Judie Kate.*

Joe started to speak and then caught himself, reminded of what he decided last night. Still, he couldn't help it.

"Would the proper answer be both?"

"You betcha!" she answered, putting the bag down on the table and then slipping off her backpack. "Ham and egg biscuits. You like?" Judie Kate asked, turning around for Joe to admire. "It's called an overall dress. They're all the rage this year."

Joe looked as she did her model imitation.

"Yep, red overalls with a short skirt and a white T-shirt," she said.

He looked at her shoes. "Really, red Converse! That is cool!"

They sat on two folding chairs at the sound table. Joe reached down and switched the amps on and then the board and finally the CD player. Then he turned up the volume on the amps. Breakfast was eaten with soft banjo music in the background, Tim O'Brien singing Steve Martin and Gary Scruggs' "Daddy Played the Banjo."

Judie Kate looked up and then out as if the music could be seen somewhere under the tent. "Hmm. Kinda nice." She listened some more.

Joe took a bite out of his biscuit as Judie Kate stood up and looked at the sound board.

"This looks complicated, Joe." She ran her fingers up and down the myriad of knobs.

Joe jumped at the chance to talk sound, even to a neophyte. "Well, yes, it looks complicated, but once you get the knack of it and get over the initial fear of all the controls, it is not that complicated."

"Show me, Joe," she asked, looking for any way to be close to him, to hear him, to just feel like he wanted her around.

Unknowingly, Joe took the bait.

He showed and explained to her the sound equipment, and Judie Kate nodded her head at first, but she soon tired from the complications of sound mixing and equipment. She sat back down and watched as Joe picked up his biscuit. She grabbed hers and both enjoyed the silence. Some early birds were marking their seats with festival programs.

"What time do you start?" an elderly man asked.

"Nine," Joe called out. "We have the folk song sing-along." The man nodded and then ambled off.

"Joe?" Judie Kate asked, swallowing. "Thank you for taking care of me last night. Who knows what would have happened if you had not come in my room." She crossed her legs, and Joe noticed that two buttons on the skirt were not buttoned at all. She noticed that he noticed. *I am Judie Kate. I am Judie Kate.*

"Well, Judie Kate, I think that Killer had a little part in that as well," he said.

She recrossed her legs once more, less for comfort, more to keep his attention.

"And, about last night. I didn't mean to hurt you. There were, just, well ... things did not go well last night. I was confused, hurt, embarrassed. I only meant—"

Joe abruptly interrupted. "Judie Kate, I understand, but I need you to do something for me today. I need to stay focused until about nine thirty tonight. So for my sake, can we talk about anything else but this today? I can't be distracted by this right now. Usually, your dad helps me here, but it looks like that ain't happening now. So, I am solo today. I promise you, we will talk about it after I finish tonight."

Judie Kate was hurt, but deep inside, she knew he was right. She wanted to make her promise to herself into actions today. But Joe had nixed that.

Take care of Boo Bird.

I am Judie Kate.

"I can help, Joe!" she responded with the excitement of a tail-wagging dog.

"Well, as it turns out, I need to do a sound check. You can certainly help with that."

"What is a sound check?" Judie Kate said.

"Go up on stage and stand in front of that mic," he said, pointing to one. "That one closest to us. Stand about six inches back from the mic and talk strongly, not loud, into the mic. I'll tell you what to do from there."

She tentatively stepped up onto the stage, looking anxious, not quite sure what to do next. While she was on stage, some people were milling about, and they looked at her. Suddenly, it was like stage fright overwhelmed her. Her face said "now what" as she looked over at Joe.

"Talk to me, Judie Kate," he said.

She rambled on, trying to act like an announcer at a ball game, describing the scene around her, in front of her. "And here in the third row, we have a nice-looking couple finding their seat."

Joe adjusted the volume until it sounded about right. Then he walked around the seating area, standing in various spots, listening as he encouraged Judie Kate to talk on. She gabbed about the weather, the tent, the chairs. He came back to the sound board, made an adjustment, and sat back down.

"Okay, Judie Kate, now speak into the instrument mic below the vocal mic." She did and Joe adjusted the volume as well. "Okay, next set of mics."

"Am I doing okay, Joe?" Judie Kate asked a bit sheepishly.

"Just fine, sound girl."

"Sound *woman*," she corrected. The couple laughed. She talked again as Joe made the adjustments.

"Instrument mic?" Judie Kate, gaining confidence, bent over and spoke into that one. On down the line she went until all the mics had been checked.

"Now what?" Judie Kate asked.

"Okay, stay right there. Now, we are going to check the monitors, which are the speakers in front of you. Those are what the performers listen to when they play. I want you to talk into the mics again, but this time, listen until you hear yourself clearly in the monitors. When you do, let me know."

She talked into the mic again, not real sure about this new assignment, as Joe brought up the monitor volume. "I can hear it Joe, but it's weak," she said. Joe turned the knob further. "Okay, I think that's good."

Joe adjusted the volume again. "Sound okay to you now?" She nodded. Joe said, "Okay, check the instrument mic just below the vocal mic." Judie Kate did so and then, one by one, she checked all the mics down the line.

Ever the teacher, Joe continued with the sound lesson.

"Now, we change bands every hour. If we're on time—and we rarely are on time—we have fifteen minutes for the band to unplug and exit and then for the next band to come on stage, tell me what they need, move around the mics and set their heights, plug in, tune up, and do the sound check. Everything that we just did, from EQ to checking the mics, is done in about five minutes." Joe paused. "The problem is, they all want to talk, meet the crowd, mingle. It is a workshop stage after all. The other band is waiting; we have to get them up there." Joe shook his head in anticipation of the impending mayhem.

Judie Kate looked at Joe in awe. "I didn't know it was so complicated. That's a lot of pressure, isn't it?"

"And that is why I need to stay focused for the rest of the day, Judie Kate."

She awkwardly stepped back down off the stage, unknowingly showing more leg than was comfortable in public, and came over to the table. "Now what?" she said.

Joe took his place at the sound board and patted the seat beside him. She sat down and looked over at him in wonder. He was in a different world now. He stared at the stage like a lover entranced. Joe was in the zone.

He turned the music back on and answered, "Now, we listen to the music and leave our cares behind." As he settled back, Abner came up and hopped into his lap.

Judie Kate was startled, jumped, and then laughed. "Where did he come from?"

Joe introduced her to Abner the Sound Dog. He told her about how he lived on the island, was everybody's pet and nobody's dog.

"Every year, he always helps with the sound. He's already checked on Rex up there at the Live Oak Stage, then he went to Howard Street to check on Darren. Now, he is here."

He broke off a piece of biscuit and gave it to Abner. "Best sound dog ever, right, Abner?" Abner barked and then put a paw on the sound board.

* * *

A still sleepy George ambled up to the Howard Street Stage as Darren finished plugging the mic cords into the snake.

"Running a bit late there?" Darren said.

"Long night," George answered. "Abner checked on you yet?"

Darren nodded, then George called out, "Ready for the sound check?"

Sound check completed, Darren walked back up to the stage and saw consternation written all over George's face. "Let me guess, Joe and Judie Kate?" Darren said.

"It got more complicated last night." George replied.

"Yeah, I saw Judie Kate with you and the Winstons. Looked like their son was there too. From what Joe told me, you guys were hoping to set those two up. How'd that go?"

"Drake assaulted Judie Kate. Sexual assault. In the bathroom of Lane's house," George said.

Darren reeled back, like he was dodging a bullet. "You're kidding? Drake? Mister pre-med Drake? Drake *Winston*?"

George related the whole incident in minute detail, pausing occasionally. Darren interrupted George midstory. "George, isn't that a felony? What happened?"

George continued. "She was really bruised. Susan was there. She figured it out first. It was all I could do to keep from punching that kid in the face."

"That must have really embarrassed Lane and Brooklyn. What did you and Ellie do, George?"

George looked down at the ground, scooted his shoes back and forth, rubbed his beard, and then shook his head. His lips quivered as he answered. "I'll tell you what we did. We let her down, Darren. We let her down."

They sat there awhile, Darren still in utter disbelief, George reliving the nightmare again.

"What happened after that?" Darren asked.

"Apparently, she had texted Joe somewhere in the fray, and he picked her up and took her home. Ellie and I said some things to Lane and Brooklyn. It got ugly. We rushed home, and when we got there, Judie Kate went ballistic. I have never seen her like that, ever. She chewed us up and spit us out." George paused a bit. "It hurt, Darren, it hurt a lot. For one, it was our daughter taking us on. Two, she was right. We meddled when we should have left things alone."

Darren remembered that Lane had sent him a text early that morning about having to leave for home for an emergency. He told that to George.

"Emergency my eye. They're trying to keep Drake out of jail."

"Is Judie Kate going to press charges?" Darren looked directly at George.

George looked back at Darren and paused as a young man, oblivious, walked right in front of them, stepping on the snake cable and the power cord. George and Darren both shook their heads. "We have not crossed that bridge yet."

* * *

Back at the Workshop Stage, Billy and Janie Sands arrived. Fans loved Billy's laid-back manner and his encyclopedic knowledge of folk songs and the stories behind them. He was a master of numerous instruments, and Janie was lugging quite a few of them toward the stage. She dropped them on the table by the stage and paused to catch her breath.

"You guys get all your things ready, and I'll get you set up," Joe said.

As he stooped down to rearrange cables on the ground, he saw two feet with turquoise nails and one silver toe ring in dainty sandals and then two tanned legs that rose into a white jean skirt with a front slit standing in front of him. He looked up to see Pamela wearing a soft turquoise blouse with her hair pulled back into a ponytail with a turquoise bow.

"Hey, stranger," she said. She took delight in his stare.

Joe caught himself. He was so in the zone that, at first, he did not recognize her. "Oh, hi, sorry, I was so busy I didn't … " He caught himself again staring. Joe, so enmeshed in Judie Kate, had not admitted to himself that Pamela was quite attractive. Now that Judie Kate was all but over, he paused for small talk. It was not to be.

An arm slipped into his as Judie Kate quickly but quietly walked up from behind.

"Hi, Joe, who is your friend here?" She remembered her from last night, how she had come up to the sound table and invited him over to her table with her friends. She saw the look in her eyes then, and she could feel it in Joe's body now.

Joe was caught off guard, stuck between two women, one he thought was behind a door he had shut and the other who was opening a door for him to walk through. Pam's green eyes, filled with darts, stared at Judie Kate. She saw the look in her eyes as well. *Is he one of those cradle robbers?* Then she saw the bruises. *What on earth?*

Joe remembered his manners. "Sorry, Pamela, this is Judie Kate, daughter of a good friend. Judie Kate, this is Pamela. We met at the bookstore on Thursday."

Judie Kate stuck out her hand, but she did not let loose of Joe's arm. She shook Pamela's hand strongly. "I remember you. You were at the restaurant last night."

Pamela was cordial but now wary, if for no other reason than the bruises. Judie Kate looked her over. She was what one would expect of a forty-ish trendy woman. Fit but not gaunt, tanned but not too much. Cute, quietly sexy, somewhat strong yet able to put on a needy face to get her a man. Professional but could do yard work if she had the right clothes for the task. Wine, cheese, and a nice magazine in the sunroom type. *Everything I'm not ...*

Joe tried to wriggle out of what was becoming a very embarrassing situation. "Pamela, you've heard about the rapist, right?" She nodded. "We've found out that he is targeting Judie Kate here. My friend is really busy with the show, and so he asked her to stay with me." He paused, not knowing if this was working or not. He wanted to pursue Pamela some more but realized the winds were not blowing his way. "It's, uh, complicated."

She could see that quite clearly. She saw the way Judie Kate looked at him, and she saw the faint glow of affection he still had for her as well. Friend or more than that? But she wondered about the sadness in his eyes as well. *More.*

Billy broke the tension. "Hey, Joe, I think it's time."

Joe woke up from the awkwardness, thankful he had an out. "Well, ladies, it's show time. Gotta go." And with that, he turned and took his seat at the sound board. *Let them duke it out.*

Judie Kate left Pamela to her thoughts and moved her chair closer and sat beside Joe. Pamela walked away, grabbed her program from her seat, and left for the Live Oak Stage. Joe watched her body, her hips, her legs, her hair, fade into a memory and tried not to wonder what might have been.

Judie Kate watched Joe as he stared at Pamela and saw the pain in his eyes. She realized she might have just shooed away the one hope Joe had for a happy life. For a moment, she felt sorry for him. She tried to smooth it over, but she only made it worse.

"She is very pretty, Joe."

He stared at the stage. "I'm sure that does not matter anymore now." He looked at his phone for the time and then back at Billy. A forced smile came across his face. "Showtime!"

The crowd of mostly older folks were suddenly back in the '60s and '70s. Vietnam, miniskirts, tie-die, drugs, civil rights. Billy and Janie led them through the stories and songs that got America through the angst. The set finished up with "This Land Is Your Land." The only thing missing was the smell of pot in the air.

Joe quickly got up and moved the mics around while the next act prepared for their set. Judie Kate watched as he shooed Billy and Janie off the stage as friends and fans clogged up the area, recalling yesteryear. A dapper young man in black slacks, tan shirt, and black vest walked up, followed by a cute young lady in a short, floral baby doll dress and cowgirl boots.

After a quick sound check, all was ready. The duo performed all originals, talking with the audience, answering questions, living out their dreams of being stars. When the set was over, both thanked Joe.

* * *

As Joe ran the stage by himself, Tyler and Miller searched all around for Zach. They stood in the back at the Live Oak Stage area, scouting for his head of thick black hair.

"He was supposed to meet us here," Tyler moaned. "Eleven o'clock. We agreed."

"Let's get some coffee," Miller said, turning around to cross the street. Tyler followed her friend, still scanning the masses for Zach.

Iced coffees in hand, they found a bench under the live oaks and watched the people go by, music from the Live Oak Stage wafting over the street, mixing with the weak sounds coming from the Howard Street Stage. Tyler was bent over, elbows on her knees, turning the coffee cup in her hands, looking more like a jock than a musician or the fantasy of every boy's dreams. She turned back and looked at Miller, who stared back at her with a question mark rising on her face.

"What?" Tyler asked. "Spill it."

Miller feigned spilling her coffee, grinned, and then sipped it instead, dodging the request, looking the other way.

"What's on your mind, Miller? I know that look."

Miller looked back, her eyes watering up slightly. "Why doesn't he like me?"

Tyler gazed out over the street and then swigged her brew. She waited a moment, collecting her thoughts. "Because he doesn't like himself."

"What do you mean?" Miller was very bright in school, having won an academic scholarship as well as an athletic one. But, sometimes, Tyler swore she had the brains of a post.

Filled with the Muse and the mystical whimsy of a gypsy, she could read people like a book. "He thinks if he can save the world, that will give him release from his own guilt. Deep down inside, he doesn't like himself, what he feels, what he thinks. The guilt he feels he tries to ignore. If he is so religious, so perfect, then it must be something else that is causing him to sin, to feel guilt. Rather than deal with that, he tries to get other people to get rid of their sins, which are really his sins. If he saves the world, he saves himself."

Tyler looked over at Miller whose raised eyebrows and twisted lips and blank look said "I don't get it" all over her pretty face. Tyler sipped her coffee while Miller computed her observations. Sometimes, it just took a while for it to sink in. After a long moment, there was liftoff.

"So, is that why he keeps staring at that other girl? Every time she's around, he's looking at her. I wish he would look at me," Miller said.

Miller was a natural beauty, the proverbial girl next door. Her cheeks were always rosy, her smile, accented by perfect rose-colored lips, was like the Mona Lisa, and her walk and quiet demeanor was full of grace. She looked like the soft, cuddly type. She was tall like a model, and her long, black hair, which she fiddled with constantly, was always brushed and often in some form of a ponytail or braids or had a bow in it. But the boys mistook her shyness for being a snob. And because she was a brainiac and tall, boys were intimidated.

When you first met her, the image of a giraffe appeared in your mind, and when she was not on the volleyball court, where her fierce coordination was dominant, she was gangly and had a goofy propensity for clumsiness. And she could be a great airhead, good for a laugh until she finally got it. Her favorite maxim was one she made up, sounding like Yogi Berra. "It doesn't make sense until it makes sense."

Tyler grabbed her hand and looked at her best friend. "He will. Soon."

They wandered over to the Howard Street Stage and scanned the faces there but, again, no luck. Miller asked Darren who said that Zach had just left. She turned away, disappointed.

"Where is he?" an exasperated and increasingly frustrated Miller asked, stomping her foot and causing some people on the back row to turn their heads. "Ugh! Men are *so* frustrating!"

Tyler tried to calm her down. When Miller was exasperated, she could turn thirteen.

"He's here somewhere. We'll find him."

"I'm texting him," Miller said, pulling her phone from her back pocket. *Where R U???*

Tyler pulled her back down the sandy path of Howard Street to the vendors. "If we don't find him soon, I'll miss the next set. That Appalachian guy is there, the one who plays the dulcimers and guitar. I need to see him." Miller had paused, staring at her phone as if Zach might answer if she just looked at it long enough.

"Would you come on?" Tyler said, yanking her back to life. Miller nearly tripped on her own feet and looked like she was accidently falling off a diving board into a pool. The flapping of her flops drew stares from everybody. "Today, Miller, today."

* * *

Joe finished up with Cane Ridge Express. The set went well, and the boys were happy with the sound. Their dad walked up and thanked Joe as the band packed up and tried to answer questions from a small crowd of young, doting girls. All had to be pushed away from the stage.

"Great job, thanks." Joe nodded, no time for chit chat as the next act showed up late. And he was hungry, and it was time for lunch. In times past, if George was not with him at the stage, Joe would call or text him. Within two hours, a paper plate with a sandwich, chips, pickle, and cookie would appear from the green room via George. Not this year. Joe explained the situation to Judie Kate as he ran through the sound check for the next group.

"I can go get some lunch. Where is the green room, Joe?"

Joe looked back at her. "A, the green room is one hundred feet from where your dad is and, B, you're not going anywhere without me or another man."

Judie Kate looked like a scolded puppy. "I'm sorry, Joe. I forgot."

He looked back at her, realizing that he had been too curt with her. "I'm sorry, too, Judie Kate. Didn't mean to snap." He adjusted channel five and nodded to the Latin guitar duo. Billy introduced the group as Joe grabbed his phone.

"Who you calling, Joe?" Judie Kate whispered as the guitarists broke into a flamenco number. "Grubhub?" She tried to smile.

George felt his phone vibrate and looked at it. Joe. "What does he want?" he muttered with consternation, unaware of the time. More out of habit than care, he swiped the screen and looked at the text.

So, here's the deal. We're hungry, and you know I can't leave the stage. So, you can bring us something or arrange for somebody to bring us something. Your call. This is about Judie Kate, your daughter, not me anymore!

George stuffed the phone in his pocket and thought it through.

Darren saw the confusion and frustration on his face. "What?" he asked while watching the stage.

George shook his head. "Joe's hungry, Judie Kate is hungry. Usually, I get him food, but there's a bit of an issue here. Joe can't leave the stage; Judie Kate can't come by herself. Joe says I'm supposed to fix this."

"Well, she *is* your daughter, you know?" Darren adjusted the midrange on channel seven, listened to the mix, and looked back at George. "Call Bow String Bill and get him to get one of his guys to pick up their lunch."

George nodded his head. "Hadn't thought of that."

Darren nodded. "That's why I am in charge." He grinned at his jibe, but George was not grinning at all as he dialed the number.

Thirty minutes later, a Gator pulled close to the sound trailer, and the volunteers carried two plates over to the sound table. Joe handed one plate to Judie Kate.

"Grubhub," he grinned at her. He placed his plate on the EQ case and reached down into his cooler for his Pepsis.

"I can't believe my dad's acting like this," Judie Kate said.

Suddenly, Joe was sad again. The bruise on her neck and the red patches on her arms angered him. He wanted to protect her, beat Drake into little pieces. But, he needed to call the whole thing off. A faint hum caught his attention, and he looked on stage, saw the guitarist frown, and quickly reached for the midrange on channel three. The hum immediately disappeared. Mostly, he just wanted the day, the weekend, to end. The show he looked forward to so much year after year was the worst of his life.

"Joe, you okay?" Judie Kate asked.

Joe didn't want to hurt her anymore, so he lied. "The roast beef is a bit tough."

She could see the lines on his face, and she wished she had never pushed him away.

The fourth act was a trio from the band that was playing '50s rockabilly at the Berkley Barn that evening. While Joe readied the stage, Judie Kate stood, yawned, and stretched. She was bored. *How does he do this all day long?* She picked up the festival program and flipped through the pages until she found the artisans listed. Then, she looked at the vendors nearby and wanted to peruse, shop, just talk to anybody about anything that wasn't music or sound-related. *Oh well.*

She turned and looked out over the crowd. Their smiles, laughter, their relaxed demeanors, enjoying their weekend away, lost in the sun, the sounds, the sights. Life and cares were left behind, and for a weekend, all was joy and contentment. The humidity was cranking up, so she grabbed her bottle of water and drank while she scanned the Workshop Stage area. Some folks were eating nachos, Thai food, or BBQ sandwiches at the picnic tables in the shade.

She picked up the program again, as if the contents might have suddenly changed, and flipped through it once more, pausing at the schedule in the back. Then, she tossed the program down and crossed her arms over her chest. *It's like I'm a dog on a chain.*

She thought about the rapist and how it was so unfair that she could not wander about and feel the freedom of life away from life. How she had to worry about whether her outfits, her body, her hair, whatever, were going to cause some misfit to pull her off into an alley.

As she looked into the crowd, she saw him, the Christian guy, and he was staring right at her. Then it hit her. What if *he* was the real stalker? What if the creepy tattoo man was just some sort of jerk, the kind that made off-color come-on lines at the bar? The kind who religiously bought the *Sports Illustrated Swimsuit Issue* or drove around college campuses, gawking at the girls tanning on the lawns. The kind who went to the malls and stared at fifteen-year-olds in tight leggings or short shorts. What if the sheriffs were chasing the wrong guy?

"Joe?" He paused as he tweaked the levels once more. "That Christian guy is in the back and he's staring at me. What if he is the rapist?"

Joe looked out into the crowd and spotted him. "Never thought about that."

Zach saw Joe looking at him and then quickly looked the other way, but moments later, as Joe concentrated on the stage, he was staring at Judie Kate again. Joe looked up, and spotting him once more, reached for his phone to snap a pic, but then two girls grabbed the guy and pulled him away before he could get the camera on. He didn't even get a good look at what kind of T-shirt he had on.

"If you see him staring again, we call the sheriff," Joe responded and then sat for the set.

After forty minutes, he waved at the trio and noted that they had time for one more song. He had to cut the set right at 2:45 because the Paper Hand Puppets would be coming by, drums a pounding, children in tow, smiling, laughing, screeching, and making a noise that would drown out the group. The trio finished their tune, and right on cue, the percussion started up. All under the tent, those standing by the artists' stations and folks walking by, stopped and turned and stared and smiled as the line of kids, grotesque puppets, and percussion instruments of all stripes, sounds, and pitches, marched in cacophonous cadence up School Road.

The Workshop Stage portion of the festival ended at 3:45 p.m. with local favorite Jordy Johns and friends finishing their set. His music was a throwback to the old days, '50s and rockabilly, '60s and folk songs, as well as coastal tunes. Joe had worked with him several times over the years. Set over, the band cleared out, and the small crowd went away. After a while, Billy and Janie came over to Joe.

"Well, another year," Billy said, looking tired, aged.

Joe nodded, worn out from the day's work, anticipating the storytelling at eight that evening. He wondered how many more years Billy had in him.

"Well," Joe paused. "I've got the storytelling tonight and then I'm done." Janie and Billy, fading fast, nodded, and then they finished packing up their hoard of instruments.

"Joe, we'll see you next year," Janie called out as they walked away.

"Judie Kate?" Joe called out, "I need to visit the boy's room." She dutifully followed him to the theater. What else could she do? They stole a Coke on the way back out and then Joe sat down and patted the stage for her to sit beside him.

"Joe, you look tired," Judie Kate said.

"I was tired before the show started today." He didn't mean for it to sound so curt, but at this point, he didn't care either.

"I'm sorry, Joe. I feel like this is all my fault."

"We'll talk about that later. Right now, I just need to sit and breathe for a bit." He took a swallow and looked around.

Up the road, they could hear Ditchville12 playing and the crowd clapping with the song and then applauding afterward. It was quite a contrast to their stage, which was now lonely, desolate, and quiet. Joe was pensive, almost philosophical.

"'The Load-Out,' Judie Kate." He sipped some more. "'The Load-Out.'"

"What Joe?" She was not following him yet. He could be cryptic, but this was worse.

"Jackson Browne's 'The Load-Out.' Remember the song? It's about after the show when the crowd is gone, and the venue is empty, and all is being packed up. The quiet after the show is a sound that very few people ever hear, and one they will never understand."

Joe took another sip and looked out over the empty chairs, programs on the ground, water bottles strewn here and there, one stray shirt on a chair, the sun blasting in from the left.

Judie Kate looked behind her, all the stands, cables, a few chairs, and nobody on the stage. What was once bustling with entertainers, emcees, strings tuning up, cables being plugged in, questions and problems being solved accompanied by the buzz of the crowd, *the whole energy of the stage*, was now just dead silence. "Wow, Joe, I never thought of that before. It's kind of sad, huh?"

"Now you get it." The crowd up the road roared again as the band finished a number.

Joe was feeling sorry for himself. He leaned over and started pulling cables out of the snake box.

"I once did a show, all day long, ten in the morning to about nine at night. Band after band. Not one of them thanked the sound man. Not one. The sound was great. Everybody, including the promoter, told me so. But not one band member said anything about the sound." He stood and walked over to the row of mic stands and disconnected the mic cables from the mics. "Judie Kate, can you wrap these cables up for me?" He showed her how to wrap one and then left her to finish the task.

Joe unplugged the power cords and then went to the main speakers and stood on tiptoe to unplug them. He looked back over his shoulder as he continued.

"Today, three different people asked me if I had seen their hat. Am I the lost-and-found department? One musician asked me if I had seen his cajon. How do you lose a cajon?" Judie Kate asked what that was, and Joe explained that it was a percussion instrument. As he walked away, he called back.

"One time, a man walked up and asked if I had an extra power cable. When I asked why, he said that his electric car was running low, and he needed to charge it up." Joe paused and shook his head while he wrapped the cables up. "No one ever says, 'Looks like you've been here all day. Have you had any lunch? Can I get you something?'" He walked over to the mic stands and showed Judie Kate how to break them down.

After a while, he sat down on the stage again and took a last sip from his Coke. "All the people love the band. Nobody loves the sound man." The crowd applauded as a popular tune was introduced. And Judie Kate suddenly understood what Joe was really talking about.

He stood up, held out his hand, and pulled her off the stage. "Let's go see your dad's band. I think you will see a different side of him there."

Judie Kate scowled and pulled back. "How in the world can you go see Dad? He's not exactly on my list of must-sees."

Joe did not answer. Instead, he pulled her along, and Judie Kate so wanted to be with him that she dutifully followed without hesitation. She wanted to hook her arm in his, squeeze his hand, sidle up close to him, hold him as tight as she could, maybe squeeze him back to life, but she was not sure where things stood. Instead, she walked beside him like the loyal wife or obedient daughter. When they arrived at the

Live Oak Stage area, Joe took her under the sound man's canopy.

"Rex, you doing okay?" Rex nodded, hands on the faders, Abner the Sound Dog in full control. "Abner, where were you when I needed to pack up, huh?" Abner blankly stared at Joe and then looked back at the stage. Joe paused for a moment. "Oh, sorry, this is Judie Kate, George's daughter." Rex nodded at her.

"Good to meet you. Your dad's really good on that mandolin."

While the two sound men talked shop, Judie Kate watched her dad on stage. He was dapper in his red shirt, black pants, smiling, fully caught up in the moment. She had never seen him perform, never wanted to see him perform, because she so resented his absence from her life every weekend. He took a mandolin break between lyrics, and she watched his fingers deftly move up and down the neck of the mandolin. She didn't know they could move that fast.

His body swayed back and forth to the beat, flowing fluidly with every note, like he was dancing in the clouds. He made the old wooden mandolin come alive. When his break was over, and Bow String Bill started his fiddle break, George stepped back from the mic and nodded to the crowd as they cheered his performance. A smile broke the intense focus on his face. On stage, he was a different person than the father she knew.

Ditchville12 played a medley of fiddle tunes next, and George and Bow String Bill traded licks as Kimber Lee and Darren kept the beat driving and hot.

"He's really good, Judie Kate," Rex said again. "Really good!"

After the medley, Darren gazed back at the sound tent and noticed Joe and Judie Kate. Then he introduced George again to the crowd.

"George, how about you play that new song you wrote, that waltz. What's the name of it?"

George meekly walked up to the main mic. "'If Only You Knew.'"

Darren continued the banter. "Sounds like it is for somebody special, there, George."

George leaned forward to the mic with a more serious face. "Yes, very special." Then George grinned a bit devilishly. "If only you knew, Darren."

The crowd caught the pun and laughed. Darren ran his hand through his hair and stepped back, and George counted it off. Soon, the band was in the middle of a lovely, romantic, and yet mournful instrumental. Whey they finished, the crowd, deeply moved by the emotions of the song, showed it's approval with a great round of applause. George bowed humbly and stepped back to his instrument mic.

Darren stepped forward again. "How about that, folks? Was it beautiful or what? Give another hand for Grammy Award-winning George Wilson." The crowd erupted once more and ever so subtly, imperceptibly, in a movement only a sound man could catch, he nodded at Joe.

Joe took Judie Kate's hand. "Time to get packed up. I have to be at the Community Center at seven to set up for the storytelling." He paused. "Rex, I guess

I'll see you tomorrow morning." He patted Abner on the head.

* * *

As they walked back down the now-desolate School Road, a puzzled Judie Kate looked over at Joe.

"Joe, why did you do that? With all the mess between us and him, why did you take me to see Dad play?"

"I needed you to see how much he loves music, the mandolin, the band, the crowd. And how much the band, the crowd, loves him."

Judie Kate couldn't have cared less. "So what?"

They walked a little farther, and then Joe paused as they arrived at the Workshop Stage, turned, and looked her directly in the eyes. It was a face she had never seen in all her years of knowing and interacting with him.

"Despite everything that has happened this weekend, your father loves you even more than that."

She was taken off guard, and her jaw dropped. She couldn't comprehend what Joe was saying.

"You're kidding me, right? What do I do to get him to show me that, Joe?" Her voice was filled with years of pain, frustration, and loneliness. And, indignation.

"Show some interest in his playing. Ask him about his mandolin. Ask him how he wrote his songs. Ask him *why* he wrote his songs. Ask him why he rides all night long to play for two hours and then rides back all night. Show some interest in his life."

"But I don't like his music, Joe. How can I do this when I don't like bluegrass? And, excuse me, but when will *he* show some interest in *my* life?"

Joe ignored her last question. "Did you know he plays other styles? Ask him to play some blues on the guitar. Ask him to play some blues on the mandolin. Ask him to play 'Sweet Home Alabama' on the mandolin. Ask him to finger pick that song by Orleans, 'Dance with Me,' on the guitar. Be his crowd, Judie Kate. Be his crowd."

Judie Kate suddenly stood stock still, incensed that Joe blamed her for the cold relationship between her and her father. "That's unfair to me, Joe. You're asking me to give into him. Why can't he be a father and give into me?"

Joe hesitated, choosing his words carefully. "Because he's a musician, Judie Kate," he answered as if pleading with her to understand, "and musicians have a very difficult time saying what's on their mind. That's why they play. They express their words, their thoughts, their feelings, through their music. It's the only language they can speak fluently. Ask a musician to say something. They stumble, they fumble, they rattle off showbiz speak that really amounts to nothing. But ask them to play and suddenly they make sense."

Judie Kate welled up with tears and hugged Joe tightly. "I just wish he would start the conversation, Joe, that's all."

Then Joe, unexpectedly, held her close, comforting her as she sobbed. When she settled down, he placed his hands on her shaking shoulders, and gently pushed her back so he could look her straight in the eyes.

"He just did, Judie Kate."

She looked up at him, tears in her eyes. "I don't understand, Joe."

"Judie Kate, why do you think you are here this week?"

She looked up at him with a puzzled expression. "Daddy called me last week and asked if I wanted to come to the festival. He said he had something he wanted me to hear. I just figured it was some of his bluegrass mess, and I wasn't going to come until he mentioned you were going to be here."

Joe saw the tears streaking down her face again and, overwhelmed with compassion, wiped them away with his thumb.

"Judie Kate, he wrote that song for you. He told me Thursday he had written a song for you and had invited you to come down. He asked me if I would bring you up to the stage during their performance this afternoon. He's starting the conversation, Judie Kate. Now it's your turn."

She looked down, up, over to the right, and back to Joe again. Her eyes showed hurt, then excitement, then loss. Her lips quivered, smiled, then drooped down in confusion. Hopeful and yet clueless, she pulled Joe close again and wept into his chest, soaking his stained, sweaty, and wrinkled shirt.

"I just don't know what to say, Joe," she said.

He instinctively hugged her even tighter, holding her close, like the old times when the lonely, obese, and insecure high school girl could not make sense of life, and then spoke into her ear. "How about, 'Daddy, would you play that song for me again?'"

When Joe finished packing the trailer and the truck, Judie Kate grabbed her backpack.

"Joe, I want to change for the storytelling. Have we got time for that?"

Joe grimaced inside. "Five minutes, Judie Kate."

* * *

They hurried to the theater, and she stepped inside the small bathroom and took off her dress and top. She looked at herself in the mirror, grabbed some paper towels, wetted them, and then wiped off her arms, face, and legs. Then, she pulled out her dress, put it on, fluffed up her hair, and smiled at what was reflected in the mirror. *Please, Jay Jay. Please!* Then, she repeated the mantra one more time. *I am Judie Kate, and I love Judie Kate.*

She stepped outside as Joe finished a conversation on the phone, facing the other way.

"We'll be there in five minutes." He turned around, and once again, time stood still. He saw a beautiful, if sheepish, woman in a lavender, floral, off-the-shoulder dress that stopped right at her knees. White, thong sandals finished the outfit that whispered dainty, delicate, demure. The dress was somewhat fitted at her waist, which allowed her curving body to perform its magic. In Joe's eyes, it was a bit much for the storytelling. Most in the audience would be very casually dressed, if that much.

She saw his face. She knew it was daring for her, and suddenly, she had doubts. "Too much, Joe?"

Overcome with the confusions of last night and the emotions and desires from the days before, Joe could not decide what to say.

"I could put back on my overall dress," she said.

But her shoulders, those magical soft shoulders, freed of fabric, called to him, and before he could catch himself, he answered, "Just beautiful, Judie Kate, just beautiful."

It took more than five minutes, and after they stopped to get their sandwiches, they were running a bit late. He and Judie Kate hauled in the equipment, working their way through the people who were lined up, waiting for the doors to open. The Historian was not helping. A small class of students was listening, rapt in attention, at the bottom of the ramp, now a makeshift auditorium.

Joe was impatient. "Excuse me, folks, but if I don't get in there, we don't have story time tonight."

A small split formed in the Red Sea of adepts, and he and Judie Kate proceeded inside. While Joe hooked everything up, Judie Kate sat at the side of the stage, munching her sub sandwich. Satisfied that all looked clean, organized, and professional, Joe clicked the power head on, turned up the controls, and asked Judie Kate to do the sound check.

As she took the stage, the crowd hushed. From the way she was dressed, they thought she was the hostess for the event. In the back, Ellie, sitting with George, scowled when she saw her daughter's dress.

Judie Kate saw her mother's disapproval, but she smiled anyway and spoke into the mic, now more comfortable and confident with her role as sound woman and informed everybody it was just a sound check. Joe gave her a thumbs up, and Judie Kate carefully, daintily, stepped off the stage and took her seat beside him and fluffed out her dress as politely as a debutante while he hurriedly and unprofessionally stuffed the last bite of his sub into his mouth like a hungry farm boy. *Five minutes to spare!*

An older woman on the front row scooted over to Judie Kate and whispered, "That's a beautiful dress!"

"Thank you, ma'am."

"Might that be the young man you are trying to catch with it?"

Judie Kate paused, suddenly aware of what her answer would mean for her, for Joe, for her Momma and Daddy. She breathed in—*Don't get in the way of true love*—and then admitted what she really wanted.

"Yes, ma'am."

Her weathered face with slightly misplaced makeup was full of joy and devilment at the same time, and her faded blue eyes still had a sparkle in them. She grinned wide and then patted Judie Kate on the leg.

"Show him some more of this." The woman grinned as her arthritic fingers with blue nail polish pulled her dress hem back a bit. "Good luck!"

She sat back in her seat and grabbed the wrinkled and mottled hand of her husband like they were still in high school. He smiled as if he owned the whole world and patted her hand. She winked at Judie Kate and mouthed out, "Fifty-three years."

Judie Kate pulled her dress up a bit, crossed her legs for dramatic effect, and patted Joe on the leg. It worked.

The Community Center was filled with expectant listeners. Inside, fragrances of several desserts, coffee, and an odd blend of cologne and aftershaves filled the cool air. There was a buzz, an electricity in the packed room. Two hundred people waited to hear the world-famous storyteller, Riley Do Tell.

Riley Do Tell was the stage name for Abner Stokes. He originally hailed from the western part of North Carolina, and after he retired from a lucrative insurance sales career, he bought a dream cottage on Ocracoke Island. He had told stories all his life, and slowly, he was in demand throughout the state, then in the South and, eventually, in various parts of the nation. Every year, he went to Europe, where he shared his stories about the everyday stupidities of southern American life. And every year, he told his stories and sold his books at the Ocrafolk Festival.

Andy Howard, a good storyteller himself, walked down the aisle and came over to Joe. "Everything set?"

Joe nodded and Andy took the stage. The crowd hushed in anticipation.

"Welcome, all, to the Community Center." Andy thanked the Ocracoke Alive volunteers who had prepared the desserts, thanked all who came and paid the price of admission. "We all know why we are here, right? Riley Do Tell is a world-famous storyteller, and he is going to share his wits and wisdom with us tonight. Be prepared to laugh your heads off and take away a memory. Ladies and gentlemen, Riley Do Tell!"

Riley slinked over to the steps, looking like a vine searching for something to climb and then took the stage. He had been talking with folks in the audience, and some just assumed he was a polite and talkative local. Little did they know, they were talking to the man himself.

"Thank you kindly, folks. You'll wish you hadn't wasted your time clapping so much after I'm done." Everyone laughed and settled back in their seats. Riley assumed his western North Carolina twang.

"Anyway, speaking of health care," Riley continued, "the other day, I got bit by a chicken."

Joe, caught up in the performance, elbowed Judie Kate. "This is funny. Heard it last year."

* * *

Zach's phone buzzed. It was Tyler.

"What?" he answered in a huff.

"You're an idiot!" Tyler shot back.

Zach looked at his phone in a somewhat stupefied manner. "What do you mean?"

"Miller. She's here crying. Why are you so mean to her?" Tyler said.

Zach was confused, so he explained himself. He was not mean. He felt he was doing what God wanted him to do. He was supposed to find the woman with the black hair and minister to her. That is what he did. He found Judie Kate on the beach. He was sure God had led him to her. How else would he keep running into her?

"You ever look at Miller's hair? It's dark, you idiot. Ever think that maybe you got the wrong gal?"

Zach paused and thought through the last few days.

The silence gave Tyler a moment to remember a Bible verse. "Saul, Saul, why do you kick against the goads?" When Zach did not respond, she immediately fired back. "Miller's been goading you for three days. And what do you do? You still keep following that other girl."

Zach could hear Miller crying in the background. He did not want to hurt her, but the ministry of God could be demanding. Sometimes, you had to bear a cross.

"God would never mislead me," Zach defiantly responded.

Tyler had had enough of Zach's self-righteousness. She shifted to language he might understand better.

"Satan misleads people, Zach, not God. You ever wonder why that girl has not responded to you? Satan, Zach, Satan. Why do you kick against the obvious goads? You need to end whatever this is. You ever think she is part of the devil's plan? End this stuff, Zach, end it. You're killing Miller!" Tyler hung up.

Zach sat on the edge of the bed. Could the girl be part of Satan's plan? Was he pursuing Satan? Was Miller the woman in the dream? If so, then was the other girl sent by Satan to thwart God's mission for Zach, for Miller?

Suddenly, a fear swept over him. Had he become part of the devil's lies? Was the other woman leading him astray? If God wanted him to be with Miller, then the other woman had to be part of a demonic plot to interfere with God's plan. He had been Satan's tool. And she was the one responsible! Satan lived in her! He stood up and headed out the door, down the stairs, and stopped at his car. He reached inside and grabbed his knife, the Sword of the Spirit.

"Time to slay a demon!" he hissed, heading down the dark highway.

* * *

After the storytelling, Joe and Judie Kate gathered all the sound equipment and headed back to the trailer at the Workshop Stage. They packed it up and locked the doors to the trailer, and then Joe sat on the stage. He breathed in while Judie Kate devotedly, perhaps dejectedly, sat next to him, waiting for whatever was next, worried about what would take place between them. In the darkness, he saw once again her shoulders and her dress. They lingered in his mind all night long.

It was eleven o'clock, and it had been a long day, and now she understood what Joe meant when he said he had to be focused. She didn't know just how much he had to do, how many problems he would have to solve, how many entertainers with a zillion quirks he would have to work with. Now, she understood the pressure of changing out one band after another, rushing from one event to another. She was tired and all she did was tag along.

"Wow, Joe, you must be exhausted. This has been a long day."

Joe looked out over the empty venue. "Actually, it is early. For the last couple years, I got in at two thirty on Sunday morning. This year's schedule was easy."

She wanted to touch him, feel him, but she was not sure where the line was anymore. *Did my dress have any effect at all?* Then it hit her. She needed to thank him for taking care of her throughout the day. Surely, that deserved a hug. She put her arm around him and pulled him close in a friendly way.

"Thanks for watching over me today. It meant a lot to me. I know it was difficult with everything else you had going on." She pulled him close again and then let him go, like a sister would her older brother.

He patted her on the leg, accidently causing her dress to ride up a bit. "You've been a good sound woman, Judie Kate."

The pat had no energy in it: it was just a perfunctory gesture. She was disappointed. *Maybe he's just tired.* They sat there in the silence, slowing down from the day, reluctant to talk, avoiding the next step in whatever was left of their peculiar relationship.

Joe stood and took Judie Kate's hand. "Well, guess we'd better head home and face the music."

She hesitated. "Joe, I know it's been a long day, and what lies ahead of us is not going to be pleasant, but before we do that, can we walk on the beach? We need to straighten things out between us before we face Momma and Daddy. Please?"

* * *

The beach was empty. The waves seemed agitated, as if there was a problem to be solved, tension in the air, disruptions in the soul. Judie Kate led him up the beach a ways.

"Sit," she commanded, as she plopped cross-legged in the sand across from him, her pretty dress now an afterthought. The stars shone to the east as the quarter moon sank toward the west with scattered clouds in between. A wind blew, at once chilly and then warm, indecisive about what to be, how to be it.

She stared at him, reached out, and took his hands. Her fingers were soft, warm, yet they were shaking.

"Are you cold?" he asked. He stared at her off-the-shoulder dress as her body started quivering, and then she began crying. He was not sure what to do. He had seen this before, years ago. When she talked about the bullying, about her parents, about the kids at church who made fun of her. About her weight, her wish to go to the prom, the three times he talked her out of leaving her parents.

Her body heaved as she let out deep frustrations, pains, desires, needs. He held her hands tighter, wanted to pull her close but refrained, not wanting to cross the line of his own doubts, his passions, his loss, his hopes, his decision to end the relationship. She felt he was oblivious to her line of hope, love. Why couldn't he see? But the problem was, he did see, and it was pushing him away.

Joe was tired and increasingly frustrated. "Judie Kate, after last night, when you pushed me away, I am not sure what you want anymore. Tell me what you want."

She released his hands and leaned back a bit. "I'm sorry, Joe. After Drake and the fight with my parents last night, I just gave up. I needed space. What I said came out all wrong. I know you're confused. I was too." She paused for a moment and gathered her wits. It was time to admit the obvious. "I get the feeling that, after today, this is over." She began weeping softly, head down, letting go of her true love.

"Judie Kate, when all this started, I first thought it was infatuation. You have always had this thing for me. I saw it when you were fourteen. I passed it off then as a teenage crush ... "

A surge of fire suddenly blew away her cold sadness. "I'm twenty-five now! Do you think this is a crush?"

Joe did not want to admit he knew the answer. "Do you think I don't want you? Do you know how hard it has been to refrain myself? Thursday, when we embraced under the house, and you placed my hands on you. I wanted you then. When you lay in the bed with me, I so wanted you. It's hard, Judie Kate, it is just hard to move into that realm. You have to see it from my side. How many people have called us father and daughter, grandfather and granddaughter? You've seen the looks from others. If I give in, then I will have to live with that all my life.

"Then there is the question of life itself. In twenty years, I will start becoming a burden to you. I am not sure I want to put you through that. My coldness is a way of saying I love you too much to put you through that. I would rather hurt you now than have you go through the best years of your life taking care of an old man."

She sobbed even louder, quaking all over. The winds picked up and clouds covered the moon.

"Then there are connections between you and Jay Jay. Nearly everything you do reminds me of her. It is like she was reincarnated into you."

"What is wrong with that?"

"Judie Kate, you have never been married. It is a pain you cannot know, a memory you do not have. A sense of loyalty that you have never endured for years, decades."

"I knew Don!" She fired back. "Don't tell me I don't know what loss is!

"For a few months, Judie Kate. I'm not downplaying your loss. I know it was devastating. I was there, remember? But I'm talking years. *Years*, Judie Kate." His mind fled to the past.

Judie Kate reached for his hands. Still, nothing came from him. Was he running from his feelings?

"Please talk to me!" she cried, sniffing, trying to get her breath. "Don't you dare clam up like my Daddy!"

The pause seemed eternal.

Still he fought it.

"Our age, being loyal to Jay Jay, your parents. What will people say?" Joe asked.

"I don't give a damn about that! Why do you let those things get in your way?"

Her words stung but slowly soaked in, steeping like tea leaves in a cup of hot water. He had never heard her curse with this much intensity before. She squeezed his hands tightly, feeling the pulses of the past surge up from three years of suppression.

He took a deep breath. It came to him now. He shifted his legs, one of them having fallen asleep, but never turned her hands loose.

"She used to say the same thing. All during our marriage, she said the same thing. I always let people dictate my life." He could hear Jay Jay when they dated, when they faced hardships, when times of laughter seemed appropriate, but he never gave in.

Judy Kate let the silence build, the quiet heal, the stillness transform. The waves came in, crashed, receded, regrouped, and resurged. The moon reappeared. She could see his face in the moonlight, the pain slowly turning to peace.

"When she was dying, she asked me to come near. I could barely hear her. She whispered to me, 'I am going now. I have loved you all these years, but it is time for me to go. I know sometimes I have disappointed you, but I have always loved you and always will. I will send someone to you, and you will know when she comes. She will be your dream come true.'"

"Can't you see, Joe? All the resemblances to her? Saying things that she said. I am that someone!"

He rehashed the arguments of the last three days. "How do I know that? You're so young. The few times I let myself dream about someone else, I expected someone older. My age." He thought of Pamela, and he could still see her walking away that morning.

"Are we back to that again?" She turned his hands loose. "Why can't you be *my* dream come true?"

The question caught him off guard. Could someone's dream come true be waiting for someone else's dream to come true? Could dreams be intertwined? Connected in a spiritual sense?

"I never thought of it that way." He looked back over the last four days. "You've never told me what your dream is. How can I help your dream come true if I don't know what it is? It's like you know something I don't."

Now it was Judie Kate's turn to reflect. Why hadn't she been right up front? *I've wanted you all my life.*

"I'm sorry, Joe. I guess that, for whatever reason, I thought you would just reach out to me if I opened the door. Sometimes, you are so like my Daddy. Just like years ago, when I called and asked for help, you always came. Now I am reaching out again, gaining confidence yet in need of reassurance. I want you to affirm what I feel, what I know. But I had not realized that in seven years, things had changed. I did not understand that walking through changes is difficult without knowing the paths. I have the dream of youth, but you know the map of experience." Judie Kate had calmed down. Things were becoming clearer.

"Remember when you said that Don would come back to me in a dream? Well, he did. He said, 'When the old becomes new, your dream will come true; she will tell you when your new dream begins.' I did not know what that meant, but three years ago, I had another dream. Remember? I told you about it

Thursday when we walked on the beach. Your wife came to me and said, 'Take care of Joe. He is yours now. You will have to change. When the numbers add up, then it is time.'"

Judie Kate paused to let Joe think about this again. Then she resumed.

"But I had questions. How could I take the place of your wife? Was it some kind of wishful thinking, that infatuation you were talking about? When Daddy and Momma finally told me about Jay Jay that weekend, I made a pact with myself. I would get in shape. I would remember all the things you told me: how to hold my head high, think positive thoughts, that I was someone special, but I had to believe in it myself. But the numbers had not yet added up."

The wind shifted to the south. The air was warmer now, the waves moved up the coast, not down.

Joe was backing up, fighting, resisting what he knew to be true. "How did you know it was my wife?"

Judie Kate described the woman in her dream for Joe.

"But you've met her, Judie Kate. That does not prove anything."

"She wore red overalls."

Red overalls. The first time he met Jay Jay she had worn red overalls. Even George did not know this. There was no way Judie Kate could have known.

"Red overalls, Joe! Why do you think I wore that outfit today? Think, Joe, *think*!" She shook his hands to make the point. He was so close to understanding.

"Don't you believe in dreams?" She shook his hands again, trying to wake him up to the connections in the visions. She could feel it; he was so close to finally knowing what she had known for three years.

A burst of warm air flew by. Judie Kate felt a tingle, felt taken back in time. Then, she took a dare. A last attempt. If this did not work, she would give up. If she truly believed in dreams, then this would confirm her convictions or deny them.

"You told me that, after Jay Jay died, the girl in your nightmares changed. The girl in your nightmare Wednesday night. Who did she look like?

"What?"

"*Who* did she look like?"

He paused. Judie Kate shook all over, waiting, hoping he would say the right thing. She was on the verge of getting up, running away, leaving it all behind for good. *Please, Jay Jay, please!*

"Oh my God." He looked far away, recalling all the nightmares. How they changed when Jay Jay died. For three years, it was a young girl who was being taken away from him. In black leggings and a white top. Now, he realized it. "You." He thought about it, now understanding why it had not made sense. "For three years now, Jay Jay has been turning into you. And, I was afraid that someone was going to take her away."

"See? Jay Jay put this whole thing together. She has been taking care of you, preparing me, all for this moment. The dreams, the numbers. Now does it make sense?"

It did, and yet it still didn't. He knew from his studies of religion, spirituality, dreams, that all of this made perfect sense in the greater purpose of life. But the skeptic in him was reluctant to admit there were Forces beyond our control or comprehension. To admit this would also mean he would have to believe in a power that was ultimately in control of life, but this would mean that this power permitted the abuses that haunted him still. That was the ultimate line. He could not go any further. He stood up.

"I'm sorry, Judie Kate. I just can't." He began to walk off. His abrupt decision hit her hard, an errant wave sinking a ship. She was so caught off guard, she could not respond as Joe slowly, head down in defeat, walked down the beach. Her body shook as tears poured out in disbelief. The wind picked back up and she felt chills all over.

Call him Boo Bird.

She desperately screamed out, "What does Boo Bird mean?"

Joe immediately turned around and headed back to her in an obvious huff.

"How do you know about Boo Bird?" he demanded, eyes glaring.

"What does Boo Bird mean, Joe?" she cried out over the crashing waves.

"Tell me how you know about Boo Bird!"

She caught up to Joe still in tears. He looked angry.

"She said to take care of Boo Bird, Joe. Maybe she did not mean you. Who is Boo Bird, Joe? Do you know?"

Joe collapsed onto the sand and wailed in grief. Judie Kate fell beside him and took his hands, watching and feeling him shake. Minutes dragged on as three years of tears slowly subsided. The shifting winds settled briefly, the clouds seemed to pause, and the quarter moon lit up the beach. An eternity passed and then another. Finally, he spoke.

"Only two people know about Boo Bird: Jay Jay and me. It was our secret term of endearment. She called me Boo Bird. It was what she always called me. I called her Butterfly Girl." Joe paused and thought very carefully and then admitted what he had refused to believe in order to protect his own soul. There was something greater at work here. "The only way you could know about Boo Bird is if Jay Jay told you."

He now held her hands firmly. She felt the strength of his soul coming out. This was what she knew was in him. This is what she had been trying to coax out of him all week. Just like he had seen things in her and tried to bring them out, now it was her turn. *Nothing will get in the way of my true love!*

The nightmare of three years had been broken. Judie Kate had tried for four days to be a part of a new dream. He reached out to her and pulled her close.

"I'm so sorry, Judie Kate." The embrace was momentous, deep, filling. Three years left behind for good. She shifted, put her legs around his body, and sat on his lap, fell into him, feeling him breathe. He kissed her, first softly but then with a passion that threw away his cares. The kiss was daring, deep, eternal. The chase was over, and a new dream began.

The moment lasted both a lifetime and not long enough. The moon slid behind the clouds.

"We should go. Your parents will be worried," Joe said.

They stood up, pulled each other close, brushed off the sand on each other, then touched each other in special, beautiful places. Intimately, lovingly, with curiosity. Each kiss was a caress, a promise. Each touch was a wish for the future. Now, they had to convince her parents.

* * *

As they climbed the steps to the upper deck, Joe noticed that all the lights were on. *This is not good.* George and Ellie were sitting in separate chairs, and they were staring heatedly at the sliding glass door as he and Judie Kate stepped inside.

"Where have you been?" Ellie called out. "Do you know what time it is?"

"Momma, I'm an adult now," Judie Kate responded flatly, "and I do indeed know exactly what time it is." She tossed her backpack on the floor, pushed Joe on the couch, sat close to him, took his hand, and placed it firmly on her lap, making a strong statement. Killer jumped on the couch, settled on the couple's hands, as if to affirm the new relationship. "We want to talk about something."

"*We* want to talk about something!" George shot back. "What is going on here? Are you two an item now? Are you dating, in love, getting married?"

Ellie chimed in. "What is going on with the new clothes, all the skin showing, sitting close together? People are talking, men are looking, this is embarrassing. There are too many years between you two. I don't know what is happening to my little girl! I don't approve at all!"

George bluntly cut to the chase. "This stops now!"

Judie Kate was incensed; Joe was caught between his love for her and his appreciation and friendship with George and Ellie, especially with George. Judie Kate moved to the edge of the couch and breathed in and out several times, her face getting redder and redder. It had been two thousand years, but now Mount Vesuvius was about to blow again.

"I can't believe what I'm hearing! Your little girl, Momma? *Little girl?* I am your daughter, for God's sake, not a little girl. Joe is not some stupid boy chasing a *little* girl. He has fought me all week long, but we finally got it figured out. We are in love. We understand your point of view. But this is about us. Joe is my dream come true." She patted his hand in a show of solidarity.

"Dream come true?" George fired back. "Are we listening to dreams now rather than common sense? You need a plan for your life, not some new age inspiration to chase someone who could be your father!"

Judie Kate ignored the jab. "Plan? What plan? The one you had for me? Momma, you wanted me to be a teacher. That is the only thing I was ever encouraged to be. I got my degree, and I hate teaching! What about *my* plan, *my* dreams? Why can't my dreams come true?"

Ellie was stunned. "You never told me this, Judie Kate. How was I supposed to know?"

"Momma, I have tried to tell you since I was thirteen, but you were so caught up in your precious educational career that you never heard me. Didn't you see it in my eyes, my posture, my weight?"

Ellie could not take it in. She sat in silence, staring at her Judie Kate, suddenly understanding that she was an adult but still not able to let go of her little girl.

"What are these dreams you keep talking about?" George asked

"Tell them, Joe," Judie Kate cried, letting her face fall into her hands. "Tell them!" she mumbled. "Maybe they'll listen to you. They've never listened to me."

Joe took them through the dreams, the past, the last four days. He thought he explained everything carefully, logically, step by step. He put his arm around Judie Kate.

"It seems like Jay Jay, in some strange, spiritual way, was putting all of this together." He squeezed her again. "It finally made sense to me."

George was not buying any of it. "I think you are using Jay Jay as an excuse to fulfill some juvenile fantasy. Judie Kate, I've had enough of this fairy tale, children's charade. It is time for you to grow up." George got up and walked to the kitchen, putting some distance between himself and his daughter.

Judie Kate seethed. "Excuse me! What did you say? Grow up? Look at me, Daddy! I am grown up!" She paused and looked at George, who stared out the window into the darkness. "I said look at me, for God's sake. For once, quit running away from looking at the real me! I am twenty-five, not fourteen. I make my decisions now, not you, not Momma, not Joe!"

"Judie Kate, who are you?" Ellie demanded, full of confusion. "This is not the Judie Kate we know, we raised up." Ellie shook her head as if in defeat, despair.

"The Judie Kate you know? The Judie Kate *you know*? You're kidding me, right? You think you know me? You know the Judie Kate you wanted me to be. That is all you've ever known. You don't know me at all!"

There was a long silence. The words stung and her parents reeled back a bit, taking it all in. Killer went to his bed, not sure whose side to take. Ellie looked down at the floor, then back up to her daughter. She glared at Joe, not giving up the fight.

"This is your fault," Ellie said.

"Joe?" George called out. "There is a ferry leaving at seven thirty in the morning. Be on that ferry." George turned around, the conversation done. Ellie rose and began walking toward the stairs.

Then Judie Kate stood up.

"Both of you, listen to me and listen to me very closely!" She paused, catching her breath, getting ready to cross the last line of the past. Her face was red, angry, teeth clenched in rage. *I am Judie Kate!*

Nobody was going to get in the way of her dream now, not even her parents. She stared directly at George and then back at Ellie. She looked at the floor and then raised her head up defiantly. "If he's on that ferry at seven thirty, I will be too! How is that? You two have a decision to make. Am I your daughter or your little girl? If Joe goes, I go. If Joe stays, I stay. You decide!" She stomped off to her room.

"Give up this silly dream of yours, Judie Kate!" Ellie fired off.

"Like hell I will!" She slammed the door behind her.

The silence was thick, still, hot. George looked at Ellie. The insolence of Judie Kate cut hard.

"She never cursed until this silly dream started up!" Ellie sneered at Joe.

"You don't know how many times she cursed you two when we went out for ice cream." Joe turned to go outside on the deck.

"So, now you're saying that we don't even know our daughter? Who do you think you are?" Ellie was incensed.

Joe turned back, now full of rage, a side of him that George and Ellie had never seen. All the times he listened to Judie Kate, all the times he helped her when her parents were away. All the times he kept her from running away. He knew her fantasies, her dreams, her hurts, her loneliness better than anybody.

"If you knew your daughter like I know her, we would not be having this conversation right now." He slammed shut the glass door behind him and sat on the bench. The breeze was picking up, and the sound was filled with waves slapping against the shore. Killer scratched at the door.

"What do we do now?" Ellie asked George.

"Give her a few minutes to cool off and then go and check on her. I've got to get some sleep." He went up the stairs. Ellie stared out the glass windows at Joe, her mind racing, wondering how on earth could he go after her daughter. *What kind of man is he? Was he after Judie Kate all those years he took her out for ice cream? Did he do something to her?*

"I trusted you," she whispered out loud, staring at his image outside the glass door.

* * *

After fifteen minutes, Ellie went to Judie Kate's room and knocked on the door.

"Judie Kate? Can I come in?" There was no answer. "Judie Kate?" She knocked on the door again and then slowly turned the rusty knob, sticking her head inside. There was no Judie Kate.

Worried, Ellie rushed to the bathroom, saw the open door, peeked inside. No Judie Kate. She pushed open Joe's door. Nobody there. She went back to the kitchen, hoping that Judie Kate had come back out there. Nobody.

"George!" she hollered. "She's gone!"

Joe heard her and rushed inside. "What do you mean she's gone?"

"I went to check on her. She's not in her room." Ellie went back again, as if maybe Judie Kate had snuck back inside.

"Is she on her deck?" Joe asked, rushing to the room. The door was unlocked. He looked outside. Empty. "This isn't good."

Ellie was panicking. "George!" Ellie ran back into the kitchen.

By that time, George was coming back down the steps, still pulling up his pants, tightening his belt. "Is her car still here?" he called out.

Joe stood on the deck and saw her Mustang in the driveway. "Car is still here," he called back.

"Maybe she's gone for a walk to cool off," George wondered. "Ellie, call her phone." Ellie picked up her phone and scrolled to Judie Kate's number. She pressed the screen. They all heard her phone go off in her room. "That ain't good," George called out.

"George, the attacker!" Ellie screamed.

He grabbed his keys and phone and rushed for the door. "Call 911."

"I'll go look too," Joe called out. He started for his room to get his phone.

"You leave her alone!" George shot back, pausing at the door. He pointed a shaking finger at Joe. "This started with you. This has been going on long enough! Stay away from my girl!" He clomped down the deck steps, and then they heard the truck start and gravel fly as he spun out of the driveway.

Joe looked back at Ellie and she glared back at him.

"She's never run away before, Joe. This is your fault!" Ellie said.

Joe caught himself, calmed down, and looked directly at Ellie. "Ellie?" He paused a bit. "She tried to run away three times when she was in high school. Every time, I talked her out of it."

This revelation hit Ellie hard, making her realize that maybe she was not the mother she had convinced herself she was. "I never knew that, Joe."

"Ellie, I am not the enemy here." He walked across the room. "Two can find her quicker than one," Joe offered. "Besides, I know where she went." Joe pulled his truck keys out of his pocket and rushed out the door.

"Where, Joe, where?" Ellie called out.

"Try the theater! She knows the code to get in," he hollered back, lying. There was no way he was going to let George get to her first.

When Ellie got to the deck, she saw Joe head down the steps. She looked at her phone and punched 911.

***

Joe raced to the Ice Cream Shack. He pulled in the empty parking lot, jumped out, and looked around. Nobody! He saw a bicycle on its side, and he slowly walked to the Shack, keeping his eyes peeled, hoping the stalker was not around, praying to God, to anyone, that Judie Kate was safe. He aimed for the dark corner beside and behind the Shack where they had shared ice cream together. As he neared the corner, he heard someone whimpering.

"Please, God let her be okay!" he whispered. He feared for the worse.

Joe dodged a full trashcan, looked behind a tall bush, and found her, crying, at a picnic table, completely in the dark.

"Judie Kate?" His words startled her, and she jumped, then she realized it was Joe.

"How did you know where I was?" she cried, getting up, running to him, and holding him tightly. "How did you know?"

He held her tightly, safely, feeling her heave with heavy sobs, his shirt once more soaked with her tears.

"What are we going to do, Joe? What are we going to do?" She pulled back and sniffed several times, rubbing her nose with her hands. "I've never seen Daddy so mad."

"We'll figure that out later. Right now, we have to get you out of here. The rapist, remember?"

They turned and headed around the corner.

"Well, what do we have here?" sneered a silhouette. Judie Kate screamed. Joe could just make out a skinny man with a beard and a college ball cap.

"Get behind me, Judie Kate!" Joe commanded.

"Got me a dirty old man who's gonna get him some young nookie tonight, huh?" The man pulled out a knife, waved it at the couple. "Well, old man, I'm gonna get me some too!" He shook the knife at him. "Only problem is, she's always around you. Every time I seen her, she was with you. At the stores, on the streets, at the show, this here ice cream stand, at the beach. So, you got to go, old man!"

Joe circled to his right, and the stalker turned, following him. The streetlight shone on his face, and the stalker squinted. *Just what I wanted.*

Joe reached into his back pocket and pulled out his wallet. "Here, take this and leave the girl alone. There's cash, credit cards. Just leave her alone."

"It's not the wallet I want, old man. It's her."

"That ain't gonna happen," Joe responded.

"Judie Kate. Isn't that a sweet name?" the stalker jeered. "Sounds like a good old country girl. You got some mighty perty curves there, Miss Judie Kate. So, here is what we gonna do. I get my way with Judie Kate, and nobody gets hurt. Granddaddy, you mess with me, and she gets sliced up like sandwich meat after I carve you up like a big, fat turkey." He waved the knife threateningly.

Joe made sure the light was still in the stalker's face. He glared at the stalker. "Nobody touches her, period."

The stalker stepped closer, waving the knife, staring at Joe, glancing around him at Judie Kate. "Come on, old man," the stalker echoed. "Me and her and nobody gets hurt."

"Over my dead body!"

"That can be arranged, buddy!" The stalker took one step closer.

"Judie Kate, back up."

"I'm not leaving you Joe!"

"Just back up. Now!"

The stalker lunged toward Joe, swinging his knife. Judie Kate instinctively backed up and screamed again.

Joe kicked him in the groin.

"Agh!" the stalker hollered. He bent over and the knife clinked on the pavement. He grabbed himself, feeling his testicles in his throat, every man's nightmare. Still bent over, his fighter instincts, honed from years of barroom brawls, kicked in, and he punched Joe in the stomach.

Pain shot through Joe, pain he had never felt before in his protected world. He gasped for breath as the stalker, still leaning over, lunged forward. Joe kicked his face, but the stalker's momentum carried him into Joe. Both fell to the pavement in a collective thud. The stalker, sitting on top of Joe, cried out "Aaaggghhh!" as he grabbed his head, but he still got in two punches to Joe's face.

Judie Kate, seeing the trash can lid, ran over and grabbed it, rushed back, and slammed it against the man's head. Joe, still reeling from the blows, tossed the stalker off, jumped up, and immediately kicked him in the stomach and then rushed around and kicked him in the back. The stalker grabbed his bloody and broken nose with one hand, held his crotch with the other, and writhed all over the pavement. Joe then sat on him, punching him repeatedly in the face.

"I got forty-four years of mad-as-hell in me," Joe hollered out. "You picked the wrong day to piss me off!"

Joe punched the man again and again. Years of frustrations, abuse, neglect, grief over Jay Jay, and his anger toward George and Ellie came out.

Judie Kate screamed out, "Joe, Joe, stop! They'll put you in jail too!" She grabbed him and pulled him off the man. Joe fell backward, knocking her down on her bottom, her skirt splayed outward. She got on her knees and desperately crawled over to Joe. "It's okay, Joe. It's okay! Look, he's not moving. You can stop now." *I hope to God he isn't dead.* She hugged him as hard as she could, her fears subsiding.

Joe came to his senses.

"It's not okay yet." He pulled his belt off, crawled over to the stalker, and tied the man's legs together. "Give me your belt, Judie Kate!" She untied the belt of her dress and handed it to Joe, who wound up the stalker's hands behind his back. "You try to take that off, and I'll kick your face in!" he hollered to the motionless figure. He stood up and stepped back, but the adrenaline surged in him, making him look for someone, something, to hit next.

Judie Kate grabbed him, held his hands, looked him in the eyes, trying to calm him down.

"Joe, it's okay now, it's over, we're safe!" She hugged him close, shaking, sobbing again, this time over what might have happened. Rape, knife wounds, savagery, death.

Joe pulled out his phone, his hurting hand shaking. He found George's number, but it took several attempts to touch the text icon: *ice cream shack. safe.* Next, he called 911 and gave the dispatcher the information. Then, he took Judie Kate to a bench in the light, held her close, and waited.

A minute later, George came flying up in his truck. He jumped out and hollered, "I told you to leave her alone!" He came at the couple in a rage.

Judie Kate jumped up and defiantly stood between Joe and her seething father.

"Leave him alone, Daddy! He saved my life!" She pointed over to the body on the ground in the shadows.

George stopped, stared, took in the situation, saw the knife, and looked back at Judie Kate. George stared at Joe, who was still on the bench, looking down at his feet, rubbing his head with his swelling hands.

"Joe did this?" George asked with an incredulous voice. "Joe?"

"Yes." Judie Kate went back to her savior, sat down on the bench, and held him close. "Daddy, I would have been the next victim. Joe saved my life!" She started crying again. George stepped closer to the couple as Judie Kate suddenly pulled back. "Oh my God, Joe, you're bleeding!"

She looked at her right arm, and it was covered in blood. "Daddy, get a paper towel, a rag, something!"

George rushed to his truck, scrounged around in the back, pulled up a box of CDs, and found a roll of paper towels on the floorboard.

"Hurry!" Judie Kate said.

* * *

About that time, a sheriff careened into the parking lot, blue lights flashing. He jumped out of his car, weapon drawn just in case. He looked at George first.

"Sir, who are you?" the sheriff asked. George identified himself and then noted that Judie Kate was his daughter. The sheriff looked down at Joe. "Sir, who are you?"

"Sheriff," George butted in, pausing a moment, looking first at Judie Kate and then back to Joe, a slight grin emerging on his otherwise ever-stoic face. "I think this is my new son-in-law."

Another sheriff arrived, and minutes later, the EMTs were on the scene. The two sheriffs talked briefly while the EMTs rushed to the man on the ground and then attended to Joe's wound.

The stalker, awake, blood now cleaned up, was placed in handcuffs and taken to the sheriff's cruiser, where he was questioned.

Judie Kate looked up at the other sheriff, suddenly horrified. "Oh my God, can Joe be charged? He was defending himself; he was defending me, sheriff! He was cut by the stalker!" She held Joe tighter, as if to keep him from being arrested.

"Ma'am, I don't think Joe has anything to worry about. We have the knife; Joe clearly was attacked in some way, as the wound on his arm shows. It was self-defense. And," the sheriff paused, "he was defending you as well."

Hours later, the sheriff closed his notebook. "Okay, folks, that's it for tonight. Judie Kate, you are a lucky lady. I worked the attack the other night. It was ugly." She hugged up close to Joe on the bench. "Joe, good job. The folks on Ocracoke give you their thanks. But be careful being that hero. This one ended well, but you never know." Joe nodded back, the pain starting to kick in a bit, his head now pounding, his stomach roiling, too weary to answer. "Mr. Wilson, you might want to keep this one." The sheriff smiled, pointing to Joe. He climbed back into his cruiser, cut off the emergency lights, and radioed in.

Judie Kate looked at the cruiser. "Joe!" she tugged on his arm.

"Not that arm, Judie Kate!"

"I'm sorry, Joe." She patted his leg several times in excitement. "Look at the number on the cruiser!"

156.

* * *

Judie Kate pulled a battered Joe into the kitchen and sat him on the couch. Ellie rushed over, shaking, tears in her eyes, and reached out to her daughter.

"Judie Kate! I was so worried! You could have been killed!" She hugged her close.

"Not one of my best decisions, Momma." She sat by Joe, who was bent over, elbows on his knees, looking at the floor, and rubbed his back.

Ellie, assured that her daughter was safe, then saw Joe's face, hands, and arm. She cringed at the sight and sat on the other side and stared at the gauze on Joe's arm, the purpling bruise on his face, his red hands. *He did this for my daughter.* "How bad are you hurt, Joe?"

He looked up and slowly shook his pounding head sideways.

"Just a scratch, Ellie."

Judie Kate jumped in and gave her the play-by-play as Killer rushed over and plopped on Joe's leg, licking his hands. Ellie's eyes grew wide and teared up as the story unfolded, and she realized how close to disaster the two had come. George stood to the side, his pride, his thanks, not showing.

"Momma," Judie Kate concluded, "he almost killed Joe!"

George butted in like he was correcting Judie Kate. "Uh, Judie Kate, from what I saw, Joe almost killed the stalker!"

She carefully hugged Joe's arm, cringed at the sight of the bruises and welts, and held him tightly. There was quiet in the room, as if all were silently giving thanks, appreciating the gift of life, acknowledging what could have been, and remembering what started it all.

Ellie breathed in, wondering if she should admit she was wrong about Joe, about Judie Kate, about the whole situation. Back to her stoic self-composure, she offered a thank you olive branch.

"We're glad you are both safe." She took Joe's swollen hand and shook her head. Worry came over her face, manifested in a very wrinkled brow. "George, would you get some ice in three plastic bags? This looks awful."

George returned in a moment with the ice packs, handed them to Ellie, and stood back a bit. Ellie gave one to Judie Kate, who held it on Joe's face. Then Ellie applied the others to Joe's quivering hands and held them there, as if giving them her blessing. After a moment, a new Ellie appeared, mother-in-law Ellie. "Thank you, Joe."

He nodded.

"I'm glad she's safe." He paused as Judie Kate reassuringly patted him on his leg. "Got any Aleve, Excedrin, Advil, whiskey, a bullet to bite?"

Ellie got up and searched around. "I know we brought some. I'll have to find it."

The silence allowed for introspection, a time to breathe in and exhale, moving away from the excitement, the danger, into the safety of family, freedom from fear, the hope of a new beginning for all of them. The darkness outside the windows only amplified the light within the room, a light that seemed filled with a new life, a new day. *Heaven?* Judie Kate looked up.

"Daddy, don't you have anything to say?" She stared at George. *Of all the times to be silent.*

George looked at Joe, then at Judie Kate. He saw her face, her hands on Joe's hands. Her compassion and care. There was indeed something different about her. The look of her eyes, the way she carried herself. The clothes, the makeup, the confidence all exuded a Judie Kate he had never seen, nor even wanted to see. This young woman was no longer his little girl. She was an adult. She was confident, sure, strong, herself. Now he understood. It was time to let her go, to leave the past behind. To welcome home the little girl who was now a young woman, a woman he almost lost before he saw her for who she was.

And, it was time to welcome a new member to the family.

"Thank you, Joe." The tone said everything he couldn't.

"I'll send you a bill." Joe winced a bit. "Cash only."

Ellie came down the stairs. "I have some aspirin, Joe." Judie Kate got up, found a glass, filled it with water, and came back to her hero. Ellie stood in front of Joe and extended her hand. "Here's two for you."

"Four please." He reached out two black and blue hands, grabbed the cup of water, and took the pills, swallowed them all, then fell back on the cushion. Judie Kate returned the glass to the sink while Ellie and George headed to the stairs, glad to know it was all over, still a bit leery of what the future held.

"Give thanks to Jesus," Ellie called back to Judie Kate.

"Already did, Momma." She turned to check on Joe. He was fast asleep, Killer curled up right beside him.

Sunday

T yler's phone buzzed her awake. It was 6:30 a.m.

Miller: *u awake*

Tyler: *Now I am.*

Miller: *meet me at the stage at 8?*

Tyler: *Why?*

Miller: *I need a fishtail braid*

Tyler: *Do it yourself.*

Miller: *It needs to be perfect*

Tyler: *Why?*

Miller: *for zach*

Tyler: *You guys patch things up?*

Miller: *yes. i want to look good this morning*

Tyler: *See you there but you owe me!*

* * *

George, not convinced he was awake, much less alive, came back down the steps, bleary from just a few hours of sleep, cloudy from the emotions of the night, thankful for the new day and his daughter's life. The bobbleheads, warmed by the sun's rays, clicked out a good morning as he glanced over at the couch. His little girl was snuggled around his soon-to-be son-in-law, who was covered in a sheet. *She must have wrapped him up last night.* She was still in her dress, dirty and blood-stained. Both were asleep, out cold, all four legs on the ottoman. He quietly let Killer out and breathed in the humid morning air.

"Hardly a cloud in the sky," he happily mumbled to himself. He stumbled back to the kitchen and opened a can of cat food and placed it in Killer's bowl, then shuffled back to the glass door and let the unkempt furball back in. Killer raced to his breakfast. *Salmon at the beach!*

George quietly gathered his instruments and his gig bag and went to the truck. Ellie was in the room when he came back in. She looked at the couple, marveled at their innocence, and then gave a quiet thanks once more for their safety. She rubbed Judie Kate's hair and pulled the sheet up on Joe. Killer, now back on guard, looked up, waiting for his special treatment too.

"Okay, *Killer.*" Ellie petted his scruffy head.

* * *

The Wild Herd Restaurant was alive with the clanking of utensils on plates, plates on tables, coffee cups on saucers, and conversation. A few early risers looked at the old pictures of the island on the walls and smelled ham, sausage, omelets, coffee, biscuits, syrup. Vacationers enjoying their last meal, sunburned fishermen gobbling up man-sized portions, women searching for a healthy item on the menu. Children dropped food on the floor, made a mess of the butter, asked for even more syrup on their soaked pancakes, and wiped grape jelly on everything but their toast.

Darren and Mike Scott were already seated when George and Ellie came in.

"Looks like you two stayed up all night," Mike, eyes full of their usual mischief, quipped. "Waiting on the children to come home?" he teased. "Is Judie Kate on probation now? Did you send Junior to his room?"

George and Ellie took their seats, and both ordered coffee.

Darren looked confused.

"George, you never drink coffee." George looked back at him. "Long night." Ellie placed her head in her hands and rubbed her eyes.

Darren broke the silence.

"Radio announced that the rapist was apprehended last night." He took another forkful of Western omelet. "You can feel the relief. Maybe folks can enjoy what's left of the show."

"Joe caught him," George responded nonchalantly, as if he were describing how to change a string on a guitar.

"Joe?" Mike asked, incredulous. "Joe? Sound man Joe?"

"George, was he after Judie Kate?" Darren asked. He didn't wait for the response. "Is she okay, Ellie?" Darren paused. "Is Joe okay?"

Mike was about to break. "Silence is not golden, George."

Ellie teared up, again realizing what could have been.

"We had an argument late last night or early this morning. I don't remember. This whole romance thing—it's complicated. Anyway, it got ugly real fast. Judie Kate ran off. Joe found her, and that's when they were attacked by the rapist."

"Oh my gosh!" Darren replied. "They're okay, right?"

George beamed a bit. "Joe beat the snot out of that guy."

"Boy, that image makes these eggs look all the more pleasing," Mike teased, taking another forkful. "Our Joe?" he asked again, surprised.

Ellie brought them back to earth. "He saved our little girl," she sobbed.

"Our daughter," George reminded her. "Joe got a pretty nasty cut on his arm. Black eye. The man slashed him with a knife. We need to get him checked out by someone."

Mike asked, "You think Lane might help out here?"

George rolled his eyes. "After Friday night, not sure. Anyway, he's not on the island anymore."

Mike interrupted. "Friday night? Is there something I don't know about here?"

George retold the whole ordeal of the date gone bad.

Mike shook his head. "Poor Judie Kate."

Mike chomped down some toast while George and Ellie picked at their breakfast. Darren was thinking.

"I guess we could get Susan to come and check on Joe. Hate to mess up her weekend though," Darren said. He finished off the last bite of omelet.

Then Ellie spoke up. "Did I see Tom Landers at the ticket booth yesterday?"

Darren perked up. "Yes, Ellie, he's down here volunteering. Sometimes he fills in for Susan as well. I'll text him and see if he can help us with Joe." He sipped more coffee. "Good one, Ellie!"

The table was quiet as the import of the events and the need for nourishment settled among the four diners. After a few moments, Darren brought out the set list for the gospel show and handed a copy to Mike and George. They both looked it over, nodded in approval.

"I put in that Zach guy after the Assembly of God sings. Did I tell you all about him? He was busking on the corner Friday, had a bit of a crowd around him. Handing out water in the name of Jesus. Actually, pretty good idea. Anyway, he's good, great spirituals, phenomenal picker," Darren said.

Mike looked at Darren with a surprised face. "You're going to put a Christian busker on stage? Those are your two pet peeves."

Darren took a bite of toast. "Mike, he's *really* good. Thinking about asking him to come back next year. Maybe do a workshop on spirituals." Darren swallowed. "Plus, that will keep us in the good graces of the church folks here as well."

Mike shook his head as if to wake up. He forked in some more eggs and then swigged his tea. After a moment, his face lit up, an eyebrow raised, and he looked over at Darren.

"You know, we got us a hero here. We should honor Joe at the show," Mike said.

"I like that, Mike. First decent idea you've had since I've known you." He looked over at Ellie. "You think you can get them here to the show in time?"

"They were sleeping this morning when we left," Ellie said. She called Judie Kate, but nobody answered.

* * *

Judie Kate was dreaming. It was one of those dreams where you can't get to where you need to go. In the dream, she could hear the phone ringing, but she could not find it. The more she searched, the louder the phone got, and the farther it moved away. She desperately lunged for it and woke herself up.

She looked at Joe. He had not moved from the position he fell asleep in that morning. She shook her head, got up, searched around the kitchen and then her room, and found her phone, the green light flashing. Text. She swiped the face and saw the message.

Darren wants to honor Joe at the gospel sing. He wants it to be a surprise. Can you make it?

Judie Kate called Ellie. "Where are you now, Momma?"

"At the Wild Herd," Ellie answered.

"How do I get him there without him knowing?"

Ellie asked George, who came up with a quick answer.

"Tell her that Rex might need him for sound this morning. That'll wake him up," Ellie said.

"Got it, Momma. Get us two sausage biscuits. We'll be there as soon as possible."

"You're going to eat a sausage biscuit?"

"No time to explain, Momma!"

Judie Kate ran back and shook Joe. "Joe, Joe. Wake up. We gotta go!" She cringed when she saw his face. She shook him again, and Joe slowly opened his eyes.

"The ferry, I know, I have to get going."

"No, Joe, we have to go to the gospel show. Daddy said Rex might need help with sound, something like that. Hurry! You need to get cleaned up. Shave and brush your teeth."

Joe, sensing the sound emergency, quickly woke up and stood, felt a bit woozy, and then sat back down.

Judie Kate saw his bandaged arm and blue hands. She remembered something about not getting his arm wet. "I'll help you!"

As she helped him with a sink bath, she looked at her arms in the mirror and the dried blood on them, then she saw her ruined clothes. There was blood all over them too. She sent Joe to his room to dry himself off, then she rushed to her bedroom and yanked off her clothes, and then saw her knees, bruised and scratched.

"What am I going to wear?" She ran back to the bathroom and hurriedly rinsed off, looked around, and found her black leggings. "What goes on top?" she wondered. She pulled out a white bra, found a white cami in her suitcase, and then pulled on a tight, white tank top. "White top, black leggings. Joe's dream come true!" Then, she remembered her red Converse shoes in her backpack. *For Jay Jay!* "Perfect."

She hollered through the bathroom. "You done in there? You gonna be okay?"

"The show must go on, Judie Kate."

She applied some minimal makeup and then walked into Joe's room. "We need to go!"

* * *

Miller excitedly yet cautiously walked up to the stage and looked around for Tyler. All was quiet except for the sound crew connecting mics and cables, some festival helpers wiping off the dew from the chairs, and the small din of artisans setting up their wares on School Road. Tyler walked up. She wore a flowing, long, light yellow sun dress and was barefoot. She looked at Miller.

"Wow, you went all the way there, didn't you?" Tyler said.

Miller looked wonderful. Her light blue, sleeveless dress was highlighted with faded red and green flowers and tiny lace around the hem and the shoulder straps. The dress stopped just above her knees, and thong sandals complemented the whole ensemble. Tyler looked her over, as if carefully inspecting her.

"That should keep his attention for a while," Tyler said.

Meanwhile, Miller found a chair, and Tyler sat behind her and began the braid.

"Did you say fishtail or mermaid's braid?" Tyler asked. Miller was confused.

"Aren't they the same thing?"

Tyler nodded, not that Miller could see her. "I know exactly the style you want." Tyler took two strands of hair from the front of Miller's head and twisted them like small ropes, pulled them above her ears to the back, and then started the fishtail braid. When she finished, she looked at the end result. From the side, it looked like a dark laurel wreath around her head, like a Roman goddess might wear. From the back, Miller's long, black hair was accented with an elegant braid that cascaded down her back. "We need a mirror," Tyler thought out loud.

Miller thought of something. "Take a picture!"

Tyler took out her phone, snapped a pic, and showed it to Miller.

"Perfect!" Miller shouted, a bit too loud.

A helper paused to look up, shrugged, then resumed wiping off the seats. "Kids."

Miller hugged Tyler. "I hope he doesn't chicken out," she worried.

* * *

Judie Kate skidded her Mustang into a small space behind the school, jumped out, and slammed the door. Joe was not quite so fast.

"I need caffeine," Joe called out as they headed for the Live Oak Stage.

"I need some too!" Judie Kate answered, thinking about breakfast. Joe hurriedly pulled her to the left toward the theater and reaching the back door, punched in the code and went inside. He reemerged with two Pepsis, handed one to Judie Kate, pulled the door shut, and on a mission to save the sound crew, pulled her along to the stage area.

There was a quiet electricity in the air as people gathered for the Sunday morning gospel sing under the live oaks. The morning sun peeked through the leaves, leaving patches of light and shadows on the white chairs. Birds chirped and doves cooed. A soft breeze eased the morning humidity. Some folks were slow to wake up, some a bit reverent, anticipating the old-time feelings the music would bring. Many knew they had to get there early to get a seat, and they had been there since 8:30 a.m. Others walked about the vendors, some went into Read A Bit More. There were people on their phones, dogs looking for a place to nap or being overly protective of their owners, babies in strollers, and kids climbing the trees.

Tyler eyed Zach before Miller did. He was dressed in jeans and his new Ocrafolk T-shirt. He looked lost, so Tyler sent Miller the opposite way to look for him while she came over to him. He spotted a familiar face as Tyler walked up.

"Hey, Zach," Tyler called out. "You ready to sing?" It was more of a command than a question. As Zach got ready to answer, she stared him in the face.

"All right, look, I know you and Miller got it straightened out last night, but here's the deal. You blow this one, and I'm gonna break your left hand. Got it?"

Something about Tyler scared Zach. He was not quite on the same page. "Blow it?" He looked confused.

Tyler turned around and pointed to Miller across the yard. Zach spotted her too.

Tyler said, "You see her, Zach? See how dressed up she is? She looks beautiful, right?"

Suddenly, it hit Zach full force. Miller was dressed in blue, like the ocean of the woman in his dream. Her hair looked like it had a laurel wreath around it, and her dress had green and red flowers on it. She was the one who encouraged him to sing. She was the one in the dream. Now he understood.

"Like an angel from God," he answered.

"That angel needs a hand to hold. You've got two hands. Got it?"

About that time, Miller spotted the two of them and came running over.

"There you are. I was worried you weren't going to show up." She stared at Zach with big puppy eyes full of hope, joy, love. "Do you like my hair?" She turned all the way around so he could see it.

Tyler moved behind Miller, looked at Zach, nodded her head toward Miller, and then turned away. "I've got to get some water, guys. I'll see you at the stage."

Zach was nervous. Another demon, but this time, it was him. He needed to defeat this last one. He reached for his knife in his pocket and squeezed it tightly. Then, he worked up his courage to break a barrier that had held him captive for too long.

"Uh, Miller, do you think it would be okay if I held your hand?"

Miller beamed. "Yes, Zach!" It was like a prayer come true. He slowly reached out, as if her hand was the serpent of Eden that might bite him, but Miller softly took his hand and held it tight. It was warm, a bit clammy, but strong and assured. She squeezed it more and moved beside him. Miller's face was brighter than the morning sun.

Zach felt things he had never felt before, but this time, it did not bother him. This was a gift from the sea, from God. He looked at her, absorbed her, felt her life come to him through her soft hand, and then realized he had not answered her question.

"Your hair is beautiful."

* * *

Judie Kate let Joe walk over to the sound booth, where he found Rex in a whirl, doing the sound check. Abner the Sound Dog was hard at work, too, standing on the chair, front paws on the sound board, twenty-four channels at his command. Joe looked up on stage and saw George working with the tech, arranging the mics.

"Hi, Rex. George called, said you might need some help this morning," Joe said.

Rex looked over at him, took a drag from his cigarette, and emerged out of his sound zone with a puzzled look on his sweaty brow.

"Hey, buddy, good to see you!" He reached out to shake Joe's hand, noticed the bandage and the black and blue hands. "What the hell?"

Joe answered, "Nothing much. Little excitement last night. What do you need help with?"

Then Rex saw the other side of his face.

"Damn! Speakers fall on you last night?"

Joe ignored the question and asked again if Rex needed help.

"Nothing here. George called you? Maybe he knows something I don't." Rex exhaled from his cigarette, adjusted the midrange on channel four, and rubbed Abner on the head. He patted Joe on the back and went back to work. The show deadline of 9:15 a.m. was approaching fast, and he was worried about a bad mic cable on channel ten.

Joe, now confused, wandered over to the performer's tent, looking lost. Everybody was walking around, warming up on their instruments, wandering in thought as they rehearsed lyrics from songs that were not sung too often on their regular gigs. He knew better than to interrupt. Performers want their space before a show, so best leave them alone unless it was a specific sound matter. He saw George and walked over to him, even though he was still leery of him.

"You called?" Joe said.

George looked at him funny while he ran through a lick on his mandolin. "What?" he answered.

"Judie Kate said you called and that you needed help with something, or Rex needed help with something."

George looked away for a moment, then turned back around. "I think Darren fixed it."

George walked off, conversation ended even though the situation was not resolved. Joe felt his phone go off. His hands were so swollen, he could barely get it out of his back pocket. He looked at the text from Judie Kate. *You gonna sit with me or what?* He turned around, and he saw her standing up, waving in the crowd. He waved back and wove his way through the maze of people and chairs and three dogs to where Judie Kate and Ellie were sitting. She patted the empty seat beside her as Joe made his way over other people.

"Sit." As he did, she handed him a wrapped-up sausage biscuit. "Eat." She opened hers up and then handed him his soda and some napkins.

"Joe," Ellie called out, "How are you feeling?" He had a mouthful of biscuit, so he pointed at his mouth and chewed some more and then swallowed. He was feeling a bit woppy-headed.

"Sore, but okay for now. Music should be good this morning. A very nice day for gospel music." He knew Ellie loved the gospel music portion of the festival.

Darren walked out to the main mic, carefully adjusted it to his height, looked at Rex at the sound table, and got the nod he wanted. Abner barked his readiness.

"Well, good morning, folks! I hope you are ready for the Sunday gospel music portion of the festival!" The crowd politely answered, not quite sure if reverence or an inspired rowdiness was the order of the day.

Mike Scott walked up to the mic. "Darren, let's try this again. I think we have a few folks who are getting over their Saturday night hangovers and are still praying for forgiveness." The crowd laughed, waking up to the casual and festive mood. "Better," Mike said. "Now, are you ready for the gospel music portion of the festival?" He got many "amens" and a heartier applause.

Darren moved back over to the mic. "So, folks, some of you may have heard on WOVV, but most do not know: the rapist was apprehended last night." There was a gasp and then a sigh of collective relief as some clapped their approval. George walked up on the stage as Darren continued. "He attacked a couple, but he was disabled and then arrested." More applause.

Ellie looked over at Joe, who was finishing off the biscuit and grinned a big yet silent "thank you" to him. Judie Kate, proud of her knight, hugged his good arm.

"What you don't know is that the hero is here among us this morning." There was more applause, but now heads were turning everywhere, as if Santa Claus might walk into the room at any moment. Joe, still dull from the battle, was oblivious. "Our sound guy at the Workshop Stage ... anybody go to the Workshop Stage yesterday?" Darren paused for a moment. Numerous hands shot up. "Well, Joe Clark, our sound man subdued the stalker last night ..."

George then walked up with a rare show of emotion, a big grin on his face. "He beat the snot out of him is what he did!" The crowd laughed, now really looking around.

"Thank you for that very graphic play-by-play," Mike answered. "That's what we in the trade call professionalism."

Darren continued. "Joe has not had much sleep, he's cut and banged up pretty bad, but we tricked him into coming out this morning. Joe, stand up for us, would you? Give him a round of thanks, folks!"

Joe reluctantly stood up, looked around in embarrassment, swallowed, and painfully took off his hat as people applauded. Several gasped when they saw his face as he turned around. Those around him patted him on the back and stared at his bandaged arm. Judie Kate beamed brighter than the summer sun. Ellie glanced over at him with pride. George looked out from the stage and smiled.

As George looked out, Mike stepped back up to the mic again.

"Uh, George, isn't there something else we should know about?" Mike said.

George looked at Mike with a puzzled face, and Mike moved his lips: *Judie Kate.* Suddenly, George teared up.

Darren, noting the problem, took over. "Folks, the stalker was after George's daughter. Joe saved the day." There was a collective gasp and then thunderous applause from the fans.

Then Mike intervened, trying to get George back into show mood. "Uh, George, might there be one more very important thing we need to know this morning?"

Having recovered his composure, George now realized he had to admit the obvious. "Well," he answered, looking out over the crowd and then directly at Joe. "It pains me to say this, but Joe is going to be my future son-in-law." Applause erupted once more as the crowd celebrated the great announcement. Judie Kate patted Ellie on her leg and hooked her arm around Joe's good arm.

Mike stepped back to the mic. "Judie Kate, why don't you stand up for us?"

She was completely caught off guard, not expecting her time in the sun. She slowly, shyly, rose up as people nearby shouted out congratulations to her and Joe.

"Isn't she beautiful, ladies and gentlemen," Mike called out. The applause increased. "George, you and Ellie did a good job on that one, right folks?" Ellie was embarrassed and George just shrugged his shoulders. "Joe's a lucky man, right, everybody?"

Judie Kate quickly sat back down, leaned over to Joe, and whispered, "Nobody has ever said I was beautiful in public, Joe." A tear came to her eye.

"Enjoy it, Judie Kate," Joe answered back, "because you are."

As the applause ended, George came up to the microphone and looked like he wanted to say something very serious. Everybody quieted down, waiting for a solemn, reflective thought, perhaps a time of thanks.

He waited and waited, letting the tension build. Then, he looked very serious. "Joe, you know I'm not going to call you son." Everybody remained quiet, all looking in Joe's direction.

Joe, likewise, waited before giving his response. "I love you, too, Dad," he hollered out, throwing it right back at his buddy and now his future father-in-law.

Three hundred people laughed and applauded at his humor. Judie Kate beamed. It was like old times again.

Darren stepped back up to the mic, realizing that time was slipping away. "Okay, folks, let's get going. This first song is a great one to honor Joe and even Judie Kate. You'll see why as we sing it. Join in if you know it." Then he started off "A Beautiful Life."

After the warm-up tune, Mike walked up to the mic, adjusted it upward a bit, looked at the crowd, and then began his portion of the gospel sing. "Y'all ready to sing along?"

They called out a hearty "yes," and Mike told them they all knew the songs he was going to lead them in. "If you went to summer camp, you learned all these songs." He began with "This Little Light of Mine." The crowd was immediately into the medley of old campfire tunes. Soon, they were singing "Down by the Riverside" and "Do Lord" and then "Michael Row Your Boat Ashore."

The folks from the Assembly of God Church took the stage, led by Tyler and Reverend Baylor. Each checked the tuning of their guitars while the children, youth, and adults got in their places and arranged their sheet music. Zach, guitar in hand, joined them as well, right beside a radiant Miller, who reached over and briefly took his free hand and held it tight.

Judie Kate elbowed Joe. "Look at that, Joe, the Christian guy. He's holding hands with a young lady!"

Rev. Baylor nodded at Tyler, who moved over to the mic and confidently looked out over the crowd.

"Hi, folks. We are going to sing our version of Crowder's song 'I Am.' We hope you enjoy it!" Tyler said.

After the Assembly of God choir finished and was walking off, Darren walked onstage. "Uh, Zach, come over here." Zach shyly walked over to Darren, a bit unsure of the situation, glancing briefly at the crowd, then down at his feet. It was one thing to busker on the street and hand out water and tracts. Now, he was standing in front of three hundred people. Stage fright washed over him like a rough wave.

Darren sensed his increasing fears and put his arm around him, noticed his Ocrafolk shirt, and whispered, "Nice shirt." Suddenly, Zach felt welcomed but not quite relaxed.

"Folks, how many of you have seen Zach busking around Ocracoke this weekend?" Darren said. Many applauded, nodding their heads.

"Well, we don't usually have uninvited singers on stage, but after I heard Zach the other day, I felt we had to give this young man a listen. You all agree?" The applause was more intense, an affirmation of Zach's abilities.

"Ladies and gentlemen, Zach Daniels."

Zach centered himself before the large condenser mic. The crowd stared in anticipation, and suddenly, Zach was afraid. He could not remember the song he had chosen; his hands were clammy, and his face began to perspire. He reached into his pocket for his pick and felt his knife. The Sword of the Spirit. He squeezed it and immediately felt empowered. A cool and comforting calm swept over him, and as if he was born again, as if he was a new person, he became a different man. He looked over to the right and saw Miller standing there in her blue dress, her long hair and pretty braid, looking like a woman out of the Bible. She smiled her affirmation and sent him a prayer.

It worked. When he finished, the crowd showed their appreciation. Some stood up, so powerful was the song. Zach had never performed this way before, and when he finished, he was overwhelmed with emotions, even confusion. *Now what?*

Even Darren was moved, as were many of the seasoned performers under the tent. He walked back onto the stage and put his arm around Zach. "Wow, that was stunning, wasn't it, folks?" The crowd affirmed his observation. "Now, Zach, one of our groups could not make it this morning, so we've got time for another song. Got another one in you?"

Zach froze, and the audience saw his deer-in-the-headlights look.

Darren caught his hesitancy. "How about that Appalachian thing I heard you do the other day? The one with the open tuning?"

Suddenly, Zach felt reassured. "'Two Coats?'"

"Yes, that one," Darren said.

Miller wandered to the front of the crowd and stooped down, phone in hand, and started videoing her new man. She was about to pop. Darren walked away and the crowd grinned in anticipation.

Zach began his intro, and the crowd settled back as he mournfully related the story of two coats being worn by the sinners of the world. One was the tattered old coat of the original sinner, Adam, and the other was the new coat of salvation brought by Jesus. When he finished, he was met with firm applause. He looked down, and Miller was beaming with pride and love.

Darren walked back over to the mic. "Zach Daniels, everybody. Should we bring him back next year?" The folks hollered their answer. Darren nodded, acknowledging their appreciation. "Thank you, Zach!"

The gospel show continued as other groups sang the old standards. "Precious Memories," "Amazing Grace," "I Saw the Light," "Angel Band," "In the Garden." Time was running out, so Darren called all the entertainers out for the finale. They gathered around whatever mic they could get close to as he closed out the show.

"Okay, folks, that will wrap it up for this morning. Sing with us, won't you?" Darren called out "Will the Circle Be Unbroken," and all jumped into the song, ending up with "I'll Fly Away."

* * *

The theater was a cool relief from the humidity outside. Joe, George, and Judie Kate stood before a tall, lanky, unassuming man. George introduced them to Dr. Todd Landers and explained that he was a general practitioner from Greensboro who focused on women's health issues.

"You guys can just call me Dr. Todd," the doctor said.

Everything about him was long except his hair. Long fingers, long arms and legs, long feet, long eyebrows, all complimented with a long nose to boot. He wore wrinkled shorts and a shirt that should have been tossed away a few years ago. He moved a bit slow, like a sloth, and time seemed to stand still all around him. He talked even slower.

"Joe, let me look at your arm," he said as he came over, pulling on two latex gloves. Dr. Todd unwrapped the gauze and carefully inspected Joe's arm. Joe winced as Dr. Todd squirted antiseptic deep into the cut. The doctor let the liquid run, cleansing the wound once more. Then he rubbed ointment over it and deep into the cut. He dried the skin and then applied fifteen steri-strips to keep the wound together. "This wound probably could have used stitches. I think the steri-strips will do. They'll fall off in about seven to ten days. From what I see here, the EMT did an excellent job, Joe." He then rewrapped the wound in gauze and taped the end down.

"I believe this will heal up fine. You need to be careful for the next few days. I brought some antibacterial ointment for you. Apply this several times a day and change the dressing every day." Dr. Todd pulled out a bottle from his bag. "Here are some antibiotics. If the wound gets red or starts oozing anything, head to a doctor or emergency clinic." Finished with the arm, Dr. Todd reexamined Joe's face and hands. "I think you'll live, young man," he concluded dryly.

Joe nodded a silent "thank you" as the doctor packed his bag. Dr. Todd then turned and looked over at Judie Kate. "Now, Judie Kate, I talked with Susan yesterday when I filled in for her—boy, that was a day! I've never had so many jelly fish stings!—so, can I do anything for you?" She was still not sure about wanting to share anything with anyone about Friday night, but something about Dr. Todd seemed welcoming, compassionate, genuine, like he and she had been friends for quite some time. Quite different from Lane and Brooklyn.

"I see the bruises. They will heal up in a few days," He looked at the side of her face. "Looks like the imprint is gone. Are you feeling any pain in your jaw? Any headaches?" She shook her head no.

"Good." Then he pulled a chair over, sat down beside her, and crossed one leg over the other. "George, you and Joe join us."

Judie Kate was not sure about this. What was the powwow about?

"George, does Judie Kate know about the job?"

The blunt question caught her off guard, and she glared at her father. "Daddy, what's going on?" Judie Kate crossed her arms over her chest. Joe, trying to keep from falling asleep in the cool room, perked up.

"Hmm. Well, this is a bit difficult for me, given the events of Friday night." Dr. Todd's droll voice made everyone lean forward, wishing he would speak up, not to mention speed up. "Judie Kate, several of us were working on a venture. Lane was in charge. But after Friday, he backed out for professional and personal reasons that he felt would put the whole thing in jeopardy. We also lost his investment money as well, but I hope to keep this going. So, Judie Kate, I have a very humble request. This is part of a long story, one that George knows about, but I need you to work with me here if you will."

He shifted his body in the chair and looked over at George.

"What you don't know is that in a casual phone call with George a few weeks ago, Lane was informed about your situation, how your job was not very fulfilling, about your MBA, blah blah. Just talking about the family, kids, that sort of thing." Dr. Todd was failing in trying to smooth over the potential bumps and bombs in this situation. He could see Judie Kate becoming agitated. "Anyway, your father suggested that if the right situation came up, you might try another career. Lane told him of an idea that I and my colleagues were bandying about."

Judie Kate cringed. *Just as I thought.* She recrossed her arms over her chest, more defiant, face becoming red.

Dr. Todd continued. "We were dreaming of opening up a clinic for women who had identity and self-esteem issues, those who were abused and even rape victims. Not exactly a safe house, but a place where women, and even teens, could come and get help and support with all kinds of issues that are not being addressed adequately by the health-care industry, politicians, and even religions. Things like obesity, self-image, neglect, abuse, date rape, and more. Lane asked to meet you and open the discussion about helping us. He thought, with your educational background and your focus on nonprofits in your MBA, you might be good for us. He just assumed that you always come down here for the festival."

George interrupted. "Judie Kate, I know this sounds like my meddling into your affairs and your life, but this time, it was different. This sounded like you, not the you Ellie and I had pushed for. But I knew that you really didn't care for the music or the festival and anything I had to do with it. To you, it would be just another gig and another time wasted with your father. So, I told you that Joe would be here in the hope that it would bring you here. I did not foresee anything else. Probably should have though."

Dr. Todd, sensing an old tension between father and daughter, smiled slightly, hopefully, and continued.

"Now, with Lane out of the picture, I don't know where we quite stand—I guess we'll have to back up and punt here—but I want to continue the project. We will have to come up with funds to replace what Lane was going to contribute."

Judie Kate squirmed, less defiant, but still cautious, not talking, a bit curious.

"Right now, with the departure of Lane, we have five professionals on board: a doctor, a lawyer, a social worker, a counselor, and a nurse. We need an educator, an advocate, kind of an inspirational leader. Your experience would be beneficial. Your background in education would give us someone who can teach our clients. I understand you have a basic knowledge of the nonprofit world and business in general from your MBA. I know we will need help to get grants and navigate the politics and legal issues, but I think that in a few years, with the proper grooming, you can take over as the director of the clinic. So, I think that six professionals will give us the staff and tools to handle the case load. We already have five who are ready to go. One added to five makes six."

Judie Kate, still a bit incensed, took all the information in as her emotions whirled around. The whole conversation brought back up the pain and fury of Friday night, not to mention her battle with weight and self-esteem. But, a rainbow was beginning to appear after the torrential and destructive storm. The prospect of a new job was intriguing and refreshing. Finally, it seemed she might have a purpose, indeed, that all the events in her life, the loneliness, parental issues, even Don and now Joe, everything had a reason, as if all her life had been leading up to this, as if her life was part of a master plan. The tension in her face and body language eased, and the beginnings of a smile found their way to her lips. Dr. Todd saw her relaxing and waited, hoping. George exhaled. Joe looked at her.

Then, it hit her. *When the numbers add up ...*

"I'm sorry. You said you have five already, and you wanted six. So, one added to five will make your six?"

Dr. Todd looked confused. The math seemed simple, so what was Judie Kate after? "Yes," he answered in a puzzled voice.

Judie Kate slowly grinned and then looked over

to Joe. She nudged him into her thinking zone. "Joe? Joe? Did you catch that? One plus five equals six."

Joe answered sarcastically. "Yes, Judie Kate, the math is not that complicated. I think it can be calculated on mere fingers. Your education has done you well."

"Joe," Judie Kate answered, poking him in the ribs. "It's not the math, silly. One plus five equals six. One fifty-six, Joe. One-five-six, Joe! Jay Jay is here. She is the one behind this, Joe!" She patted him on the arm exuberantly, smiling.

"Ow, not that arm, Judie Kate!"

Dr. Todd looked at George, who looked at Judie Kate and then shook his head and looked back at the doctor. Joe was now smiling.

Judie Kate was a birthday balloon about to bust. "Yes, I will think about this. I need some more information, like where will this office be, when does it start, and so on. We can talk about this." She paused and looked at Joe again with the excitement of a child in a toy store and then back to Dr. Todd. "Thank you for thinking of me, for your consideration, and," she paused to breathe in, "for this opportunity."

Dr. Todd finally exhaled, relaxed, and smiled. "Judie Kate, I really want you to be our director. I'll be in touch in the next few days regarding the details." He stepped forward and reached out his hand.

Judie Kate shook it heartily and smiled. "Thank you, again, for this opportunity. This sounds very exciting!" She vigorously shook his hand again and looked back at Joe. Dr. Todd leisurely headed to the door.

As the door shut, Judie Kate honed in on George. "Why didn't you tell me, Daddy? When I let you have it the other night, why didn't you say something?" She ran over and gave her father a big hug and then stepped back from him.

George smiled and then looked serious. "Judie Kate, I know that I have not been the most attentive father you ever had, and I apologize for that. But, I do worry about you, and when Lane mentioned his idea to me, I immediately thought of you. That is why I asked you to come, but I wasn't sure you would, so I mentioned that Joe would be here. I figured that would get you down here, but I didn't expect this romance thing to come along. When it did, Ellie and I worried that you had fallen back into the old emotions and feelings. We also worried that it might get you sidetracked from this opportunity. We wanted you to meet Drake, to get your mind off Joe. We meant no harm in asking you to meet Drake and we are sorry that it turned out so bad. I will never forgive myself for that night, ever. Joe, I hope you will forgive us for meddling. We were just worried about our little girl."

"*Daughter*," Judie Kate corrected. "Daughter. Let's move on from little girl."

George continued. "Judie Kate, you were perfect for the job. I knew it. And given all that happened this weekend, you are the best qualified for the job as well."

She hugged George again. "Thank you, Daddy." She turned to Joe. "Now what?"

Joe was feeling tired. "Let's get a sandwich and head to the house. I think I need to get some rest."

* * *

Back at the house, Joe and Judie Kate sat outside on the picnic table. She was nestled as close as she could get to Joe as they ate their lunch. She looked at the wound on his arm, his bruised hands trying to hold his sandwich, the black eye, and thought again how Joe risked his life to save her.

"Thank you, Joe," she said quietly, holding his arm carefully. "This picnic right here would not be happening if it weren't for you."

He munched on a pickle and looked pensive while staring out over the sound. He put his sore arm around Judie Kate and pulled her closer. Then he turned and looked at her intently, as if he had never seen her before, taking in every bit of her face, lips, nose, eyes.

She couldn't tell if there was joy or pain in his eyes, his face. "What, Joe?"

He worked up his courage and then spoke. "Judie Kate, after Jay Jay died, I thought I would never say this again to a woman, but," he paused, looked down and then away, and then, with watery eyes, looked back into her face, "I love you."

She broke down in joyful tears, reached over to Joe, and gave him the biggest hug she had ever given anyone. Three words that meant the ordeal was over, the dream had come true; her life now made sense. All the years of loneliness and shame and heartache erased with three simple words. "I love you too!"

The embrace relaxed them both and at the same time energized them. Suddenly, there was a new life to plan, new adventures awaiting them.

Judie Kate patted Joe's leg incessantly, happily.

"Joe, do you know what this means?" she said.

He winced as she continued patting his leg harder as her excitement grew. "Yes, I do. It means now my leg hurts."

Judie Kate realized she had been hitting Joe's leg for quite a while.

"I'm sorry, Joe!"

He got up, picked up the wrappers and glasses, and headed into the house, Judie Kate following him. "Judie Kate, I need to take some aspirin and go to sleep. I am really tired," Joe said. She found the aspirin bottle, and Joe took several. Then, he gave her a hug and turned and then paused and turned around. "I would be honored if you would take that nap with me," he added.

She beamed and rushed over to him. "I was hoping you would ask." She took his good arm and led him into the room and shut the door. Soon, she cuddled up to her hero and held him close. "I love you, Joe Clark." He was already snoring.

* * *

"Wake up Joe, you're going to miss the after-party!" It was Judie Kate. Joe looked like he was in a faraway land, stunned, dazed, stuck in the middle of a dream. He wiped his eyes as if to see something else.

"Where's the gingerbread?" he asked, looking far beyond Judie Kate.

"What gingerbread, Joe?" she said. He missed her disappointed look. Joe looked around the bedroom, sniffed the air, looking confused. "There was gingerbread, I know it. You made it and put it in a small, brown bag with your pink panties and some soap."

Judie Kate now realized he had been dreaming, but she played along. "My panties? You having fantasies about me now, Joe? Hmm? You been in my room looking in my *drawers for my drawers* when I was not around? What other colors did you find?"

Finally, he woke up, realizing what he had said, now embarrassed with the contents of his dream. "I'm sorry, Judie Kate, I didn't—"

She put her finger to his lips, shushed him, settled by him in the bed, and whispered in his ear in her best lusty voice, "If we were alone for sure, I would show you some more colors." Then she kissed him deeply. The kiss was over far too soon for Joe. "C'mon, kinky man, let's eat and then go to the beach." She got up and helped him out of bed. Then she suddenly stopped, as if on a whim, and wrapped her arms around him tightly and flirtingly said, "I'm wearing red today."

She walked away into the bathroom. "I'm going to change into something pretty so you can feel proud to be seen with me!" After a few minutes, the door to the bathroom opened slightly and red panties sailed into his room as the door closed quickly. "Changed my mind."

* * *

They took his truck over to the after-party at the Howard's house and parked by the school, then walked up Howard Street. Judie Kate looked stylish in her blush capris and black blouse with floral patterns. Her copper jewelry added a mystical, earthy, indigenous touch. Joe looked as unkempt as ever despite his new Ocrafolk shirt. Her dainty sandals contrasted markedly with Joe's ever-clean New Balance shoes.

The musicians remaining on the island were squashed like sardines into the screened-in porch, trying to escape the mosquitoes, and squeezed into the other porch as well where the food was, recounting the weekend, getting ready for the next gig down the road. Rex and Bill were loading their plates, taking a rest from breaking down the stage and packing up, Abner the Sound Dog in tow, dodging feet and looking for handouts. George was talking with Darren and Bow String Bill. Kimber Lee walked up, and soon, they were rehashing their performance the day before. Ellie found a lost and lonely wife of a musician who was an educator, and both were soon caught up in theory, politics, and laments. Eventually, there would be impromptu playing and singing as the musicians relaxed and came down from the excitement of the show. When Joe and Judie Kate walked up, hand in sore hand, several migrated over to them to hear the whole story.

Eventually, the lovers made their way to the food. Judie Kate had never seen such a spread. Shrimp larger than a big man's thumb. Meats, salads, breads, pastas, desserts. No plate was big enough to carry the fare. Three trips would only be a start. As she walked down the steps, she saw Dr. Todd and someone she assumed was his wife. She was shorter than her husband and big and soft in a huggy bear way. Dr. Todd spotted Joe and Judie Kate and headed for them.

"This is my wife, Sherry. Sherry, this is Joe and Judie Kate," Dr. Todd said.

Judie Kate wanted to be professional, but Sherry reached around her and gave her a hug that said "old friends" and did the same to Joe. They exchanged pleasantries.

Sherry related that she was a social worker. She applauded Judie Kate's outfit and then said in a voice of concern and sympathy, "Judie Kate, you and Joe have been through quite a lot this weekend. I hope things are calming down now."

Judie Kate nodded, mouthful of shrimp, holding a finger up to show she was trying to swallow.

"Yes, ma'am, quite a lot."

Sherry came a little closer. "Tell you what, let's get out of here and do some girlie talk. It'll be good for both of us."

As they walked off, Dr. Todd inquired about Joe's wounds. The two talked generalities and then Dr. Todd asked if Joe and Judie Kate had talked about the position, and Joe related that they had not had the time but would be discussing it soon. As they gobbled up the fare, Joe talked with other musicians, and Dr. Todd found Darren and discussed ideas for the show next year.

Soon, the two ladies came back. Judie Kate was about to speak when a sad and lonely elderly woman appeared. Those gathered for the party immediately hushed while others continued their conversations. Still, there was a faint tension in the air. The woman filled her plate her way, organizing it precisely to her culinary specifications while those in line waited with consternation.

Judie Kate was bewildered. "Why do people treat her as if she has the plague?" Judie Kate said.

Darren sidled over to the group, who looked at the woman, and caught the tail end of their conversation. "Did they tell you she's crazy, Judie Kate? After her husband died, she just lost her mind."

Darren related that she and her husband had moved to Ocracoke a few years ago, that the man had patented several apps and became filthy rich. But, suddenly, the man died. The woman became eccentric, odd, even confrontational. But the island put up with her because she generously gave to the show and donated money for several community building projects.

Judie Kate's complexion turned a bit red. Joe had seen that face before.

"Judie Kate," Joe said, "what are you thinking?"

"I'm thinking that maybe she is filled with grief and that is why she is acting out. Has anybody ever asked about her after her husband died?" Judie Kate said. With that, she walked off, stopped to get a drink, and then caught up with the woman.

* * *

"Joe?" Darren asked, one eyebrow higher than the other, "are you sure you're ready for this?" It was a rhetorical question. All stared in wonder, waiting for the woman to blow a fuse and start fuming over anything irrelevant. Darren saw a hand wave him over, so he walked away, and Sherry renewed the conversation.

"Joe, we really want her to take over the clinic. Anything you can do to convince her would be appreciated," Sherry said.

"Honey?" Dr. Todd asked, "were you twisting her arm over there?"

Sherry smiled and looked at Joe. "We need her. I told her I would help in any way I could. I've got some contacts. I'm a member of various organizations, and they have contacts as well. We think we can make this work; we just need someone to take charge."

All three paused and watched with open jaws as Judie Kate continued talking with the woman with no sign of World War III in sight. After a few more moments, she gave her a hug, creating gasps and dropped jaws among the observers, and returned with a smile on her face.

* * *

"She has a name," Judie Kate said indignantly, as if their discussion had never ended. "It is Margie Waller. And once you get past her brassiness and eccentricities, she is an interesting person. She is a women's advocate, has an advocacy blog, and writes under a pseudonym for women's rights."

Judie Kate paused, as if waiting for an apology. When none came, she continued.

"And, Dr. Todd, if you'll do four things, I'll take that job."

The doctor slowly smiled, and Sherry hugged Judie Kate and thanked her several times.

Then, Dr. Todd became cautious and said, "Wait a minute, not so fast. We have not heard the four things. What are they, Judie Kate?"

"Number one. We broaden the scope of the clinic to include elderly women's issues as well. Grief, health, legal advocacy, end of life issues," Judie Kate said. Doctor and social worker looked at her. Judie Kate politely but forcefully reminded all of them that elderly women were women too.

"Number two. Name the place Monica Center," Judie Kate said.

Dr. Todd interrupted. "Well, we already had some names in mind. Why Monica?"

Judie Kate continued. "Because according to Margie, it is a Latin, female name, and it means advise, counsel. The center is about advising and counseling women, right?"

Sherry and Dr. Todd looked at each other, and they, for some reason, looked at Joe, then back at each other again.

"Okay," Dr. Todd said, "what is number three?"

Judie Kate answered. "If you name the clinic Monica Center, Margie will donate five hundred thousand dollars to the cause."

Sherry's eyes opened wide, and Dr. Todd slowly clapped his hands. Joe was smiling, more that Judie Kate had pulled this off than in glee that the center would be funded.

Dr. Todd came back down to earth, like he had gotten very far from it. "What's number four, Judie Kate?"

"You go over there and tell her who to make the check out to. When you do that, consider me hired," Judie Kate said.

Dr. Todd, professionalism suddenly aside, opened his arms as if asking to give Judie Kate a hug. She walked over and embraced him and made the same overture to Sherry as well. The doctor was incredulous.

"Judie Kate, how did you pull this off?" Dr. Todd asked.

She smiled and then gave him a stern but passionate look. "It was very simple. She's not a can of nuts. She's a person. I just went over there and said, 'Hi, I am Judie Kate.'"

Dr. Todd's droll face with a subtle grin said it all. "Lesson learned, Judie Kate! Thank you for accepting our offer. Now," he hooked his arm into Sherry's, "my dear, we have a job to do."

As both cautiously moved over to Margie, Dr. Todd confided to his wife. "That's the amount Lane was going to give. She's amazing, Sherry. Absolutely amazing."

Judie Kate, tired of musicians, clinics, and people in general, asked to go to the beach and take a walk. "I have something I need to do there," she said.

* * *

The sun was heading down but still in full force, yet the wind took away some of the heat. The waves crashed onto the beach, sending salty spray even farther. It was refreshing given the temperature. The two lovers walked far up the beach, both quiet, pensive, coming down from the chaos and tumult and moving into their new life together.

"Let's sit for a bit, Joe," Judie Kate said.

He followed the request, and both sat side by side, taking in the waves, the spray, the wind, the moment, the whole weekend. Judie Kate briefly looked at Joe, saw the gauze on his arm and the bruise around his eye. Minutes passed, then she broke the silence.

"Were you scared, Joe?" she said.

It took a while before he answered as he relived the moment again. She looked over at him and gave him time to formulate his thoughts.

He breathed in. "I was madder than anything else. Mad that someone would think of a woman as just an object, as another conquest, as someone he could bully into his sexual submission. Mad that he was coward enough to have to attack someone to get the twisted pleasure he wanted. And on top of that, I was just mad. I didn't know what we were since George and Ellie were fighting us tooth and nail. Then, I was defiant. There was no way he was going to harm you, no way I would ever let him hurt George and Ellie's daughter."

She looked up at him like a little child who had just seen a fireman pull a person from a burning building. "Joe, he could have killed you."

He looked out over the ocean like a weathered cowboy gazes out over the range. He glanced down at the sand and then back out again. Then, he turned to Judie Kate and spoke with a resolute voice. "That thought *never* occurred to me."

She moved closer and then held him tightly in a way that said she would never let him go. "Thanks, Joe."

As Joe stared over the ocean, Judie Kate began digging out a hole in the sand. After a while, he became curious.

"Looking for buried treasure? You know Blackbeard hung around here before he died. If the Historian were here, he could fill you in," Joe said.

Judie Kate ignored him for a while, her face focused on the sand, like a child on a mission digging up a bucket of sand for the castle she was building. She reached into her pocket and pulled out something.

Joe was trying to give her some space, but curiosity had now caught up with him. It looked like a necklace and a ring. Finally, he couldn't stand it any longer. "What are you doing?"

"Burying the past, Joe," Judie Kate said.

Then, he saw the diamond ring and the shark's tooth necklace. "Wait a minute. Why are you doing that?"

Judie Kate paused. "These are from Don, Joe. They are the past. They are like a stone I carry with me all the time. It's holding me down, Joe. The weight from all the grief, the loneliness. There's a saying: 'the only thing standing between you and true love is you.' It's time to bury it and move on." She dropped the items into the hole, but Joe quickly reached into the hole and grabbed them. She wasn't sure why he did so and gave him a curious stare.

He held them in his hand for a long time, like he was analyzing them, looking for a secret, exploring a distant mystery. Then, he looked at her as if a revelation had come.

"There is a Chinese Zen koan about four students who come to a master's home and ask to stay there overnight. They build a fire in the yard and are warming themselves by it when the master comes out and, in typical teacher fashion, asks them a question. Looking at a large stone on the ground, he asks, 'Gentlemen, is that stone on the ground or in your mind?' Buddhism teaches that all things are perceptions and that our mind determines how we see things, so a proper answer is 'it is in our minds.' One student responds thusly. The Master responds, 'Your head must be very heavy from carrying around such a stone like that in your mind.'"

Joe remained quiet while Judie Kate pondered the implications. Then he continued, still gazing out at the sea.

"A stone can be a burden if you carry it long enough. There are three things you can do with the stones of memory, the stones of grief. You can carry them with you, losing energy and being slowly worn down; you can toss them aside and leave them behind, making them useless; or you can put them to good use. They can be a foundation for the next part of your life. You don't want to leave Don behind.

That's part of your life, part of your foundation for further living. Don't carry the stone, Judie Kate. Don't bury the stone. Put it to good use."

She looked up at him, then back at the jewelry, then out to the ocean. Joe could be like a Zen master, spouting off riddles that took too long to understand. She didn't get it.

Then he said, "Come here." She sidled over to him, and he wiped off the necklace and hooked it around her neck, then he leaned back and looked at it. "Beautiful. He had good taste." Then he reached for her left hand, wiped the sand off the glimmering stone on the ring on his shorts, placed it on her third finger, and smiled. "Judie Kate, will you marry me?"

Seeing Joe's smile, she thought he was playing with her. "Silly, what are you doing?"

Joe then firmly held her hand, squeezed the ring tightly onto her finger, looked her in the eyes with a face that was both serious and expectant, and asked again. "Judie Kate, will you *marry* me?"

It hit her like a rogue broiling breaker. Her eyes grew wide, her mouth grinned with excitement and then jubilation. She screamed out loud, and people on the beach stopped and stared.

"Are you serious? Joe, are you serious? Do you really mean this?"

Joe looked at her and smiled at her smile. "I was hoping for a simple yes."

She jumped onto him and held him with all her might. "Yes, Joe, yes! I will marry you!" She kissed him like he was a sailor finally coming home.

It was long, strong, passionate, and had the force of each one slowly passing into each other, two becoming one. She saw an elderly couple walking by out of the corner of her eye. "He asked me to marry him!" she hollered out.

The woman paused. "Well, honey, I hope you said yes!"

Her husband of many years smiled. "I hope you two will be as happy as we have been all our lives." He took his wife's hand and pulled her along. "I think they need some alone time, dear." He winked at Judie Kate and walked off.

"Congratulations," the woman said.

Judie Kate was like a child on Christmas morning. She looked at her ring and then at Joe and did so again and again.

"You don't mind using Don's ring, Joe?"

"Something old, something new?"

Judie Kate beamed a sheepish grin. "I love you, Joe!"

***

Back at the house, it was time to begin packing up. Joe asked George if he could help him hook up the trailer.

"You got you a woman now. Put her to work," George said.

"Daddy!" Judie Kate exclaimed. "Not nice!"

Yes, things were normal again.

When they left, Judie Kate grabbed a bottle of water, went out on the deck, and sat down. Ellie came down from the bedroom and soon joined her.

She noticed the ring and raised an eyebrow.

"What's with the ring?"

"Momma, I need to tell you about a man named Don."

* * *

Later at the house, Darren stopped by for a beer and to relax. Soon, Kimber Lee walked through the door, found the fridge, and settled down, beer in hand. Ellie came down from the bedroom, made some coffee, and joined the group. After a while, instrument cases were opened and music began to flow. Bow String Bill strolled in late, pulled out his fiddle, rosined up the bow, and joined in. Darren had a new song, and while George was in town, he wanted to go over it. Kimber Lee and Ellie talked about the weekend and Joe and Judie Kate.

The new lovers arrived from their last walk to the Ice Cream Shack and came into the room. Heads turned briefly as they sat down, but all were beginning to accept the new relationship, even Ellie. As the men played, Joe nudged Judie Kate. She thought it was a love nudge and elbowed him back. Joe nudged her again and nodded over to George. Judie Kate smiled and elbowed him again and then leaned into him. Then Joe leaned over to her and whispered into her ear. She looked surprised, but then her face turned into one of a little girl's. When George and Darren finished playing, Joe elbowed her once more.

Judie Kate took a deep breath. *Here goes.* "Daddy, could you play that song for me?"

Joe knew the look he saw on George's face. George loved the attention when on stage, but off stage, he was shy and bashful. Not to mention that he was absolutely no good with emotions and deep feelings. Touchy, feely, mushy were not in George's emotional vocabulary. In asking George to play her song, Judie Kate had just asked him to share his deepest thoughts for her and walk a tightrope across a Grand Canyon of years of misunderstandings, mistrust, and misery. Judie Kate had opened a long-closed door. Now, it was time for George to come in. The question was, would he?

Everyone in the room knew what the silence was about. All knew George intimately from years on the road to and from gigs and a marriage of many years. They knew this was awkward, scary, momentous. Judie Kate and George were now in no-man's-land. What would he say?

Father looked at daughter and then at his future son-in-law. He knew Joe was his biggest fan, but now there was another person in the crowd. Judie Kate had joined with his best friend. It was time to win her applause as well.

"Sure."

* * *

The house was quiet. Bow String Bill, Darren, and Kimber Lee had left, and George and Ellie were calling it good-night. As they ambled up the stairs, Joe and Judie Kate were left all alone with Killer close beside. It had been a long day, a longer weekend, and a very long week. Weariness drifted in over them like a morning fog.

Joe broke the silence. "Judie Kate, I hate to end this, but I need to be up early tomorrow morning for the ferry. Better head to bed."

She held him closer, not wanting to turn him loose. Finally, she gave in. She walked him to his room, holding him around his waist. She knew he would leave tomorrow and didn't want to let him go. She kissed him good-night and then headed to her room through the bathroom.

As Joe lay there in bed, he couldn't fall asleep. He turned one way and then the other, but all he could think of was the woman in the other room who would one day be his new wife. *This is nuts*. He got up, went through the bathroom, and quietly stepped into Judie Kate's room.

She heard him and whispered, "I was hoping you would come in." She opened the sheets and motioned for him to join her. As he lay down, she pulled the covers back over them and snuggled up to him. Kisses and caresses produced waves in the sheets.

Intimacy increased as inhibitions ebbed away. Their lips pressed closer and held longer, their bodies melded into one as they hugged, touched, and began the slow process of learning beautiful secrets about each other. Then, there was a scratch on the door and a low bark.

"Killer, go to bed," Judie Kate called out. She resumed her embrace of Joe.

Scratch, scratch, scratch ... bark.

This time, it was Joe's turn. "Killer, go to sleep."

He resumed kissing Judie Kate.

Scratch, scratch, scratch … bark.

Judie Kate gave in, got up, and opened the door, and Killer rushed in, jumped on the bed, and stood at full attention. She sat back down on the bed and pulled the sheets over her and reached out for Joe, but Killer immediately jumped between them. Joe tried to pull Judie Kate closer, but when he did, Killer growled quietly. Joe backed off, but then Judie Kate reached out to Joe and tried to snuggle, but again Killer growled, this time a bit louder. Joe and Judie Kate momentarily gave up, sighed, and leaned back from each other.

"Killer, are you chaperoning us?" Judie Kate asked. Killer wagged his tail. She tried one more time, teasing Killer, and reached for Joe again, but Killer growled softly. "Okay, I get it." She pulled away, and Killer nestled himself between the disappointed would-be lovers and curled up for the night.

"I'm sorry, Joe," Judie Kate whispered. There was a bit of silence.

"Given what I'm feeling for you right now, Killer is probably the wiser of us three."

"Good-night, Joe."

"Love you, Judie Kate."

Killer's tail thumped on the covers.

Tomorrows

Joe hurriedly checked his emails and his online classes and then closed his computer and packed it away in his shoulder bag. He was gathering up his food when Judie Kate appeared, still fluffing her hair, flannel shorts just barely visible from underneath an oversized, long-sleeved shirt, all doing their simple magic on Joe.

"Good morning, would-be lover." She gave him a hug. "Killer kind of ruined the mood last night, huh?" She didn't wait for an answer but kissed him again and then pulled back. "Ready for your ferry ride, mister?"

Joe leaned over for one more kiss. "Not really. Want to stay here with you."

She looked him in the eyes and answered, "We'll take care of that real soon."

She told him of her plan to stop and get themselves something to eat and wait on the ferry together.

"Isn't there a bakery behind the Community Store?" Judie Kate said.

They grabbed Joe's things and tossed them in the Mustang and drove off to the bakery. Ocracoke was desolate, emptied of tourists at this early hour. Inside the bakery, they breathed in all the fresh aromas, sugary, salty, and in between, made their order, and then rushed out. She dropped him off at his truck in the Park Service parking lot and then watched as he drove to the ferry service and got in line.

She walked over to his truck, carrying two bags, and together they found a seat in the picnic area of the Park Service and enjoyed fresh-baked cinnamon rolls, hot coffee, and their last few moments together. Crows cawed, mourning doves sang, and seagulls flew by as the morning swept over the sound. The sun had been up only an hour, but it was already shining bright. Sleepy drivers dozed in their cars, waiting for the ferry gates to open. The day was beautiful except for the clouds of good-byes.

The silence spoke for both as if words might go by too fast and not convey their real intent. Rolls done, Judie Kate took his sticky fingers and licked them off in a sexy way, looking up at him with longing eyes all the while.

"Your turn," she said, poking her fingers into his mouth. The tease done, both were not satisfied with the result. "Didn't do the trick, huh?" she said, flexing her still-sticky fingers. "Oh well." She held his hand, fingers intertwined, and they enjoyed the moment. The morning breeze was picking up, bringing with it the fresh scent of the sound.

Judie Kate broke the silence. "I'm coming up to see you this weekend if that is okay."

"*If?*"

"I didn't want to assume anything."

"I want you to assume everything."

Car engines began starting up and Joe stood. "Gotta go, Judie Kate." He pulled her along as they walked back to his truck. They embraced once more, and their final kiss was way too long and uncomfortable for the people around them.

"I love you, Uncle Joe," Judie Kate said teasingly, intentionally a bit too loud, as he got into his truck. She handed him a package. "For the trip home. Drive safe. Text me when you get to Swan Quarter."

As she turned to walk away, two young men in an old Honda who heard her good-bye stared in disbelief, jaws dropped.

Judie Kate looked back at them. "What? We're from Arkansas. Nieces kiss their uncles. It's what we do." She turned back and winked at Joe and then walked off, briefly pulling up her shirt, making her hips wiggle for him.

What is it about flannel shorts? Joe looked at the two men in the car beside him and decided to keep up the ruse. "Her sister's hotter than she is!"

As the ferry backed out of the mooring, Joe looked back to the island and saw a hand waving at him. He waved back, sad but full of joy. This good-bye was just the beginning of hello.

**

Curious, Joe investigated the bag and pulled out a treat. Gingerbread! He unwrapped it and took a bite. Crunchy and chewy. Just right. He grabbed his phone and called, and Judie Kate answered.

"Yes?"

"Yum!"

"I see you found your treats!"

"Treats? Plural? I found the gingerbread. You are wonderful!"

"That all you found?"

He scrounged around in the bag, felt a chunk, pulled it out. "Soap!"

"And?"

He reached deep into the bag and pulled out pink panties.

**

Judie Kate thought about all the emails, phone calls, video chats, and texts of the week as she headed to Joe's house on Friday. The drive from Wilmington took about four hours, but that was too long. Interstate 40 was packed all the way to Raleigh, but Highway 64 west was smooth sailing.

She drove through the country on the winding backroads and remembered her younger days with her parents. Suddenly, a rush of insecurities hit her. *What is this all about?* She looked at herself in the mirror and smiled. *Don't get in your way, Judie Kate.* All of that was in the past now. A new life lay before her.

Cows and trees and fields of two-feet-high cornstalks framed with miles of rusted barbed-wire fence used to be symbols of an embarrassing life with her rural parents. Now, their tranquility renewed her soul. "In a quarter mile, turn left on Old Mill Road," the GPS woman politely directed. It dawned on her: in all her years of knowing Joe, she had never been to his house. Log cabin? Split-level? Ranch? Old farmhouse with wrap-around porch? She made three more turns, dodged an errant groundhog, and then heard the words she longed for. "In three hundred yards, your destination is on the left."

She pulled into a long, gravel driveway lined with railroad ties and then saw a modest ranch house accented with black shutters and an empty carport. The green, recently mowed yard was bordered with a split rail fence and then pine woods. There was Joe's truck and sound trailer to the side of the carport. *My car will look good in there!* Bushes lined the front of the house with bright zinnias and then marigolds of many colors in front of them. As she shut off the car, Joe came out the side door, brown shorts and blue pullover shirt on, hair disheveled but in an outdoorsy kind of way. Judie Kate could not get to him fast enough, and Joe could not smile big enough. It was like the reunion of two longtime friends who had not seen each other in years.

"Joe! I missed you so much!" Judie Kate slammed into her lover with a body hug that would have squashed a bear. He pulled her as close as he could, breathing in her very essence, feeling the energy and passion he had missed for four long days. He couldn't touch her enough. He held her arms, her waist, her hips, and then wrapped his arms all around her once more as if to make sure she was real. Again and again he touched those shoulders that had moved him since the Wednesday before. Judie Kate reveled in the grasp of her man.

The four days of distance and longing temporarily resolved, Joe helped her with her things.

"All this for three days?" he asked.

"I have an image to keep up," she teased. As he reached for her bags, she noticed his hands were still faintly blue, and then she looked at his face and saw the last remnants of his black eye. As they walked to the house, she looked around. "Wow, Joe, I had always pictured you in a two-story, Cape Cod kind of house, you know?"

"Well, this is my winter home. I'll be heading north next week for some R&R." Joe stared at her, taking her in as if it was the first time he had seen her.

"What?" she asked.

He looked her over from head to toe once more, just in case he had missed something. The radiance of her smile, fire and compassion in her eyes, a presence that exuded beauty in every way. Voluptuous and quietly seductive, like a woman in a Renaissance painting, yet strong and secure for the demands of a new day.

"I'm a lucky man, Judie Kate."

"Don't you forget it either, buster!" responded a very confident and happy Judie Kate.

They walked into the house, and Joe gave her the grand tour. He started with the den and from there, he went into his music room. As he walked down the hall, he pointed to the guest bedroom.

"I won't be needing that," Judie Kate smiled.

"I was just being a gentleman," he responded, "and a good host." Then he passed the bathroom, turned for his bedroom, and plopped her bag down.

"Better," she approved, giving him a huge hug while she checked out the room. Yellow walls, pine furniture, one thirsty begonia on a stand, a nightstand with a lamp, and some paperback books. A faded quilt graced an old poster bed that begged for refinishing. No pictures on the walls, but there was a small nail hole in one wall and an empty space on the dresser. Something felt odd, empty. Then it hit her: there were no pictures of Jay Jay anywhere in the house.

"Joe?" she asked, looking around once more. "Not one picture of Jay Jay?"

He looked around as if he had misplaced them. "Well, I was not sure about that. You know, starting over and all."

She held him more, but this time, it was not love. It was reassurance that all was well.

"You know, if it weren't for her, we would not be doing this," she said.

Joe, now filled with her permission, went over to the dresser and opened an otherwise empty bottom drawer and pulled out a picture of Jay Jay on their wedding day and another picture of her in the mountains.

Judie Kate took the mountain one from him and looked at her carefully. "You know, Joe, the few times I met her, I never really looked at her." She stared at the picture for quite a while, refreshing herself with the person of Jay Jay. Joe stood back, as if afraid to get to close to the memory. Then she hooked her arm in his and pulled him along. "C'mon, Joe, let's put her in the den."

Still, something did not seem right. For some reason, she expected to see a clump of dirty clothes on the floor in the bedroom, a soda can and a leftover bowl of popcorn in the den, cables and CDs in his music room. It was too …

"Are you always this, uh, neat, Joe Clark?"

He looked around the den, shrugged his shoulders, and confessed. "I was trying to impress you."

"Impress your lips onto mine." He did.

Later, they walked about the yard. Judie Kate was amazed at the flowers, how manicured the whole yard was. Then she spotted them: butterflies. All over the flower blooms. Small ones, large ones, orange, yellow, brown. Some fought each other over multicolored turf. Some flickered and wafted about. In and out, then back again.

"Wow, Joe, I've never seen so many butterflies at one time," she said.

He paused and watched them feed on the marigolds and zinnias. "Just this year, there seem to be more than ever. When I got home from the festival, I couldn't believe how many there were."

She looked at him and wondered to herself. "Joe, do you think it is a sign? Didn't you tell me that Jay Jay loved butterflies?"

He put his arm around her shoulders and held her close. "Hmm," was all he could say, and Judie Kate left it at that, but she knew the answer.

As they walked on, hand in hand, she renewed the conversation. "I never pictured you for a flower kind of man."

He paused and looked around, as if assessing her conclusion. "Well, you are correct. But Jay Jay was, so I have a yard man keep them up. The one way I keep her memory alive, I guess." She thought about how sweet that was, how sweet Joe was, and had been all his life. "But I do the grass and weed eat and all the other man stuff." It came out in a sarcastic, self-deprecating air.

"Yes, you da man!" Judie Kate affirmed. "Such a big man too!" She patted his stomach. "Big man!" she reaffirmed. "Now, let's check out the deck."

They stood by the rail and looked out over the backyard as two squirrels chased each other around a white oak tree. Judie Kate began thinking of ways to make the yard her yard without losing the memory of Jay Jay. A gray cat, ignoring the squirrels, sauntered up from out of the woods, headed their way.

"Is that your cat?" Judie Kate asked.

"That," Joe answered, "is Rats. Yes, he's my cat." Joe explained that after Jay Jay died, the cat appeared on his deck at the door with a dead rat in front of him, something like a gift. He was scraggly, thin, and a bit beaten up, and despite the gesture, quite spooky. Joe gave him some milk in a saucer, and he lapped it up. Joe then found some tuna and offered it to him, and he ate it all up as well. Then, as if satisfied, he walked away back into the woods. For several days, he would bring up a dead rat or sometimes, a bird or mouse, and Joe would return the favor with a bowl of food. Once, Rats brought the gift of a snake.

Finally, one day, he stood at the door and meowed until Joe opened the door, and he walked inside like he owned the house. After a few days, he stood by the back door and meowed until Joe let him out. And now, that was the routine.

"Rats? Seriously?" Judie Kate asked.

Rats climbed the steps to the deck, parked his gray body right at Judie Kate's feet, and stared at her.

"He wants you to pick him up, Judie Kate."

"And if I don't?"

"He will stare at you, glare at you, and then follow you everywhere you go until you pick him up. Minutes, hours, days, it does not matter to him."

She tentatively picked him and held him at bay until she warmed up to him. "My God, you could hear him purr a mile away," she said.

Joe roughed him up on the head. "Well, Rats, is she welcome or not?" Rats's tail swished from side to side, the purr became even more audible, and he winked his eyes. "You're in," Joe announced. With that, Rats wriggled to get down and then stood by the door. "Time to play fetch?" Joe asked.

He opened the door and Rats walked inside.

"You're kidding, right? He plays fetch like a dog?" Judie Kate asked. Joe reached down inside the kitchen and picked up a toy mouse off the floor. "Watch this. Ready, Rats?" He tossed the mouse down the hallway. Rats raced off, and seconds later, he came back with the mouse and dropped it at Joe's feet. He tossed it down the hall again, and Rats brought it back. This time, he dropped it at Judie Kate's feet. "Your turn," Joe said. She tossed it, and sure enough, he brought it back and plopped it at her feet. "Well, Judie Kate, you have passed the test. Rats says you are now part of the family." Rats walked back to the door and sat down until Joe opened it and then sauntered off back to the woods, a mockingbird dive-bombing him all the way.

"Where does he sleep when he comes inside? Surely not with you?"

"Sometimes, but, generally, he sleeps on top of the fridge."

Judie Kate walked over to the fridge as if inspecting the space. "Seriously, on *top* of the fridge?"

"He's a cat."

She wrapped her arms around him and snuggled up. "Interesting how he just came up after Jay Jay died."

"They say the animal knows when you need him. He's been a good friend."

"I need you, Joe Clark." She nuzzled up to him like a cat would its owner. "Meow."

"I'm right here."

"I'm also hungry. What's for dinner?" She pulled away and looked around the small kitchen, and here she saw the organized mess that was so Joe Clark.

It was quite a contrast to the perfectly manicured yard outside or even his clean and precise stage at the festival, not to mention the house itself.

Chips and cookies pushed into a corner of the counter. Scrunched-up loaf bread and a long loaf of French bread in a clear wrapper by the toaster oven that could use some cleaning. Some glasses and spoons awaited washing someday by the sink that had a dirty bar of soap in a smudgy, soap holder. A coffee mug on the windowsill. A towel hung from the handle on the fridge, another towel hung from the oven door, and two more towels were on the countertop. A nearly empty jar of barbecue sauce was on the counter by a small Corningware dish. The wrapper from a half-eaten 3 Musketeers bar completed the whole scene. By all of this was an open book on healthy Mediterranean cooking.

"Got a thing for towels there, Joe?" She walked over and folded two of them, straightened up the counter to her liking, and then turned around. "Dinner."

"Welcome to Ristorante Clark," he answered in his best southern French accent. "Tonight, we tour several countries for our cuisine." Joe opened the top of the dish and a vinegary smell erupted. "Chicken basted with Eastern barbecue sauce on the grill is our Southern dish, along with asparagus and squash brushed in olive oil, basil and oregano for a taste of Italy, some French bread toasted with garlic butter, and ..." He paused and then opened the freezer door with a flourish. "Voila! Ice cream, of course, which originated from either China, the Middle East, France, or the local grocery store!"

"Wow, Joe, ignoring the ice cream, when did you get so healthy?"

He opened the refrigerator door and showed her the collection of yogurts in the fridge and then opened the cabinet door where he had granola.

"When I met a sweet young thing."

"Aw, Joe!" She hugged him again. Together, they relished the moment, the day, all their tomorrows lining up in the stars.

"Thought you were hungry," Joe asked.

"I am, but I want some food first," she winked, squeezing him once more before turning him loose. "What can I help with?"

Dinner was out on the deck on the picnic table. The weather was not so intense and there was a breeze from the west. A bluebird, flitting up and down from a limb and catching worms, provided the entertainment, and a hummingbird danced all around the flowers. The aroma from the grill wafted all around them.

Judie Kate took a bite of her chicken. "This is good, Joe. Spicy, vinegary."

"Got the sauce from the store. George's Sauce. Pretty good, huh?"

She swallowed. "Never pictured you for an asparagus person."

Joe took a swig of his tea. "Me neither, but after dinner with some friends who served it, I thought I would give it a shot. Cover it with enough goo, it is not too bad."

Judie Kate shifted the conversation.

"Talked with Dr. Todd the other day." She broke off a large piece of French bread and put some lite spread on it.

"Okay," Joe answered, "how'd that go?" He stuffed more chicken into his mouth and then remembered his manners. She explained the conversation.

Dr. Todd wanted to open the clinic in Greensboro. With the money from Margie, the project was moving forward. He was hoping for a January first date. He had a building selected. It was on the major bus route, the parking lot was well-lit, and there was an ample back lot they would landscape into a garden and walking path. It would be surrounded with a high wrought iron fence with only one entrance. It would be a clinic, sanctuary, safe place, and education center all in one.

"Wow," Joe responded, forcing down another mouthful of asparagus, "sounds like they have it all planned."

"That's just the outside. Inside, we'll have a clinic, of course, plus an education center with plenty of computers, small dormitory, showers, mailboxes, food pantry, kitchen, washers, and dryers. We've partnered with a local chaplaincy training center for a part-time chaplain to be available. The local community college will provide back-to-work training and even scholarships for those who need education but can't afford it. And there's daycare, in house, and a small chapel and prayer room as well."

Joe's face was covered with awe. "That sounds great. Dr. Todd has really thought this thing through."

Judie Kate corrected him. "Judie Kate and Dr. Todd have really thought this thing through."

"Noted. So, when do you start?" He forked some squash.

"Yesterday," Judie Kate answered. "Already on the payroll. Speaking of which, I have to learn how to do that."

Joe nodded and swallowed some bread and reached for his tea. "Google it," he answered sarcastically.

She ignored him. "Which means I need to move up here and find a place to stay." She looked at him with a you-know-what-I-mean face.

"Whooo, that's fast!" he answered back. Devilment filled his eyes. "They have some new apartments outside of Greensboro that are nice, according to my students."

Judie Kate stood up and reached for his empty plate. "I really prefer small ranch houses with really nice stereos and beautiful flowers. Know where I can find one?" She opened the deck door and took the plates inside. "Where are the ice cream bowls?" she hollered back.

Joe called out, "Stove, up to the left in the cabinet." He heard the clinking of dinnerware. "Two scoops, right?"

The ice cream melted in the heat as they enjoyed the dessert and each other. They recalled the many times they talked through her problems over scoops of ice cream. Family, self, church, school. Clothes, weight, esteem. Boys and the lack thereof. Dreams.

"How did you do it, Joe? How did you put up with me all those years?" she said.

Joe spooned around in the bowl to get the last bit, licked it, and tossed the spoon back in the bowl with a precise clink.

"I guess I thought of you as my daughter, or my sister. You needed help, and I was there." He paused as she looked up at him. "And," he continued, "George and Ellie needed help too. They're good people, Judie Kate, but frankly, they had no clue."

Judie Kate wiped her mouth with her napkin and pushed her bowl away. "You know, I had a major crush on you for a while." She grinned and her eyebrows scrunched as if she wasn't sure that was a good thing to admit.

Joe leaned back in his chair as if to put distance between him and the teenage girl.

"Yup."

Then, she became serious.

"Joe, why did you agree to take me to the prom? I mean, I had pimples, I didn't really know how to do my hair, people were going to talk. You know ... Wasn't it embarrassing for you?"

He looked up at the blue sky as though the night was playing out in front of him once more. He hesitated and then answered. "With all the bad things in my life, I never got to go to a prom."

She scooted her chair over to him and took his hand. "It meant the world to me, Joe. It was a dream come true." She let the moment and the memories settle down. "Joe, one day, I hope you will feel comfortable enough with me to tell me about those days."

Joe looked away from her for quite a while as if ashamed and then he looked her way again. "One day. Maybe."

Things were getting too serious. A question mark filled her round face. "Do you remember saying that if Jay Jay left, you would marry me?"

"I said that? I probably shouldn't have. That was a boundary that … "

She held his hand tighter and teared up ever so slightly. "Joe, that was when I realized, deep down inside, that I was pretty enough to be married. I doubted it many times, but I never forgot that, ever." She looked at him and then grabbed her napkin and wiped her dark eyes. Then she looked at her ring. "Who knew, right?"

Tummies full, they snuggled on the couch in the den as the evening sun went down, sending scant rays through the sheers on the windows. They sat in silence, watching the shadows slowly creep across the carpet, slide over the furniture, and then fade out of sight. No parents, no Killer, no festival, no stalkers, nothing but themselves.

"You want some music?" Joe asked.

"Of course."

He reached for the remote and turned on the Bose Wave stereo. Soon, there were sultry saxophone sounds filling the room.

"Coltrane?" Judie Kate asked. "You trying to seduce me?"

"Better. Grover Washington's 'Winelight.' And, yes."

Attraction and affection soon gave way to deepening arousal as the sensuous, then sensual, and finally sexual saxophone music wafted around the room, building in rhythm, intensity, and volume, drowning out inhibitions. Judie Kate caressed Joe's face, and Joe's hands flirted around her body, on her legs, around her waist. She leaned over and kissed him.

"Joe?"

"Yes?" He pulled her closer with purpose, intention, desire, positioning her body on top of him. He wanted to feel all of her, every inch of her, pressing downward onto him, into him. No more gentleman, just man. She followed his desire, nestling slowly, suggestively until her body, like a soft and warm pillow, rested on top of him, conforming to him. She moved her head close to his face, felt the heat from his neck and hair, and then placed her lips softly against his ear.

"Do you remember last Thursday night when we were under the house and I said, 'Not yet?'"

Joe thought back and recalled his feelings for her, how he fondled her until she pulled away. He could still feel her hips, her back, her sides, her body pushing into his. He had thought about that moment all this week.

"Oh yes, I remember it too well."

She rubbed his face softly with her fingers, pushed her lips into his ear, and whispered, "Yet."

* * *

Fresh from the shower, Judie Kate remembered something. She reached into her travel bag and took out a small package. She unwrapped it, and finding

Joe's wash cloth, placed the soap inside it, much like at a fancy hotel.

She looked in the mirror at herself, diamond ring glistening on her finger, breathed in the lavender scent, and realized that life was good, that the only thing that stood between her and her true love was her Self. Dreams come true. Waking up is the hard part.

Seeing herself in the mirror, she smiled at the mysterious eyes that looked back at her.

"I *am* Judie Kate."

There was one more thing to do. Judie Kate brushed off the wooden box and took out her diary. It was like an old friend who had kept her company for many years. How many times had she held it close, cried tears onto it, fallen asleep with it? She thought about her life and how much of it was shared in pages between flowery covers that disguised the winters of her true life. She opened it up, turned the pages slowly until she came upon her bookmark, the note Don had left her that Christmas long ago.

Friday, June 14, 2018

Tonight, I feel wonderful, whole, complete. Tonight, I finally feel like a woman, a beautiful woman. I never in my wildest dreams, ever, thought this would be possible. I am like the ugly duckling who became the swan, the caterpillar to the beautiful butterfly, the maid who became a Cinderella.

The fairy tale is over. My life is truly a dream come true.

I didn't know my Knight in Shining Armor would snore. LOL.

So, my good friend, it is time for us to part. You have been my constant and never-complaining companion since I was thirteen. The times we shared, right? The dates we never had, the insecurities we told each other. Dreams, nightmares, broken hearts, confidential secrets just between you and me. You got me through all those years. But, I have found the love of my life, the one I dreamed about in your pages years ago.

From now on, I will be writing my story, my thoughts, on the heart of my Joe. I will come back and visit you as the days and months and years go by. I will never forget all our times together.

Thank you, my friend.

Love,
Judie Kate

About the Author

J.T. Allen is a professor of religion, history, and humanities, as well as a musician and sound man. He has written humor, local interest, history, and religion for over thirty years under the pen name J. Timothy Allen. This is his first novel. He lives with his wife, two horses, two dogs, and two cats on a small farm near historic Snow Camp, North Carolina.

CPSIA information can be obtained
at www.ICGtesting.com
Printed in the USA
FSHW011533221020
75012FS